"SIMON LEONIDO

PLACE IN THE THRI

ALONGSIDE CUSSLI

JACK RYAN, AND LU

—Brad Thor, bestselling author of *Takedown*

THE COURIER

"A perfect thriller. There is no putting this book down once it's opened."

—Bookreporter.com

"An edgy debut. . . . Leonidovich is a fascinating character. . . . A taut, enjoyable ride."

—*Publishers Weekly*

BAGMAN

"Razor sharp . . . equal parts Dashiell Hammett and James Patterson. . . . Heart-pounding, brilliantly paced. . . . An unmatchable, edge-of-your-seat thriller."

—Brad Thor

"MacLarty's writing is crisp and colorful. All of his characters, especially Simon, are carefully drawn with depth and complexity."

—*The Oakland Press*

"Well-rounded and compelling. [*Bagman*] has all the elements of a great thriller—and MacLarty balances these components expertly. . . . Simon [is] a character worth following."

—*Publishers Weekly*

LIVE WIRE

"Intricate, fast-moving and . . . a whole lot of fun."

—*The Oakland Press*

Choke Point **is also available as an eBook**

Also by Jay MacLarty:

Live Wire

Bagman

The Courier

JAY MACLARTY

CHOKEPOINT

POCKET BOOKS
New York London Toronto Sydney

An *Original* Publication of POCKET BOOKS

POCKET BOOKS, a division of Simon & Schuster, Inc.
1230 Avenue of the Americas, New York, NY 10020

ISBN-13: 978-1-4165-0348-4
ISBN-10: 1-4165-0348-X

This Pocket Books paperback edition February 2007

10 9 8 7 6 5 4 3 2 1

POCKET and colophon are registered trademarks of Simon & Schuster, Inc.

Art and design by Carlos Beltran

Manufactured in the United States of America

For information regarding special discounts for bulk purchases, please contact Simon & Schuster Special Sales at 1-800-456-6798 or business@simonandschuster.com.

This book is dedicated to:

Miles & Ian
my daughter's best work to date.

Acknowledgments

The author wishes to thank the following people for their help with this novel:

John Hill
a great writer, with big ideas,
and a willingness to share.

Lew Nelson
for his review of all things aeronautical, and for his ability to cry silently when I pull out my literary license and fly around the edges.

Jill Kelly & Marc Horowitz
they know why.

And always, my literary compatriots,
who never fail to offer good and honest advice.
Gene Munger
Louise Crawford
Mark and Sunny Nelsen
Vic Cravello
Holly McKinnis

ChokePoint

Chapter One

The Pacific Pearl, Taipa Island, Macau

Wednesday, 27 June 16:22:51 GMT +0800

"Everything is now better," Quan said, turning over another page of blueprints. A slight man in his mid forties, rather formal in manner, with high cheek-bones and saffron-colored skin, he was dressed in a custom-tailored linen suit and soft leather brogues. "Much better."

Better! Patience was not one of Jake Rynerson's virtues and it took all his willpower just to remain seated at the table while Li Quan methodically recounted everything that was being done to accelerate the pace of construction. *Better* wasn't good enough, not when a new world order hung in the balance.

As he continued, Quan delicately smoothed down the large dappled sheet of paper. "Interior work should be back on schedule within ten days." He spoke with an unusual accent, not quite Chinese, not quite English, a by-product of his Oxford education. "As you see—" His voice echoed through the cavity of unfinished space, a revolving cocktail lounge two hundred feet above the casino floor. "We have tripled our work-force." He motioned toward the teakwood balustrade, an intricately carved serpentine of dragons.

Though Jake hardly needed anyone to point out the obvious, he realized his attention was expected, and glanced down at the beehive of workers and craftsmen swarming over his masterpiece, and what he now feared would be his albatross. The main tower was a typical John Portman design—a huge open atrium with plants hanging off the indoor balconies—except nothing about the Pacific Pearl was *typical.* Every suite offered two breathtaking views: outward, over the Pearl River Delta, and inward, over five acres of green felt tables. It was by far the most spectacular of all the new resorts in Macau, exceeding even his own lofty expectations, but he was already late to the party, the last of the large gaming corporations to open in what was predicted to be the new Mecca of gambling. If he hoped to lure the high rollers away from the other resorts, he needed to open with a splash . . . and if he hoped to save the Pacific Rim Alliance, he needed to open on time, something that no longer seemed possible. *Holy mother of Texas!*—he couldn't imagine the ramifications. The hotel booked to capacity . . . Streisand coming out of retirement to open the showroom . . . the collapse of a yearlong secret negotiation between China, Taiwan, and United States.

"Three shifts," Quan continued, "working twenty-four hours a day."

Nothing Jake didn't already know. He would have cut the man off, but the Chinese were different from Westerners, they didn't understand his mercurial temperament, and he couldn't afford to offend his general manager a month before the scheduled opening. Billie, sitting between the men like a bridge between East and West, dipped her chin, acknowledging her husband's unusual restraint, her subtle way of telling him to keep his yap shut. He took a deep breath, then let it out long and slow, all the way to the bottom, trying to control his anxiety. How could he have been so confident? The secret was too big, the time too short. All those bigger-than-life headlines must have turned his brain into bullcrap.

BIG JAKE RYNERSON, BUSINESSMAN AND BILLIONAIRE, TAKES ON SOCIALIST CHINA.

VEGAS COWBOY RIDES INTO MACAU—CAN HE DELIVER?

Yup, that was it, his balls had finally outgrown his brain. He had clearly succumbed to the myth of his own infallibility. What did he know about Chinese politics? About Chinese superstition? How was a dumb ol' West Texas cowboy supposed to *appease the Gods, blow away the bad spirits, and sooth the sleeping dragons?* Of all the stupid things he'd done in his life, this had to be the worst—not counting wives two, three, and four—three acts of lunacy he preferred not to think about. At least he'd been smart enough to marry his first wife twice—he gave Billie a little wink—the *best* decision he ever made.

"Of course," Quan went on, "much depends on the weather."

Jake swiveled toward the windows—a three-hundred-and-sixty-degree panorama overlooking the Chinese mainland, the islands, and the South China Sea—a spectacular view if not for the onslaught of rain hammering away at the glass, a two-day downpour that showed no signs of retreat.

"It won't last," Billie said, sounding more hopeful than confident. "We're going to make it."

Jake nodded, trying to put on a good face, but he didn't believe it; it was the beginning of typhoon season, the time of black rain, and the onslaught could last for days. *Weeks maybe,* and if the problems continued . . . they were already $82 million over budget . . . but that was only money, *that* he could handle . . . it was all the political bullshit . . . the set-in-stone timetable established by some feng shui master . . . that's what he couldn't handle.

Li Quan stared at the rivulets of water streaming down the glass, then turned over his hands, a gesture of helplessness. "Very bad joss."

Jake kept his eyes fixed on the gray horizon, barely able to restrain his desire to grab the man by the shoulders and shake some sense into him. Quan was an excellent administrator, but his Chinese mind-set, his propensity to blame all problems on *bad joss,* was almost too much. Luck had nothing to do with it. Too many things had gone wrong. *Big things*: a crane buckling under the weight of an air-conditioning unit and crushing two welders; a misplaced wrench tearing out the guts of the hotel's grand escalator, a curving triple-wide mechanical marvel that cost over eight million dollars; the sudden collapse of a construction elevator that killed four workers; and two days ago—only hours after the security netting had been removed from the tower—a building inspector had somehow gotten past the retainment barrier and fallen off the roof. Problems that were costing him a fortune to keep out of the press, and far too many to be written off as *bad joss.* "No, Mr. Quan, I don't believe luck has anything to do with it. Someone's behind this."

A wave of confusion rolled across Li Quan's face. "Behind this . . . ?" He turned to the window, obviously wondering how *someone* could control the weather. "I don't—"

Billie, who had an aggravating and somewhat mystic insight into exactly what her husband was thinking, interrupted. "Excuse me, Mr. Quan—" She glanced at her watch, a gold, wafer-thin Gondolo by Patek Philippe. "But I think it's time for the uniform review." She nudged Jake's boot with her foot, a reminder that Li Quan knew nothing about the secret negotiations, the proposed alliance, or the true significance of the opening date.

"Right," Jake said, more in answer to Billie's unspoken warning than to what she had said. "Let's get that over with."

"Hai," Quan responded, a relieved lift in his voice. "We should not keep them waiting." He snatched up his two-way radio and began chattering away in rapid-fire Cantonese, the most common dialect within the province. It was that single talent—Li Quan's ability to communicate with the Macanese

staff—that kept Jake from making an immediate management change.

Within minutes people began streaming out of the crystal-domed glass elevators that ascended silently along one side of the atrium. There was a male and female employee from each department: bellhops and parking valets, hosts and hostesses, janitors and maids, dealers and croupiers, bartenders and cocktail servers, and at least a dozen more. As Li Quan began lining everyone up along the front of the balustrade, Billie leaned over and whispered, "You have to be careful, Jake, you can't afford to offend the man. We need him."

He nodded, not about to argue, but knowing what he really needed was a hard-charging ballbuster like Caitlin Wells to get the place open.

"And," Billie added, "you can forget about Caitlin. She can't speak the language."

Damn woman, he was starting to think she could read his mind. "Give me a little rope, darlin', I ain't senile yet."

"Besides, you need her in Vegas. She's got enough to handle with the expansion of the Sand Castle."

As if he needed to be told. "I know that, Billie."

"I know you know, but you look a bit short on patience." She gave him a teasing smile, the kind that could still make his old heart giddy-up and gallop. "So, I'm *reminding* you."

"Well I don't need *remindin',*" he whispered back, though they both knew that wasn't true. "But if I hear *bad joss* one more time, that boy's gonna be wearing one of my boots up the backside of his fundament."

She chuckled and patted his knee as Li Quan began his fashion parade. Though Jake smiled and nodded to each team as they paraded past the table, nothing registered, his mind struggling to find some way to speed up the construction process. He wanted to pick up a hammer, do something with his own hands, but that would look desperate, and all it would take for the press to unleash their bloodhounds. That's the way it worked—one minute he was that loveable Vegas cowboy, and the next just another dumbass cowpoke from West Texas—but either way, up or down, Big Jake Rynerson made good copy for the tabloids, and their minions were always watching. So he was stuck, hoping Mother Nature would turn her wrath elsewhere, hoping the contractor could finish before anything else went wrong, hoping the press . . .

"What do you think?" Billie asked as a casino hostess in a micro-short dress of shimmering gold stepped forward.

He felt like a lecher just looking at the girl, who couldn't have been more than eighteen, with perfect golden brown skin and sparkling black eyes. "About what?"

"The dress. You think it's too flashy?" Billie pointed toward the heavens and made a circling motion with her finger. The girl executed a graceful pirouette, her pixie-cut black hair spiking outward as if charged with electricity.

Jake tried to concentrate on the dress but couldn't move his eyes beyond the hemline. "It's awful damn short."

"These girls don't have breasts, Jake, and they're not very tall. They need to show some leg."

"I got no problem with legs, Billie. We just don't want 'em flashing their fannies around, that's all."

Billie tilted her head, a look of amusement. "Jake, honey, you're blushing like a schoolboy."

And feeling like one. Embarrassed, he pushed himself back from the table. "It's almost nine o'clock in Vegas. I promised Caity I'd call before breakfast."

"What about the dress?"

"Whatever you think." He grabbed his cellular and started toward the back of the room, but before he could punch in Caitlin's number, the tiny unit began to vibrate. The number on the display, a Macau prefix, was not one he recognized. "Hello."

"Mr. B. J. Rynerson, this I presume?" Despite the awkward syntax, the soft feminine voice was both confident and seductive, with only a hint of Cantonese accent.

Jake hesitated, moving deeper into the room. Only three women knew his private number, and this was not one of them. "And who is this?"

"My name Mei-li Chiang. Perhaps you have heard this name?"

"It's possible," he answered cautiously, though he knew the woman by reputation: a well-known power broker, and one of the few Macanese who had managed to maintain influence in the new Special Administrative Region—the SAR—that guaranteed Macau a "high degree of autonomy" when Portugal turned the province over to China in '99. "What can I do for you, Madame Chiang?"

"It is more what I can do for you, taipan."

He hated the title—*big boss*—and tried to discourage its use. "Please call me Jake."

"Jake," she repeated, turning his hard-edged name into something soft and provocative. "I understand you are having problems."

Was she guessing—he knew the Macau grapevine was healthy and well entrenched—or did she really know something? "The usual construction delays."

"Not so usual, I am told."

He wanted to know exactly what she had heard and who had said it, but was positive she would never divulge a source or any details of what she knew. That was the crux of her power—*secrets*—and she would know how to keep them and use them. "Nothing we can't handle."

"That is most gratifying to hear, taipan. I thought perhaps I could be of some small service . . ." She paused, her voice a teasing mixture of promise and provocation.

He could already feel her hand in his pocket and knew he was being sucked toward a vortex of Chinese graft and corruption. Given a choice, he would have told her to take a flying leap off the Taipa Bridge, but if she did know something, he needed to quash the story before it spread. "Yes, it's true, we've had a few unfortunate accidents." Nothing, he was sure, she didn't already know.

"Accidents," she repeated, as if the word amused her. "I think it is more than that, taipan."

"And you could help?"

"Perhaps. I have some small experience in these matters. There are people I could speak with about these . . . *unfortunate accidents.*"

"And what's this here 'small experience' going to cost?"

She made a little sound, a disapproving exhale of breath, offended that he should be so blatant and boorish. "This is not about money, taipan."

He knew better. Once a person acquired that ludicrous title of *businessman and billionaire,* it was always about money. "Please excuse my ignorance, Madame Chiang. I'm just a simple *qai loh,* and a cowboy to boot."

"A foreigner, yes, but we both know you are neither ignorant nor simple, taipan. You misunderstood my offer."

"Which was?"

"To welcome a new friend into the colony. To provide assistance. Your problems are my problems."

He didn't believe a word of it. "That's much appreciated, ma'am. Sure is."

"We should discuss these problems."

Or more accurately, the cost of eliminating them, a situation he could see no way to avoid. If he went to the police—who cared nothing about the problems of a rich *qai loh*—the story would leak out; and if he didn't pay, the *accidents* would continue. The only question was the amount it would take to make the problems go away. "Yes, ma'am. I'm listening."

"These are not matters to be discussed over the phone."

Right, you don't discuss bribes and offshore bank accounts over the airwaves. "What do you suggest?"

"A private meeting."

And you don't discuss such matters in front of witnesses, which was perfectly fine with him. "When and where?"

"I am at your service, taipan."

He glanced at his watch—4:51—realized the day was rapidly slipping away, and the Alliance that much closer to dissolving. "Is today convenient?" He tried not to sound as desperate as he felt, but could hear it in his own voice. "Say nine o'clock?"

"Ten," she answered instantly, obviously aware she had him on the hook, and could reel him in at will. "You are familiar with the *Leal Senado*?"

"The old senate building?"

"*Hai.* From there you must walk."

He pressed the RECORD button on his smartphone. "Give me directions, I'll find you."

Billie leaned forward over the white tablecloth, her whispered voice as tight as the string on a new guitar. "This isn't like you, Jake. You've never paid a bribe in your life."

He shrugged, trying to keep it casual, nothing he couldn't handle. "I've never done business in China."

"It's too dangerous," she snapped back, her voice rising, the words echoing through the dimly lit bistro. "Forget it, Jake. Please."

He gave her his best good ol' boy smile, trying to dampen the fire in her eyes. "You sure do look spectacular when you're angry, darlin'."

"Don't you try and sell me with that cowboy bullshit. Don't even try. I'm too old to buy, and too smart to believe."

"I mean it, Billie." And he did. She might have acquired a few wrinkles around the eyes and mouth, but it was a face built on a magnificent superstructure of bones that didn't depend on makeup and perfect skin. "You look as good as the day we got married."

She frowned in mock disgust, though her eyes sparkled with affection. "Like that's a big whoop. We've only been married two years."

"I meant the first time."

"You're so full of bullshit, I'm surprised those baby blues haven't turned brown over the years." She dropped her voice another notch. "What else did he say?"

She assumed it was a man and he saw no reason to say otherwise. That would only exacerbate the problem, her thinking he was meeting some Chinese seductress in the backstreets of Macau. "That was it. The person who called was just a go-between."

"You don't know that."

No, but he believed it. Mei-li Chiang was a political parasite; she didn't create problems, she lived off them. "It doesn't matter."

"It does matter. You're one of the richest men in the world; you can't start paying bribes to everyone who tries to shake you down. For all you know it's the Triad."

"The Triad hasn't operated in Macau since '98. These are just some local yahoos trying to score a few bucks from the newest *qai loh* wanting to play in their sandbox."

"I don't think so."

That was the problem with Billie, too damn smart. They both realized the *accidents* were too severe for a bunch of local yahoos. "Why?"

"If this was just about money," she answered, "they would have made a try after the escalator got trashed and before a bunch of innocent people got killed."

He shook his head, but that was exactly his thinking. There was something else going on, something he didn't understand. "There's no reason to worry, they just want to be sure nothing is being recorded. They'll give me an amount and the number of some offshore account and I'll be back at the hotel in less than an hour. Besides—" He glanced around, making sure no one was eavesdropping on their conversation. "—I don't really have a choice. If these accidents continue we'll never get the place open in time. The Alliance will fail."

"That's not your problem."

"The President made it my problem. I gave my word."

"Don't do it, Jake." She reached out and clutched his hand, the way a person does at thirty thousand feet in bad weather. "Please, I've got a very bad feeling about this."

"I've got to, honey. You know I do." He gave her fingers a reassuring squeeze. "I'll be careful."

She cocked her head toward the three-man security team near the door. "At least take one of them."

"Can't do it. The instructions were very specific. Private. If I don't show up alone there'll be another accident tomorrow, you can bet on it."

She released his hand and slumped back into her chair, resigned.

Ten minutes later he was on the Avenida de Almeida Ribeiro, the main thoroughfare dividing the narrow southern peninsula from northern Macau. Despite the late hour and the rain, there was still an abundance of foot traffic, a combination of tourists and locals. Jake pulled the collar of his Gore-Tex jacket up around his neck and hunched over, trying to conceal his massive frame, but it was hopeless, like trying to hide Paul Bunyan in a land of midgets, and he gave up the effort. Guided by street names etched onto azulejos—the distinctive blue-enameled tiles of Portugal—he turned north on Rua de Camilo Pessanha, then west toward the inner harbor, moving deeper into old Macau: a maze of narrow, cobbled streets offering a colorful mixture of shops, churches, and small cafés.

After twenty minutes of back and forth and around, he was thoroughly confused, blindly following Madame Chiang's directions into the hodgepodge of alleyways and backstreets, away from the tourists and pedicabs. From time to time he had the feeling of being watched, eyes following his every move, but saw nothing and dismissed the apparitions as the fruit of an over-stressed imagination.

Another few turns and he found himself in a dimly lit area of closed shops, the foggy street empty of people. Though the rain had eased to a drizzle, the humidity was thick enough to chew, and his shirt was now soaked with sweat. He stepped into the covered entryway of a Chinese apothecary and checked his notes in the reflected glow of his cell phone. *Almost there.* He leaned into the misty rain, checking the street for any sign of activity. *Nothing,* but he could feel something, or someone, and didn't like it. The place was too dark and remote, the whole scenario too much like an old Charlie Chan movie the moment before everything went bad. But what choice did he have? If he didn't show up, there would be another accident, more innocent people dead. And that's all it would take, one more accident and they would miss that magic feng shui timetable; and then the dominos would fall, Taiwan would blame Beijing, Beijing would blame the United States, and the President would have no choice but to blame that dumb 'ol West Texas cowboy. *Shit.*

He stepped back into the narrow street, moving cautiously toward the hazy glimmer of a streetlamp about a hundred yards ahead. It was like moving underwater, the fog softening the harsh lines of the shops into muted shades of gray, the sound of his own footsteps muffled and distant. At exactly ten o'clock a woman stepped out of the fog and into the yellow cone of light beneath the streetlamp. She was dressed in a shapeless silk chemise, as garishly colored as a macaw, a cream-colored shawl draped over one arm. "Good evening, taipan." Her soft, sensual voice dissolved into the heavy air, barely spanning the short distance between them.

"Nei ho ma?" he answered, the standard *Hello, how are you?* greeting of the province. She was a short woman, not more than five foot, early forties, with black hair pulled back into a bun at the back of her head, and thick black eyebrows that arched together like bat wings over sharp, black eyes—ugly as a Komodo dragon. "Madame Chiang?"

She smiled coquettishly and dipped her head. *"Hai."*

He returned the bow and stepped forward into the light. He wanted to get straight to the point, the money—the how much, the when, and the where—but that was not the way of business in China. "It is generous of you to meet me on such a night."

She smiled again, the cryptic grin of a gambler with aces in the hole. "It is my honor to serve the great taipan."

Honor. Great taipan. The bullshit and exaggerated politeness made his skin crawl. "And it is my—" From the corner of his eye he saw a man step from the shadows, not more than ten yards away, his skin so white it seemed transparent. Dressed in a dark jogging suit and black running shoes, he had the broad shoulders and narrow hips of an athlete, and the steady hand—which contained a black machine pistol—of a professional. Before Jake could react there was another sound, from behind, someone light on their feet, coming fast, emerging out of the fog, arm outstretched, a small chrome-plated automatic waving erratically with each step.

Twisting his body to avoid a direct hit, Jake shoved Madame Chiang out of the way, but he was too slow and too late, a lightning bolt of fire burning through his chest as both guns fired simultaneously. He felt the air leave his lungs, the blood draining from his legs, the earth rising to meet him as he pitched forward onto the wet cobblestones. *You dumbass cowboy!*

He landed with a hard, dull thud, but felt nothing, his body already numb. He could see the hem of Madame Chiang's dress, her booted feet as they peddled backward out of the light.

"Billie . . ." He gasped her name with his last bit of air, knowing it would be the final word to cross his lips.

Chapter Two

Manhattan Island, New York City, New York

Wednesday, 27 June 10:53:32 GMT -0500

Lara dropped the deli bag onto the small glass table next to the window, and pulled the mouthpiece of her head-mike down below her chin. "Let's eat."

Simon glanced over at the wall-mounted clock—a new two-thousand-dollar global time indicator—located above Lara's equally new twelve-thousand-dollar, ultramodern, ultra high-tech desk. *Her command center.* In fact, everything in the place was new and expensive and high-tech: his blatant attempt to overcome her resistance to their new office. Despite her assurances that she never thought of Eth Jäger and what happened, he didn't really believe it and wanted the added protection of a building with full-time security. "It's not even eleven o'clock."

"I don't care. We've been moving this crap around for hours." Though dressed in a lightweight tank top and loose-fitting khaki shorts, her tan skin glistened with perspiration. "I'm hungry and tired and I need a break."

He wanted to point out that the *moving around* was her doing, that no matter where he put things, she wanted them somewhere else. That was the problem with having your sister manage your business: she felt an inherent right to bitch, and he felt a familial obligation to let her get away with it. "Okay, we'll take an early lunch."

She pulled out two of the unborn chairs, still wrapped in their thick plastic membranes, but before she could peel away the covering, a tall man with broad shoulders and brown curly hair stepped through the open hallway door. His coffee-colored eyes made a quick sweep of the room, lingering for an extra microsecond on Lara's slim figure. "Excuse me." Dressed in tan slacks and a blue blazer, he was holding a clipboard in his left hand. "Is this a bad time?"

"Of course not," Lara answered, her voice suddenly perky and full of energy. "What can I do for you?"

He reached inside his coat—exposing the butt end of an automatic pistol holstered beneath his left arm—and pulled his identification: a laminated PVC card with photo ID, and an embedded hologram of the building. "I'm Bill Rapp, head of security. I just need a few more details for our records. Number of employees, that kind of thing."

"Sure, no problem," she answered, as her tiny hand disappeared into his large one. "I'm Lara. Lara Quinn."

He flashed a boyish grin. "Nice to meet you, Ms. . . . I'm sorry, is that Ms. or Mrs. Quinn?"

"It's Ms." she answered. "But call me Lara."

"I will, thank you." He released her hand and turned to Simon. "And . . . ?"

Simon stepped forward and extended his hand. "Simon Leonidovich." He pronounced his name slowly and distinctly—Le-on-o-vich—letting the man know the *d* was silent. "That's L-E-O-N-I-D-O-V-I-C-H."

Rapp recorded the information on his clipboard. "I've got you listed here as Worldwide SD. What's the SD stand for?"

"Special delivery," Simon answered. "We're a courier service. Most of our work is international."

Rapp's pupils expanded with interest, as if he had just stumbled across the Playboy Channel on his television. "You ever transport valuables? Jewelry or bonds, that sort of thing?"

Simon smiled to himself, thinking of Lara's common refrain: *At ten thousand a pop, you don't hire the man who can deliver anything, anywhere, to haul toilet paper.* "Sometimes."

"Will valuables ever be stored here on the premises?"

"Never." *Almost never.* He wasn't about to divulge that kind of information to a stranger—security service or not.

Rapp recorded the information on his form. "And your position with the firm, Mr. Leonidovich?"

"He's one of our delivery people," Lara answered before Simon could speak up, "and a general pain in the ass."

Rapp's gaze bounced back and forth between them, clearly wondering what kind of weird relationship he had just stepped into.

"She's my sister," Simon explained before the man became overly confused, "and I own the company."

"Aaah." Rapp expelled a faint sigh of relief and turned his attention to Lara. "So you're . . . ?"

"My secretary," Simon answered in quick retaliation. Of all his sister's self-anointed titles, *secretary* was most decidedly not on the list. "But you might want to put her down as the office manager. She's very sensitive about job titles."

"Thank you, Boris."

Though tempted to strike back, he realized that's exactly what she wanted—an excuse to embarrass him with the story of how Boris Leonidovich Pasternak Simon became Simon Leonidovich—and he wasn't about to step into that trap. "You're welcome, Sissie."

Rapp took a step back, as if wanting to extract himself from a situation he didn't understand. "That's all I need." He pulled a couple of business cards from the breast pocket of his blazer. "Any questions or concerns about security—" He leveled his eyes on Lara, his tone going from helpful to inviting. "I'm the man to call."

Eating her lunch—a footlong Italian sub that miraculously disappeared into the confines of her tiny stomach—Lara stared out the window and tried to hide her interest in the handsome Bill Rapp. "This really is a nice view."

Simon suppressed a smile. He would have teased her about the obvious attraction, but the last thing he wanted was to dampen any possible relationship. It had been seven years since Jack's death, Allie and Jack Jr. would soon be teenagers, and she deserved to have a life beyond work and kids. He followed her gaze down to the small community park, eight stories below. The patch of green, a pleasant little garden surrounded by ornamental wrought iron, offered a welcome respite from the surrounding towers of steel and concrete. Under the watchful eyes of mothers and nannies, children scampered back and forth through the playground, a pinball movement of colorful little bodies bouncing from swings to slides to climbing bars. "Yeah, sure is."

"It looks hot."

"Sure does." He could see the heat shimmering off the hot cement; could almost smell the hydrocarbons through the glass.

"Bill seemed nice."

He forked another scoop of salad into his mouth, trying hard to conceal his amusement. "Mmm-hmm."

"This place might not be so bad."

Not so bad! The building was newly remodeled with plenty of underground parking, the offices were light and airy, the security chief handsome and friendly—what more did she want? "If you decide you don't like it, we'll move."

She gave him a suspicious look, realized he was yanking her chain, and immediately changed the subject. "What's with you and the salad? You lose any more weight, you'll need a new wardrobe."

Wardrobe. He could barely keep from laughing.

"Men don't have wardrobes, Sissie. As long as we're covered and comfortable, we're good to go."

"Yeah, well . . ." She leaned to the side, giving his ratty T-shirt and paint-spattered gym shorts the evil eye. "That's probably the reason you keep getting dumped."

"I didn't get—" The sharp buzz of the phone saved him from once again having to explain his breakup with Caitlin Wells.

Lara pulled the tiny head-mike up from under her chin and toggled the switch on the wireless receiver attached to her belt. "Worldwide SD. How may I help you?" As she listened, her expression mutated from happy recognition to puzzlement. "Yes, he's right here." She pressed the HOLD button on her controller. "It's Billie Rynerson. She sounds . . . odd."

"Odd?" Simon was already up and moving toward his office. "What do you mean by 'odd'?"

"I think something's wrong."

He leaned over his desk from the front side and snatched up the phone. "Billie, what's up?"

"Jake's been shot."

The unexpected words hit like a gut punch, and for several eternity-in-an-instant heartbeats he couldn't muster a response. Without conscious thought, he reached over and pressed the INTER-LINK button on the phone, automatically recording the call on his computer. "Is he okay?"

"No," she answered, in what sounded like a major understatement. "He can't breathe. They've got him on a ventilator."

This time he noticed the distinct intercontinental hiccup between question and answer, and remembered they were in Macau. "Is he conscious?"

"No, but he's hanging on. He's fighting."

Of course he was fighting; she was talking about Big Jake Rynerson, a man who didn't know the meaning of quit. "Then he'll make it, Billie. Jake's got the heart of an elephant."

"Absolutely," she answered with a confidence that failed to hide the truth: hope mixed with fear, mixed with panic. "That's exactly what I told the doctor."

"What happened? Tell me everything."

As she started into the medical details, Simon printed four words on a scratchpad—JAKE SHOT, HANGING ON—and handed it to Lara, who had followed him into his office and looked ready to burst with questions.

By the time Billie finished, her voice was edgy with impatience. "That's everything."

But it wasn't, not even close. She hadn't said anything about the shooting, and Simon could think of a dozen unanswered questions. How did it happen? Where did it happen? Was the shooting random or intentional? What happened to Jake's security? But Billie Rynerson was a tough old West Texas broad, and he knew better than to push too hard or too fast. "What can I do?"

"I need you to pick something up in D.C.," she answered instantly, "and bring it out here. Jake was going to call, but . . . well, anyway, it's very important. All the arrangements have been made. They'll be expecting you."

"Sure. No problem. What—"

"And I need you to stay here awhile. We need your help."

Of course he would go, as a friend, someone to hold her hand and help her through, but there was something in her voice, the way she said *help* that told him it wasn't moral support she had in mind. "Is there something . . ." He didn't know how to say it, didn't want to sound reluctant. "Something specific . . . ?"

"We need you at the Pearl. The grand opening is less than a month off and we're having problems."

"What kind of problems?"

"Never mind that," she responded, her tone impatient. "We'll talk about that when you get here."

He hesitated, trying to read some meaning into her reluctance to say more. Were the problems and the shooting connected? "Billie, I'll come, of course I will, but if you're having problems at the Pearl, you need to get Caitlin out there."

"No," she answered without a moment's consideration, "we need Caity in Vegas."

"But—"

"We're at a chokepoint." She hit *chokepoint* hard enough to make it echo over the line, a warning ping that had nothing to do with Jake's current state of health. "We need someone we can trust."

"But—"

"Kyra is already on the way. She'll have all the details about the pickup in D.C. She'll be at Teterboro Airport in two hours."

He realized it was useless to argue. Hurricane Billie was at full blow, her mind made up, and nothing he could say would alter her path. "Sure, I'll be there. You just take care of—"

She interrupted a third time, clearly wanting to end the conversation. "Gotta go, Simon. I'll tell you everything when you get here."

Before he could respond, there was a soft click and the line went silent. Something about the way she said it—*tell you everything*—reverberated with innuendo. Billie Rynerson was not the kind to mince words, and she didn't lie, which meant there were things she wouldn't, or couldn't, say over the phone.

CHAPTER THREE

Central Macau, northern peninsula

Thursday, 28 June 02:01:16 GMT +0800

Thirty years of battles and skirmishes—big wars, small wars, and more hand-to-hand encounters than Bricker Mawl cared to remember—and never once in all that time had he been hit. Until now. It was ridiculous, more embarrassing than painful, and a blow to his image of invincibility.

Robert Joseph Kelts, known to everyone on the five-man team as "Robbie" or "Jocko" or "the kid," ripped another strip of camouflage tape off the roll. "A little more, sir. I'm almost done."

Mawl raised his arm another couple inches, trying but failing to ignore the explosion of heat that spread down the side of his abdominal wall. *Bloody hell!*

Robbie leaned forward, carefully smoothing the tape along the top edge of the trauma bandage, then stepped back and smiled, admiring his handiwork. "That should do it."

Mawl nodded once, showing his approval, but careful not to make too much of it. "Thanks, Jocko." The nickname had nothing to do with the kid's athletic ability—they were all athletes, or former athletes—but everything to do with his gung-ho, buddy-up enthusiasm. At twenty-four he was the newest and youngest of the group, and still thought being a commando mercenary the *most crackin'* job on the planet. Mawl knew better, and taking a bullet in the side had been a good reminder. Though he was still in excellent shape, he suddenly felt every one of his fifty years, and realized he was pushing the envelope of a young man's game.

Robbie held up the tiny lump of gray metal. "Aye, you're lucky it was small-caliber."

Mawl nodded again. *Damn lucky.* Another inch to the right and . . .

"I'm thinkin' you should have taken backup."

Mawl took a deep breath and counted to five, fighting to control his anger. Of course he should have taken backup. That was obvious—*now!* He should have worn body armor. He should have had the gun set to semi instead of single shot. Lots of mistakes. And if Rynerson survived, such mistakes could magnify themselves into a full-blown catastrophe. Getting to such a man twice would not be easy, and making it look like an accident would be impossible. "It was supposed to look like a bungled nick. A snatch job that went bad." He realized he was explaining his actions, something he made a habit of never doing. "He was supposed to be alone." Which didn't excuse his lack of foresight; he could have taken at least two members of the team without jeopardizing the mission.

The furrow between Robbie's eyebrows deepened to a trench. "Aye, but—"

Mawl never allowed backtalk, but let it go with a look. *The look* was always enough.

Robbie took a step back, finally realizing he had ventured into a minefield. "I mean . . . I—"

Mawl held up a hand, cutting off the words. "You're dismissed."

Robbie started to salute, then remembered that such displays of military protocol were never allowed—a dead giveaway of the team's background—and quickly retreated into the adjoining room, closing the door behind him. Mawl smiled to himself. Jocko was a good kid, fearless and blindly loyal, but like most pumped-up and puffed-up young men, his ability to think was hampered by an overabundance of testosterone. *Assets and liabilities,* Mawl thought, the yin and yang of his high-risk profession.

He pushed himself away from the cheap wooden table and stood up, a fresh jolt of pain pulsating down his side and into his groin. *Bloody hell,* it felt like he had just taken a hard kick in the goolies. He waited, letting the fire dampen, then crossed to the single window and carefully peeled back the curtain. The guesthouse was old and shabby, only six rooms, located in a run-down neighborhood near the border that separated the Macau province from the rest of socialist China—well away from the casinos and tourist hotels, and well away from their private security and the notice of local police. The street was dark and quiet, not a whisper of movement. Confident that no one had followed—that the police would never look for a *qai loh* in such an out-of-the-way flea trap—Mawl dropped the curtain back in place, then stepped into the bathroom: nothing more than a dimly lit corner, separated from the main room by a thin parchment partition.

The meager facilities were old and limited—a squat toilet, a cold-water sink, a cracked mirror—and it took a moment for his eyes to adjust, and a moment longer to mentally block out the pungent odor of stale urine that embedded the floorboards. Breathing through his mouth, Mawl slowly raised his arm, gently probing the area around the dressing for any swelling or other signs of internal bleeding. The kid had done a good job, the bandage dry and tight, the skin tender but not swollen. *Very lucky.*

Satisfied, he studied himself in the mirror, measuring himself against the memory of his youth. On the outside he looked as tough and toned as any of his men, but below the surface he could feel a bit of softness, the subtle changes of age that couldn't be held back no matter how much he exercised. It would start to show soon enough, and he hated the thought of it, the loss of his warrior edge. Though only five-ten, he was tall for that part of the world and the teahouse girls still found him attractive. They liked his shaved head, his pale-blue eyes, his washboard gut, the protection and warmth of his strong arms. That too would change. It was time to find a new profession. *But what?* There weren't many choices in the New Territories for old soldiers, especially ex-Brits, who had ruled the area for nearly a century. Unfortunately, after thirty years, Mawl couldn't imagine living anywhere other than Hong Kong, a city of magic and mystery.

He took a deep breath, the pungent odor stinging his eyes, and forced himself to focus on a more immediate problem: the client. Returning to the main room, he quickly calculated the time difference to the States, attached a digital micro-recorder to his scrambler phone, and punched in the number. As the call worked its way around the planet, Mawl carefully lowered himself into one of the molded plastic chairs and prepared his mind for what he knew would be a very uncomfortable conversation. It wouldn't take long for word to slip out that Rynerson had been shot, and was clinging to life—not the kind of news Mawl wanted the client to receive secondhand.

Calm. Center. Focus.

The phone rang four times, followed by a faint click as the call was automatically routed to another location, followed by another click, followed by the client's familiar voice and code name. "This is Trader."

"And this is English," Mawl responded.

"Is it over?"

"Yes," Mawl answered, "but not done."

There was a long pause, far beyond the normal hesitation of global long-distance. "What . . . do . . . you . . . mean . . . by . . . that?" Each word came slow and hard, verbal bullets searching for a target.

Determined not to lose control, Mawl waited a good five seconds before responding. "It means things went bad." He could have said more, but wanted to wait for the right moment, to save the only positive news until it would do some good.

"What happened?"

"He didn't follow instructions," Mawl answered, trying to deflect some of the blame without making it sound like an excuse. "His security team showed up before I could close the deal." From what he had seen—though it was difficult to be sure in the fog—there had been no *team,* but with one bullet in his side and others flying, he wasn't about to hang around and count heads.

Trader's voice dropped to a lockjaw growl, his tone accusatory. "You said he would be alone."

"That was our mistake," Mawl admitted, "thinking we could trust him."

"I was *assured—*" He accentuated the word, a climbing sarcastic drawl. "—you people don't make mistakes."

Mawl took a deep breath, long and slow, suppressing the urge to snap back. "We guarantee our work."

"Guarantee." Trader snorted, as if the word gave him a bad taste. "You missed your chance. You'll never get close to him again."

It was time, Mawl realized, to play his last card, the only good-news card he had in what was otherwise a busted hand. "There's an excellent chance we won't need to. He may already be dead."

"You hit him?"

"That's affirmative," Mawl answered, keeping his voice matter-of-fact. "I saw him go down."

"You're quite sure?"

Mawl found the question insulting—he always hit what he aimed at—but realized this was no time to make the point. "I have a source at the hospital. I should know something soon."

"I'll expect a call the minute you do. The *very* minute."

"Of course. And what about the hotel?" Mawl hated having to ask; it made him feel like a lackey. "Is it time for another problem?"

"No! Absolutely not. After the shooting, that would be too suspicious."

"That's not a concern. It'll look like an accident."

"No! The press is going to be all over this. I don't want to draw any kind of negative attention."

The man was half a world away, clearly beyond "attention," but Mawl made it a rule never to argue with a client, especially those with deep pockets and shallow tempers. "So what do you want us to do?"

"Do?" The answer came hissing back over the line. "I want you to finish the fucking job! That's what I want you to do!"

There was a faint click and the line went silent.

Chapter Four

Teterboro Airport, Teterboro, New Jersey

Wednesday, 27 June 13:26:21 GMT -0500

Simon watched as the small jet completed its rollout and turned onto the taxiway, directly toward his courtesy car parked at the edge of the tarmac. Though nowhere near the size or opulence of Jake's *whale taxi*—used to ferry high-rollers to his gaming Mecca in the desert—the Gulfstream G550 was no less impressive. Sleek and fast, with skin the color of champagne, it only whispered of the power and wealth it represented.

The cabin door was open and the stairway extended even before the twin Rolls-Royce turbofans quit spinning. Looking no less impressive than her father's plane, Kyra Rynerson stepped into the doorway and waved. "Hiya." Dressed in a white button-down oxford shirt and khaki wash pants, she looked both stylish and casual, a woman in her mid thirties with the body of a college athlete.

Forcing a cheerful smile, Simon scrambled up the steps with his luggage. "Hiya to you."

She gave him a peck on the cheek and stepped back. "Thanks for coming."

It never occurred to him that he had a choice.

"Thanks for picking me up." He stepped inside, she punched a button next to the door, and the stairs instantly began to fold up and retract into the fuselage. He dropped his bags and leaned forward, giving her the eye-to-eye. "You okay?"

"Oh sure." She glanced away. "I'm fine."

But what he saw was a little girl playing brave soldier, and what he heard was: *Hell no, I'm not okay—my father's been shot and I don't think he's going to make it.* He reached out and pulled her into his arms. "Don't worry, kiddo, your dad's the toughest guy I know. He's going to be fine." And he believed it; to think of Big Jake Rynerson losing a battle, even a battle with the Almighty, was inconceivable.

Her stoic resolve seemed to crumble, her body melting into his, silent tears dripping onto his shirt. He waited, saying nothing, letting her get it out. After a minute, maybe two, he felt her body stiffen and grow taller as she gathered herself, drawing on that deep genetic pool of Rynerson strength. Finally she stepped back, took a deep breath, and wiped her eyes with the back of her hand. "Sorry."

"No need. If you can't shed a few tears when—"

She cut him off, clearly not trusting her emotions to talk about it. "Hey, what's with you?" She gave his belly a playful jab. "You've shrunk."

Embarrassed, though he didn't know why, he had certainly worked hard enough to shed the pounds. He gave a little shrug, as if the dramatic change to his physique had snuck up without notice. "You think?"

"Don't play coy with me, Leonidovich—"

For some reason, all the women he had ever been intimate with, called him Leonidovich. Kyra, of course, was not one of those women, but the two of them had shared an experience that seemed to exceed even the most intimate emotions, bonding them in a way that most people could never understand.

"—you look really good."

And he felt it: stronger and more energetic, at least a decade younger than his forty-three years. "Thanks."

"Great in fact."

Even better, and hearing it from a beauty like Kyra Rynerson was almost enough to make him forget all the rabbit food and all the sweaty hours at the gym. "I've been watching my diet a bit."

She rolled her eyes and turned toward the back of the plane. "Yeah, right, a bit."

A young man dressed in the blue uniform of a flight steward suddenly materialized from the galley. "I'll take your bags, sir."

"Thanks." Simon grabbed his security case, empty except for his laptop, and followed Kyra through the cabin. The Gulf 5 was Jake's personal toy, the colors and fabrics done in shades of brown mustard, everything solid and warm and masculine, like the man himself. They settled into one of the conversational areas near the back, away from the galley and flight steward, who had taken a seat directly behind the cockpit. Kyra swiveled her recliner toward the communication console and pressed the FLIGHT-DECK button. "We're all set, guys. Let's get this thing back in the air."

A tiny indicator light marked CO-PILOT flashed green, the man's crisp reply pulsing through the overhead speaker. "Roger that, Ms. Rynerson. We've already gotten clearance. Flight time to Washington is ninety minutes."

Simon buckled his seat belt and leaned back into the soft calfskin. "I'm surprised you're not up there yourself."

"It's a twenty-plus hour flight," she answered. "I'll take a shift after we leave D.C." She gave him a little smile. "You can take the right seat."

"I hope you're kidding." But he knew better, could see it in the flashing glint of her sea-green eyes.

"Why not? This thing isn't any harder to fly than that Beech King turboprop you used to get your multi-engine."

"I'll tell you why not. It's—"

"That was rhetorical," she interrupted. "It'll be a good first lesson."

"Yeah but—"

"No buts, Leonidovich. This thing is easy to fly."

"That's what you told me the first time." He regretted the words instantly, knowing it would conjure up memories of her dead husband: a day and place neither of them wanted to revisit.

Her eyes seemed to drift, the way a person does when they look back, remembering things both sad and pleasant, then she shook her head, as if to amputate that dangling appendage of her past. "We survived."

He nodded. That was the quality he admired most

about her, her indomitable will to survive. Not many people could have endured such an experience and kept their sanity.

"So what's the deal?" she asked, making a rather clumsy effort to change the subject. "You've got a new friend?"

"What?" He hesitated, not expecting the question. "Why would you think that?"

"Isn't that why most people our age lose weight?"

The words surprised him, the fact that she thought of him as a contemporary. "Not in my case." If anything, he suspected it was exactly the opposite, that he was using diet and exercise as a substitution, at least a diversion, from the reality of his celibate and solitary life. "I haven't had a date in months."

"Really?" She raised an eyebrow, inviting a response, then saw she wasn't going to get one and pressed harder. "You're not seeing anyone?"

He suddenly realized where she was heading—an excursion into Caitlin Wells territory—a journey he had no intention of taking. "Nope."

"So what happened between you and Caitlin?"

He gave a little shrug, as if the reasons were too obscure to quantify. "You'll have to ask her."

"I did." She leaned forward, curious and friendly, like a dog sniffing out a new treat. "Now I'm asking you."

Caitlin Wells was not a subject he cared to discuss, least of all with one of her friends, but he couldn't resist the bait. "What did she say?"

She drew a finger across her lips, like closing a zipper. "I want to hear your side."

"There is no *side.*" It came out harsher than intended, and he quickly dialed back the emotion, a little surprised that it still bothered him after ten months. "Things happen."

"Like what?"

Like he wanted children and she didn't. Like she cared more about the House of Rynerson, than making one of her own. Like . . . hell, he couldn't even remember all the reasons, and didn't want to. "Little things, nothing special."

"Oh, right, little things." She smiled, a knowing, heavy lidded look. "Like she'll always put you second to my father?"

And that, another issue he wasn't about to discuss. "Like who cares? It's over."

"Okay, okay." She held up her hands, palms out, as if to physically push the issue away. "I get the picture. You don't want to talk about it."

"Exactly."

"Sorry." She swiveled toward the window just as the plane hit rotation. "I forgot, the male species doesn't like to talk about *feelings.*"

"Okay, smartass, what about you? Have you been dating?"

"I've got a man," she answered, not taking her eyes off the receding runway. "And I miss him already."

He knew, of course, who she was talking about—Tony Jr.—but suspected she was also avoiding a sensitive issue. "TJ doesn't count."

She swiveled around, trying but failing to look offended. "Of course he counts."

"You know what I mean, Kyra."

"I don't want to talk about it."

Touché. "Okay, let's talk about TJ. How is he? Where is he? What's his latest trick?"

She smiled at the thought of her son; a smile not conveyed solely by the curve of her lips, but by her entire being, which seemed to glow with affection. "He's great. He's with Tony's mother, and he's just starting to talk in sentences."

"Wow, that's impressive. Watching his progress must be a neat experience."

"More than you could imagine. You should get yourself one, Leonidovich."

He nodded and forced a smile. Unfortunately, though he couldn't imagine anything better, he had reached that stage in life when a man must face the possibility that love and family might never happen.

Exactly ninety minutes later the Gulf 5 rolled to a stop at the end of a remote taxiway at Ronald Reagan Airport. Simon peered out at the Wells Fargo armored truck, at the four uniformed and well-armed guards standing post at each fender, and wondered what he was picking up that demanded so much security. "You know what this is about?"

Kyra shook her head. "Mother just said there would be someone here with a package. I was too upset about my father to ask questions."

Simon grabbed his security case, which he now had a feeling wouldn't be large enough, and stood up. "This shouldn't take more than a few minutes."

As he stepped onto the tarmac, one of the guards unlocked and opened the truck's interlocking rear doors. "This way, sir."

Except for a slight, pinched-faced man sitting in a bolted down chair just inside the door, the interior of the truck appeared to be empty. "Mr. Leonidovich?"

Simon stared up at the man, who looked decidedly out of place with his red bow tie, dark business suit, and round wire-frame spectacles. "That's me."

"I'm George Hulburt, Assistant Director of Antiquities for the Smithsonian." He paused, clearly wanting Simon to take note of his importance. "May I see your identification, please?"

Simon handed over his passport and driver's license, plus a business card. The man carefully inspected all three, then returned the first two, keeping the business card. "Please step inside."

Simon grabbed the steel handrail and pulled himself up into the interior, which was cool and well lit. The walls were lined with lockers of various sizes, the fronts covered in steel mesh. Not until the doors closed, did Hulburt finally stand and extend his hand. "I believe you've done work for us in the past, Mr. Leonidovich."

"Many times," Simon answered. "The Smithsonian is one of my best customers."

"Though I have no idea what this is all about, I want you to know that I strenuously disapprove."

"Is that so?" Simon responded, trying to hide his confusion.

"This exquisite treasure is the property of the Smithsonian Institution, and by extension, the citizens of the United States. It should *not*—" He hammered the word. "—under any circumstances, be removed from this country."

Simon still had no idea what the man was talking about, or why he felt compelled to share his opinion. "Mr. Hulburt, with all due respect, I suggest you take that up with the person who authorized the transfer."

The little man puffed out his chest, the look of a banty rooster just spoiling for a fight. "Don't you think that I wouldn't. That's exactly what I'd like to do."

"So why don't you?"

The man's eyes widened behind his thick glasses, almost as if he were unable to blink. "I'm hardly in a position to question the President."

Simon almost asked, *President of what?* then realized if you worked for the Smithsonian, there was only *one* president. "Mr. Hulburt, if it makes you feel any better, I have no idea what you're talking about. I was told when and where, nothing more. Until this moment, I had no idea who authorized this consignment, or what I was to pick up. I can only assume from the size of this truck, that whatever this 'exquisite treasure' is, it's not going to fit in my security case."

Hulburt's autocratic outrage dissolved like quicksand beneath his tiny feet. "Oh . . . I'm sorry . . . I assumed . . . I'm so sorry. Please accept my apology. I should not have spoken so . . . it was not my place to—"

"Apology accepted."

But Hulburt realized he had overstepped his position, that such imprudent remarks could return to bite his bureaucratic ass, and was not quite ready to let it go. "I would very much appreciate . . . you understand . . . if you would consider my remarks as confidential."

"Of course."

Clearly wanting to put the conversation behind him, Hulburt glanced down at Simon's security case. "Yes, that will do nicely. No problem at all." He smiled obsequiously. "May I ask . . . you understand . . . the deterrents?"

Though it was not the kind of information Simon would normally provide, the client did in fact, have a legal right to know. "It's got all the typical bells and whistles. The shell is reinforced with titanium mesh and lined with aramid fiber. Both waterproof and fireproof, of course, and loaded with antitheft deterrents." He pulled his key ring and showed the man his electronic controller, designed to look like a car-door remote. "With this, I'm able to control all functions: homing transmitter, antitheft siren, dye bomb, etcetera, etcetera."

"Dye bomb?"

"Small bomb, big boom. Lots of glow-in-the-dark pink dye."

"Oh, I see." Hulburt tapped a finger against his pursed lips, thinking about it. "It might be best if you disabled the bomb. I'm not sure our receptacle is airtight. Any leakage of dye into the—"

"I understand. No problem."

"Excellent." Hulburt pulled a key from his pocket, opened one of the lockers, and extracted a black molded case, about the size and shape of a pregnant Frisbee. Except for a golden sunburst, the logo of the Smithsonian, the outer cover was unmarked, providing no clue to its contents. "The case is made of high-impact titanium, and coated with silica fiber."

Judging from the size and shape of the case, Simon suspected it contained some kind of necklace or pendant. "Silica. Isn't that what the tiles on the space shuttle are made of?"

"Exactly. Fireproof up to twelve hundred degrees Fahrenheit." Hulburt smiled with obvious pride and placed his fingers on the twist latch. "Want to see it?"

Simon almost laughed—that was like asking a teenage boy if he wanted to grab a peek into the girls' locker room—but he suspected Billie hadn't told him for a reason. "No, thanks. It's really none of my business."

Chapter Five

Macau

Friday, 29 June 00:12:15 GMT +0800

Before opening his eyes, Simon could feel the change in air pressure and knew the pilot had put the plane into a long, slow descent. He reached down, found the seat's power button, and pushed it forward, bringing the lounger to an upright position. The bulkhead lights had been dimmed, casting a soft yellow glow over the cabin. "Are we there yet?"

Kyra looked up from her book: *Women Who Run With the Wolves—Myths and Stories of the Wild Woman Archetype,* a testes-twisting title if ever one existed. "Good morning." Despite the long flight she looked fresh and pressed and ready to go, and was now wearing a pair of lightweight tan slacks and a sleeveless emerald-green blouse. She somehow managed to look both casual and chic.

He took a deep breath, struggling to clear the valerian from his brain. "That pill really worked."

"And it's all natural."

He looked out the window, into a sea of darkness, not a twinkle of light above or below. "What do you mean, *morning*?"

"Friday morning to be exact." She glanced at her

watch, a customized petite-sized Omega Flightmaster. "Just a little after midnight."

"What happened to Thursday?"

She splayed her fingers into the air. *"Poof."*

"I'm getting to old to be *poofing* away the days."

"Old!" She gave a little snort. "You're not old. Besides, you'll gain it back on the way home."

"Right," though he had a bad feeling that that wouldn't be anytime soon. "Where are we?"

"About two hundred miles out. We should be on the ground in about thirty minutes."

He released his seat belt and pushed himself out of the chair. "Just time enough for a quick shower."

Mr. Gao Wu, a representative of the SAR—which governed the province under China's one-country, two-systems mandate—scrambled onto the plane the moment the stairs hit the tarmac. A slight man, extremely formal in manner, he handed Kyra a business card, made a shallow bow, and then with the condescending aloofness typical of bureaucrats everywhere, managed to express his government's deep concern without the slightest hint of sympathy. "These things do not happen in my country." The unspoken "unlike yours" seemed to echo through the cabin.

Kyra smiled without warmth, and handed the man her passport. "Apparently they do."

"Some minor incidence of street crime," Wu admitted, "but Chinese citizens are not allowed the ownership of firearms. The penalties are most severe—" He bobbed his head, as if to endorse the wisdom of this policy. "—and such crimes most rare."

Though Simon wanted to defend his country, when it came to guns, America was indefensible. Any idiot could own one, and most of them did. In the land of equal justice and political correctness, every psychopath, gangbanger, and junkie had their constitutional right to bear arms, forcing the general population into a hopeless arms race—it was simply a matter of self-defense. "Have you apprehended the person responsible?"

"Not to this moment," Wu answered. "But I have been assured by the commissioner of police that this occurrence is only a matter of time."

"Excellent," Simon said, as if he actually believed Wu's straight-out-of-the-movies answer. "If there's a problem, I'm sure the FBI would be happy to help with your investigation. Mr. Rynerson is a very important person in our country."

Wu's face tightened, as if someone had just rammed a hot poker up his ass. "I assure you, sir, this *help* will not be necessary."

Simon nodded, quite certain that was exactly the message Mr. Gao Wu had been sent to deliver. "That's good to hear."

Mission accomplished, Wu stamped their passports and welcomed them to Macau, as if they were tourists on holiday.

"Thank you," Kyra said, stuffing the passport into her shoulder bag. "I don't mean to be rude, Mr. Wu, but I would like to get to the hospital."

"Of course," Wu answered, backing toward the door. He made another shallow bow, repeated his concern for "the great taipan," then disappeared into the darkness.

Five minutes later they were on their way to the Conde São Januário Central Hospital, their limousine bracketed between two black Land Rovers, each containing a driver and three security guards. Kyra reached over and pressed a button on the door panel, lowering the privacy window. "Excuse me, do either of you gentlemen speak English?"

The man riding shotgun, a stocky fellow with high cheekbones and Mongolian features, glanced over his shoulder. "Yes, ma'am, what can I do for you?"

"What's with all the security? Has something happened?"

"Couldn't tell you, ma'am. You'd have to ask Mrs. Rynerson about that."

"Thank you." She closed the window and leaned back into the corner. "Should have guessed."

Simon tried to read her expression, but could barely make out her face in the car's dark interior. "After what happened to your father, you can't blame her for worrying."

She expelled a frustrated sigh. "She knows how I hate their fishbowl lifestyle."

"Get used to it."

"Why should I?" she demanded, her voice suddenly sharp. "It's not my life. I didn't choose it. It's not what I want."

"Kyra, with all due respect, it's about time you

pulled that pretty head of yours out of your hinder."

She leaned forward, her green eyes flashing in the soft glow of the streetlights. "Just what the hell do you mean by that?"

"You're heir to the kingdom. You may not have chosen it, you may not like it, but that's the way it is. So live with it, learn to enjoy it, or retire to some nunnery in the French Alps. Either way, it's time you decide who you want to be, and stop blaming others for who you are.

"You don't understand what it's like being the daughter of—"

"And don't," he interrupted, "give me that I-don't-understand bullshit. Yes, you had a terrible experience. Yes, it happened because of your father's wealth. And yes, you lost your husband. But that's all in the past—get over it! There are way too many people who go to bed hungry every night. There are babies born every minute with physical and mental handicaps. There are—"

"Okay, okay." She held up a hand, as if to ward off a blow. "I get the picture."

But these were things he should have said long ago, and he wasn't about to be put off. "It's time for you to see things for what they are, Kyra. You've got a wonderful little boy, healthy and bright. You've got parents who love you, and who, ironically enough, *because* of what happened to you, are back together. You're so pretty you make a man's eyes hurt. You're funny and smart and—"

"Stop it! Please! I understand. I get it. I'm an ungrateful bitch. I need to . . ." The sentence died in her mouth. "Pretty? What's this about pretty, Leonidovich?"

Uh-oh, that wasn't the response he expected. He gave her a look of admonishment, trying to avoid the minefield. "Come on, Kyra, stop fishing for compliments. You know damn well—"

"I am *not* fishing for compliments. I'm . . . I'm curious, that's all. I haven't had a date since Tony died. I have no idea how men look at me. And if you remember, you're the only man who's seen me naked in the past two years."

Now there was a memory, about as asexual as one could get, and he realized her interest had nothing to do with him. He was her safety net—the man who had pulled her out of El Pato prison—but he was certainly not her vision of a knight in shining armor. "Well of course I think you're pretty." He kept his tone impersonal. "You *should* be dating." And then, to be absolutely sure he had eviscerated all possible misunderstanding, he added a final knife thrust. "There are plenty of guys out there who would leap at the opportunity."

"Great, that's nice to hear." She expelled a deep breath and slumped back into the corner. "That's what I like about you, Leonidovich, you always tell the truth."

Right, so why did he feel like such a dishonest jerk?

CHAPTER SIX

Hospitalar Centro Conde São Januário de Macau

Friday, 29 June 01:42:12 GMT +0800

Robbie levered himself out from behind the wheel, squeezed between the seats, and duck-walked his way into the van's makeshift kitchen, which was nothing more than an ice chest, a one-burner propane stove, a box of assorted snacks, and twelve liters of water. "Ya wanna drab of tea?"

Mawl shook his head. It was bad enough being cooped up in a muggy VW Transporter for eight hours without having to piss in a plastic bottle. Especially in front of Jocko, who still had the gusty stream of a young stallion. Mawl glanced back and forth between the side mirrors, checking the parking lot for any activity before flipping on the wipers. One swipe only, not wanting to do anything that might draw attention to their vehicle. *Bloody rain,* it never stopped.

Robbie refilled his travel mug—his fourth double cup in the last hour—and returned to his seat. "This is bollocks. We'll never be gettin' to him here. Not with all this security."

Mawl ignored the comment; he suspected as much, and finished wiping the fog off the inside of the windshield. "Something's going on."

Robbie snatched up his night-vision scope and trained it on the hospital's main entrance. "I'm not seeing anything."

"Check out the guards."

Robbie moved the scope back and forth, scrutinizing the two men flanking the doors. "Aye, they're not lookin' any different to me."

"See how they're standing?" It was a foolish question; Jocko was too gung-ho-warrior to notice the subtle things. "They're expecting something. Someone."

"I don't see . . ." The kid's voice trailed away as a three-car caravan turned off the Estrada do Visconde and circled toward the entrance. "Must be someone important."

Mawl laid the crosshairs of his telephoto lens directly on the limousine, one of the six champagne-colored DTS Presidential models that made up the new Pacific Pearl courtesy fleet. "Probably Li Quan." The Pearl's general manager was the only major player in the world of Macau gaming who had not yet joined the deathwatch. As the security men moved into protective positions, Mawl zeroed in on the limousine's rear door, the camera automatically adjusting to the distance and light.

"Those buggers are good," Robbie whispered, as if his voice might carry the hundred meters. "Very good, aye?"

Mawl nodded. "The best."

"Maybe the old boy's gone toes up."

"Maybe," Mawl agreed, but he didn't think so. His

inside man, a male nurse with a taste for drugs and gambling, had orders to call the minute Rynerson's condition took a turn. Up or down.

One of the security men popped an umbrella and pulled open the door. Mawl clicked off a couple quick profile shots before a head of honey-blond hair disappeared beneath the cone of black silk. "Not Li Quan, that's for sure."

Staring into the optic tubes of his binoculars, Robbie whistled softly. "Pretty damn sweet for an old bird."

Old! The woman didn't look more than thirty-five, but to Jocko, who had never shagged anything older than a teenager, she must have looked like a golden oldie. "Rynerson's daughter, that's my guess."

"Who's the fella?"

Mawl clicked off a half-dozen more shots before they disappeared into the lobby. "Not a clue."

"Husband?"

"Not if it's Rynerson's daughter. She's a widow."

"That right? She looks pretty young to be a widow."

Mawl smiled to himself—from *old bird* to *pretty young* in a heartbeat—and began paging through his background file on Rynerson. "Yeah, that's her. Kyra Rynerson. I want you on her security team."

Robbie stared across the narrow space, his eyes devoid of understanding. "And just how am I supposed to be doing that?"

"You have the perfect profile," Mawl answered. "Ex-military. Young. English speaking. That's exactly what they'll be looking for. Most important, when they call the Kowloon Security Service to check your references—" He tapped the cell phone on his belt. "It'll be me they're talking to."

"Well sure, that sounds great," Robbie said, sounding anything but confident. "But what if they're not hiring."

Mawl smiled to himself. The kid was so bloody naïve. "Trust me, they'll have an opening."

CHAPTER SEVEN

Hospitalar Centro Conde São Januário de Macau

Friday, 29 June 01:51:38 GMT +0800

Hospitals, Simon thought, they were all the same, the air thick with the smell of antiseptics and disinfectants, everything gray and white and sterile—including the people. Without so much as a pause, the security team escorted them through the reception area, up the elevator, and down a long hall to a door marked in both Chinese and English: ICU OBSERVATION. The room was nondescript and sparsely furnished—a small gray table with a phone, sandwiched between two gray chairs—about the size of a jail cell.

Simon closed the door behind him, feeling a little awkward and out of place as Kyra embraced her mother. Though the Rynersons had always treated him with great kindness, he wasn't exactly sure how he fit in, where that dividing line came between friendship and hired help. Finally, after a long, silent minute, Billie turned and took both his hands. "Thanks for coming." She squeezed hard, the way a person does when they're hanging on to a life preserver. "I knew we could count on you."

"Of course." For exactly what, he had no idea, but

suspected the answer to that question would come soon enough. "Any change?"

"Absolutely." She reached over and pulled open a short miniblind that covered most of one wall. "All good."

Kyra took a step back, stricken by the scene beyond the glass: her father, the indomitable Big Jake Rynerson, reduced to a comatose mass, his great body being fed through tubes of plastic, his head covered with silver electrodes, his vital signs monitored by an array of electronic meters and monitors. "Daddy . . ." The word squeezed past her lips in a gasp, like she'd been holding it in for hours.

"No, honey, it's not as bad as it looks," Billie said, putting an arm around her daughter's waist. "Really."

"How?" Kyra demanded, pulling away from her mother's grasp. "How could it look any worse?"

Exactly what Simon was asking himself. To his untrained eyes it looked worse than *bad*—it looked fatal.

"He's breathing on his own," Billie answered, "and his vital signs are strong. That's a big improvement."

Kyra shook her head, not buying any of it. "You told me he had a mild concussion. The only worry was the gunshot wound." She stabbed a finger at the glass. "Look at him. Wired up like a damn switchboard. That doesn't look *mild* to me."

Billie, not the kind to take backtalk from anyone, including her daughter, took a deep breath and held it, a rumbling volcano struggling to hold back its lava. "I . . .

didn't—" She hammered each word. "—want . . . you . . . to . . . worry."

"For Christ's sake, Mother, I'm thirty-seven years old, not some child!"

Before Billie could respond, Simon edged his way between them. "Okay, okay." The last thing they needed was a mother-daughter war. "Let's all take a deep breath and—"

"I'm not interested in some feel-good version of the truth," Kyra interrupted, her voice tight with anger. "I want to see the doctor."

"And why shouldn't you?" Billie fired back. She snatched the phone off the table and punched in three numbers. "This is Billie Rynerson. Would y'all ask Dr. Yuan to step in here when he has a moment?"

The door opened almost before she cradled the receiver. "You wished to see me, Mrs. Rynerson?" He spoke in the clear, measured way of someone speaking a second language.

"Please." Billie motioned him forward.

Yuan squeezed into the tiny room and closed the door. He was a short man, middle-aged, with a round somber face and small alert eyes, his stout body covered neck to knee in a white lab coat. Billie inclined her head toward Kyra. "This here is my daughter, Kyra Rynerson." Another nod. "And our friend, Simon Leonidovich."

The doctor bowed his head, a small and dignified acknowledgment. "How may I be of assistance?"

"My daughter," Billie answered, "would like an *unbiased* evaluation of her father's condition."

"Of course." The doctor's thick eyebrows drew together, as if trying to decide where to begin. "You know, of course, that your father sustained two gunshot wounds. One to the—"

"No," Kyra interrupted, cutting an accusatory glance toward her mother. "I *didn't* know."

The doctor hesitated, realized he had stepped into a combat zone and looked at Billie, clearly hoping for some guidance. After an awkward moment of silence, with no help offered, he cleared his throat and continued. "Yes, that is correct. Two shots. One to the thorax area, missing his heart but puncturing his left lung. And one here." He raised his right arm, indicating a spot about twelve inches below his armpit. "This wound was the most troublesome, severing the superior mesenteric vein and penetrating both the ascending colon and small intestine. The blood loss was significant."

Kyra nodded thoughtfully. "And these wounds are life-threatening?"

"Not at the moment," Yuan answered. "Fortunately, your father is a very strong man." The doctor spread his hands, a gesture of helplessness. "But there was considerable fecal contamination within the abdominal cavity. Infection is always a concern."

"What about brain damage?" Kyra nodded toward her father and his crown of electrodes. "I assume he went without oxygen for a time."

"Unfortunately," Yuan confirmed, "resulting in a coma. But—" He raised a finger in warning. "It is still very early. Very important we not jump to conclusions."

"But you know something?"

A reluctant frown creased Yuan's forehead. "The tests are complicated and difficult for a layperson to understand. I would not wish to give the wrong impression."

"And I appreciate that," Kyra responded, her tone conciliatory, yet persistent, "but I have a bachelor's degree in virology and a doctorate in zoology. Though I'm hardly an expert, I do have some understanding of human physiology: enough to know that you're using a geodesic net to map brainwave activity." She leaned forward, laying a hand on the man's forearm, as if they were old colleagues discussing a case. "So, what's the status, Doc? Have you determined a GCS?"

Yuan stared at her as if she had suddenly materialized from another dimension. "You are familiar with Glasgow Coma Scoring?"

"I am."

The conversation immediately dissolved into a complicated discussion of neurological scales, both of them talking in medical shorthand—incomprehensible acronyms and inexplicable synonyms—all of which meant nothing to Simon, and only added to the confusion about Big Jake's condition. Billie looked equally bewildered, her attention drawn to the scene beyond the glass: a nurse changing one of the IV bags feeding life into her husband's arm. Simon tried to concentrate on other things, not wanting to think of Big Jake Rynerson lying in a vegetative state for the rest of his life, but his mind kept spinning back to that very thought, the way a tongue keeps picking at a popcorn husk caught between the teeth. A sudden change in the medical debate refocused his attention.

"Move?" Kyra stared at the doctor in bewilderment. "What are you talking about? Move him where?"

Dr. Yuan looked at Billie, who looked at her daughter. "We're moving him to Bangkok."

"Bangkok?" Kyra repeated, her voice rising in disbelief. "Why?"

Billie turned back to the doctor. "Thank you, Dr. Yuan. We sure do appreciate all you're doing here."

Yuan not only took the hint, he couldn't escape fast enough, bowing and backing his way out of the room. Kyra waited until the door closed before going on the attack. "Is this some kind of joke?"

"Well, ah course it is," Billie answered, her West Texas twang flat with sarcasm. "I can't imagine a more appropriate time for humor."

"He's in no condition to travel."

"It's only a two-hour flight. They've got a first-rate medical facility."

"But why take the risk?"

Billie raised her chin, the expression of someone sitting with crossed arms. "Dr. Yuan assures me the risk is minimal."

"We're talking about Dad's life," Kyra shot back. "There is no *minimal*."

"You're right, it's his life, and I don't believe he's safe here."

"What are you talking about? Why wouldn't he be safe?"

"Don't be obtuse, Kyra, your father was shot."

"A random shooting, you said. A botched robbery. It wasn't personal."

"Well, yes," Billie answered, "but it's not that simple." She motioned toward the pair of tubular metal chairs. "Let's sit down."

Kyra expelled a deep breath—the exasperated sigh of an adult child when they're being pushed into something by a parent—and lowered herself onto the vinyl cushion. Simon edged back against the door, hoping neither of them would try to enlist his support—a no-win entanglement, no matter what he said.

Billie slid into the second chair. "What I'm about to tell you—" She glanced at Simon, letting him know the admonition was all-inclusive. "Can't leave this room."

"Oh for God's sake, Mother, don't be so dramatic. It's not your style."

"I assure you, I am not being dramatic, Kyra. This is serious. I mean it. I want your word . . . both of you . . . nothing will leave this room."

"Of course," Simon answered without hesitation, hoping Kyra would take the hint and give her mother some slack. "Whatever you say, Billie."

Kyra shrugged wearily and sat back. "Okay. Sure. What's the big secret?"

Billie glared back at her, ready to pounce, then apparently thought better of it and simply responded to her daughter's sarcasm. "Yes, Kyra, that's exactly what it is . . . a secret." She paused, still groping for the right words. "Your father's been working on something very important with the President."

Kyra glanced at Simon, then back to her mother. "The president of what?"

"The president of the United States."

"Oh." She gave her mother a puzzled, somewhat mistrustful look. "I thought Daddy hated politicians?"

"Normally that's true, but he seems to have a special affinity for this one."

Kyra's expression went from skeptical to one of intense interest. "Does that mean those old rumors are true? That he was responsible for putting the President in office?"

Simon found himself holding his breath, wondering if Jake had broken their vow of silence, and had exposed their secret to Billie. A secret, Simon knew, that if it ever slipped out, would change his life forever—and not in a good way.

"I asked him point blank," Billie answered. "He denied having anything to do with it."

Kyra frowned, a cheated look, and Simon jumped in, trying to steer the conversation away from *old rumors.* "So what's going on, Billie?"

"The President has been working on a trade agreement between the United States, mainland China, and Taiwan.

"Are you saying—" Simon hesitated, considering the ramifications. "You mean China is finally going to recognize Taiwan?"

"No," Billie answered. "Not exactly. That's why I said *mainland* China. It's all a matter of semantics. They both consider themselves to be the legitimate government of the Chinese people. Officially this is only a trade agreement, the Pacific Rim Alliance, but even that's a huge concession on the part of Beijing."

"And what," Kyra asked, "does Daddy have to do with all this?"

"For want of a better term, let's say he's the glue. The incentive package. In return for their cooperation, I'm talking about Beijing, he's agreed to help with their petroleum problem."

"I thought Daddy was pretty much out of the oil business."

"He's been in and out. Presently in. Most of his holdings are now in South America."

"But why should he—"

"Because," Billie interrupted, "Congress would never agree to relinquish any of our reserves. The President needed an independent. Someone big enough to take the heat."

"That's Daddy." She glanced toward the comatose figure beyond the glass. "But why hasn't this been in the news?"

"They're trying to keep a lid on the negotiations. Too many things can still go wrong. Half the world would like to see this thing fail, and some of them would do about anything to make that happen. Hell, half the Chinese Politburo would rather drop bombs than trade food with Taiwan." She nodded toward the inert figure of her husband. "I'm afraid this won't help. That's why we need to keep the seriousness of Jake's condition to ourselves, and just hope he recovers in time."

"In time?" Kyra asked. "In time for what?"

"The signing ceremony is scheduled for the twenty-first of July."

"You must be kidding! There's no way he's going to be in any condition to—"

"Your father's a bull," Billie interrupted. "If he comes out of this coma . . . *when* he comes out . . . there's no reason he can't—"

"Now you're the one being obtuse, Mother. Just look at him. He's—"

"Okay," Simon cut in, "that's enough. If I know Jake, he'll sit up when he feels like it, and there's nothing the two of you can do to change that." Though somewhat simplistic, it was a statement neither of them could challenge. "What's so important about the twenty-first of July? I thought that's when the Pearl was scheduled to open?"

Billie nodded. "The opening, the signing, the whole damn thing. Everything is tied together."

Simon pulled a small notebook from his pocket, ready to take down the details. "We've got a month. Why can't the ceremony be pushed back?"

"If only we could. The date was established by some famous feng shui master. Something to do with geology. It's all gobbledygook to me."

Wrong science, Simon thought, but he couldn't disagree with the gobbledygook assessment. "I think you're talking about the Chinese art of geomancy. It's a method of foretelling the future by reading the geographic patterns produced by small particles thrown at random onto the ground."

"Yeah, yeah, that's it. Geomancy. Jake calls it 'reading dirt.'"

Simon smiled to himself—Jake did have a way of getting to the essence. "You said 'the whole damn thing.' Is there something else besides the signing and opening?"

"Unfortunately, yes. That's where you come in. You know anything about Chao Cheng?"

"A little. Isn't he the warlord who unified China into one nation, built the Great Wall, and declared himself Shih Huang-Ti, First Sovereign Emperor?"

Billie nodded. "That's the guy."

"Right. That was about 220 B.C., I think. The Ch'in dynasty. He's entombed near Xi'an, along with his army of six thousand terra-cotta soldiers."

Kyra rolled her eyes. "A little! *Sheesh.* Remind me never to play Trivial Pursuit with you."

Billie ignored the interruption. "You're exactly right. In 221, Cheng had a hallmark carved out of green jade to commemorate his achievement, the unification of all China. It's commonly referred to as the Crest of Ch'in. Shortly after his death, the dynasty collapsed and the crest was broken into pieces . . . three to be exact, and carried off by the conquering armies. To make a long story short, only one section of the crest remains in China. One of the pieces was taken to Taiwan by Chiang Kai-shek when he abandoned the mainland. Another piece was captured by the Japanese during World War II, and was subsequently *appropriated—*" She gave the word a sarcastic twang. "—by MacArthur, who turned it over to the Smithsonian."

Simon suppressed a groan. It didn't take a genius to figure out what he had in his security case, and where it was going. "And what? I'm supposed to return our *appropriated* piece back to the land of the dragon? A peace offering, so to speak."

Billie nodded. "Both pieces, actually. It's all very ritualistic, from the Smithsonian, to Taiwan, to China. You're to be in Taipei August seventeenth to pick up the second artifact, and then deliver both pieces to Beijing the following day. Ironically, it will be brought back here and unveiled to the world during the signing ceremony at the Pearl."

"You must be kidding. You're saying I'm taking these things to Beijing, just so *they* can bring them back?"

"With the Chinese it's all about face." She threw up some quotation marks with her fingers. "*Mianzi.* It's the only way the Politburo would agree to the Alliance."

"Incredible."

"It gets better," Billie went on. "The crest will remain on permanent display here at the Pearl. We're using it as our logo. You'll see duplicates displayed throughout the resort."

"And this has all been agreed to?"

"Yes."

"So what's the problem?"

"Who said anything about a problem?"

"When you called, you said Jake was at his chokepoint. You weren't referring to his condition."

She hesitated, then shook her head. "We should talk about this tomorrow."

"For god's sake, Mother, it *is* tomorrow. What's going on?"

Billie took a deep breath, then launched into her story. She talked nonstop for twenty minutes, detailing each of the so-called accidents at the Pearl, and Jake's efforts to keep the information out of the press.

"So what are you saying?" Kyra asked. "You don't believe these *accidents* were accidental?"

"No," Billie answered, "and neither does your father. That building inspector didn't slip off the roof, that's for damn sure. His body landed twelve feet from the base of the building."

Despite Billie's certainty, Simon knew it was easy to turn problems into conspiracy when things went wrong. "Maybe the guy was suicidal. He could have taken a run and jumped."

"We considered that," Billie answered, "but it's not possible. There's a three-foot retaining wall around the perimeter of the roof. He was thrown."

"Twelve feet? It would take at least two people to throw someone that far."

"Precisely."

"And your general manager—" Simon glanced at his notes. "Mr. Quan. He agrees?"

Billie hesitated, carefully considering her answer.

"Li Quan is a good man, but he . . ." She hesitated again, clearly struggling to find the right words, the politically correct words. "It's a cultural thing. He has a propensity to attribute all things to fate and fortune." She threw up her hands in exasperation. *"Joss."*

"So he thinks the accidents are nothing more than bad luck?"

Billie nodded. "*Joss* is like a religion here, good luck, bad luck, it all flows from the same river of faith. And like all religions, you can't argue faith with fact. It's foolish to even try."

"But you think the accidents have something to do with the Alliance? Someone literally trying to throw a wrench into the works?"

"No. Absolutely not. Besides the people in this room, there's only one other person in all Macau who knows about the negotiations."

"And that is?"

"A man by the name of Atherton. James Atherton. He runs an international consulting firm. The State Department hired him to act as an undercover liaison between us and the three countries involved. He's a straight shooter. Very professional."

Simon nodded, being careful not to show his growing skepticism. "Okay, so if it's not about the Alliance, what is it about? Who would benefit from these accidents? Your competition?"

Billie shook her head emphatically, her silver-blond hair swirling around her finely chiseled face. "It's true, if that *bad-joss* tag became synonymous with the Pearl, it would hurt us . . . no one believes in luck, good or bad, like an Asian gambler . . . but our competition is well established, they're not afraid of us, nor should they be. The Pearl will attract droves of new customers to the province. It's going to help everyone."

He couldn't argue with that. It wasn't like the old days in Vegas, when the Mafia ran everything. Most of the gaming now was controlled by large international conglomerates. "Okay, so if it's not the competition, and it's not the trade agreement . . . ?"

"Extortion," Billie answered without hesitation. "Someone looking for a payoff to make the accidents go away."

"Have there been demands?"

"No, but Jake received a call intimating as much. He got it the same day he was shot."

Kyra jerked upright in her chair, as if someone had injected hot lead into her veins. "Are you saying it wasn't a random street crime? That there's a link between the accidents and the shooting?"

"No, I didn't mean it like that," Billie answered. "The shooting had nothing to do with the problems at the Pearl."

But the answer came too quick, and Simon had a feeling she was holding back. "How can you be so sure?"

"Because I was there, dammit! We were taking a walk and ended up in a maze of backstreets where we shouldn't have been. Before we could find our way back, some guy popped out of the shadows and demanded Jake's wallet." She shook her head, as if to erase the memory. "You know Jake, he didn't take kindly to that. He pushed me aside and tried to grab the guy." She glanced toward her unconscious husband. "You can see how that turned out."

But what he saw and what he heard didn't make sense. Something about the street-crime scenario didn't fit. Jake had been hit twice, from two sides, which meant the impact of the first bullet had spun him around before the second found its target, or—a *big* or—there were two shooters. And two shooters did not sound random or botched. "The guy was alone?"

Billie dipped her head, her lips set in a tight seam.

"Where was your security?" he asked, being careful to keep his tone inquisitive, not accusatory.

"Jake had already dismissed them for the night. Taking a walk was a spur-of-the-moment decision. Nobody really knows us here. We had no reason to expect trouble."

Simon nodded, as if her explanation made perfect sense, but he was now positive she wasn't being entirely candid. Jake was bold, but he was never careless, especially where Billie was concerned. "It must have been terrible."

"It was. I don't like to talk about it."

Whether her back-off warning was intentional or not, Simon realized there were some answers he would have to obtain on his own. "So what can we do to help?"

"The President is depending on us. You have to stop these accidents. We have to make the deadline."

You, not exactly what he wanted to hear—that he was now responsible for holding together a trade alliance he wasn't aware existed until ten minutes ago. "Where do we start?"

"With a good show." She hooked a thumb in the general direction of the lobby. "There are representatives from every major casino in Macau out there. Plus the press. It's a goddamned deathwatch. Don't get me wrong, I don't have anything against the press, and a lot of them love Jake, but they're reporters, with their noses in the wind, just waiting for that first whiff of blood. We need to put on a good face. A little *mianzi* of our own. Business as usual."

"Okay." If he had to lie to the press, at least it would be for his country. "Then what?"

"Then I get Jake out of town. Away from prying eyes."

"What's your timetable."

"Two days," she answered. "Maybe three. I need to get the two of you up to speed on the Pearl before leaving."

Kyra stared incredulously at her mother, as if this were the greatest foolishness she had ever heard. "You don't really think I'm going to stay here if you're taking Daddy to Bangkok?"

"What I think is not important," Billie answered, her voice taking on an edge. "It's what your father would expect."

"Don't play that card, Mother. You don't know—"

"Yes, Kyra, I do. This is crunch time, your father's down, and it's time you stepped into the ring."

There was a long, uncomfortable moment of silence, then Kyra looked at Simon and smiled ruefully, like someone trapped in a dental chair. "Hell of a choice, a prizefighter or a nun."

Billie glanced back and forth between them. "A nun?"

"Simon suggested I get on board the Rynerson Express, or retire to a nunnery in the French Alps."

"Aaah." Billie nodded approvingly. "Simon's a very smart man. So, what's your decision, little girl? You getting into the ring, or should we shave your head and call you Sister?"

Kyra took a deep breath and expelled it: the sound of surrender. "What do you want me to do?"

"Whatever it takes. We've only got four weeks to get the Pearl open."

"But I don't know anything about the resort business." She gave Simon a sidelong glance. "Neither of us do."

"You don't need to," Billie answered. "The management team is in place. They're good people, ready and willing to do the job. Unfortunately—" She glanced again toward her husband. "—the taipan is down, and you have to take his place."

Chapter Eight

Hospitalar Centro Conde São Januário de Macau

Friday, 29 June 02:55:16 GMT +0800

The hospital had converted the staff dining room into a private waiting area for the unexpected onslaught of visitors, all of whom glowed a sickly shade of green in the reflected glare of the fluorescent lights and baby-shit-yellow walls. As Billie entered the room, Kyra and Simon a step behind, the weary murmur of conversation dissolved into a hushed silence, everyone expecting to hear the final death knell for Big Jake Rynerson.

Billie eased in behind a small lectern at the front of the room, adjusted the microphone, then looked up and scanned the somewhat bizarre gathering: the captains of Macau gaming, all middle-aged men, most of them dressed in expensive, lightweight summer suits; and the media, a mixture of electronic and print, male and female, young and old, most of them dressed in T-shirts and shorts. "Ladies and gentlemen, I do wanna thank y'all for being here." Her words vibrated with the twang of a West Texas cowhand. "Your concern for my husband is so very much appreciated." She paused and smiled. "And I know you'll be happy to hear that

Jake's condition has improved dramatically in the last six hours."

There was an audible release of breath: universal relief, interspersed with a few soft murmurs from the press: *Headline lost.*

"He's off ventilation," Billie went on, "and breathing on his own." She paused again, letting the news sink in. "Though he has not yet regained consciousness." She flashed another smile, as if this were nothing more than an annoyance, something to be expected. "His vital signs are strong and it should be only a matter of hours before he's barkin' orders and charmin' all the nurses."

This prompted an abbreviated rumble of laughter, the tone somewhat awkward and strained.

"Now before y'all leave." She made it sound like this was not only appropriate, but expected. "I'd like y'all to say howdy to my daughter, Dr. Kyra Rynerson." Kyra tipped her head and smiled confidently, playing the game. "And our good friend, Simon Leonidovich. They'll be standing in for Jake until he's back on his feet."

She spoke with such conviction and confidence, Simon could almost believe it, could almost see Big Jake striding through the door, taking command, making everyone look small but feel big just to be in the same room with the celebrated Vegas cowboy.

"So," Billie continued, "on your way out, if you'll leave a business card, they'll be sure you're notified of any change in Jake's condition."

Instantly, three reporters were on their feet, firing questions:

"Mrs. Rynerson, what can you tell us about the shooting?"

"What were you doing in that neighborhood alone at night?

"When can we talk to the doctors?"

Billie waved them off with another charming smile. "I'm very sorry, but I want to be there when my husband wakes up. I'm sure y'all understand." Without waiting for a response, she turned and disappeared through a door marked STAFF ONLY.

It was, Simon thought, a masterful performance and a perfect escape—no one daring to keep her from the side of her ailing husband. And somehow, despite her overly optimistic presentation, she had managed to do it without actually lying.

There was an immediate frenzy of movement as the press people gathered their equipment and hurried toward an exit at the back of the room, anxious to file their stories. In no apparent hurry, the captains of gaming stood and straightened and began moving toward the front of the room, where Simon and Kyra had taken up flanking positions on each side of the wide double doors.

One by one the men filed past, expressing their concern and offering their support. It was clear they not only considered Big Jake a friend and a colleague—"one of us"—but that the shooting, which had received worldwide attention, was "bad for business." Simon nodded and smiled and shook hands, accepted their business cards, and promised to keep each man informed.

The president and general manager of Wynn Macau leaned in close, his voice low. "Mr. Wynn is very concerned. I wrote his private number on the back of my card. Please call him direct if anything changes."

"Thank you, I will."

"And you need any help getting the Pearl open, you call me. I'll do what I can."

Though Simon had a feeling they would need all the help they could get to make the deadline, he felt compelled to maintain Billie's all-is-good facade. "Thank you, that's very generous, but I understand everything is on schedule."

"Oh . . . that's good to hear." It was clear from the man's reaction—the momentary hesitation and involuntary contraction of muscles around the eyes—he had heard otherwise.

Ten minutes later everyone was gone, except for one man Simon had noticed lingering at the back of the crowd, and who was now talking to Kyra. Tall and handsome, with straw-colored hair and pale amber eyes, he couldn't have been more enthralled if Cleopatra herself had suddenly emerged from the hereafter.

"Simon." Kyra motioned him over. "This is the gentleman mother was telling us about. James Atherton. Mr. Atherton, say hello to Simon Leonidovich."

Atherton extended his hand, his smile open and friendly. "My pleasure. Kyra tells me you're the man who saved her bacon in Ecuador." Though he was casually dressed in lightweight designer jeans and a linen sport coat over a crisp blue oxford shirt, open at the collar, everything fit like a fine leather glove.

"Not really," Simon answered. "I was only part of the team." He gave Kyra an admonishing glance—she knew how he hated that hero crap—and tried to change the subject. "So you're our go-to guy with this trade-agreement thing."

Atherton glanced around, as if he expected a reporter to suddenly burst out from beneath one of the tables, microphone in hand. "From now on, it might be better if we referred to it as—" He lowered his voice. "—the grand opening." His tone was polite and without disapproval. "Just to be on the safe side."

"Good idea," Kyra said, apparently charmed by the man's gracious manner. "We can't be too careful."

Simon nodded, trying to suppress a sudden and surprising twinge of jealousy. "But isn't your being here a risk? If I know reporters, they were checking out everyone in the room, asking about their connection to Jake."

"Excellent point. And you're right, that's exactly what they did. It's a relief to know I'll be working with someone who understands these things."

The man was a true politician, Simon thought, handing out compliments and avoiding answers. "So, how *did* you explain your presence here?"

"I told them the truth. That I was hired by Jake to help with any bureaucratic hurdles that may arise. It's a job I've performed for many foreign corporations wishing to do business here in the SAR. That's one of the reasons the SD retained my services." He looked at Kyra and smiled, a thousand-watt beamer. "It's not only the truth, it's an excellent cover that gives me an excuse to stay on top of things."

The way he looked at Kyra, Simon could only imagine what *things* Atherton wanted to get on top of. "I didn't realize that's what you did."

Atherton nodded. "That's it exactly. Most of my clients are international companies expanding into the East. I help open doors."

Kyra stared up at the man, her eyes full of interest. "I'm sure you're very good at it."

Atherton smiled, the impish grin of a college jock who had just made points with the hottest cheerleader on campus. "I try."

Trying, Simon thought, to impress the heiress to an empire. An effort that appeared to be working. "So, about this . . . this grand opening. Anything we need to know? Any problems?"

"No problems at all," Atherton answered without hesitation, the confident look of a man who knew how to get things done. "As long you get the place open."

Right, no problems at all. So why did everything feel wrong? Why were people dying at the Pearl? Why was Big Jake lying in a coma? And what was Billie holding back?

Chapter Nine

Hospitalar Centro Conde São Januário de Macau

Friday, 29 June 03:14:47 GMT +0800

The moment Robbie snatched up his night-vision scope, Mawl was awake, fully alert. It was something he had trained himself to do, to survive on catnaps, part of his brain going into hibernation, the other part alert and ready, attuned to any unusual sound or movement. "What's happening, kid?"

"It's that Rynerson bird. The daughter."

Mawl flipped on the wipers, letting them go one stroke, then centered his camera over the hospital entrance, zooming in on the two figures standing just inside the glass doors. "That's not the bloke she came with."

"Nope," Robbie answered. "Must be one of the security boys."

Mawl knew better. The guy was too well groomed, his attire too perfectly casual. "With those shoes?"

Robbie angled his scope slightly downward. "What's wrong with his shoes?"

"Security people don't wear five-hundred-dollar Italian loafers with wafer-thin soles."

Robbie nodded slowly, the wheels turning as he considered this new bit of tradecraft. "Aye. So who is he?"

"Not a clue," Mawl answered. "That's why I want you on that detail. I need to know everything that's happening in the House of Rynerson."

Kyra stared straight ahead, as if she found the rain fascinating, though she couldn't take her eyes off the image of James Atherton reflecting back off the glass doors. *Ridiculous,* at her age, to be nervous around a man, but he was gorgeous and smart and obviously interested. Not that there hadn't been *some* interest in the two years since Tony's death, but the motivation was always difficult to judge: Was it her, or was it the Rynerson fortune? But Atherton seemed different. He obviously had money, and beyond his initial expression of concern, hadn't uttered the name *Big Jake* a single time, something few people could manage. "I feel guilty about leaving Simon."

"I don't see why," Atherton said, his tone puzzled. "It was his suggestion."

"I know, but it's my mother. I should have taken the first shift."

"Your mother's a wonderful woman, she'll understand."

Kyra nodded, not about to debate the point, but when it came to her mother, nothing was understood. For the last couple of years it seemed like all they did was pick at each other—mother-daughter bullshit. Not that she didn't understand the dynamic, it was typical animal behavior, and the human species wasn't much different from any other: everyone trying to establish their territory. But why now, twenty years after she left the nest? "Yes, but that doesn't make her Simon's responsibility."

"I'm sure he's being well compensated."

"That's not true." She heard the defensiveness in her voice and quickly softened her tone. "He's here as a friend." An innocent phrase, she realized, with modern-day implications. "To my father."

"Oh." He smiled awkwardly, clearly embarrassed. "I'm sorry. I didn't mean to imply—"

"It's okay," she interrupted, trying to refocus the conversation. "You didn't understand the relationship." *Relationship,* now why did she use that word?

"Clearly." He smiled tentatively, eyes curious but friendly, like a dog approaching a stranger. "I had no idea you were so close."

She heard the question in his voice but chose to ignore it. "Here's my ride."

Even before the wheels stopped turning, the security men were out of their vehicles and taking up protective positions. The two men stationed outside the entrance immediately converged on the door, one with a large umbrella. Atherton barked a one-note laugh, an eruption of surprise. "Wow, I didn't realize you were so—" He hesitated, searching for the right words. "So well protected."

Kyra could feel a wave of heat rising up the back of her neck. "Mother's a little paranoid after what happened."

He nodded in an understanding way. "Can't blame her." Then he smiled, just a little, as if struck by an amusing thought.

"What?"

"I was going to offer you and Mr. Leonidovich a tour of the city, but—" He motioned toward the phalanx of bodyguards standing patiently in the rain. "I guess you don't need me for that."

Though she suspected the offer was not really intended for Simon, she appreciated the man's quick recovery and gracious manner. "On the contrary, a personal tour by someone who knows the area sounds great."

CHAPTER TEN

The Pacific Pearl, Taipa Island, Macau

Friday, 29 June 10:02:54 GMT +0800

Simon stepped off the elevator and stopped, momentarily stunned by the sweeping view and vast expanse of open space. The place was truly spectacular, even beyond Billie's gushing description.

Everywhere he looked there were people, from the casino floor far below, to the revolving cocktail lounge high above, craftsman of every ilk—electricians and carpenters; audio and video techs; carpet layers stretching out giant rolls of material; painters painting; stencilers stenciling; women on their hands and knees cleaning grout and shining tiles; men on short aluminum stilts hanging wallpaper—everyone intent on their task, all working like bees in a hive, their efforts coalescing into one deep sonorous drone.

And there was nothing, he realized, he could do to prevent another accident. There were too many people, too many opportunities for mayhem, too many ways something could happen. If he was going to help, he would need to figure out who was behind the mayhem *before* something happened.

Despite the frenzy of activity, most of the open walkways that circled the atrium were deserted, all the guest rooms finished and locked and sealed with tape, ready for the initial onslaught of visitors. Trying not to spill the two large, open-topped containers of café mocha, Simon made his way toward a broad-shouldered Caucasian man in a blazer and slacks standing post outside Kyra's suite. "Good morning."

The young man dipped his chin, his expression as impassive as a stone god. "What can I do for you, sir?"

Juggling the two Styrofoam cups into one hand, Simon pulled his new security badge and clipped it to his pocket. "You could open the door."

"Sorry, sir, but no one is to be admitted without a verbal confirmation from the occupant."

Simon eyed the man's name tag, pleased that he had not given up *the occupant*'s name to a complete stranger, security pass or not. "That's right, Paul, and I'm the one who issued that order. Would you please check with Ms. Rynerson?"

Without taking his eyes off the containers of hot liquid, the man pulled a small two-way radio off his belt and pressed the TALK button. "Excuse me, ma'am."

A good fifteen seconds ticked by before a soft, croaking "yes" reverberated back through the tiny speaker.

"I have a Mr.—" He paused, a frown of consternation as he studied Simon's badge.

"Le-on-o-vich," Simon offered, enunciating each syllable.

"He's okay," Kyra answered before the guard had a

chance to repeat it. "Just a sec." There was a shuffle of bed covers, followed by a soft buzz as she unlocked the door with a remote. The guard gave Simon a little salute, finger to brow, and pushed open the door.

Simon stepped inside and the sounds of construction faded to a distant purr as the door closed behind him. The air smelled pure and clean, with the faint scent of fresh-cut flowers. From what he could see in the dim light the suite was moderate in size—central living area, small dining room, four-stool bar, two bedrooms—decorated with floral prints and Chinese watercolors. "Where are you?"

"In here," she answered, her words almost swallowed up by the plush fabrics and blackout drapes that covered the windows. "And unless you have coffee, I'm going to order that nice young man to shoot you."

He followed her voice into the room and snapped on the light. She was sitting slumped on the edge of the bed, eyes closed, head drooping, blond hair spiking out in every direction, hands dangling between her legs. "I feel like roadkill."

"You sound more like a wounded frog." A very attractive frog wearing white drawstring shorts and a pink tank-top camisole. "And you look even worse," which wasn't exactly true. Somehow, despite the tornado-victim appearance, she looked sexy and virginal, more like a teenager than a mother in her thirties.

"I'll get you for that, Leonidovich."

"You should be so lucky." He said it without thinking—some knee-jerk, competitive reaction to the thought of her and Atherton leaving the hospital together—and immediately tried to turn it into a joke. "Because contrary to what you might think, *Rynerson*—" He punched the name, forcing her to look up. "I'm better than *okay*. Much better."

"What?" She squinted at him, a bewildered frown creasing her forehead. "What the hell are you talking about?"

"You just told yon gatekeeper I was 'okay.' A measure of mediocrity to which I take great umbrage."

"*Aaah,* the fragile ego of the hairy beast." She shook her head in mock disappointment. "And I thought you were different, Leonidovich."

He held up the two grande-sized containers. "Play nice, Rynerson, I come bearing gifts."

She grinned, placed her hands on her knees, and levered herself to her feet. "You are my god, Simon Leonidovich. I bow to your wisdom and benevolence."

"That's all I ask, a modicum of devotion and worship."

She stretched, a graceful cat waking up after a long nap, then snatched away one of the mochas. "What happened? Someone was supposed to wake me at six."

"I asserted my new authority and countermanded the order." Though she was wearing more than most women did at the beach, it was difficult not to take a little sightseeing tour. "I knew that flight was going to catch up with you sooner or later."

"Apparently it did." She sipped at the coffee, checking the temperature, then with a robust slurp inhaled an inch off the top. "What about you? Get any sleep?"

"Some." If a twenty-minute catnap on the ride between the hospital and hotel qualified as sleep. "I'm okay."

She fluttered her eyelashes. "Oh, no, sir, you're so much better than *okay*."

Smartass. "That was a test. I was just checking to see if you were paying attention."

Her expression suddenly mutated from teasing to troubled, as if the caffeine had finally reached her brain receptors. "What about my father? Any change?"

He shook his head.

"Mother?"

"Still there. I tried to get her to leave, but . . . well, you know Billie."

She turned and started toward the bathroom. "I need to get over there."

"Not this morning. We have a meeting with Li Quan at eleven o'clock."

She spun around, her silk camisole twirling up and exposing her flat stomach. "You can do that without me."

"I could, but I won't. It doesn't take a genius to figure out that Mr. Li Quan is not going to appreciate some idiot who doesn't know a damn thing about the resort business looking over his shoulder. You're a Rynerson, he's got no choice but to accept your presence."

"But—"

"No buts," he interrupted. "We have to do this as a team."

"But what about mother? She's got to sleep sometime. She can't just—"

"*Can't* is not a word you'll find in the Billie Rynerson dictionary. She won't leave, whether you're there or not, and your father doesn't know the difference. The only way you can help him, is to help me."

She hesitated, as if searching her brain for an argument, then apparently gave up the quest and agreed. "You're right." She shook her head, the expression in her eyes remote and reflective. "I shouldn't have been so tough on her last night."

"Trust me, she understands."

"Not likely."

"No, really, we talked most of the night. She gets it. You're worried about your father. She's worried about her husband. It's as simple as that."

She rolled her eyes. "Yeah, right, simple as that."

"Exactly," though it was obvious they both knew better.

"She didn't sleep at all?"

"No, but I had an orderly put a cot in the observation room. She promised to use it."

"Fat chance." She took a deep breath and let it go, a sigh of resignation. "What did you think of James Atherton?"

He shrugged, the abrupt change of subject catching him off guard, then realized how petty such a casual show of indifference might appear. "He seemed like a nice guy." *If you like tall, suave, and good-looking.*

"He offered to give us a tour of Macau."

An offer, Simon was sure, meant for two, not three. "That was nice of him. When?"

"Five this afternoon."

"Sounds good." More than enough time to come up with a reasonable excuse.

CHAPTER ELEVEN

The Pacific Pearl, Taipa Island, Macau

Friday, 29 June 10:58:36 GMT +0800

Never moving from behind his desk, Li Quan stood and bowed his head in welcome. A small man, with intelligent eyes and amber-colored skin, he was dressed in a dark navy suit over a starched white shirt and matching navy tie. He extended his hand toward two stylish but very uncomfortable-looking steel-mesh chairs facing the desk. “Please.” In sharp contrast to the frenzy of activity taking place just beyond the door, the office was silent and serene—incredibly stark, sterile, and well organized. Decorated in pastel shades of gray, with glass and chrome furnishings, the room seemed perfectly suited to its occupant’s formal manner. “I understand your father’s condition has improved dramatically.”

Kyra nodded. “That’s correct.” Dressed in an open-neck cotton blouse and tailored slacks, she looked fresh and rested, her damp hair combed straight back from her face, giving her the chiseled look of a high-fashion model. “The doctor is very optimistic.”

“This is good to hear. Your mother has tried to keep me informed. Unfortunately, I have not yet had time to visit the hospital and pay my respects.”

"We understand. You have a hotel to open."

"There is still much to be accomplished," he continued, obviously feeling the need to explain. "With all the rain . . ." He gestured toward the window, then rolled his eyes heavenward, as if to say: *It is in the hands of God.* "We have crews working around the clock, but . . ."

Simon hardly listened to the words, they sounded rehearsed, and concentrated on the man's verbal intonations and body language, hoping for some insight into his character. Quan continued unabated—all his attention and comments directed toward Kyra—summarizing the progress of construction, answering questions never asked, but not once referring to the problems that threatened to delay the opening. After fifteen minutes, Simon had heard enough about nothing. "Excuse me, Mr. Quan, but what about all the accidents?"

"Most unfortunate," Quan answered. "Very bad *joss.*"

"And you believe that's all it is?" Simon asked, being careful not to sound accusatory.

"Construction accidents are common, Mr. Leonidovich. A certain number of problems are to be expected, *neh*?"

"Yes, but—" He hesitated, knowing he was venturing into unwelcome territory, and that he needed to choose his words carefully. "You don't think it's possible someone might be trying to sabotage the opening?"

"Possible?" Quan smiled tolerantly, his tone a

touch condescending. "'All things are possible until they are proved impossible.'"

Simon nodded, recognizing the quote. "'And even the impossible may only be so, as of now.' Pearl S. Buck."

"Very good, Mr. Leonidovich. You are obviously an educated man."

Kyra snorted softly, a mixture of admiration and incredulity. "The man's got a brain like an elephant. He reads everything and forgets nothing."

Simon knew better, but kept his eyes on Quan, conscious of the man's clever evasion. "So you accept the possibility?"

"Yes, Mr. Leonidovich, I accept the possibility. I reject the likelihood. The Pearl will bring worldwide attention to the province. Why would anyone wish to delay the opening?"

That, of course, was the question. "I wouldn't know," although he could think of at least six countries that would be against any kind of trade alliance that would unite Taiwan with mainland China. "But Mrs. Rynerson thinks that some of the accidents might not have been accidental."

Quan responded with a tight smile, the expression of someone reluctant to express what he truly felt. "Confucius said, 'Worry often gives a small thing a big shadow.'"

A quote for every occasion, Simon thought, though he didn't understand how Quan could view the accidents as a *small thing*, or why he would want to diminish their significance. "And we have a saying in my country: 'If you've got a problem with roaches or rats, it helps to turn on the lights.'"

Quan leaned forward over his shiny black desk, his dark eyes suddenly fiery with indignation. "I assure you, Mr. Leonidovich, the lights are on. Security is at the very highest level."

"Good. So, you're telling me there's nothing to worry about? Nothing I can do to help?"

Quan hesitated, obviously aware he had just been painted into a corner. If he refused help, and something happened, he would look incompetent. "It has not been made clear to me what kind of *help* you are here to provide, Mr. Leonidovich."

They were now into the cat-and-mouse, Simon realized, establishing territories and boundaries. "Mrs. Rynerson has asked me to assist in any way I can."

"Assist," Quan repeated, clearly wanting to emphasize that role. "What, if I may ask, is your experience in the hospitality business, Mr. Leonidovich? In what area are you most qualified to *assist* me?"

Kyra glanced back and forth between them. "Now wait just a second. Simon is here to—"

"That's okay," Simon interrupted, "it's a perfectly reasonable question." A question, he was sure, to which Quan already knew the answer. "I have no experience in this business, Mr. Quan. Absolutely none. And, just so there's no misunderstanding—" He paused to emphasize his point, to make it clear he wasn't there to play assistant. "—I'm *not* here to learn."

Quan leaned back in his chair. "*Neh* . . . ?"

"No. Mrs. Rynerson wants me to investigate the accidents and do whatever it takes to prevent any further disruption in your efforts to open the Pearl on schedule."

"I see. And what of those decisions normally reserved for Mr. Rynerson?"

It was the question Simon had been waiting for, the only question that really mattered—the question of purse strings and power. "Mrs. Rynerson has indicated—" He purposely used the word *indicated,* which was open to interpretation, since he and Billie had never actually discussed the matter. "—that Kyra and I make those decisions together, as best we can."

Though his expression never changed, the contraction of muscles around Quan's eyes was proof enough of his displeasure. Kyra, who knew nothing of this phantom discussion, looked equally unhappy. "I'm not really qualified."

"Nor I," Simon admitted, knowing he needed to offer Quan a way to save face if they were ever going to make things work between them. "It's a terrible idea. A formula for deadlock and disaster. I suggest that any major decisions be decided between the three of us."

"Sounds good to me," Kyra said without hesitation. "Majority rules."

Quan nodded thoughtfully, trying, but failing, to conceal his relief. "*Hai,* that should work."

Simon extended his hand across the desk, wanting to move on before the man began thinking about power lost, rather than power gained. "Settled then."

Quan nodded, and they all shook on the deal.

"So," Kyra asked, "where do we start?"

"Perhaps I can help," Quan answered. He reached over, pressed the intercom button on his phone, and in rapid-fire Cantonese began issuing instructions to his secretary. He released the button and sat back in his chair. "This will not take long."

Though tempted to ask *for what,* Simon thought he detected a glint of wry amusement, and decided to give the man his moment.

While they waited, Quan extracted two mag-stripe smartcards from a locked drawer in his desk, inserted one of them into a special slot on his laptop, entered a memorized string of alphanumeric characters, then rotated the laptop toward Kyra. "This will allow you access to all areas of the property. Please, place your right thumb over the touchpad and hit the ENTER key."

She did as instructed and a moment later it was done, the information embedded on a tiny chip within the plastic card. "Certain areas," he explained "require only a passkey. The more sensitive areas require both a passkey and a biometric fingerprint match."

"How much of the property," Simon asked, "do you visually monitor?"

"How much?" Quan seemed surprised by the question, at its naïveté. "We maintain video surveillance over all public areas, including the parking garage."

Simon tried to look appropriately impressed, zeroing in on something he should have considered earlier. "I'm talking back-of-house."

"Everything," Quan answered, "with the exception of changing rooms and showers." He held up the second smartcard, moving it back and forth like a windshield wiper. "But access to *all* areas are electronically controlled."

"So you're able to control which employees have access to any given area?"

"Of course." He inserted the card into his laptop and began entering code. "That's essential."

Simon nodded, being careful to keep his tone casual and curious. "So how many people have access to the entire property?"

"Only a select few," Quan answered. "The principal managers and a limited number of top-level security officers. Employees are generally restricted to their area of assignment." He turned the laptop toward Simon. "Right thumb, please."

Simon placed his thumb on the touchpad and hit the ENTER key. "How about the roof?"

The dark eyes narrowed, the man finally realizing the conversation had a definitive destination. "The roof?"

"The tower roof."

"And why would you be interested in the tower roof?"

Simon was sure the man already knew. "I would like to interview anyone who was up there when the building inspector fell to his death."

"That was an accident."

"How can you be sure? I understand his body landed twelve feet from the building."

"*Hai*, that is true, but—" Quan gestured once again toward the window and the unrelenting storm. "The man was small of frame, and the wind currents quite substantial that day. Neither the police nor the safety officials found the distance to be significant."

Wind currents, he hadn't even considered the effect. Why didn't Billie say something? She must have read the report. Did she forget, or was she overreacting, looking for some excuse to explain the accidents and delays? "I'd like to see the official report."

Before Quan could respond, the door opened and a huge man with raven-colored hair and Mongolian features came in toting two large, and obviously heavy, open-topped file boxes of tabbed and color-coded manila folders. He set the boxes in front of Quan, politely dipped his head, then withdrew without comment.

Quan pushed the boxes across the polished surface of his desk. "These are *all* the accident reports." He smiled, the same wry grin from before, though this time he didn't bother to hide his pleasure. "A good place to begin, *neh*?"

Buried in paper, Simon thought, though he suspected any real clues, if they existed, were now locked away inside Big Jake's head.

Chapter Twelve

Central Macau, northern peninsula

Saturday, 30 June 18:16:26 GMT +0800

Robbie gave the door a quick succession of coded taps, waited five seconds, then stepped into the dark room and closed the door. "Sir?"

"Here," Mawl answered, not turning from his observation spot at the window. Nothing had really changed in six days: a few locals hunched over against the downpour, the street awash with floating bits of trash. Anyone but a native would stand out like a purple cow.

Robbie pulled off his fatigue cap, slapped it against his leg, and dropped it on one of the plastic molded chairs. "Bloody rain. Worse than Cambodia."

Cambodia! Robbie had missed that action by a couple of decades, but he loved war stories and Mawl saw no reason to smother the kid's gung-ho enthusiasm. "Almost." If you didn't consider the bombs and bullets. Satisfied the kid hadn't been followed, Mawl pulled the black plastic tarp back over the curtain, carefully taped the edge, then snapped on the light. The pale yellow glow did nothing to brighten the room's seedy appearance. "Well . . . ?"

"Yessir, you were ri—" His words dissolved in a

muffle as he pulled his rain poncho over his head. "—looking for people."

"And . . . ?"

Robbie grinned, proud as a schoolboy who had just discovered he had the biggest willy in the locker room. "Aye, got the job sure enough."

Mawl smiled to himself. "When do you start?"

"Monday morning, oh-seven hundred. We're to be workin' twelve-hour shifts, seven to seven, six days a week."

"Good. Then you'll be with her most of the time."

"Yessir, up close and personal like." His eyes glowed with lascivious mischief. "Until they hire some more blokes, I'm the only one on the team speakin' English."

"Don't start getting ideas, kid. Kyra Rynerson is one smart lady. She catches you looking sideways and you'll be gone."

"Aye, I understand. No sweat."

Mawl didn't like the casual response, or that stupid Yankee idiom, and gave the kid a look hot enough to cauterize any foolish ideas he might have floating around in that boyo brain. "I mean it, kid. You mess up this job and I'll let Big Paddy turn you into one of his nancy boys."

Robbie grimaced. "Yessir, I understand."

Mawl was now sure of it. A friend since his early days in the regiment, Big Paddy had spent six years in a Cambodian prison camp, an experience that left him slightly twisted, with a distinct taste for young men. Despite his many unusual proclivities, the man was absolutely loyal, absolutely trustworthy, and willing to do whatever Mawl asked. Anything. Without question. "You better, kid. Big Paddy's got a stonker that would make a donkey jealous."

"Yessir," Robbie answered quickly. "You can count on me."

"I am," Mawl said, "that's why I picked you for this assignment." In truth, Robbie was the only one on the team with a record clean enough to get hired by such a high-end security service. "Just keep your ears open and your eyes lowered."

"Yessir, I'll be doin' that."

Mawl nodded confidently, not wanting to completely crush the kid's warrior bravado. "That's exactly what I told the client." Trader, of course, had no idea Robert Joseph Kelts inhabited the same planet. "Assured him I had one of my best men on the job."

The sun freckles on Robbie's face brightened noticeably. "You mentioned me to the client?"

"Sure did. Don't let me down."

"No, sir."

"Good." Mawl lowered himself into a chair, being careful not to aggravate the wound under his arm. "I want you to find us a new place." He pulled his wallet and counted out twenty thousand *pataca.* "Two bedrooms."

"Only two?" The kid's expression of self-assurance dissolved away, apparently afraid he might have to share a room with Big Paddy. "For five of us?"

"Paddy, Chrich, and Catman will stay here." They wouldn't like it—the place was so dirty even the cockroaches had fleas—but they were professionals and wouldn't complain. At least not to him. "We need a place that fits your cover. Decent, but not conspicuous. With at least two good exit points."

Robbie stuffed the money into his pocket, a relieved lift in his voice. "Aye. I'll be gettin' right to it."

As soon as the kid was gone, Mawl attached his micro-recorder to his scrambler phone and punched in Trader's private number. As always, the phone rang four times before an automatic router took control, followed by another distinctive click, then ten seconds of silence before the familiar voice came snapping back. "This is Trader."

"And this is English."

"I'm listening." Though it was after midnight in the States, the man sounded fresh and fully awake.

There was no good way to say it, no way to spin the bad news into something positive, and Mawl knew it would be foolish to try. "They're moving him to Bangkok."

"Continue."

Mawl hesitated—he expected an explosion, a demand to "finish the job!"—not *continue.* "He's surrounded by his own security now. A team from Las Vegas. It's unlikely we can get to him before he's out of the country."

"I understand."

Why the change of attitude, this never-before understanding? "We can follow, of course. Eventually, we'll get another—"

"Just tell me everything that's going on. I'll decide what to do."

Mawl flipped open his surveillance log and started down the list of entries. "His daughter flew in early yesterday morning. She arrived at the hospital at 1:44, accompanied by—" He flipped over to his profile notes, the information supplied by his contact at the hospital. "—a Simon Leonidovich. Identified as a family friend. They're staying at the Pearl."

"In the same room?"

"No. Separate suites. 718 and 726."

"Go on."

"They met with Quan later that morning. The meeting lasted forty-eight minutes."

"Don't suppose you have any idea what they discussed?"

Mawl smiled to himself; his first opportunity to redeem his reputation since his failure to take out Rynerson. "What do you want to know? I have a complete summary of the conversation."

"I'm impressed. Read it."

For the next five minutes, Mawl did exactly that, embellishing just enough to make it sound like he had a microphone attached to everyone's ass. "That's pretty much it."

"What will they find in those accident reports?"

"Nothing."

"You're sure?"

Mawl resented being questioned twice about anything, but swallowed his impulse to strike back. "Yes, I'm sure."

"Okay. What happened after the meeting with Quan?"

"Ms. Rynerson went directly to the hospital. Leonidovich spent most of the afternoon inspecting the resort. Roof to parking lot."

"What do you know about him?"

Mawl turned back to his profile notes. "White male, forty-three years old. Works as an international courier. Office in New York. Lives at—"

"Don't waste my time with that background crap! What's he doing in Macau? What's his role?"

Mawl hesitated, realized the man already knew *that background crap,* which meant he had another source in the province. And there could only be two reasons for that: *insurance,* a backup team in case Mawl failed; or *termination,* someone to sever the link once the hit had been finalized. And the latter, Mawl realized, would explain the bullet in his side.

"Mawl . . . ?"

"Don't!" Mawl interrupted, struggling to keep his voice steady. "Use . . . my . . . name."

There was a long silence, far beyond the normal satellite delay. "What's your problem? These conversations are secure."

"We hope," Mawl answered, working very hard to hide his anger, and the fact that he had figured out the man's game plan. "Technology changes. Can't be too careful." A piece of advice he intended to follow himself.

"You're right," the man answered, "there's no reason to get sloppy. So, what about Leonidovich? What's his role here?"

"Just what I said," Mawl answered, his subconscious struggling to process the new information, measuring risks and revising plans. "A family friend. He's insignificant."

"If he's so fucking insignificant, what's he doing poking around the Pearl? What's he looking for?"

Questions Mawl had been asking himself, but so far he had found nothing to indicate that Leonidovich was anything other than a high-class delivery boy. "He's fumbling in the dark. Probably trying to impress the Rynerson broad."

"You said they weren't together!"

"I said they weren't in the same suite," Mawl answered, not liking the man's accusatory tone. "I didn't say anything about a relationship."

"Well then say something! What is their relationship? I need information."

There seemed to be no rhyme or reason, Mawl thought, to what *background crap* the man considered important. "They're friends. It's platonic."

"You're sure?"

No, he wasn't sure, but knowing he was now competing against another intelligence source, he needed to rachet up his value, to imply he had video surveillance everywhere. "There's been no nocturnal movement between their suites." He flipped back to his surveillance log. "And she had dinner Friday evening with a guy by the name of Atherton. James Atherton. They seemed pretty cozy."

"Interesting. What else?"

"I checked the guy out." Mawl quickly scanned

the profile information, picking out the highlights. "He's from Washington, D.C. Runs an international consulting firm. Does piece work for the government from time to ti—"

"Don't bother with that. I know who he is."

Another surprise bit of intelligence. "Right."

"What are they doing today?"

"They've been alternating shifts," Mawl answered. "One at the hospital, one at the hotel." He decided to throw in another small embellishment. "Going through all those accident reports."

"Good. That was clever of Quan, a good way to keep them busy. Don't let that courier out of your sight. Add more people if you need to. I want to know what he's up to."

"What about the daughter?" Though Mawl would normally have mentioned that he already had someone on her security detail, he now realized there was no longer an upside to that kind of disclosure. "You want twenty-four/seven on her too?"

"Absolutely not. She's a fucking zoologist for Christ's sake."

Another fact Mawl hadn't mentioned, though he realized the information was readily available on the Internet. "You want another accident? Just say the word and we can set them back another week. Maybe two."

"No, I don't think that's going to be necessary."

Now Mawl was absolutely sure the man knew more than he was saying.

Chapter Thirteen

The Pacific Pearl, Taipa Island, Macau

Monday, 2 July 07:21:39 GMT +0800

The guard stiffened to attention as Simon approached with his two steaming containers of coffee. The kick-off-the-day meeting with Kyra had become routine, something he both enjoyed and dreaded, knowing that sooner or later he would find her in bed with James Atherton, her dinner companion for three straight nights. "Good morning."

The young man nodded, his smile open and friendly. "And a good one to you, sir." Broad-shouldered and muscular, with pale blue eyes and a smattering of sun freckles across his cheeks, he filled the doorway like a load of bricks.

Simon glanced at the man's security badge: R. J. Kelts. "I don't believe I've seen you before, R.J. You're new?"

"Aye. First day."

"You sound Irish."

"Aye, that I am, sir. And you are . . . ?"

Simon pulled open the front of his jacket, exposing his security badge. "I'm expected."

"Oh, yessir. I saw your name on the list." He extracted a keycard from the breast pocket of his blazer, slipped it into the magnetic card reader, waited for the click, then pushed open the door. "Have a good day, sir."

"You too." For an instant, Simon considered asking if she was alone, then thought better of it. "Good luck with the new job."

"Thank you, sir."

Simon closed the door, waited a moment for his eyes to adjust, then worked his way toward the bedroom, and the only sliver of light in the suite. Hoping her dinner with Atherton had not turned into something more carnal, he tapped lightly on the door. "You—" Distracted by images of erotic interplay, he almost said *alone.* "—decent?"

Her voice, husky from sleep, barely penetrated the door. "I may not be great, Leonidovich, but I'm better than decent, you can bet on that."

That he believed, though more information than he cared to ponder. "I'll take your word for it." He pushed open the door. She was propped up against a mountain of pillows, the bed covers pulled to her chin. She gave him the squinty eye, a feigned look of displeasure. "Don't you ever sleep, Leonidovich?"

"Five good hours. What more does a person need?"

"Six would be nice."

Meaning she hadn't gotten in before 2 A.M. "Six!" Though he had no right to be jealous, he couldn't help but envy the time she was spending with the suave James Atherton. "Six is for wimps."

"Don't pick on me, Leonidovich. I know things."

"Lies and rumors," he fired back, feeling better now that he knew she was alone. "Exaggerations and innuendo."

"That's what I thought. It was all too good to be true."

"Exactly. They don't call me bad-to-the-bone, for nothing."

"Ha! You don't know the meaning of bad, Leonidovich." One naked arm snaked out from beneath the coverlet. "Coffee! I need coffee."

He handed over one of the containers. "What's with the new guard dog."

"That's Robbie." She took a small sip of coffee, carefully checking the temperature as she always did, then sucked down a healthy gulp. "He's my new body man."

Body man, now there was a job a man could get into. "What happened to Paul?"

She shrugged, exposing her bare shoulders. "No idea. The manager of the security company called yesterday. They lost a couple of men, the only ones on my detail who spoke English. Told me to expect a couple of new faces."

"Lost . . . ?"

"That's all I know. Robbie showed at seven o'clock."

"Robbie?"

"Robert Joseph Kelts." She cocked her head toward a profile sheet laying on the nightstand. "Don't you just love his accent?"

"Heterosexual men never admit loving anything

about another man. I read it in the *Rock Hudson Guide to Machismo.*"

"Men have such silly rules."

"Don't get me started on the female species." He picked up the profile sheet and began scanning through the particulars. "I thought he looked young. Only twenty-four."

She smiled, a wicked little grin. "What you call 'young,' I call eye candy."

"I thought that was Atherton." He regretted the words instantly—a foolish, shoot from the hip remark—but they were already gone and he couldn't retract them.

She cocked her head to one side, a puzzled expression. "You don't like James?"

Afraid he would sound like a jealous schoolboy, he ignored the question, keeping his eyes on the profile of Robert Joseph Kelts, aka R.J., aka Robbie. "He does seem to have plenty of experience."

"I wouldn't know," she answered, as if they were still talking about Atherton. "We've only had dinner."

Was she purposely providing information, checking his reaction, or was he reading too much into too little? "He's been with the same security service since his discharge from the SAS. Moved here from Hong Kong about a month ago."

"I saw that. What's the SAS?"

"Special Air Service. It's a division of the British military. Small commando units. Very elite."

"Guess you'll have to start being nice to me, Leonidovich. He sounds tough."

"I'll keep that in mind."

The playful twinkle faded. "You talk to my mother yet?"

"An hour ago. The flight went well; no complications. She likes the hospital and all the doctors."

"And . . . ?"

"No change."

She emitted a long sigh, the sound of hope fading. "I should be there."

"No, you shouldn't. This competition between you and Billie isn't going to help your father."

"Competition?" She gave a little snort, as if the word gave her a bad taste. "Believe me, I'm not competing with my mother. It's just that—"

"Come on, Kyra, it's obvious. You were both out of Jake's life for years, and now you're competing for his approval and affection."

She stared back at him, as if trying to decide whether to be insulted or angry, then simply shook her head. "You really do piss me off, Leonidovich."

"Sorry." But he could tell she was only being sarcastic. "It's a special gift, the ability to say exactly the right thing at the wrong time." He hesitated, feigning a look of confusion. "Or is it the wrong thing at the right time? I can never remember."

"You're too damn smart is what you are."

"Yup, I hear that a lot. Smartass this, smartass that. It's all very gratifying."

"I can only imagine. Okay, smartass, I need to take a shower. Turn around."

He did as ordered, fixing his gaze on a molded duplicate of the Crest of Ch'in, a framed adornment in all of the executive suites. "Don't take forever, Rynerson, we need to talk. I may have discovered something important."

"I'll be quick," she answered, her voice fading toward the bathroom. "Five minutes."

Bathroom. Female. Five minutes. No way that was going to happen. He snapped on the television, a fifty-inch plasma with a wireless keyboard and Internet connection, and settled into a comfortable armchair, but before he could get halfway through his e-mail messages she was back, scampering across the room in a fluffy white towel that barely covered her *féminin délicieux*.

"Didn't think I could do it, did you?"

Despite the taunting implorations of the horny little devil whispering in his ear, Simon managed to keep his attention glued to the screen. "Never doubted you for a second."

"You're not only a smartass, Leonidovich, you're a smartass liar."

"Guilty as charged."

"You take your eyes off that television, you'll be singing soprano at the Temple of Lost Jewels."

"Don't flatter yourself, Rynerson, I've seen you naked, remember? Nothing special."

"Yeah, but back then I looked like a refugee from Dachau. Now I've got some meat on my bones."

Well-toned meat, but this time he was smart enough to keep such insightful commentary to himself. "Yes, ma'am, eyes front, mouth shut."

"What's the weather like?"

Despite his good and honorable intentions, he could see her nude reflection in the television. *Very* well-toned.

"Earth to Simon."

"What?"

"Is it still raining?"

"Yeah. I mean no. It was." *Damn,* he sounded like a junkie on crystal meth. "It stopped about an hour ago. Supposed to be dry for the next couple of days."

"Hallelujah." She turned and disappeared into the closet. "You said you may have found something important."

He tried to refocus, to erase the vision of her naked body from his mind, but knew it was hopeless, the image forever frozen in the occipital lobe of his brain. "I went to the hospital last night."

"Oh . . . ?" Her reflected image—now covered in a bra and boy-short panties—reappeared in the closet doorway.

"I wanted to talk to Dr. Yuan. Some things about the shooting didn't make sense to me."

"How's that?" She pulled on a pair of wheat-colored slacks.

"Your father was hit twice, once in the chest, once in the side. I assumed . . . I think we all did . . . the impact of the first shot spun him around before the second bullet hit his side."

"I didn't really think about it," she admitted. "But sure, that makes sense."

"Except that's not what happened."

"How . . ." Her voice momentarily faded as she pulled a sleeveless top over her head. ". . . know that?"

"Because the bullets came from different guns. One from a 9 mm. The other from a 22." There was more, odd things he couldn't explain and didn't feel comfortable discussing—not with her. Not yet. "Two bullets. Two shooters."

"Mother didn't say anything about a second gunman."

"No. She didn't." He could have said more, but wanted to give her time to work through the information.

She stood there, frozen in the doorway, the wheels turning. "Maybe she didn't see the other guy; it must have been pretty frightening."

"Probably," he agreed, though he didn't believe it. Billie Rynerson didn't frighten, and she didn't miss much. "But that's not the point."

"What is the point?"

"Two shooters from two different directions. That doesn't sound like a botched robbery to me."

"You're saying—" She hesitated, thinking about it. "A professional hit?" She shook her head, rejecting the idea. "No. You're wrong. If it was a hit, Daddy would be dead. They would have made sure."

It didn't take her long to identify *that* inconsistency, but that was only one of many, and only a small part of the wild-ass theory he wasn't about to share. "There's more." He pulled Jake's smartphone from his pocket, switched on the power, and navigated over to the appointment calendar. "Look at this."

She came across the room and leaned over his shoulder, her scent soapy and fresh, her damp hair slicked straight back from her forehead. "What?"

"It's your father's cell phone. I retrieved it from the hospital." He navigated over to the appointment calendar, tapped June 27, and pointed to the 10 P.M. entry: Mei-li Chiang. "That's Jake's last appointment. The day he was shot."

"Uh-oh." She stepped back.

That was not the reaction he expected, not even close. "You know her?"

"No, of course not. I just . . . never mind."

Never mind wasn't on the agenda—he was getting enough evasion from Billie. "What? You recognize the name?"

"No, it's not that. It's just—" She sucked her cheeks into hollows and rolled her eyes. "It's just that . . . it looks like Daddy might be up to his old ways."

It took Simon a moment to process the remark. "Are you talking about another woman?" *Stupid question,* of course that's what she was talking about. "Don't be crazy, Billie was with him."

"Unless she wasn't. That would explain why she didn't see a second gunman. She's trying to cover up for that horny old bastard, make excuses for him, just like she always has. He was out tomcatting, you can bet on it. Why else would he be meeting a woman in that neighborhood? That time of night?"

"You're way off base." At least that's what he

hoped. "I knew something was wrong with the story, and I pressed her about it. She finally admitted Jake was trying to set up a meeting."

"It sounds like she's feeding you a line. Why would she have lied in the first place?"

"She was embarrassed. Said she didn't want to admit that Jake was willing to pay a bribe."

"Mother? Embarrassed? Are we talking about the same person? That woman has balls like the Jolly Green Giant. Please, don't tell me you believe that *embarrassed* crap?"

Actually he didn't. Billie was still holding back, still waffling around the truth, but he couldn't believe Jake was on the prowl—he loved his wife too much. "It was a trap. He was lured into the area."

"And just how did you arrive at that conclusion?"

He toggled over to a text entry linked to the appointment. "Look at these directions. It took me over an hour to trace the route. Someone was running them in circles."

She stared at him, incomprehension in her eyes. "Why?"

"To make sure they didn't have security."

"That's a pretty big assumption."

No, it was experience—El Pato had done the same thing to him in Cali—but mentioning the man who had killed her husband didn't seem like such a brilliant idea. "Call it intuition." Something most woman considered completely reasonable. *Assumption, no. Intuition, yes.* The logic was beyond his neolithic comprehension.

"So you're saying . . . ?"

"I'm saying the shooting wasn't a random street crime. Maybe they were trying to kill him, maybe they only meant to scare him off, but it's all connected. We find out who's behind the shooting, we'll find out who's behind the accidents here at the Pearl."

"And just how do you plan to do that?"

He tapped his finger on Big Jake's last appointment. "Mei-li Chiang."

Chapter Fourteen

Central Macau, the old village

Wednesday, 4 July 21:18:12 GMT +0800

James Atherton pushed open the door to the underground bistro and stepped aside. "This okay?"

Kyra nodded, her saliva glands reacting instantly to the smell of grilled lamb and fresh mint. "Smells great." She paused, letting her eyes adjust to the dim light before stepping inside. "Looks even better."

The place was subdued and intimate, with lots of candles that cast soft flickering shadows across the tables and up the dark brick walls. He seemed to know all the good places. Not the ones found in guidebooks, but small and quiet. And very dark. With each successive night the places seemed to get smaller and darker and more intimate. If things got any more intimate, they would be eating breakfast in bed, and the thought of it scared the bejesus out of her. Was she ready? Was Atherton someone she could build a life with? He certainly had the assets: sophisticated and smart, with a good sense of humor and impeccable manners. All the important stuff. And it didn't hurt that it came wrapped in such a nice package. So why the hesitation?

He stepped forward, peering into her eyes. "Is everything okay?"

"Of course. Why?"

"You looked, uh . . . confused, I guess."

You have no idea, but before she could think of an appropriate response, they were facing a small man wearing a crisp white apron wrapped high across his stomach. He bowed, his wrinkled skin the color and texture of old leather, then led them to a corner table at the back of the room. He waited patiently as they settled into their seats, then took their drink order, and withdrew. Atherton leaned forward over the small table, his amber eyes sparkling in the candle-light, his voice barely a whisper. "You look especially beautiful tonight."

She smiled, trying her best to look pleased. Such compliments always made her nervous. And suspicious. Was it her, or was it the Rynerson money? Atherton was different, she knew that; he had money, had his own company, and hadn't shown the slightest interest in the Rynerson empire. *Loosen up, lady, the guy likes you.* "Thank you. You don't look so bad yourself."

He smiled, a slow tentative smile that ended before it reached his eyes. "I didn't mean to make you uncomfortable."

"You didn't." Was it that obvious? "It's just—" She could feel her face growing warm with embarrassment. "I don't take compliments very well."

"I understand. I'm sure you've heard that one a thousand times."

"It's not that. It's . . ."

"They make you suspicious," he said. "Does he

like me, or that I'm the daughter of Big Jake Rynerson?"

She nodded, feeling foolish and transparent. "Something like that."

The smile expanded to his eyes. "Maybe I'm just trying to get you into bed."

"Are you?"

"Absolutely."

"At least you're honest."

"Patient."

That she believed. Despite all the time they had spent together, the only thing that had passed between them was a good night kiss on the cheek. "Patience is good."

He nodded and sat back. "You're not ready. It's a big step."

It aggravated her—the fact that he was so right. "It's been a while."

"I understand. It was easier when we were young. No baggage. No pressure. No instant appraisal."

"Instant appraisal?"

"That's the way I see it. After a certain age, there's no such thing as a casual date. No time for that. The clock is ticking. You need to bag someone. Would this person make a good partner? What are his assets? What are his liabilities? By the second date most women are asking, 'where is this going?'" He shook his head, amused at the thought. "Hell, I was thinking dinner, a little conversation, *maaaybe* a romp between the sheets. She's thinking dinner, a white picket fence, and babies."

She could barely suppress a sigh of relief. Not only was he right, he was clearly in no rush to bag her, or the Rynerson fortune. "I get it, you don't like babies."

Though she meant to be funny, he seemed to take her seriously, his expression stony as he rolled his hand from side to side, a *comme cí, comme ça* gesture. "Depends how they're cooked."

The words, delivered in such deadpan fashion, caught her so completely off guard that for a moment she thought she might actually lose control of her bladder, but somehow managed to hold on through an uncontrollable onslaught of laughter. She had barely caught her breath when the waiter appeared with drinks and menus. Eyes still swimming, she slid her menu across the table to Atherton. "Surprise me."

He quickly scanned the single handwritten page, then without the slightest hesitation rattled off his decision in rapid-fire Cantonese. The old man nodded his approval and withdrew, silent as a ghost.

She raised her glass in salute, offering the traditional toast, *"Gon-bui."*

"Dry the cup," he responded, converting her Chinese into English, then with a single swallow drained the small glass of *Moutai,* a local wine distilled from millet.

"How many languages do you speak, anyway?"

He shrugged, as if his abilities were an embarrassment, and refilled their glasses. "Five or six. I can muddle through a few others."

From what she had seen, the man didn't *muddle through* anything, which was obviously why the State Department had chosen him to help coordinate the final details for the most important trade agreement since NAFTA.

"Any word on your father?" he asked, clearly wanting to change the subject.

She shook her head, her lighthearted feelings evaporating like water in the desert.

Atherton reached out and squeezed her hand. "He's going to make it."

She nodded. Of course he was going to make it—the infection had been subdued and his wounds were healing—but as what? A vegetable? The thought was repugnant. Unacceptable. Not her father. Not Big Jake Rynerson. Better he was dead.

"Full recovery," Atherton said, as if reading her mind. "Guaranteed."

It was one of the things she liked most about the man—his confident optimism—and she did her best to match his enthusiasm. "I'll drink to that."

As they clinked glasses, the waiter arrived with a basket of steamed bread and a cauldron of bouillabaisse. He ladled heaping portions of the pink broth overflowing with fish and lobster into large bowls, removed their half-finished drinks, replaced their glasses and the *Moutai* with a bottle of white Bordeaux, then melted into the shadows. Kyra leaned forward, savoring the spicy aroma, a tomatoey combination of fennel and garlic and saffron. "Smells wonderful."

He nodded. "It's the best in Macau. Simon doesn't know what he's missing."

Though she realized Atherton really wanted to

spend time with her, he was always gracious enough to invite Simon, who always found a reason to decline the invitation. She was tired of making excuses. "What can I say, the guy's a workaholic."

"I admire his dedication."

But it was more than dedication, she was sure of that. Both men were like a couple of wary dogs, sniffing around to see what the other was all about, not quite trusting their instincts. Similar, she realized, to her own feelings.

Atherton lifted his wine glass but didn't drink, holding it in both hands, looking at her over the rim. "Is there some problem I should know about?"

"Not at all," she answered. "These three days of dry weather have been a godsend. Mr. Quan assures me we're on schedule. Maybe a little ahead."

"That's wonderful news. Excellent. I thought something might have happened. That was the reason Simon couldn't—"

"No, no," she interrupted, "it doesn't have anything to do with the Pearl."

"It?"

"It's nothing." She didn't really believe that, but was afraid Simon's theory about the shooting would sound too far-fetched, that it would diminish him in Atherton's eyes. Why that should bother her so much, she wasn't sure, but it did. In her mind she was always comparing the two, hoping they would like each other. "Really."

"Really?" He smiled, as if he found her avoidance amusing, and crossed his eyes in mocking disbelief. "I don't *thiiii-nk* so."

She knew she was getting sucked in by his disarming smile, but couldn't resist. "Promise not to laugh?"

He held up his right arm, two fingers extended. "Scout's honor."

She took a sip of wine, gathering her thoughts, wanting to keep it simple and real. "Simon thinks the attack on my father was planned. That he was lured into a trap."

All the features on Atherton's face seemed to shift and resettle: from shock, to confusion, to skepticism. "Are you—" He shook his head, as if trying to wave off his own doubts. "You can't be serious."

"I am."

"That's no laughing matter."

"No, of course not. I was afraid—" Afraid of what, that he would think less of Simon? "Afraid you might not believe me."

"Of course I believe you. Simon's no alarmist. Has he gone to the authorities?"

"No," she answered, relieved that he was taking the idea seriously. "The details are a little fuzzy."

He leaned back and folded his arms. "Your mother said it was a botched robbery."

"Yes."

"She's changed her story?"

"No."

He nodded slowly, the picture coming into focus. "So what is it Simon intends to do?"

"He's got a name. Someone he thinks might be involved. He's trying to find her."

"Her?"

"A woman by the name of Mei-li Chiang." Atherton's mouth went a little slack. "You know her?"

"I know the name," he answered. "She's a back-alley power broker. A political chameleon with lots of contacts."

Kyra leaned forward over her untouched bowl of food, keeping her voice to a whisper. "So this really might have something to do with—"

"The grand opening," he interrupted, as if fearing she might not remember their euphemism for the trade agreement. "No, that's doubtful; the details of that event are too tightly guarded. It must be something else."

"Like . . . ?"

He shook his head. "No idea, but I'm sure of one thing, Madame Chiang won't be hard to find. And she won't run. She survived the turnover in '99—she knows how to work the system. Probably knows where more than a few bodies are buried in this town."

"What are you saying?"

"I'm saying that woman is clever and ruthless. Dangerous. Simon needs to be careful."

Chapter Fifteen

Central Macau, southern peninsula

Thursday, 5 July 13:46:53 GMT +0800

The lunch crowd had finally evaporated, the porch of the small noodle shop empty except for Simon and Kyra, and her body man, Robbie Kelts, who sat directly behind her, at the next table. The remainder of her security detail—six men, all big, all Asian, all evenly spaced along the railing, all facing outward, all wearing identical lightweight jackets to hide their weaponry—couldn't have looked any more conspicuous had they been naked. Trying to read Kyra's expression, Simon reached up and tilted the edge of the umbrella just enough to keep the sun from hitting his eyes. "I think you're being a little dramatic, Rynerson."

The skin tightened across her high cheekbones, her response a restrained hiss. "I am *not* being dramatic. Those were his exact words."

"I understand that." He should have known better than to use the word *dramatic.* To a woman like Kyra Rynerson, that was akin to *airhead.* "But 'knowing where the bodies are buried' is just an expression. He meant politically."

"I know what he meant, Simon. You think I'm an idiot?"

Christ almighty, why didn't he just dig a hole and cover himself with shit? "No, of course not. I only meant—"

She cut him off. "You think because I'm blond, I can't tell the difference between reality and drama?"

"No, I—"

"He said 'clever and *ruthless.*' " She leaned forward, drilling him with her icy-green stare. "He said 'Simon needs to be careful.' "

"I understand. I get it. I will."

"Then why not take security?" As quickly as it flared, her anger had dissipated, her tone suddenly pleading. "Please."

"Because I don't need it. I'm going to have a conversation with the lady, nothing more." He reached out, clasping her hands. "Kyra, honey, look at these guys. They're scary big. I walk in with one of these palookas and she'll clam up."

"She's not going to tell you anything anyway. She's too smart for that."

He smiled, trying to reassure her with his confidence. "She agreed to the meeting."

"Yeah, right." She rolled her eyes. "And just why do you think that is?"

The question was rhetorical, a sarcastic aside, but he pretended to take it seriously. "That's easy. She wants to know how I found her, and what I know. Until she knows that, she's at risk."

"No! You're wrong." She jerked her hands free. "It could be a trap. If she's the one who set up my father, what's to stop her from doing the same to you? She's setting you up."

"It's not like that."

"How do you know?" she demanded. "How can you be sure?"

"Because it's the middle of the day," he answered, spelling out for her what he had already worked out for himself, "and we're meeting at her house. Because, for all she knows, I've shared that information with at least a hundred of my closest friends. Because she's a woman, and that means she's snoopy curious." This earned him a little you-better-be-careful glare, but it was a smiling glare, and that's all he wanted. "And because she's a back-alley politico, not a black widow."

She took a deep breath, then let it out slow. "I'm rather of fond of you, Leonidovich. You know that?"

He reached out and patted her hand. "I kinda like you too." More than he cared to admit, even to himself. "I need to go." He glanced at his watch, more to avoid her eyes than to check the time. "I told her I'd be there by three."

"We can drop you."

He shook his head—the last thing he needed was to show up in a two-car, armor-plated caravan—and pushed himself to his feet. "It's a beautiful day. I need the exercise."

She nodded, her eyes gazing up at him from beneath her eyebrows. "Be careful."

"Of course." Beyond her shoulder, he could see

Robbie's back, his head cocked to one side, and Simon realized the kid was eavesdropping. "Always careful." Especially, he decided, whenever Robbie was around. The last thing they needed was some indiscreet bodyguard whispering secrets to his friends.

He left the shop and headed east toward the inner harbor. The narrow street, bordered on both sides by small boutiques, was loud and crowded, a cacophony of languages and colorful attire, everyone enjoying the sunshine after all the rain. When he reached the waterfront, he turned south on Rua das Lorchas, the street crowded with tourists waiting to board the floating casino, and followed the route he had mapped out in his mind before leaving the Pearl. It was one of those perfect summer days, the sky deep and blue beyond a scattering of white clouds, the heat diminished by a light breeze smelling of salt and seaweed. Perfect, except for a vague sense of being watched that kept itching across the back of his neck.

He stopped twice at small waterfront shops, casually browsing the window displays and checking the reflections in the glass, making sure Kyra hadn't decided to play nursemaid with her team of bodyguards, but he saw no sign of the black Land Rovers. Satisfied, he followed the street through a progression of name changes around the tip of the peninsula, past the Pousada de São Tiago—an incredible hotel built on the remains of a seventeenth-century Portuguese fortress, the Fortaleza de Barra—until he was heading north toward Penha Hill, into the city's most prestigious residential area. Along with the traffic and pedestrians, the sounds of the city dissolved away, the commercial buildings giving way to large colonial mansions surrounded by plush gardens.

He found the home of Mei-li Chiang on a quiet, dead-end street, surrounded by a fortress-like wall covered in vegetation. Even before he reached the gate—a narrow wooden door with iron straps thick enough to withstand a vehicular assault—at least two motion-sensitive cameras had zeroed in on his movement. Madame Chiang either liked her privacy, or feared her enemies. Probably both, he decided, considering the woman's reputation. He pushed the bell and offered up a friendly smile to the camera, knowing someone beyond the wall would be comparing his physiognomy to a database of persona non grata.

A man's nasally voice erupted from a small speaker above the door. *"Nî jiào shénme míngzi?"*

Though most of the locals spoke Cantonese, Simon recognized the words as Mandarin, and one of the few common phrases—*What is your name?*—that he could actually respond to in most languages. "*Wô jiào* Simon Leonidovich," he answered, and opened his passport to the camera.

Someone inside threw a latch, the sound heavy and muted, followed by the accelerating hiss of an air piston and the scrape of locking bolts being withdrawn. As the door moved silently inward, a disembodied hand motioned Simon to step inside. For the first time he felt a flutter of anxiety, an ominous foreboding, the way, he imagined, a convict must feel when he takes that first step behind the gray walls. *It could be a trap. She's setting you up.* He stepped forward and the door closed behind him with a dull and irrevocable *thunk.* In contrast to the fatalistic sound, the lush garden that stretched out before him—an artful coalescence of fountains, miniature fruit trees, and limpid pools of koi—was both welcoming and serene, a virtual Garden of Eden. Unfortunately, it wasn't Eve who stepped out from behind the door, but an Asian version of Mr. Clean: shaved head, gold earring, tight T-shirt over bulging muscles. Without so much as a smile or a "let's get to know each other," the man pushed Simon's arms into the air, then with the quick and thorough hands of a professional, proceeded to explore clothes and crevices, no body part left untouched. Apparently satisfied, the man turned toward the house, an impressive three-story colonial villa, and motioned for Simon to follow.

A gatekeeper with skills, Simon thought, taking note of the man's tool belt, which contained an assortment of small gardening tools and one very large handgun. When they reached the door, Mr. Clean punched a combination of numbers into a keypad, then stepped back. There was a faint but audible corresponding tap of keys from the other side, then the snapping click of electronic locks.

The man waiting inside might have been a gatekeeper clone—*Clean II*—except for his clothes: black slacks and a white Nehru-style jacket that failed to hide the bulge of a weapon beneath the hem of his coat. "Mr. Leonidovich." He bowed, the shallow bend typically reserved for foreigners. "Please welcome to this home."

Simon returned the bow, purposely giving the man a more courteous dip. "*Do je.*" Thank you.

The man smiled, a somewhat arrogant upturn of the lips. "If you would be pleased to follow this way." Without waiting for a response, the man turned and started toward the back of the house. They passed through the entry gallery, a formal waiting area, a large drawing room, and emerged onto a sweeping veranda overlooking another spectacular garden. Mei-li Chiang was waiting at one end, her back to the wall, ensconced in an extremely wide and high-backed wicker chair. So high and wide, in fact, it appeared to have wings, and might have taken flight had it not been for its short and corpulent occupant. Sitting very upright on a thick layer of colorful silk pillows, and dressed in an equally bright kimono-style robe, the woman looked like a garishly dressed Buddha.

"Mr. Leonidovich—" Her voice was soft and breathy, almost suggestive, with only a hint of accent. "Welcome." She offered her hand, palm down.

"Madame Chiang." He took her hand and affected his best imitation of a French courtier. "I am honored to make your acquaintance."

Her blood-red lips curled into a coquettish grin, the affect somewhat ghoulish with her over-rouged cheeks and bat-wing eyebrows. "Any friend of Jake Rynerson, is a friend of Mei-li Chiang." She motioned toward a chair on her left, separated from her throne by a narrow table containing a tea service and a double-tiered plate of Chinese confectioneries. "Please be comfortable."

Simon lowered himself into the chair, a miniature version of her great wingback, which left him a good two inches beneath her brightly painted eyes, and even further below the judgmental gaze of Clean II, who had stationed himself slightly behind and to the right of his mistress. "Thank you for seeing me on such short notice."

"It is of no inconvenience." She reached out, her stubby fingers surprisingly quick, and palmed one of the sweets. "May I offer you a light refreshment?"

Simon shook his head. Judging from her girth, the woman considered the tiny candies—made of glutinous rice paste and wheat flour—more of a staple, than a *light refreshment.* "No, thank you. I just finished lunch."

The bat wings curled upward, as if this reason made no sense, then she shrugged, popped the small candy into her mouth, and swallowed. "So." She leaned forward, as if to share a confidence. "How may I be of service to the great taipan? What is his condition?"

Simon knew this would be the first question and he answered without hesitation, adding a slight but enthusiastic lift to his voice. "Better every day. Since his transfer to Bangkok the improvement has been remarkable." And true enough, if one considered only the physical wounds. "We're expecting a full recovery." *Hoping* would have been a more accurate description, but he needed her to believe Jake was actually talking.

She tried to smile, an awkward attempt to pretend the information pleased her, but the effort failed before it reached her eyes. "This is most gratifying news."

"Yes. I knew you would want to be kept informed." This, he hoped, would only confuse her more.

She nodded slowly, trying to hide her consternation, the wheels spinning so fast he could almost hear the grinding. "Yes, I—" She popped another candy, the gesture instinctive and without thought. "I . . . yes . . . your courtesy is much appreciated."

"It's the least I could do." He wanted her to dig for the information, to force her, through her own questions, to expose what she knew. "Under the circumstances."

The bat wings found a new direction to flutter. "Oh, yes . . . the circumstances . . ."

He smiled innocently, letting her swing.

"So, uh . . ." She paused, just long enough to pop and swallow. "The taipan . . . he mentioned me?"

"Of course." He gave her a curious look, as if he couldn't understand why this should surprise her. "Naturally, he was worried."

"Worried?"

"That you were okay."

She looked like a woman sifting through a dozen possible responses, trying to decide which was the most appropriate, then simply gave up and admitted her confusion. "I don't understand?"

That was the last thing he wanted to hear. Now he

was really stuck, hanging over a ledge with no safety net. If he was wrong, if she hadn't been there when Jake was shot, she would know he was lying. Then what? He tried, but couldn't stop himself from stealing a glance at Clean II, who looked especially protective of his mistress. *Not good.* It was even possible she had orchestrated the attack, but that seemed unlikely; she was a power broker, not a killer. At least that's what he hoped, because if the Clean twins had done the shooting, then Simple Simon was about to get dead. And very fast. He suddenly felt cold to his bones, his bowels going to ice water. *You idiot, Leonidovich!* But it was too late now, she was waiting for an answer, and he needed to know the truth. He took a deep mental breath and stepped off the ledge. "He doesn't remember much after the first shot. Naturally, he was worried about you."

She sat there, her body locked in suspended animation, the silence thick as quicksand; then, after what seemed an eternity, but couldn't have been more than five or ten seconds, she reached down and plucked another morsel off the plate of confectioneries. "You may tell the taipan that I was unharmed in the attack."

Simon leaned forward, trying to hide his emotions, and casually selected one of the small treats. "That's excellent news." He dropped the candy into his mouth, and slowly exhaled, bubbles of relief bursting in his chest. *Thank you, God.* "Mr. Rynerson will be very happy to hear that." He sat back, gathering himself for the next round. "Is there anything you can tell me about the attack—" She started to shake her head. "—that might help with the investigation?"

Her head rotated faster, the bat wings threatening to take flight. "Very dark that night. Rain and dark. Everything very quick." She thrust out a hand, pointing it at him like a pistol. "Bang-bang-bang!"

Simon smiled and clutched at his heart, trying to keep it light. "Three shots?"

She continued to shake her head. "Two, three, don't remember. People running and shooting. Bang-bang-bang."

"That must have been very frightening."

"Aieeeeee!" She threw up her hands and shook them, as if trying to ward off an attack of killer bees. "Mei-li very frightened. Run away fast." She sank back into her nest of pillows, apparently exhausted at the thought.

"So you saw nothing? Nothing at all?"

Another shake of the head.

"Which, of course, is why you didn't go to the police." He purposely offered the excuse, not wanting her to feel that he was the enemy.

"Of course." Then she smiled, that coquettish grin, the expression completely at odds with her calculating eyes. "That would be the most important reason."

She was setting him up for something, but he couldn't avoid asking the question. "There was another?"

She glanced away, as if embarrassed. "Had the circumstance of this meeting become known—" She faltered, feigning the reluctant messenger. "If the press—" She took a deep breath and finally let it out. "This would have been most discomforting to the taipan's wife."

Though Simon recognized the words as a threat—that she was prepared to make the allegation—he could barely keep himself from laughing; as if anyone would believe Jake Rynerson would jeopardize his marriage and reputation for two seconds with this painted-up old charlatan. It was too ridiculous, except that he realized the woman had inadvertently answered one important question, and in so doing, had opened a Pandora's box of new ones. Madame Chiang would never have dared imply such a thing if Billie had been there. "That was very considerate of you."

She cocked her head and smiled, a little conspiratorial grin, letting him know the accusation would not be made unless he forced her into a corner. "You may assure the taipan of my discretion in this matter."

Knowing he needed to take away her bargaining chip, he expelled a soft but noticeable breath of disappointment. "Unfortunately, it won't matter, they're bringing in the FBI. Everything's going to come out." Despite her contacts, it was safe fabrication; the FBI never confirmed their investigations.

"American agents in the SAR?" She glanced up at Clean II, as if to assure herself this would never happen. "Never!"

"I'm afraid it's true," Simon said, trying to sound sympathetic. "That's one of the reasons I'm here. Mr. Rynerson thought you should know."

She shook her head, as if trying to convince herself. "We would never allow such a thing."

"It surprised us too. But—" He held out his hands, palms up. "You know how these things work. Mr. Rynerson is an important man. Someone called the President, the President called the Premier . . ." He could only hope her backdoor contacts did not extend all the way to Beijing.

"Impossible," but she no longer sounded confident.

He nodded agreeably, certain he had her. "That's what I thought. But apparently your government isn't willing to take the risk."

"Risk?"

"They know the kind of money American corporations are pouring into Macau. The kind of revenue gaming generates for the province." He shrugged, feigning a look of indifference. "Guess they're not willing to jeopardize all that."

She plucked another candy off the plate, sucking on it thoughtfully as she stared into the garden, the silence broken only by the soft buzz of honeybees working their way through the flower beds. Simon could almost feel her weighing options, measuring risks, considering in advance the outcome of every possible move and countermove. Clean II remained at attention, his body as stiff and attentive as a Royal Grenadier.

Knowing any determined push would only weaken his position, Simon concentrated on the movements of a small hummingbird as it flitted from one feeder to the next. The seconds lengthened into minutes, and the air seemed to take on a strange density, thick as water, the hush so pronounced it was deafening. Then, apparently having reached some kind of decision, Madame Chiang let out a thin sigh. "*Do je.* Please tell the taipan, his courtesy in sharing this information is much appreciated."

Simon realized he was being dismissed, that his efforts had failed. What little he did learn—about Billie—only confused the matter. He considered one last try, then rejected the idea, knowing it would only make the woman suspicious. He pushed himself to his feet and dipped his head. "I will convey your message."

Without waiting for a reciprocating nod, Clean II began ushering Simon back along the veranda. Just as they reached the door leading into the house, she stopped them. "Mr. Leonidovich . . ."

He turned, no idea what to expect. "Ma'am?"

She pushed herself forward off her throne of pillows, actually hopping the last couple of inches to the floor. "This thing with the American agents . . ." She came toward them, her slippers padding silently over the teakwood deck. "Such publicity as this would not reflect well on Macau."

Right, like it was Macau she was worried about. "I agree. Makes it look like you can't handle your own problems. That's why Mr. Rynerson wanted you to know." He threw up his hands, a gesture of helpless sympathy. "I'm sorry. The FBI can be ruthless sonsubitches when it comes to digging through files and records." For a back-alley power broker, he assumed that was the very last thing she wanted to hear. "Please, excuse my language."

She stepped in close, very close, and Simon had the feeling he was seeing the woman's true nature for the first time. "We must find a way to prevent this intrusion into the SAR."

We! He shook his head, giving her his best look of bewilderment. "I don't see how. Not unless those bastards who shot Mr. Rynerson suddenly decide to give themselves up."

She nodded, looking up at him from beneath her bat wings. "This would not be likely."

"Very unlikely," he agreed.

"*Hai,* this leaves only one solution."

He waited, knowing this was the moment.

"They must be apprehended before these *qai loh* agents begin their investigation."

"That's always a possibility," he said, making it clear by his tone that he doubted it would happen. "We did offer a million-dollar reward for information leading to their capture. Somebody might talk, I suppose."

She placed one of her pudgy hands on his chest, her touch soft as a flower. "It is possible I could be of some assistance in this matter."

"Oh?" *Simple Simon here,* you'll have to spell it out.

"I have, of course, no interest in this reward."

He nodded, waiting, knowing the woman was now ready to sacrifice her firstborn to save herself.

"Some time past, I received a call . . . a man asking

that I intervene on his behalf with the taipan. This is what I do, you understand . . . assist people in their business relationships here in the SAR."

Right, altruism for a price. "Who was this person?"

She stared up at him, her hand still on his chest. "Unfortunately, he refused to give me a name."

Unless he had suddenly lost his ability to read people, she was telling the truth. "And what did this person want?"

"I'm not sure." She continued to maintain eye contact, the liar's classic effort to appear forthright. "I declined his request."

He could sec that she had now ventured into makeup land, where lies were conceived. "And what does this have to do with the attack on Mr. Rynerson?"

"Perhaps nothing." She stepped back, her tone suddenly museful, as if thinking aloud. "But it now occurs to me, this person may have had ill intentions toward the taipan. That this attack may not have been the simple street crime we all assume."

Simon nodded thoughtfully, playing the game, but he *assumed* nothing, least of all the *simple* part. "Yes, I see what you're saying. But if you don't know the person's name . . ."

"I may still have notes regarding this conversation. Perhaps a telephone number, or one of those computer addresses."

"That could be helpful."

"Please—" She gestured for him to follow.

She led the way into the house, Clean II a step behind. They crossed through the drawing room and down a long gallery of original art—a nonsensical collection of old-world landscapes and pop-art convulsions—to a wide metal door at the far end of the house. Madame Chiang punched her password into the keypad and the heavy door began to move inward, slow and hushed, like a bank vault.

In contrast to the decor and scale of the home, the area was high-tech and relatively small—a combination panic room/office, without windows—a double row of fluorescent lights, reflecting off a highly polished white linoleum floor. There was little in the way of furnishings: a desk, a small refrigerator, two nonmatching chairs with casters, and a well-used leather couch. The desk, a football field of gray laminate stretching from one wall to the next, was nearly invisible, the top covered in electronic equipment and mountains of papers. A row of gray file cabinets covered the far wall, and above them, the only nonfunctional element in the room: an austere cityscape of black tubular steel, the buildings and bridges jutting out from the three-dimensional sculpture in a nightmarish depiction of futuristic existence.

Madame Chiang motioned toward the couch, indicating Simon should sit, then went to the desk and began searching through a stack of papers near the phone. Above her head, a double row of high-definition surveillance monitors displayed various views of the house and grounds. Clean II stationed himself just inside the door, his dark eyes attentive and unreadable.

Leaning back on the couch, Simon let his mind drift, hoping to sneak up on Billie's story from a new angle. If she lied, and he was almost certain of that, it had to be for a good reason. But what? Combining the various bits of information, he began to play the scene through his mind: the narrow street . . . the rain . . . the fog . . . the darkness. For a brief moment the fog started to lift—*bang-bang-bang*—a vision of what happened, or might have happened, coming into focus . . . then something on the security monitors caught his eye. Not something he saw, but a lack of something. He glanced from one screen to the next, searching for movement, a bird or a tree branch, but not until he reached the last monitor—a view of the front garden and gate—that he knew for certain. Near the edge of the screen, the gatekeeper was just coming into sight, one leg extended, his foot an inch or two above the ground . . . hovering there . . . locked in suspended animation. *Probably nothing,* an electronic glitch, but for some reason it gave him a bad feeling, a low-frequence hum that vibrated outward along his nerves. "Excuse me . . ."

Madame Chiang glanced over her shoulder.

He pointed to the monitors. "The screens are frozen."

She looked up, her head rotating slowly from one monitor to the next. *"Dee karray ray?"*

Though Simon didn't understand the words, her puzzled tone was clear enough. Clean II stepped forward, a look of annoyance as he studied the images, then his gaze settled on the last screen—the front garden and the unmoving leg of the gatekeeper—and his expression mutated from irritation to alarm. He spun around, his arm stretching out for the red panic button that controlled the vault-like door, but he was too slow and too late, someone already standing in the doorway. Except for the goalie-like Plexiglas mask that distorted his face, and a long-barreled pistol in his left hand, he looked like a mechanic or maintenance worker, his body covered neck to foot in a dark blue, zip-up-the front coverall. He smiled, the expression somewhat ghoulish beneath the thick plexi mask, and fired one quick shot—*pop*—the sound of a lightbulb breaking. Clean II stared back at the man, his expression frozen in surprise as a droplet of blood coursed down his forehead and dripped onto his nose, then his knees buckled and he pitched face-forward, his arm still extended toward the panic button—dead before he hit the floor.

Madame Chiang started to scream, but the sound died in her throat as a second bullet ripped through her trachea. Before Simon could react, the gun was pointed at his chest, the man warning him not to move with a gesture of his right hand. Simon nodded, indicating he understood, but knew if he didn't do something, no matter how rash, he would end up like Mei-li Chiang, who had collapsed to her knees, her hands clutching at her throat, trying unsuccessfully to stem the river of red blood flowing down the front of her kimono and onto the white linoleum.

The man stepped forward, glancing down to avoid the spreading pool of blood, and Simon launched himself off the couch, diving for the man's legs, bracing himself for the impact, expecting at least one bullet to find his back, but *hoping* it would miss his vital organs, *hoping* for a little luck. The moment seemed to last forever, one of those never-ending dream sequences, the colors muted, the sound turned off, the unending strain to get somewhere . . . reaching . . . reaching . . . almost there . . . and then, as quickly as it began, reality came crashing down, the searing impact on the back of his neck, the vivid explosion of colors through his head, the immutable fade into darkness.

Chapter Sixteen

Central Macau, southern peninsula

Thursday, 5 July 16:02:15 GMT +0800

Mawl waited until Fosseler—aka Catman—was in the van with the door closed before speaking. "You turn on the cameras?" Catman Fosseler was their sweep man—last in, last out—responsible for making sure no detail had been overlooked, no equipment left behind.

The man frowned, clearly irritated at the suggestion he might have forgotten anything. "Yeah, Brick, I reactivated the bloody cameras."

Mawl nodded and turned to Big Paddy. "Go."

Paddy eased the van away from the gate, which they had left slightly ajar, and slowly accelerated away. Mawl pulled his cellular and pressed SEND, the number preset and ready to go.

The woman answered on the first ring. *"Yeyyy."*

"Make the call. You'll get the rest of your money tomorrow."

"Hai." There was a soft click and the line went silent.

Mawl immediately deleted the number and call history from the phone's memory, then leaned back, closed his eyes, and methodically began to walk the dog back, making sure nothing had been overlooked. He worked every step through his mind, back and forth twice, but couldn't find a single mistake. *Perfect,* not a hitch or a hiccup, not one damn thing Trader could take exception to.

No one spoke until Paddy reached their designated disposal site—the backside of a shuttered warehouse near the waterfront—but Mawl could tell the men were jazzed, relieved and excited at the way things had turned out. Daylight assaults were always risky, especially when you were stuck on a peninsula with no way out if things went bad. He glanced over his shoulder at the two men in back, now dressed in typical tourist attire, their coveralls along with the plexi masks and latex gloves having disappeared into a black garbage bag. "Bang on job, guys."

Everyone nodded, trying unsuccessfully to hide their exuberance and maintain their professional detachment. Mawl turned to Paddy. "You too, Big."

Paddy grunted, leaned out the window and spit, obviously still upset about his watchdog role.

Mawl smiled to himself. It had been an easy choice; someone had to monitor the police channel in case they inadvertently set off a silent alarm, and Big Paddy wasn't exactly the stealthy type. "Next time—" He hoped to hell there wasn't one, not in broad daylight. "You go in."

Paddy hunched his massive shoulders, sulking like a schoolboy who had been passed over when they chose up sides for soccer.

Mawl let it go. The big man would get over it soon

enough, he always did. Opening the door, Mawl stepped onto the crushed-granite lot, peeled off his coveralls, and tossed them into the back along with his thick rubber-soled shoes. Fosseler stuffed everything into the garbage bag, added a small magnesium charge, and passed the bag up to Paddy, who walked it out to an empty oil drum near the back of the empty lot.

While the other men scrubbed down the van—removing all traces of the water-soluble paint and temporary signage—Mawl walked out near the water, far enough not to be overheard, attached the micro-recorder to his phone and punched in Trader's now familiar number. As always, the phone rang four times, followed by the sound of a relay and another click before the call was finally answered. "This is Trader."

"English," Mawl responded.

"Is it over?"

"Yes."

"Complications?"

Mawl wasn't about to make it sound easy. "A few minor surprises. Nothing we couldn't handle."

"And . . . ?"

"You don't need to worry about songbirds, if that's what you're asking." The neck shot had been his own idea; a subtle message no one would understand but his own men, which was exactly his intent.

"And the carrier pigeon?"

Mawl smiled to himself—the man was quick, no doubt about that. "Just as you ordered. I clipped his wings."

"Excellent. The money will be in your account within the hour."

That was all Mawl wanted to hear. "I need to go. All hell's about to break loose around here."

"I'll be in touch." There was a faint click followed by the sound of dead air.

Mawl pulled the jumper cable, dropped the recorder in his pocket, and jogged back to the van. "Let's move."

As Paddy wheeled the van around and headed toward the street, Mawl reached up and pressed the button on the tiny remote attached to the visor. Behind them, there was a soft *whomp* as the magnesium charge exploded.

CHAPTER SEVENTEEN

Central Macau, southern peninsula

Thursday, 5 July 16:13:34 GMT +0800

Along with the terrible roaring noise that filled Simon's head, came the realization that he was still alive. His neck felt like an elephant had stepped on it, the rest of his body numb. Afraid to move—not sure that he could—he laid there, eyes closed, listening, trying to assess the damage. He could smell blood, but couldn't taste it . . . he could even feel the dampness against his chest, but couldn't tell if the bleeding had stopped, or where it was coming from.

The internal noise slowly diminished until it was only a loud hum and all he could hear was the sound of his own shallow breathing. Confident he was alone, or the only one alive, he took a deep breath and cracked one eyelid. *Holy Jesus!* A wave of nausea welled up from his stomach, but he managed to swallow it back, the acid scorching his throat. Though he knew Madame Chiang would be there, he didn't expect her to be so close—barely a foot away—her painted eyes staring directly into his.

He forced himself to look away—at least he could move his head—enough to see Clean II, his arm still stretching out toward the panic button and the door beyond. A door that now looked firmly closed. Something felt oddly wrong about that, though he couldn't think why; it was such a small detail in comparison to being trapped and bleeding to death. What the hell happened? Robbery? No, the man had come to kill—it was in his eyes. Either a vendetta or a hit. Madame Chiang obviously had enemies—that's why she needed a panic room and a staff of armed retainers—and Simon Leonidovich just happened to be in the wrong place at the wrong time. *Story of my life.*

He tried to move his arm but couldn't. Then he noticed a slight tingle in his fingers and realized it was stuck beneath his body. Girding himself for a jolt, he edged over onto his side, relieved and more than a little surprised at the lack of pain. He waited, working his fingers until the tingling numbness began to recede, then reached up and gently probed the back of his head and neck, searching for the wound. He found it at the base of his skull, but it was only a small lump, and he suddenly realized the blood wasn't his—that the man had hit him with the gun, not shot him. *Thank you, God.*

Moving slowly, not wanting to rile the demons still humming away inside his head, he pushed himself back from the gaping, lifeless stare of Madame Chiang, and sat up. The room looked untouched, the file drawers unopened, the stacks of paper on the desk undisturbed—everything just as it was except for the phone, which Madame Chiang had apparently yanked from the wall in a last desperate attempt to call for help. No robbery, that was certain. He glanced at his watch, the face smeared with blood, but the numbers still visible beneath the glass: 4:18. How long had he been out? Twenty, thirty minutes? No more, he was sure of that. He pulled his cellular, wiped it beneath his underarm to remove the blood, and was about to call for help when he noticed the NO SERVICE display. *Great,* trapped in a steel reinforced panic room with two bodies and no phone. And the smell, the putrid miasma of death—a disgusting combination of excreted body fluids—wasn't getting better.

He pushed himself to his feet, then carefully tiptoed his way to the door, trying to avoid the blood. Though controlled by electronic keypad, he gave the door a hard tug, just to confirm what he already knew. He turned and began to scan the room, looking for an override. There had to be something, some way to get out if the electricity failed. Then, from the corner of his eye, he noticed a slight movement on one of the security monitors—a ruffling of leaves on a plum tree in the garden—and he realized the system had been reactivated. *Sonofabitch.*

He made his way to the desk, checking each of the screens. What he saw, sent a sudden, nauseating chill racing through his body. There were at least five more bodies: Mr. Clean just inside the front gate, a woman at the top of the stairs, two more in the kitchen, and another man near the back garden: another Clean type, except that his muscular arms were covered in tattoos. All dead, Simon realized, before anyone ever approached the panic room. All in broad daylight. It would have taken a team. A well-trained and well-financed team. What did Mei-li Chiang do to deserve such cold-blooded retribution? And who did she do it to?

Without moving, he resumed his search, looking for some way to escape a room that seemed to be getting smaller by the minute. Not that he was worried about being trapped; both the gate and the front door were slightly ajar, and he couldn't imagine it would be long before someone investigated and called the police.

By the time he finished scanning the walls and the underside of the desk, the headache demons were picking up steam, trying to escape their cranial prison through the front of his forehead. Being careful to avoid the blood, he pulled one of the rolling chairs over to where he was standing, then eased himself down into the seat, intending to rest his head on the desk. Unfortunately, he couldn't avoid the stack of papers Madame Chiang had been going through, or the temptation. Pulling a tissue from a nearby box, he tore it into small squares, dampened them with saliva, then layered the pieces over his thumb and index finger to avoid leaving fingerprints, and began to turn pages. Most of the material, faxes and letters, were written in Chinese, but all the handwritten notes were in English—*I may still have notes regarding this conversation*—and that's what he concentrated on. Nothing seemed to stand out—most of the notes nonsensical scribbles from telephone conversations—yet he had the feeling he had seen something and overlooked it. He ran through the pages a second time, trying to connect the disjointed phrases into something meaningful, but couldn't find anything vaguely connected to Jake or the opening of the Pearl.

Frustrated, he removed the damp tissues, absently wiping at a faint ink stain between the thumb and forefinger of his right hand. When it didn't come off, he realized it wasn't ink, but some kind of oily film. *Huh.* He leaned back, thinking about it, when a frenzy of activity drew his attention back to the monitors. Cops everywhere—a battalion of heavily armed SWAT-like troops with helmets and body armor—swarming through the gate and into the garden, moving fast toward the front door. *Too fast,* no reconnaissance, no tiptoeing through the tulips, as if they knew exactly what they were up against and what they would find. That's when it hit him . . . why leave the gate and front door ajar? . . . why wear a mask if the intent was to leave no witnesses? Or was that intention? He glanced down at the smudge on his hand, then brought it to his nose. *Gun oil!* But he was locked in, how could anyone believe . . . ? But the answer right there, Clean II pointing the way, as if he'd hit the panic button and died, trapping his killer inside. *You idiot, Leonidovich!*

He spun around, the adrenaline spike burning away the demons, his mind suddenly sharp and focused. Where was it? He forced himself to breathe, to slow down, to take his time, knowing it was there, a gun with a silencer and fingerprints—his fingerprints. *Think, Leonidovich, think!* And then he knew, even without looking, it would be close to where they left him, where they expected the police to find him, but not where he would see it if he woke up. He crouched down, and there it was, laying just beneath the edge of the couch. He glanced back at the monitors, the cops were already in the gallery, less then a minute away if they had the door code, and he knew they did. Someone had given them everything: Simple Simon on a platter. *Bad! Very bad!* And he only had seconds to make it better.

Chapter Eighteen

Coloane Island, Macau

Friday, 6 July 11:04:54 GMT +0800

Simon recognized the man the moment he stepped into the room, Mr. Gao Wu, the officious government representative who had met the plane when he and Kyra landed in Macau. He affected the same shallow bow, the same dour expression. "Mr. Leonidovich."

Simon would have laughed at the utter foolishness of the situation if he hadn't been sitting with his hands shackled to a table, in the middle of an interrogation room, in the middle of a mini prison, with his urine-stained pants stuck to a hard steel bench. He nodded, determined not to the show the man how miserable he felt, but even that small movement was enough to make his brain explode with fireworks. *Damn,* twenty hours, and the little demons with jackhammers showed no signs of retreat. "Mr. Wu."

"*Hai,* you recognize me." He looked surprised, a man not accustomed to being remembered.

"Of course. You're the one who said these kind of things don't happen in your country."

The little man sucked his cheeks into hollows, as if he had just taken a bite of lemon. "You can hardly blame the People's Republic for your actions."

"You don't really believe that."

"I'm told the facts are quite condemning."

Condemning—the man made it sound like everything had already been decided: accused and tried, convicted and sentenced. "Contrived would be a more accurate description."

Wu frowned impatiently. "We have a witness. Someone who saw you enter the room, who heard the shots and saw the door close."

Simon had heard the claim—a maid who had miraculously survived the attack—and realized that nothing he said would make the slightest bit of difference. "You know how it is, all us Caucasians look the same."

The look of impatience melted into incredulity. "Mr. Leonidovich, this is not a matter of levity."

Simon forced an agreeable smile, suppressing the rage that had been building up over a long night of intense questioning. The man was a bureaucratic gnome, without any sense of irony. "We can certainly agree on that."

Wu gestured toward the steel bench on his side of the table. "May I sit?"

"Please do, I can't very well stand."

Wu set down his briefcase, a thin attache made of faux leather, pulled a slightly yellowed handkerchief from the breast pocket of his shiny black polyester suit, and carefully wiped the steel bench before sitting. "It would be best," he began, "if you would cooperate with the investigators." He opened the handkerchief, laid it carefully on the table, and folded his right hand over his left.

"Best for who?"

"For everyone, of course."

"Really?" Simon tried to sound genuinely mystified. "I gave them a statement. It didn't seem to help."

"Mr. Leonidovich, these games are not productive. Your statement does not agree with that of the witness."

Simon nodded slowly, being careful not to arouse the demons. "So you're saying it would be best for everyone if I confirmed the woman's story?"

"Of course."

"Even though it's a complete fabrication?"

Wu frowned, his frustration etched in furrows across his forehead. "This woman has no reason to lie."

"I suggest you look under her mattress."

The furrows deepened. "Her mattress?"

"The woman was paid, Mr. Wu. She's hidden the money somewhere."

"Mr. Leonidovich, these foolish attempts to blame an innocent domestic . . ." He emitted a disappointed sigh. "This is not the conduct of an honorable man."

"Mr. Wu, do you really believe I was clever enough to kill seven people, then stupid enough to lock myself in a room with two of the victims?"

"Of course not. There were five victims outside the room. Killed with two different weapons, so we know you had at least two accomplices. Unfortunately, they escaped before the police could apprehend them."

That was a new twist; one, Simon suspected, the

police had invented to fit their imagined scenario. "And the witness? She was able to identify these men?"

"I'm sorry, I'm not at liberty to say."

"I'll bet."

Wu stared across the table, eyes blank, clearly confused by the idiom. "I assure you, Mr. Leonidovich, your cooperation in identifying these men would not go unnoticed by the People's Republic."

"I'm sorry, Mr. Wu, but I'm finding it hard to take these accusations seriously." He didn't really expect the man would fall for such an obvious ploy, but tried anyway. "I don't even own a gun."

"We have a witness, Mr. Leonidovich, we don't need a gun."

Despite his relief, Simon managed to hide his surprise. "If you believed that, Mr. Wu, you wouldn't be here."

Wu nervously kneaded the knuckles of his left hand with the fingers of his right. "I'm here to help, Mr. Leonidovich, nothing more. By your own admission, you visited the home of Madame Chiang in the belief she had somehow been involved in the attack on Mr. Rynerson, *neh*?"

"That's correct."

"Something happened in this meeting that prompted you to react in an inappropriate manner, *neh*?"

Inappropriate manner!—now that was an interesting way to describe the slaughter of seven people. "No, that is not correct."

"Yes, Mr. Leonidovich, I believe this is quite correct, and the sooner you admit this, the sooner this matter can be placed behind us."

Typical bureaucrat, would lock up his own mother if it would clear his desk. "Mr. Wu, with all due respect, this matter will be put behind us when your investigators stop trying to pin this on the dumb *qai loh,* and start looking for the guy who put the dent in my head."

"I assure you, Mr. Leonidovich, if you would cooperate with the—"

"Mr. Wu, please excuse my interruption, but I'm very tired, I haven't eaten, and I'm not interested in your assurances. When are you going to let me speak to someone at the American Embassy?"

"These things take time."

"That's what you said about finding the people who attacked Mr. Rynerson. How are you doing with that investigation?"

"I assure you, this matter—"

"Puah-leeze, enough with the assurances. I've cooperated. I've been patient. Now put me in touch with the American Embassy or bring out the rubber hoses. Until then I've got nothing more to say."

"I assure—" Wu stopped himself. "We do not physically abuse prisoners."

Simon believed it—at least the *qai loh* prisoners—the repetitive, never-ending questioning was probably more effective. "Good-bye, Mr. Wu."

Wu stood up, carefully folded his handkerchief and slipped it into his pocket. "Is there anything I can get you?"

"Besides out, you mean?"

Wu smiled tolerantly.

"Some aspirin would be appreciated."

The man nodded, made another shallow bow, and disappeared out the door.

Unable to fold his arms, Simon leaned forward and placed his head on one elbow, hoping to catch a few minutes of sleep before the next team of investigators swooped in to harass him. He had barely closed his eyes before the steel door scraped open. *Inhuman bastards!*

"You okay?"

The familiar voice brought his head up with a jerk, waking the demons with their little jackhammers. *Oooooweeeee-sonofabitch!* "Define okay."

Kyra slid onto the steel bench just vacated by Mr. Wu. She was dressed in a white, open-neck cotton blouse and khaki slacks—no purse, no makeup. "You don't look so good, Leonidovich."

"You sure know how to perk a guy up, Rynerson."

"I'm serious. You okay?"

"I'm fine, just a little tired. How did you find me? How did you get in here?"

"I'm learning how to use the Rynerson name. My father has pumped over four billion dollars into this economy; they can't just ignore me."

"Good for you. What about your father? Any change?"

She shook her head, a look of weary resignation. "Let's talk about you. What happened?"

He gave her the sanitized version, careful not to say more than what he told the investigators.

She nodded, looking more unhappy than when she first came in. "So what happened to the gun?"

So they had told her about that, hoping he would be stupid enough to incriminate himself. He lowered his head, just enough so the fisheye lens high in the corner couldn't pick up his eyes, and gave her a warning look, letting her know their conversation was being recorded. "Good question." He wasn't about to lie or say anything that could be used against him if they found the damn thing, which he assumed they would. "It sure put a dent in my head, I can tell you that."

She nodded, an acknowledgment of understanding. "You may have a concussion. Have you seen a doctor?"

He gave her a little wink and leaned back. "Not yet. If I die, make sure you sue the bastards."

"Count on it. I'll make it my mission in life to see that the warden of this joint spends the rest of his days shooing frogs out of rice paddies."

A bit racist, Simon thought, but the threat would probably buy him some sleep. "What about getting me out of here?"

"I've already spoken to the Consul General in Hong Kong. He promised to notify the State Department immediately."

More bureaucrats; by the time anything got done he'd be speaking Chinese and dribbling green tea out the end of his pecker. "That should be quick."

She rolled her eyes. "I'll stay on it."

"I have an important job coming up." He gave her

another pay-attention look, making sure she got the message. "Looks like I may have to cancel."

"That would be unfortunate. I'll mention it to Jim."

Jim now—things were obviously warming up between her and Atherton. "Good idea. And I'd appreciate it if you'd call my sister."

"I already did. Typical Lara, she wanted to jump on a plane and start dropping bombs on Beijing. I told her I thought she could accomplish more by pushing the State Department from her end."

"Good." Knowing his sister, she'd have half of Washington playing duck-and-cover by the end of the day. "I'm not sure her kind of fireworks would play very well over here."

"That's what I thought. She said to tell you she loves you." Kyra leaned forward, covering his shackled hands with her own. "I do too, you know?"

Though he knew how she meant it—like a brother—her touch still sent a flicker of heat pulsing through his body. "Thanks."

She gave his hands a reassuring squeeze, then sat back. "This is all so stupid. We shouldn't have any trouble getting you out of here."

He forced a confident smile, but doubted if that was true. The attack had been well-planned and well-executed, the gun no last-minute, take-advantage-of-the-moment decision. Someone knew he would be there, and wanted him out of the way. But out of the way for what? "Right. Shouldn't be a problem."

Chapter Nineteen

Macau

Saturday, 7 July 16:15:21 GMT +0800

"What kind of brain-dead operation are you running out there!"

Given the power, Mawl would have reached back through the phone and crushed the man's windpipe, but there was nothing he could do—not yet. "What are you talking about?"

"I'm talking about the gun! The motherfucking gun! What happened to it?"

Good question, almost as good as how Trader got his information. "It was right there. Less than a meter from where we left Leonidovich."

"Well they haven't found it!"

"That isn't my fault," Mawl answered, fighting to control his anger. "It couldn't have been any more obvious if we'd given the idiots a map."

"What's *obvious*—" The words came hissing through the phone's tiny speaker, a climbing sarcastic drawl. "—is that you got nervous and forgot to leave it."

That was exactly the accusation Mawl expected, but unless those idiot cops got busy and found the thing, there was nothing he could do to prove otherwise. "It's there. It's in that room. It has to be."

"Then Leonidovich found it before the cops got there."

"It wouldn't matter, he couldn't get out of the room." Mawl realized he was making an argument against himself. If it was there, why couldn't they find it? "It's there someplace."

"Then you underestimated the man."

Maybe, Mawl thought, but he wasn't a bloody magician. "They'll find it," he said, trying to sound confident, but now suspecting one of the SWAT cops had grabbed the gun as a souvenir. "They have to."

"But they won't," Trader snapped. "They're not even looking. When they couldn't find the gun immediately, they got suspicious and turned their attention back to the maid. She's starting to embellish, thinking that will please the investigators. Her story is breaking down."

Bloody hell! Where was this man getting his information? "You don't need to worry about her, she doesn't know anything."

"Apparently that's the problem."

Though Mawl could almost predict the response, he could think of no way to avoid the question. "What do you want us to do?"

The answer came slow and hard, as if the man were speaking to an idiot child. "I . . . want . . . you—" He screamed each word, hard verbal bullets that vibrated through Mawl's head. "—to . . . finish . . . the . . . fucking . . . job! Is that so difficult?"

Of course it was difficult, but Mawl realized he was being baited, and resisted the temptation to strike back.

"You missed Rynerson," Trader continued, "and now you've missed the opportunity to pin this thing on Leonidovich. Believe me, if the police don't connect the dots, he will. The man's no fool. We can't afford to have him sniffing around. Not after this. I want him eliminated."

"It'll take time. It won't be easy getting to him inside those walls."

"Well isn't this your lucky day—"

Mawl waited, ignoring the sarcasm.

"—because unless those investigators find that gun pretty damn quick, they'll have no choice but to release him."

Was the man guessing, or did he know something? In Mawl's experience, the Chinese could never be counted on to do the predictable when it came to civil rights. "We'll be ready."

"And he'll be expecting it," the man shot back. "Just how do you plan to accomplish this magnificent feat?"

This time the question was real, but Mawl didn't have an answer. "Does it need to look like an accident? Is that still important?" He was stalling, trying to come up with some kind of reasonable response, but as he said the word *accident,* he knew exactly how he would do it.

"More than ever," the man answered. "After this last fiasco, there's enough questions being asked."

"Then we'll do it at the hotel. They have a history of construction problems. One more won't seem unusual."

"Do it."

"What about collateral damage?" Mawl asked, not wanting to leave the man any reason to complain later. "If others are involved it won't appear personal."

"I don't care how you do it. And I don't give a fuck who gets in the way. Just get it done!"

That was all Mawl wanted to hear.

Chapter Twenty

Coloane Island, Macau

Monday, 9 July 09:32:33 GMT +0800

Sitting cross-legged on the straw sleeping mat, Simon strained to identify the approaching footsteps: the heavy-booted tread of the morning guard, and the lighter step of a second person, a woman or small man. They paused outside the steel door, a key scraped in the lock, the heavy tumblers rolled over, and the door swung open, revealing the dour and always officious Mr. Gao Wu. He dipped his head—"Mr. Leonidovich"—then took one measured step forward, stopping just inside the door.

Simon nodded, mimicking the man's less than cordial bow. "Mr. Wu, how good of you to visit. I would offer you a chair—" He motioned toward the steel toilet. "—but that's the best I can do."

Wu never diverted his eyes from Simon's face, the unassailable expression of a man on a mission. "I wish you to know, I have been doing all that is possible to obtain your release."

Simon knew better—suspected the man wanted something—but kept his thoughts hidden behind an expression of grim understanding. "I'm grateful. These things take time."

Wu nodded, not realizing his favorite bureaucratic aphorism had just been shoved into his bureaucratic face. "Unfortunately, this is true."

"Is there anything I could do to expedite the process?"

Wu hesitated, as if considering the thought for the first time. "It is a most delicate matter. The investigation is still ongoing."

"I understand."

"Any premature disclosure of information could jeopardize the investigation."

So that was it, the great and mighty People's Republic was worried about what little ol' Simple Simon might say to the press. "Yes, that would be unfortunate. In my country—" He tried to make it sound like America had an answer to everything. "—the judge would simply impose a gag order while the investigation was ongoing."

"Really?" Though Wu tried to look surprised, it was obvious he cherished the moment. "What about your famous 'freedom of the press?'"

Simon shrugged. "The order is usually lifted once the investigation is complete." And this one, he had a feeling, was now destined for the land of never-over.

"You would not find such a thing . . ." Wu paused, struggling to find the right words to express himself.

"Too restrictive?"

"Hai."

"Not for me," Simon answered, being careful not to overdo it. "But I happen to be one of those people who dislike reporters. Too damn nosy for my taste."

Wu nodded thoughtfully. "It is possible I may be able to work something out."

More than possible, Simon suspected, now certain the Rynerson Express had worked out some kind of face-saving compromise with the Chinese government. "Oh?"

"A way for you to be released that would not jeopardize the investigation."

Simon tried to look appropriately enthused, which wasn't difficult. "That would be wonderful."

"I will speak to the lead investigator."

A man, Simon was sure, who had absolutely no say in the matter. "I would appreciate any help you give me."

Wu bowed, a bit deeper this time, and backed through the door.

Thirty minutes later, in a small administrative office, Gao Wu pushed four copies of a document typed in English across the metal desk. He laid a cheap ballpoint pen on top of the papers. "If you will agree to these terms and conditions, you are free to go."

Free to go: suddenly it sounded too easy. Simon quickly but carefully read through the three-page document, which was nothing more than a gag order relating to:

- The Incident at the residence of Mei-li Chiang (now deceased);
- Any and all details relating to the protective custody of the signatory.

Simon smiled to himself, imagining how many hours the legal nitpickers had spent arguing over the words "the Incident" and "protective custody." He scratched his name on the signature line of all four documents and pushed them back across the desk.

Wu extracted an old-fashioned fountain pen from the inside pocket of his suit, unscrewed the cap, then hesitated. "You understand, you may talk to no one regarding this incident?"

"Yes, Mr. Wu, I understand English quite well."

"Including your lawyer."

"Unless you charge me with a crime." A clause, he hoped, that would act as some deterrent against that ever happening. "Then it's Katie bar the door."

Wu stared back across the desk, a puzzled, slightly wary look. *"Neh?"*

"All bets are off." Great, now he was explaining one colloquialism with another. "It means this document becomes null and void."

"Ah." Wu bent forward, added his signature to all four documents, then sat back, a look of smug satisfaction. "You must agree, the People's Republic has been most accommodating in this matter." He spoke like a man who actually believed the words that came out of his mouth.

Though he wasn't about to *agree,* Simon knew better than to offend petty bureaucrats flush with power. "Mr. Wu, you can't imagine the level of my gratitude."

Stepping through that last steel door into sunlight and freedom, Simon felt slightly intoxicated, lightheaded with relief. Barely able to contain a silly-ass smile, he headed toward the champagne-colored limousine parked at the curb, the rear door imprinted with the discreet but distinctive monogram—PPR—of Pacific Pearl Resorts. The driver, who showed absolutely no reaction to Simon's disheveled appearance, dipped his head respectfully and pulled open the door.

Simon ducked into the dim interior. "Hey—" The intended words caught in his throat, the sight of James Atherton coming as a complete surprise. In contrast to the man's normal attire—casually perfect—he seemed overdressed for the occasion: a perfectly tailored three-piece navy suit, a starched white shirt, and a tightly knotted burgundy tie. "Thanks for picking me up."

Atherton chuckled softly, friendly creases around his eyes. "You were expecting someone else?"

Simon tried not to look disappointed as he settled onto the plush seat, the softest thing to hit his backside in four days. "Apparently I was."

"She had a few last-minute things she needed to get done. She'll see you at the hotel."

Simon tried to think of something intelligent to say, but his sleep-deprived brain seemed incapable of getting past the suit, and the thought that Atherton looked dressed for either a funeral or a wedding. *A few last-minute things she needed to get done.* Had Jake taken a turn for the worse, or had things progressed that fast with Atherton? Was Kyra that impulsive? "Sure. Great." *Great,* that's the best you can do, Leonidovich? No wonder she likes the guy—rich, handsome, successful, and he could actually string words into sentences.

"So, how are you doing, buddy? You okay?"

Buddy? Now they were pals? "Well, they didn't wire my testicles up to a battery, if that's what you mean."

Atherton grinned, his white teeth flashing in the dim light that filtered through the darkened windows. "Now there's an image I'd rather not consider. No bruises, then?"

"No, nothing like that," Simon answered. "Nothing a little sleep won't cure."

"Good. The whole thing was ridiculous, to even think you were involved in something like that."

Though it was exactly what Simon would expect from someone like James Atherton—who always knew exactly what to say and how to say it—the unquestioning support felt good. "And they know it. I had to sign some stupid document about not talking to the press, but they didn't even bother to restrict my movements. I can leave the country if I want."

Atherton nodded, his lips curling slightly. "So maybe it wasn't so stupid."

The door to Simon's brain suddenly swung open. "You negotiated my release?"

"That's my job, remember? Helping clients through the Chinese maze of bureaucratic hurdles." He smiled, a good-natured flash. "Without endangering the family jewels."

Damn, it was getting awful hard not to like this guy. "Did I mention what a swell agreement I just signed?"

Atherton laughed. "Kyra said you would never go

to the press anyway, so I just gave them what they wanted."

Modest too. No wonder she liked the guy. "I'm sure it wasn't all that easy."

He waved a hand dismissively, as if his efforts were of no significance. "Without a weapon, they really didn't have much of a case."

"Even so, I appreciate the help."

"You're welcome. I'm just sorry it took so long." He reached up, loosened his tie, and pulled open his collar. "What the hell happened anyway?" Almost before the words cleared his mouth, he shook his head. "No, wait, don't answer that. You agreed not to talk about it, and I believe a man should honor his agreements."

Simon nodded, grateful not be pushed. "I agree."

"But let me put it this way," Atherton continued. "Without telling me anything about *the incident*—" He smiled, as if sharing an inside joke. "—have you formed an opinion about why it happened? Or who was behind it?"

A good question, Simon thought, one that cleverly skirted around the legal issue, if not the moral intent of the document, and that made him uncomfortable. Did he have an opinion about why it happened? *Absolutely.* After four days of thinking about nothing else, the answer to that question seemed obvious. Did he know who was behind it? *Not yet.* He glanced out the window as the car turned north onto the Taipa-Coloane Causeway, purposely avoiding Atherton's curious eyes. "Not a clue."

Chapter Twenty-one

Macau

Monday, 9 July 21:27:05 GMT +0800

Mawl waited until he heard the lock snap before turning on the light. "Where the bloody hell have you been?" He slipped his Beretta back between the cushions and pushed himself up from the couch. "You should have been here two hours ago."

Robbie, who had been playing guard dog to Kyra Rynerson since early that morning, scowled and headed for the kitchen. "There was a maintenance crew diddlin' around near the communications room." He pulled a bottle of Red Dawn from the refrigerator and collapsed into a chair at the small dinette. "Couldn't get past the buggers until they finished."

Mawl realized he was overreacting, but he didn't trust Trader, and he didn't trust the kid to recognize a threat if one developed. "You sure you weren't followed?"

"Aye, I'm sure."

Mawl knew better, but didn't say anything. It wouldn't do Robbie any good to know that Catman Fosseler had been assigned to shadow his backside. "So, did you get it?"

Robbie reached into the breast pocket of his blazer, extracted a flash-memory card, and handed it over without a word. Mawl returned to the couch, inserted the card into the multicard reader attached to his laptop, and clicked open his voice editor. The program immediately identified the source, listing seven separate files: all calls to or from the courier's suite. "Talkative bastard." The phone tap was voice-activated, each call listed in sequential order as a separate file, including the date, time, length, and size of each recording.

Record No.	**Date & Time**	**Length**	**Size**
001	9 July 13:04	00:02:38	345 KB
002	9 July 13:09	00:00:36	79 KB
003	9 July 13:30	00:28:16	3697 KB
004	9 July 14:09	00:19:51	2596 KB
005	9 July 14:44	00:01:53	247 KB
006	9 July 15:01	00:02:01	264 KB
007	9 July 15:12	00:14:18	1870 KB

Mawl highlighted the first file—recorded at 1:04 P.M.—turned up the volume so Robbie could hear the playback, and hit the PLAY button. There was a long series of separate tones, at least ten, indicating an international call, and Mawl immediately stopped the recording and started over, this time recording the tones on his micro-recorder. Once he finished listening to the calls, he could then choose the ones he wanted to trace, and use a tone identifier to convert the sounds into numbers. After the tones repeated a second time, there was a momentary pause, the familiar *brrrrappp-brrrrappp* call signal, then a faint click followed by a woman's voice. "Billie here."

Mawl hit the PAUSE button, made a quick note in his surveillance log—#001, Billie Rynerson—then clicked the PLAY button.

"Billie, it's Simon."

"So they let your sorry ass out of the hoosegow, did they?"

"Don't sound so disappointed."

"A little time behind bars never hurt anyone. You okay?"

"I'm fine. How's Jake?"

The woman's voice dropped an octave. "No change."

"You hang in there, he's going to make it."

"Of course he is," she snapped back. "The old buzzard's too ornery to go out like this."

"Billie, I may have to change the grand opening schedule."

"You can't. I told you—"

The courier interrupted. "Not the opening date, Billie. Just the, uh . . . the travel schedule is all."

"The travel schedule . . . ?"

"Think about it, Billie. *My* travel schedule."

There was a momentary pause before the woman replied. "Oh, right. I understand. I assume you have a good reason for this?"

"I think so."

"The other parties would have to agree."

"I understand that," the courier answered. "But

you have no problem with a change if I can get the schedule approved?"

The speaker went silent for a good ten seconds, the woman obviously thinking about it. "If it's approved by all parties, I don't see how that would affect anything."

"It won't."

"Well, you've got the security codes. You know who to talk to?"

"Absolutely," the courier answered. "I've got the list right in front of me."

"Make sure you use that scrambler I gave you."

"Of course."

"Then do what you have to do."

"Thanks, Billie."

"How's Li Quan doing?"

"He's uh . . . he's a hard man to read, but the place is looking good. A lot's been accomplished in the last four days."

"You're telling me things work better when you're in jail?"

The courier laughed. "Apparently so. That and a little good weather."

"Are we going to make it?"

"Yes." A slight pause. "Unless there's another accident."

"Right. What's my daughter up to?"

"I just got to the hotel. I haven't seen her yet, but she's here someplace."

"Is she okay? I know she'd rather be here with her father."

"She's doing fine. Atherton is helping to keep her mind off things."

"I wouldn't worry about that."

"Why would I worry? They seem like a good match."

The woman made a little sound, a kind of sardonic snort. "Men are so stupid."

"It's a genetic imperative, Billie, we can't help it. What's that got to do with—"

"Gotta go, Simon. Do what you have to do." There was a faint click and the speaker went silent.

Mawl looked at Robbie, who had just opened a second bottle of beer. "What's this about a travel schedule? Where's he going? Have you overheard anything?"

Robbie shook his head. "Nae. Course if I knew the plan, maybe I could help connect some dots."

Mawl opened his mouth, intending to give the kid the old need-to-know speech, then reconsidered. Playing bodyguard twelve hours a day, plus missing the assault at Mei-li Chiang's, the kid was obviously feeling left out. "That's true, but if you knew what to expect, you might inadvertently tip them off."

"I ain't stupid."

No, just young and naïve, but if the courier suddenly left the area, they would miss their best opportunity, something Mawl couldn't allow to happen. "We're planning a little accident for Mr. Leonidovich. All I need is some idea of his movements within the hotel. A meeting time or an inspection tour, so we're ready for him. That way he'll just walk into it. No one would suspect he was a target."

Robbie nodded slowly, the gears grinding. "He

meets with the bird every morning. Usually between seven and eight."

"I realize that, kid, but we need to do it in the open, with lots of witnesses. Maybe we'll get lucky with one of these calls." He reached down and double-clicked the second file.

This time the recording started with a click—an incoming call—followed immediately by the courier's voice. "Hello."

"Welcome home."

Mawl hit the PAUSE button. "Recognize the voice?"

Robbie nodded. "Aye. That's the bird."

Mawl added the note to his surveillance log and clicked the PLAY button.

"This is a little more plush," the courier answered, "than what I call home."

"You're free, that's all that's important. Sorry I wasn't there to meet you, I had a meeting with Li Quan."

"No problem. Your friend Mr. Atherton took care of everything."

"Hey, the way you say friend . . . you make it sound like a bad thing."

"Hey, yourself," the courier came back. "You're hearing something that isn't there. The guy's great. He just busted me out of jail."

She hesitated, the line silent for a couple of long beats. "I'm sorry. Maybe I overreacted."

"No problem."

"I'm in the lobby. May I come up?"

"Is it important?" the courier asked.

There was another momentary pause. "Not really. I just thought . . ."

"I haven't showered yet."

"Oh—"

"Then I need to get some sleep. I can barely think."

"Oh . . . sure . . . I understand."

Mawl chuckled to himself—the woman sounded anything *but* understanding.

"I'll see you in the morning, okay? Our regular time?"

"Absolutely. I'm glad you're back, Leonidovich."

"Thanks. See you tomorrow." *Click,* then silence.

Mawl scanned down the list of call times. "He didn't sleep, that's for sure." He highlighted the next file and hit the PLAY button. The moment he heard the long string of dial tones—another international call—he stopped the recording and started over, recording the acoustic numbers on his micro-recorder.

A machine answered, the female voice distinctly American. "You have reached the American Embassy in Beijing. Please press—" The message was interrupted by the courier as he punched a string of numbers into his keypad. After a moment of silence, the speaker hummed with a series of clicks and beeps, then a high-pitched screeching sound, similar to that of a fax machine. Mawl lowered the volume, letting the recording run.

"What the bleeding hell is that?" Robbie asked.

"He's using a scrambler. Rynerson must have set up a secure communication link with the embassy."

"Why?"

Mawl shook his head, wondering the same. "It must have something to do with the Pearl. There's a lot of legal issues involved with opening a new resort." He sat back and closed his eyes, waiting for the recording to play out. The low irritating screech lasted twenty-eight minutes before ending.

"Can you decipher it?" Robbie asked.

"Of course," Mawl answered, though he doubted if he could, and had no intention of wasting his time trying. No matter what they were talking about, it wasn't going to change his orders: *Just get it done!* He scrolled down to the next file and hit PLAY.

Another machine answered, a similar voice, followed by another scrambled conversation, only this time it was the American Institute in Taipei, and the call only lasted twenty minutes.

"What's the American Institute?" Robbie asked the minute the speaker went silent.

"The Yanks don't officially recognize the government of Taiwan," Mawl answered. "The AIT serves as a substitute embassy." He clicked open the next file, wanting to avoid any more questions—questions to which he had no answers.

A woman answered, her voice thick with sleep. "This better be good."

"I love you too, Sissie."

"Boris!" There was a faint *click*—a lamp switch—and the sound of someone sitting up in bed. "Don't tell me they let you out of jail?"

Mawl stopped the recording, made a note of the

name on the courier's profile sheet—aka: Boris—and hit the PLAY button.

"About two hours ago," the courier answered. "Everything okay back there?"

"Of course everything is okay." She sounded offended. "How about you? You still like girls, or did you become the alabaster play toy for all the boys in lockdown?"

Robbie snorted. "That's funny."

"Sorry to disappoint you, Sissie, but I still pee standing up." His voice took on a businesslike tone. "I need you to do something."

"So what's new?"

"I've got a shipment. A five- or six-day job. Something I can't do myself."

"What's this, the world's greatest courier needs a courier?"

"Don't be a smartass, Sissie. I've been locked up for four days and I haven't slept much, so unless—"

"Okay, okay, I get the picture, your summer vacation left a lot to be desired. So what's the job? When, where, what? Size, value, destination? You know the drill."

"I'll e-mail you all that. Just find me someone with no affiliations in this part of the world. Someone independent and reliable."

There was a moment of silence, a few seconds beyond the normal intercontinental delay, before her voice came back. "I've got just the man. You remember Bill Rapp?"

"Yeah, sure. Head of security there at the new building."

"Right. He just started a three-week vacation and doesn't know what to do with himself."

"Now how would you know that?"

"He's interested in doing some part-time work," she answered. "He's a former detective with the NYPD, and he's fully bonded."

"You didn't answer my question, Sissie. Are you seeing this guy?"

"I'm going back to bed now. Take care of yourself, Boris."

"No wait"—*click*—"a minute. Damn woman." There was another click and the recording ended.

Robbie levered himself up from the table. "Want a beer?"

Mawl shook his head, added the call to his surveillance log, then sat back, wondering how the courier had managed to pull it off. *Clever bastard. Clever, clever, bastard.*

Robbie opened the refrigerator and grabbed another Red Dawn. "What you think that was about? Why would a courier need another courier?"

"No idea." But he did. He was sure of it. Though he couldn't imagine how, the bastard had not only hidden the gun, but had somehow gotten it out of the house. All he needed now was someone to carry it out of the country. *Someone independent and reliable.* Mawl smiled to himself—the gun was now meaningless—the man had a date with death, and nothing could change that. He reached down and double-clicked the next file.

This time the call was local, to the *Macau Post*

Daily, the only English-printed newspaper in the province. Though Mawl didn't understand the odd transaction—a prepaid, one-month subscription, the papers to be held until Leonidovich picked them up—it did seem to confirm the man's intention to temporarily leave Macau. The next and last file, a fourteen-minute call to Macau Aviation, made it clear exactly how and when he intended to go.

"Now what?" Robbie asked. "If he leaves in the morning, we're bloody screwed."

Mawl smiled to himself. He didn't know what Leonidovich was up to, or why he would charter a small plane. But the opportunity was clear enough. "No, kid, we're not screwed. Not screwed at all."

"How's that?"

"You don't remember what Chrich did in the service?" Except for Big Paddy, Thomas Chricher had been with Mawl longer than anyone on the team. "Think about it."

Robbie took a sip of beer, stalling, the hesitant expression of a pupil wanting to please his teacher, then his eyes widened with the look of remembering. "Chopper pilot, aye?"

That's right, Jocko, Chrich flew a chopper, but the man can fly anything, fixed-wing or rotor, and he's one hell of a mechanic. He knows how to fix 'em—" Mawl paused, making sure the kid understood. "—and he knows how to break 'em."

Chapter Twenty-two

The Pacific Pearl, Taipa Island, Macau

Tuesday, 10 July 07:07:21 GMT +0800

Balancing the two cups in one hand, Simon pushed the door closed behind him, surprised that the lights were on and the curtains open. "Rynerson?"

"In here."

In here turned out to be what the new brochures referred to as "your breakfast room," a small table with four chairs overlooking the Pearl River Delta. Beyond the glass, the sun reflected off the blue-green water with a sparkling luminescence that seemed to make the boats and hovercraft quiver in the early-morning light. Kyra was sitting at the table, dressed in what he now thought of as her day uniform—a cotton blouse and khaki slacks—sipping on a large mug of steaming coffee. He feigned a look of shock. "What's this, Kyra Rynerson up and dressed at seven in the morning? You just getting in or going out?" When she didn't smile, he realized things were about to get frosty.

She stared up at him, a look of concern. "Are you angry with me?"

"Absolutely not. Why would you would think that?" But he knew, and realized he was being disingenuous.

"I'm sorry if I seemed a little short yesterday. I was pretty tired and—"

"It's not that," she interrupted. "I know you were tired. I just want to be sure that's it. There's nothing else we need to talk about?"

He heard the question, loud and clear, and in lieu of honesty, there was only one good answer: avoidance and misdirection. "As a matter of fact, there is something we need to talk about."

She nodded and glanced at her watch, as if she knew what he wanted to discuss, and how much time it would take. "We have a meeting with Li Quan at seven-thirty. Maybe we should wait until after."

"I won't be here."

"Oh?" Though her expression never changed, her pupils dilated, exposing her surprise. "And why is that?"

"That's what we need to talk about." He lowered himself into the chair facing her, and slid one of the café mochas across the table. "I'm flying to Taiwan."

"To Taiwan?" She sat back. "Why?"

"To pick up their section of the crest."

"But you're not due there until the seventeenth."

"I changed the schedule. They're expecting me in Beijing the day after tomorrow."

"Beijing?" She repeated the name as if trying to decipher the punch line to a joke. "But . . . have you discussed this with the State Department?"

"Of course. I received their final approval about thirty minutes ago. The Chinese, of course, are more than happy to take early delivery. If something goes haywire before they dot all the *i*'s on the agreement, they'll still have their crest. Once I explained the situation, both the State Department and the Taiwanese government agreed."

"The situation?"

"That someone knows about the proposed trade agreement and is trying to stop it."

"You're sure about that?"

He nodded, not really sure about anything. "Madame Chiang was about to give me some information when she was killed. They wanted to keep her quiet, and they wanted me out of the way. It's the only logical reason for such an elaborate attempt to set me up."

She nodded slowly, thinking about it. "Let's assume you're right. Who are *they*?"

"No idea," he admitted, "but they're determined and ruthless, and probably more than a little pissed that I managed to avoid their trap."

"So you intend to grab the crest and skedaddle before the bullets start flying."

"I'm a chicken at heart."

"Does Jim know about this? He's supposed to be the point man on this thing."

Knowing she would ask, he gave her a little smile, the one his sister called boyishly irresistible. "I was hoping you would tell him."

"Oh, no." She flapped a hand back and forth, as if to ward off a fly. "You're not hanging me with that job, Leonidovich."

So much for irresistible. "He's not going to like it, is he?"

"Would you?" The question was purely rhetorical and she didn't wait for an answer. "You just cut him out of the loop. It'll look like he failed at his job. Yeah, I think he might be a little upset."

"Sorry, I didn't want to put you in the middle." Though he realized that was exactly what he was doing. "I just thought—"

"Oh, don't you worry about that, Leonidovich. You're not putting me in the middle of anything." She grabbed her cell phone and began punching numbers.

"Who are you calling?" As if he couldn't guess.

She scowled at him, her green eyes firing laser shots across the table.

"I wish you—"

She held up a hand, cutting him off. "Can you come over here? . . . Yes, right now . . . No, not over the phone . . . Room 718 . . ."

It surprised him that Atherton had never been to her suite, and embarrassed him that he should feel so good about it. *Leonidovich, you're pathetic.*

". . . Yes, they'll be expecting you . . . Okay, thanks." She set down the phone, took a deep breath, then let it go with a disappointed sigh. "Simon, why did you do this? Jim's the one who got you out of jail for Christ's sake. What the hell were you thinking?"

He hated the way she said *Simon,* which somehow sounded more impersonal than her saucy and sarcastic *Leonidovich.* "Apparently I wasn't." But he knew exactly what he was thinking, that the last time he said anything—about his intended visit to Mei-li Chiang's—somebody had overheard, or inadvertently shared the information; a mistake that had nearly landed him in a Chinese prison doing twenty-five to life. "I'm sorry."

"Tell it to, Jim. He's on his way." She made two quick calls: one to the security kiosk at the front gate, authorizing Atherton's access to the property; and one to Li Quan, telling him they would have to reschedule their meeting. She pushed herself up from the table. "I'll make more coffee."

They waited silently, drinking their coffee and watching a line of gray-white clouds spill over the horizon. He wanted to explain, but couldn't think of anything that wouldn't sound like a self-serving excuse. "I'm sorry, Kyra. It's not what you think."

She didn't look at him, her eyes fixed on the darkening skyline. "Don't tell me what I think, Leonidovich."

At least she was back to *Leonidovich,* and he knew enough about that fiery Rynerson temper not to push harder. She would cool down soon enough, that was her nature, though he had no idea if she would forgive him.

Finally, after what seemed an eternity but couldn't have been more than fifteen minutes, Robbie's familiar Irish brogue broke the uncomfortable silence, his voice squawking from the two-way radio attached to Kyra's belt. "Ms. Rynerson?"

Kyra reach down and pressed the talk button. "Yes, Robbie."

"Just got a call from downstairs. Mr. Atherton is on his way up. Says you're expecting him."

"Thank you, Robbie. Please let him in when he gets here."

"Aye. Will do, ma'am."

She turned, her eyes boring in. "You think I look like a *ma'am*, Leonidovich?"

He heard the challenge, but knew better than to give her some kissass, I-want-to-get-back-on-your-good-side answer. "No, ma'am, you sure don't."

"You're a shit, did I ever tell you that?"

"Yes, ma'am. Stupid too."

"Don't think you're forgiven, smartass."

"No, ma'am."

"You call me ma'am again, and you'll be singing soprano at the—"

"Yeah, I remember. The Temple of Lost Jewels."

"That's right." She pushed back her chair back and stood. "I think it would be better if we were in the living room when he got here."

Better? Better that Atherton didn't see them having coffee in the breakfast room, like it was some postcoital ritual?

They had barely gotten seated when Atherton came in, bubbling with enthusiasm. "Wow, this place is really something." Dressed in a cream-colored silk pullover shirt and tailored slacks that perfectly matched his caramel-colored shoes, he looked all smooth and shiny, like a melting cone of vanilla ice cream. He stopped in the center of the room and did a complete three-sixty, his gaze taking in the lush furnishings, the original art, the panoramic view, and finally landing directly on Kyra as he delivered the benediction. "Absolutely spectacular!" Then he smiled, a thousand-watt dazzler, stepped forward, and brushed a kiss across her cheek before turning to Simon. "Hey there, good buddy, you're looking better this morning."

Good buddy! In twenty-four hours they had apparently gone from casual acquaintances, to friends, to ride-the-hog buddies. Simon forced a smile and took the man's outstretched hand. "A good mattress is a highly underrated thing in this part of the world."

Atherton chuckled sympathetically. "I hear that. I've slept on a few mats in my time." He grabbed an armchair and pulled it around, until they were sitting knee-to-knee in a triangle. "Okay." He glanced from Simon to Kyra, then back to Simon. "What's the problem?"

"No problem," Simon answered, "just a small change in the schedule."

Atherton leaned forward in his chair, his expression attentive and curious. "What kind of change?"

Simon began to lay out the details, waiting for the man to explode, but he showed no emotion, absorbing the information without any sign of annoyance. "I'm sorry, Jim—" The casual familiarity echoed through Simon's head with a camaraderie he didn't feel. "—if this puts you in an awkward position."

Atherton waved a hand dismissively. "Of course not." He glanced at Kyra, who looked stonier than Washington on Rushmore. "We're all on the same team here."

Simon felt an unexpected sense of relief, hoping the man's understanding attitude might help soften

Mount Rynerson. "I didn't want to say anything until I received approval from the State Department."

"I understand," Atherton answered. "You'll probably think I'm crazy, but it's occurred to me that 'the incident'—" He said the words as if they were written in italics. "—at Madame Chiang's might somehow be connected to the trade agreement."

Though sure of it, Simon had purposely avoided making the connection. The further he stayed away from that subject, and the gun, the better.

"The sooner we make the transfer," Atherton continued, "the better I'll feel about it."

Simon nodded, hoping the *we* was nothing more than a casual turn of phrase. "I'm glad we're in agreement."

"Absolutely. So what's your timetable?"

Your. Much better. "I should be in the air by eleven."

"Today?" The man's expression went from full-steam-ahead to you-must-be-kidding. "This morning?"

"Yes."

You-must-be-kidding turned to you-must-be-crazy. "There's no eleven o'clock flight to Taipei."

"I chartered a plane." He kept his voice casual, as if he did that kind of thing all the time. "I thought it might be safer if my name didn't show up on any passenger manifest."

Atherton frowned. "What are you saying? You think the police might go back on their agreement and not let you out of the country?"

Simon nodded, though he was more concerned about the people who had done the shooting and tried to set him up, than the ones who were trying to find the shooters. "I don't want to take any chances with the crest."

Kyra rotated her chair toward the window. "What kind of plane?"

"A Beech King 90," Simon answered, afraid that things were about to get dicey. "The same plane I used to get my multiengine."

She dipped her head, looking at him from beneath her eyebrows, her expression frozen in a shadowed look of suspicion. "And does this charter come with or without a pilot?"

"It's only a three-hour flight."

"Three hours over water, Simon. You don't have that kind of experience."

Back to *Simon.* "You said I was your best student ever." He grinned, trying to keep it light. "Besides, I plan to follow the coast north. It's barely a hundred miles between the mainland and Taiwan."

Atherton stared at Simon, as if seeing him for the first time. "You're a pilot, too?"

"A rookie," Kyra snapped, never taking her eyes off Simon. "I don't care if it's twenty damn miles." She hooked a thumb toward the window. "Look at that cloud bank."

"Which is not supposed to move inland until late afternoon," Simon answered. "That's why I need to get out of here now." Even more important, he wanted to get out before anyone knew he was leaving.

"Then we better get moving," she said, as if they had already agreed that she was going. "I'll take the right-hand seat."

He groaned inwardly, not really surprised, but knowing that once an idea got stuck in that pretty head, it would not be easy to dislodge. "You need to stay here. We can't leave Li Quan alone."

"Mr. Quan is doing just fine. He can call if anything big comes up."

"You really need to stay here." *Brilliant, Leonidovich,* not exactly the kind of argument that made him captain of his college debate team. "What if there's another accident?"

"Then it's too late," she fired back. "I'm tired of sitting around here doing nothing. Let's get moving."

Atherton rotated his head back and forth between them. "Are you people serious? This is all too quick. Why not wait until the weather clears?"

Simon cocked his head toward the bank of clouds. "That's the leading edge of another typhoon. There won't be another window for at least—"

"So what?" Atherton interrupted, an unfamiliar tightness in his voice. "The Chinese have been waiting for this thing since World War II. It won't hurt them to wait a few more days. What's the rush?"

"I think there may be an information leak. I want to move the crest now, when no one's expecting it."

"You talked to the embassy," Atherton responded, a rising inflection that made the act sound foolish. "God knows how many people listened in on that."

"I used a scrambler," Simon answered, being careful not to show any irritation. He suspected the man hated small planes, and was trying to hide his fear behind security concerns. "No one listened in."

Atherton hesitated, his face flushed, the desperate look of someone trapped in an elevator. “I still don’t like it.” He glanced at Kyra, smiled weakly, then shook his head. “I think we should wait until after the storm.”

We? It was, Simon realized, the first time he had seen the man nervous about anything. “Jim, there’s no reason for you to go. This is what I do for a living. It’s routine.”

“Of course I’m going,” he fired back. “That’s *my* job. And unless you’ve got some other secret talent you failed to mention, I’m the only one in this group who speaks both Mandarin and Cantonese.”

Simon ignored the sarcastic dig, trying to be diplomatic. “We don’t need to worry about that. The embassy has everything worked out.”

“Sounds to me,” Kyra said, “like you’re the one who has everything worked out. Why shouldn’t Jim go?”

Simon heard the challenge and realized she had boxed him into a corner. He didn’t have a good reason, nothing beyond his penchant to work alone, to worry about nothing beyond *the package*; but he was already stuck with Kyra and couldn’t use that as an excuse. *God hates you, Leonidovich.*

Chapter Twenty-three

Macau

Tuesday, 10 July 08:14:16 GMT +0800

With practiced ease, Thomas Chricher ducked his head and pulled his lean frame into the pilot's seat. "We're ready."

Sitting sideways in the helicopter's passenger seat, Mawl lowered his binoculars and twisted around. "You're late."

"Bleedin' hell, man, you rather they grabbed my ass? I had to wait until they finished fueling the bloody thing."

Mawl ignored the sarcasm. "Anyone notice you?"

Chricher rolled his eyes. "What security they have is tutti-frutti. A bunch of wankers who wouldn't know Osama if he showed up with a crate of box cutters." He chuckled and unzipped his coveralls, neck to crotch, then arched his back and shoved the mechanic's uniform down over his body, until it lay heaped in a puddle around his ankles. His T-shirt and SeV cargo pants were both stained with sweat. "Once I got past the gate, no one gave me a second look." Using first one foot, then the other, he pushed the blue fabric down over his shoes. "What's the status?"

Mawl twisted around and gave the main access road leading to Macau International another sweep with his binoculars. “No sign of him. He should have left the hotel thirty minutes ago.”

“Big Paddy could have missed him.” Chricher pulled a small tracking device from his pocket, peeled the film off the sticky back, then pressed it to the instrument panel, directly between the two seats. “Or he might have taken a taxi instead of one of those hotel limos.”

“Maybe.” Mawl didn’t really care; Big Paddy had become irrelevant, an early-warning system in case Chricher got delayed at the airport.

“Doesn’t matter now.” Chricher tapped the transponder’s ON button and the tiny gridlined screen blossomed to life: a red dot marking the target as south-southwest of their location, four digital readouts indicating the exact location, distance, and altitude.

Latitude: 22° Ø9' N Distance: 2.43 nautical miles
Longitude: 113° 34' E Altitude: Ø.ØØ feet

“The minute that plane moves we’ll know it.” He bent forward around the pitch lever, picked up his coveralls, and tossed them into the storage area behind the seats. “That courier man is already dead. He just don’t know it yet.”

Right, except that’s what they thought when they left the man trapped in a panic room with a gun and two bodies. “You better be right, Chrich. Getting this machine in less than twenty-four hours cost me an extra five thousand quid."

"You wanna see the splash, you gotta pay the cash."

Mawl wasn't worried, but he wasn't about to take any more chances with Houdini Leonidovich. "I just want to see his body floating facedown."

"Doubt if you're gonna see that." Chricher pulled a mechanical pencil and a small leatherbound notebook from a side pocket in his cargo pants, carefully adjusted the lead, then began updating his calculations. "Okay . . . lemme see here . . . ten to fifteen minutes before the heat builds up enough to melt the wax . . . another five or ten before the acid burns through the panel. By then he should be at cruising speed . . . 230 knots, give or take . . . we'll be doing 130, 135 . . . so . . . lemme see here . . . rate of climb . . . weight—" He looked up. "You sure he's going alone? No cargo?"

"That's what he told the leasing company."

"So why's he need that size of plane? That thing can hold eight people."

Mawl had no idea, but after listening to nearly an hour of scrambled conversations, he suspected Leonidovich had more than a trip to Taiwan on his agenda. "So what?"

"Weight can make a difference," Chricher answered. "The heaver the load, the longer it'll take to reach cruising altitude. Could make a difference in my calculations."

"No passengers, no cargo—that's what the man said."

Chricher shrugged and resumed his calculations.

"Okay, lemme see . . . uh huh, uh huh . . . considering all the variables, we should be somewhere between twenty and fifty nautical miles when he takes the dive. So . . . lemme see . . . at max speed, depending on the wind and distance between aircraft . . . we should . . . lemme see—" He added a few more numbers to his page of calculations, multiplying and dividing. "Okay . . . best I can figure . . . we should be over the scene within—" He rolled his hand back and forth, a give-or-take gesture. "Ten to twenty minutes. Don't think there's gonna be much to see."

"I'm not looking for entertainment, Chrich. I just don't want to find that bastard hanging on to a seat cushion."

Chricher snorted. "Not likely. By the time that acid does its work, he'll be up around . . . lemme see here—" He paged through his notes. "Twenty-three, twenty-four thousand feet."

"And what if he hugs the coast?" Mawl cocked his head toward the bank of clouds building along the eastern horizon. "That looks pretty nasty. What if he manages to put it down on the beach?"

"First of all—" Chricher straightened his thumb. "—that ain't no glider he's flyin'. From that altitude, he's not gonna *manage* to put it down anywhere. Second—" He extended his index finger. "—I'm pretty sure the Chinese aren't about to let him fly over their coastline. And third—" Middle finger. "—that front's not supposed to move inland until late afternoon."

"Weather changes."

"He's gonna end up in pieces. Little pieces. On the

beach or in some shark's belly. Does it matter which?"

"No," Mawl answered. "As long as it looks like an accident."

"Don't worry, there won't be enough left of that plane to figure out what happened. This time the guy is going down." He smiled, baring a mouthful of stained teeth. "And I mean that literally."

Mawl nodded—another cluster fuck and they'd be the ones getting hunted—but Chrich didn't need to know that. The portable two-way gave a short squelch and Mawl pressed the TALK button. "What's going on?"

The radio beeped, followed by Big Paddy's deep voice. "How long you want me to sit here?" *Beep.*

In his mind Mawl could see Big leaning over a hot engine, the van conveniently disabled just beyond the Pearl's main security gate. "Anyone giving you the eyeball?

Beep. "Negative." *Beep.*

Mawl hesitated. He still wanted a visual, still wanted to be sure Leonidovich got on the plane, but if Big stayed there long enough, someone would eventually get suspicious. "Lay chilly for another fifteen, then get out of there."

Beep. "Fifteen minutes," Big Paddy repeated. *Beep.*

"So." Chricher shifted uneasily, as if trying to hollow a new spot in the seat. "Whatcha think?"

Mawl shrugged, hiding his anxiety behind an expressionless mask. "Maybe the bleedin' trip got canceled."

Chricher grinned, as if he found the possibility highly amusing. "Then the next person who charters that plane is in for one big surprise."

Before Mawl could respond, the two-way gave another sharp squelch. "Talk to me."

Beep. "I think he just went by," Big Paddy answered back. "In one of those hotel limos." *Beep.*

"How many in the vehicle?"

Beep. "Hard to tell with those dark windows. The kid was riding up front." *Beep.*

Bloody hell, that meant Rynerson's daughter was in the car. "Okay. Follow them, but don't get too close. See if you can get a visual on the plane and the number of passengers."

Beep. "Roger that." *Beep.*

Chricher opened his notebook. "Sounds like I better go back to work."

"They're probably just dropping him off." It made perfect sense, but nothing had gone right so far, and Mawl didn't feel especially confident.

"Does it matter?" Chricher looked up from his calculations, his expression indifferent, no concern one way or the other. "Him being alone or not?"

Mawl thought back to his last conversation with Trader. *I don't give a fuck who gets in the way. Just get it done!* "Nope. Doesn't matter at all."

Robbie Kelts, sitting in the front passenger seat, twisted around and gave the privacy glass a couple of sharp raps, the sound barely penetrating the thick Cyrolon-over-glass laminate.

"Excuse me." Kyra reached across Atherton, to the control panel on the door, and lowered the partition. "What is it, Robbie?"

"Beggin' your pardon, ma'am, but I don't think you should be goin' anywhere before we've had a chance to make security arrangements at the other end."

Kyra smiled, her eyes glowing with a kind of big-sister affection. "You looking to take a trip, Robbie?"

"No, ma'am, really, I don't like to fly. I just don't think you should be going anywhere before we've had a chance to set something up. Maybe you could catch another flight." His gaze swept back and forth, from Atherton on her left, to Simon on her right. "Join these gentlemen later."

"I appreciate your concern, Robbie, but no one knows I'm leaving the province. You can't get better security than that."

"Yes, ma'am, but—"

"If you want to tag along, you're welcome to join us."

The young man grimaced, obviously uncomfortable with the thought. "No, ma'am. Like I said, I—"

"I understand," Kyra interrupted, "you don't like to fly. Don't worry about it." She reached out and simultaneously patted the two knees on each side of her own. "These gentlemen will take good care of me."

He opened his mouth, clearly intending to argue the point, then nodded reluctantly and turned back to the front. "Yes, ma'am."

Atherton raised the partition. "Presumptuous bastard."

She cut the man a hard look. "Robbie's a good kid. He's just doing his job." She turned, as if expecting an attack from both flanks. "What about you, Leonidovich? You want to add your two cents?"

"No, ma'am." Though he knew it was coming, she was too quick, jabbing her elbow into his ribs. "Damn, Rynerson, those elbows are as sharp as your tongue."

"Remember that the next time you think about using that word."

Atherton leaned forward, his expression puzzled. "What word?"

"Trust me," Simon answered, trying to rub away the sting. "You don't want to know."

Atherton hesitated, his eyes bouncing from Simon to Kyra, then back again. "I believe you." He started to sit back, then noticed the titanium cable running from Simon's left wrist to the black case at his feet. "That it?"

"It is," Simon answered, already knowing what the next question would be.

"Can I see it?"

"Sure." Simon pulled the case between his legs, just enough to shield his hands, and quickly sequenced through the unlocking procedure: right latch toward the handle, foot-lock one-half turn clockwise, left latch outward. Reaching inside, he extracted the Frisbee-sized high-impact repository and unsnapped the latch, exposing the lower right section of the carving embedded within its molded impression.

Atherton frowned, a slightly cheated look. "Looks just like that reproduction in the suite."

"Exactly," Simon agreed. "The ones at the Pearl were cast from molds of the original three pieces."

"I expected more for some reason."

Exactly what Simon thought when he first saw it.

"It's the smallest section. The one in Taipei is considerably larger." He closed the cover, slipped the container back into his security case, reactivated the alarm, then reached across Kyra and snap-locked the cuff around Atherton's wrist before he realized what was happening. "You're the man, Jim. Don't lose it."

"Hey! What the . . . what's the idea?"

"You wanted to come." Simon cracked a little smile—the one Lara called his snake charmer—letting the man know it was all in good fun. "You might as well make yourself useful."

"Well, yeah but—"

"I'm the pilot. Need both hands."

Kyra gave Simon a conspiratorial nudge. "And I have to make sure he doesn't fly us off into never-never land."

Atherton shrugged, his lips curling into a good-natured grin. "Do I get hazard pay?"

"Only if I forget the combination," Simon answered, "and we have to cut off your hand."

Atherton grimaced. "How's your memory?"

"Pretty good until that guy hit me in the head."

"Sorry I asked."

"Asked what?"

Kyra snorted a laugh, and then they were all laughing together, like old school chums sharing an inside joke. Beyond the privacy glass, in the visor mirror above his head, the eyes of Robbie Kelts watched this lighthearted display of camaraderie with an odd expression of fatalistic regret.

Chapter Twenty-four

Macau

Tuesday, 10 July 08:59:05 GMT +0800

Standing beneath the five-blade rotor, Mawl read the pulsating display on his cellular—Jocko—and knew it wouldn't be good news. "Talk to me, kid."

"I've only got a second," Robbie whispered. "I'm in the WC at the charter service."

"So what's the problem?"

"He's not flying alone," Robbie answered. "Ms. Rynerson and that Atherton bloke are going with him."

Mawl noticed "the Rynerson bird" had suddenly become "Ms. Rynerson," and decided the kid was taking his bodyguard role a little too seriously. "That's not a problem." He glanced at the darkening cloud bank, afraid if they didn't leave soon, they might cancel the flight. "Why haven't they left? What's the holdup?"

"But I thought—"

"Don't," Mawl interrupted, "that's my job. I repeat, what's the holdup?"

"But what about Ms. Rynerson?" Robbie persisted. "She's not the target."

Mawl forced himself to take a breath, to give the

kid some slack. "Listen up, Jocko, you have to forget the bird. She's CD." It was the kid's first big test, and to write off someone he knew as collateral damage—especially a woman, and someone he had been charged to protect—would stretch his concept of commando warrior. "It's unfortunate. It's not your fault. That's just the way things worked out. Okay?"

There was a long beat of silence, then a temperate, "Yessir, I understand."

Obviously not, Mawl thought, but he decided to let it go. The kid could bury his guilt in money once the job was over. "So what's the holdup?" he repeated. "Why haven't they left?"

"They're signin' papers now," Robbie whispered, his voice heavy with resignation. "Don't think it'll be much longer."

Mawl glanced again at the gray wall of clouds, which seemed stalled about fifty kilometers off the coast, and hoped the kid was right.

Simon nudged the yoke forward, leveling off at 24,000 feet, the roar of the dual Pratt & Whitney engines dropping to a steady growl. "Handles real well."

Kyra nodded. "Want me to take over?"

"Fifteen minutes in, and already you want to play Sky Queen?"

"I'm bored."

"Well, you can forget it, Rynerson, I need the hours." More than hours, he needed the distraction. Over the last couple of years, flying had become his favored escape, his best means of clearing away the cerebral roadblocks. He glanced toward the north: a sweeping panorama of the China coastline and the South China Sea, its dark-blue surface speckled with islands of green and brown. Leaning forward, he looked past Kyra to the huge bank of dark clouds off the right wingtip. "Just keep your eyes on the weather, okay?"

"*Whoop-de-do!* If you had told me about this little excursion, I could have had them send the Gulf 5 up from Bangkok. We could have flown right over those babies."

"Yeah, and I could have called a press conference, too."

"Oh, right, clandestine mission." She flashed one of her sassy smiles and *du-dummed* the theme music from *Mission: Impossible.* "I forgot."

"That's right, Rynerson, it was supposed to be a . . ." He was about to say "secret," but the word got hung up in his brain as a collection of random images and displaced bits of information came together in a disturbing collage.

"Simon . . . ?"

"What's the nearest airport?"

Her expression mutated instantly from playful to stony serious, her right hand going for the portfolio of maps in the expansion pocket next to her seat. "Why?"

"There may be a problem with the plane."

Her gaze swept the instrument panel. "Everything looks normal. What are you talking about?"

He ignored the question and began banking the

plane toward the coast. "Just find me a place to land."

Atherton, who was sitting in a rear-facing seat immediately behind the cockpit, poked his head through the open door. "What's going on?"

"Simon thinks we may have a problem."

"What kind of problem?"

Simon glanced at Kyra, who had the portfolio open and was looking for the right map. "Didn't you think it was odd the way Robbie tried so hard to talk you out of going?"

She pondered the question for no more than a second. "No. He wasn't concerned about the flight. He wanted to make sure I had security when we landed."

"Yet he didn't ask where you were going."

"He didn't?"

"No."

She hesitated, thinking about it. "I don't remember . . . but even so, he's just a kid. Who knows what—"

"A former member of the SAS."

"So?"

"You ever hear of someone in the Special Air Service who didn't like to fly?"

She frowned in disbelief. "Oh, hell, Leonidovich, lots of people don't like to fly."

Atherton glanced back and forth between them, his tan face suddenly ashen. "What are you saying? You think that security guy might have done something to the plane?"

"No," Simon answered, "I don't see how that's possible. He didn't have an opportunity, but . . ." He hesitated, his mind still splicing the various bits of information into something that sounded reasonable.

"But what?" Kyra demanded. "Just because he's worried about me, doesn't mean—"

"It's more than that," Simon interrupted. "I always thought it was odd the way two members of your security detail disappeared on the same day. The only ones who spoke English."

She shook her head, as if trying to wave off her own doubts. "I think your imagination is working overtime."

"There's something else. Something I saw at Madame Chiang's. A note with a name and phone number. I knew I'd seen the name somewhere, but I didn't put it together until now. The Kowloon Security Service. It was on Robbie's profile sheet—the company he worked for in Hong Kong."

The last of the color drained from Atherton's face. "Oh, Jesus."

It took Kyra another second to grasp the significance. "Holy shit! Now you remember! What the hell happened to that photographic memory of yours, Leonidovich?"

Good question, though he felt certain it had something to do with a very large lump on the back of his head. "Momentarily out of film, I guess."

"Find us a place to land!" She slapped the map portfolio onto his lap. "I'm taking control."

"Took you long enough."

She grabbed the yoke on her side, pushing it forward in the same motion. "Hang on, I'm going to put this thing on the deck!"

Simon glanced back, but Atherton had already withdrawn into his seat, only his right arm and the titanium cable attached to the security case still visible through the narrow opening.

"What do you think?" Kyra asked, her voice rising as she increased power. "Should we call it in?"

He knew what she was asking. Was he sure? Was he confident enough in his theory to declare an emergency before they really had one? Did he want to explain why, and risk sounding like an idiot? Even more important, did he want to try and explain to some low-level bureaucratic investigator why he was transporting a priceless Chinese artifact to Taiwan? "We're not that far out of Hong Kong. Maybe we should wait."

"Okay by me. Check the map, see if there's any place to put down between here and there. Maybe one of those islands has a strip."

It took him less than a minute to find the right map and determine that the only thing flat between them and Hong Kong International was a very deep ocean. "Nope. Kia Tak's our best bet."

She nodded, an expression that could have taught stoniness to a mountain. "It's probably nothing." She sounded more hopeful than confident.

"Right." Never in his life had he wanted so much to be so wrong. He took a deep breath, trying to control the rising pace of his heart. "What's your plan?"

"I'll level off at a thousand feet," she answered. "If something happens, I should be able to control the glide from that altitude."

"Sounds good," but they both knew if something happened to the flight controls, there would be no *glide,* and even from a thousand feet the water would be like cement. "Maybe we should island hop our way in . . . just in case."

She cut a glance back and forth across the seascape. "It would take longer."

"Not much, and if we go down, we might be close enough to something to get ashore."

They passed through 4,000 feet and she started to ease back on the yoke. "Okay. You pick the route, but keep us in as straight a line as possible."

He began to trace a route with his finger, a connect-the-dots island hop right into Hong Kong. "This shouldn't add more than a couple minutes to our time."

She leveled off at a thousand feet, not more than thirty miles and ten minutes out of Kia Tak. "I need to call in."

He nodded, his heart rate beginning to settle. "I'll do it." He felt responsible. The plane, he suspected, would be okay, and all he had done was scare the bejesus out of everyone by twisting a bunch of innocent remarks into a conspiracy.

She shook her head. "No, let me. I've got the seniority. I'll just tell them we're experiencing some sporadic instrumentation problems. That we want to get on the ground before—" Without so much as a sputter or cough, both engines shut down, every needle and light on the instrument panel going dead and dark. Her final words—"something happens"—loud and ominous in the eerie silence.

Before her words faded, Simon had his fingers on the ignition switch. The faint *click-click-click* confirmed what already seemed obvious: complete electrical failure. "Dead." *Clever choice of words, Leonidovich.*

Behind them, Atherton groaned, the pitiful sound of a wounded animal caught in a trap.

"Help me!" Kyra yelled, struggling to keep the nose up. "I can barely hold it."

"There!" Simon answered, pointing his chin toward an island less than a mile in the distance. "Two o'clock!"

Working together they managed to ease the plane toward the slender mountain of vegetation, but it was hopeless, the dark-blue sea rising to meet them faster than they could close the distance.

Chapter Twenty-Five

South China Sea

Tuesday, 10 July 09:32:18 GMT +0800

From the moment they took off, Mawl had kept his attention glued to the tracking device attached to the instrument panel. At one hundred and thirty knots, a mere fifty feet above the water, just looking at the dark, undulating surface for more than a few seconds gave him a feeling of vertigo. Determined not to expose his weakness, he concentrated on the transponder's small red dot and waited for it to disappear.

For twenty minutes, the distance between the helicopter and the plane had continued to widen, then the Beech King took a sudden and unexpected turn toward the coast. Mawl pressed the COM button on his headphones. "What's going on?"

Chricher shook his head, not taking his eyes off the horizon.

"Well, something's not right. Maybe the acid only took out part of the circuitry."

Chricher shook his head again.

"How do you know? They could be trying to make an emergency landing in Hong Kong."

Chricher reached up and tapped one of the bubble

earphones that covered his ears. "There's been no emergency call. I would have heard it."

"Their radio might be out."

"They haven't changed altitude," Chricher answered. He pointed to the altimeter reading on the transponder. "I don't know what they're doing, but it hasn't happened yet."

Mawl nodded and glanced at his watch. *Twenty-one minutes.* They would know soon enough.

Two minutes later it happened; the altimeter reading on the transponder rolling downward like an out-of-control slot machine. "You were right," Mawl shouted, barely able to contain his excitement. "They're going down."

Chricher's lips curled slightly, a look of vindication.

"How long will it take us to get there?"

Chricher glanced at the transponder, mentally calculating the distance against the speed of the helicopter. "Fifteen minutes." He took one hand off the pitch lever and rolled it back and forth. "Give or take."

Mawl nodded, unable to take his eyes off the plunging numbers. It must be strange, he thought, to know the exact moment of death, to see it hurtling toward you, knowing you could do nothing to stop it. Not the way he wanted to go. Too much time. Too much thinking and waiting. He could visualize exactly what they were going through: the uncontrollable panic, the frantic effort to gain control, the erosion of hope, and finally . . . *splish, splash, you is takin' a bath.* He smiled to himself; no playing hide-the-gun this time, Leonidovich. Then, as the numbers rolled past 4,000 feet, they began to slow dramatically, as if the plane had suddenly hit a layer of thick air. "What the . . . ?"

Chricher cut a look toward the transponder. "Bloody hell."

"Bloody hell what! What's going on, Chrich? Talk to me."

"They're leveling off. It looks like they've gained control."

"You said—"

"I know what I said," Chricher interrupted. "It's not possible. Something must have—"

"Don't bloody fucking tell me it's not possible! Look at that!" He pointed at the numbers, which had stopped at a thousand feet, moving neither up or down. *Leonidovich!* Somehow that Houdini bastard had managed to do it again. "Now what?"

Chricher shrugged, his eyes shifting back and forth between the transponder and the horizon. "That's awful damn low. They still might—" He hesitated as the numbers on the altimeter suddenly renewed their downward spiral.

800

500

300

100

Then the red dot disappeared and the final readings on the transponder locked in place. "That's it. Splashdown."

Mawl nodded. But were they dead? He reached down, unzipped the small flight bag lying between his feet, and began pulling together the items he might need: a 9mm Micro Uzi, two twenty-round clips, and two five-hundred-gram concussion grenades. "Just get me there."

CHAPTER TWENTY-SIX

South China Sea

Tuesday, 10 July 09:37:35 GMT +0800

Too late, Simon thought, as they struggled to bring up the nose. For one heart-stopping moment nothing happened, the dark water rushing toward them like a tsunami, then they caught an updraft off the water and the plane flared, the nose rising just enough for the main fuselage to take the impact, momentarily launching them back into the air. Though teeth rattling, the jolt was less than Simon expected, and for a few seconds he thought they might actually survive; then the left wingtip dipped beneath the surface and they were cartwheeling across the water.

Somewhere in the middle of a roll, the windscreen popped, and for the second time in a week something slammed into the back of his head. *No-Noo-Noooo . . .* He tried to fight the darkness, that fade into oblivion, but he could feel the weight leaving his body . . . his face going numb . . .

He came awake with a jolt, the plane lying dead in the water—a wingless tube of aluminum—floating right-side up, the pilot seat empty. "Kyra!"

"Back here." Her voice seemed far away, as if coming from the back of a deep cave. "You okay?"

He had no idea, but he was still alive and that was enough for the moment. "I think so." He reached down to release his seatbelt, then realized his watch was missing and his left arm was broken, halfway between the elbow and wrist. *Damn!* "You?"

"I'm fine. See if you can help Jim. He's still in his seat."

"Yeah, sure." He popped the belt with his right hand and stood up, being careful not to bang his head on the overhead. "Where—" Then he saw her, near the back of the cabin, a dark silhouette beyond the odd reflections of fluttering sunlight streaming through the small windows along the top of the fuselage. "What are you doing back there?"

"I'm checking the storage closet. There's supposed to be a raft somewhere. I thought I better find it before it was too late."

"Oh, right." Nice to know someone could think. He squeezed past the control console, his feet sloshing through ankle-deep water. "We need to get out of this thing! It's a floating coffin."

"Don't panic," she answered. "As long as we don't open the door, I think we're good for a few minutes. We can exit through the cockpit window."

Panic? Did he sound panicky? He stepped into the cabin—which, despite its post-tornado appearance, had managed to survive its loop-to-loop tumble without breaking apart—and bent down next to Atherton. The man looked undamaged except for a vagueness in his amber eyes. "Jim, you okay?"

A confused frown creased the man's forehead. "What?"

"It's time to go," Simon answered, being careful to keep his voice calm and matter-of-fact. "Can you stand?"

"Stand?" He looked down, his eyes growing wider as he stared at the smear of vomit covering the front of his shirt. "What happened?"

"We made an unscheduled stop. We're going to exit through the cockpit."

Atherton nodded, as if this made perfect sense. "Okay. Sure." He tried to push himself up, the effort stymied by his seatbelt.

Simon snapped the buckle and pulled the man to his feet. "How do you feel?"

Atherton stared in bewilderment at his right arm and the cable that stretched downward to the security case lying half submerged on the floor. Simon grabbed the case with his good arm, placed it against Atherton's chest, and gave the man a gentle shove toward the cockpit. "I need to help Kyra."

Atherton turned back, the light in his eyes finally coming full beam. "Where is she? Is she okay?"

"I'm right here," Kyra answered. "I'm fine. Just do what Simon says."

Simon says: Let's get the hell out of here! The water, he noticed, had risen at least three inches in the last minute, and his broken arm had become more than an irritation—the throbbing pain echoing through his banged-up skull like a kettle drum. He reached out, dialed the numbers on the wrist cuff attached to Atherton's arm, took the case, and gave the man another gentle push. "See if you can get yourself up in that window. We may not have a lot of time. I'll be right back." He tossed the case onto the pilot's seat, then turned and began to slosh his way toward the rear, which was riding noticeably lower in the water. With every step the water became deeper, the ocean now slapping against the windows. Bending down, he could see the island off to one side. Not that far, maybe a quarter mile, but against the waves with a broken arm, he doubted if he could make the swim. "Any luck there, Rynerson?"

"Maybe." Standing knee-deep in the narrowest part of the cabin, she was straining to extract a large yellow duffle from the bottom of a half-submerged cabinet attached to the opposite wall. "Jim okay?"

"A little disoriented. He'll be fine." Moving in close, Simon dropped to his knees, the water rising to his chest, and found a good grip on one of the duffle's thick straps. "Okay, Rynerson, put your butt into it."

Leaning back against the bulkhead, she brought her feet up, one at a time, planting a foot on each side of the cabinet door—until she was literally stretched out over his head—and began to pull. The bag moved an inch or two, then caught in the narrow opening and refused to budge. "It's hopeless."

Despite the circumstances, he couldn't resist the opportunity. "Don't panic, Rynerson. Wait five seconds, then give it everything you've got."

"I'm not panicking," she snapped back. "I'm just stating the—"

He didn't wait to hear. Taking a deep breath, he dropped beneath the water, wedged his right hand under the duffle and began to push upward. For a few long seconds nothing happened, then when he was about to give up, his lungs ready to burst, it moved . . . slowly . . . reluctantly . . . then, like a stubborn wine cork, burst free. As it popped loose, Kyra collapsed onto his back, crushing his broken arm beneath him. He screamed, couldn't help it, but the sound was lost in the water and his desperate scramble for air.

Kyra rolled into the water, and for a few moments they were both flailing around like inverted crabs, struggling to get their feet under them. When they finally managed to surface—both of them sputtering and spitting and gasping for air—the water was up to their waists, the plane tilting precariously toward the tail. Simon reached down, found the duffle, and pulled it to the surface. Stenciled in black across the yellow fabric was a string of unintelligible Chinese characters, the international symbol for first aid, and one encouraging word in English: SURVIVAL. "Gotta be it."

Kyra nodded, grabbed a nylon strap, and turned toward the front. "Let's get out of here."

As they neared the cockpit, the plane leveled slightly, but the water was still rising, and Simon figured they didn't have more than a minute, two at the most. "In case I forgot to mention it, Rynerson, that was one hell of a landing."

Without turning, her right arm shot up, middle finger extended. "Screw you, Leonidovich."

That, he had a feeling, would not be such a bad way to go. Better than drowning like a rat in a can. "I was serious."

"Yeah, me too."

Right, nothing like a little flirtatious humor to obscure the thought of death.

"Come on!" Atherton shouted. He had managed to get himself through the narrow opening, and was straddling the nose and hanging on to the window strut like a bronc rider in fear of losing his mount. "This thing's about to go down!"

Kyra pulled herself up onto the co-pilot's seat and turned, but Simon ignored her outstretched hands and unzipped the duffle. "We need to get it out of the bag first. It'll be too hard to open in the water. We could lose it."

She nodded, bent down, and frantically began pulling at the polyurethane-coated fabric. As hoped, the duffle contained an inflatable raft and an emergency survival pack. Working together, they quickly stuffed half the material through the window. "Okay," Simon said, "out you go. I'll feed you the rest." She opened her mouth, clearly intending to argue the point, but he cut her off. "I'm the pilot of record." He gave her a hard, don't-screw-with-me look. "And that's an order."

She hesitated, but only a second, then reached out, grabbed Atherton's belt, and shimmied out through the window and onto the nose. Simon grabbed his security case and stepped onto the co-pilot's seat. The plane immediately dipped forward, a huge wave of water surging from the cabin into the cockpit. For a moment he thought he was dead, then he relaxed—*Go with it! Go with it!*—and with surprisingly little effort floated out through the opening.

Chapter Twenty-seven

South China Sea

Tuesday, 10 July 09:53:11 GMT +0800

Mawl glanced at his watch. *Sixteen minutes.* "How much longer?"

"Almost there," Chricher answered, his eyes intense and feral, searching for their target.

"That's what you said three minutes ago. We should be able to see it by now."

"Doubt if there's gonna be anything to—" He sat up straighter in his seat. "Right there! Twelve o'clock!"

Mawl tried to shield his eyes against the glare, but couldn't see anything but blue water and a small island in the distance. "Where? I don't see anything!"

"Saw it just for a second," Chricher answered. "A nice white line. Then it disappeared."

Mawl strained forward against his seatbelt, searching for some sign of the wreckage, but the waves were just high enough to create a froth—a thousand white lines in a sea of blue. "Are you sure? I don't see it!"

"You will." Chricher pulled back on the pitch lever and the helicopter darted upward, giving them a better overview. "See it now?"

Mawl nodded, though there wasn't much to see: only the fuselage, and most of that was underwater.

Although both wings and the tail assembly had broken off, there was no debris in the water. And no bodies. "Could anyone survive that?"

"Depends how they hit." Chricher eased the pitch lever forward, the tail of the chopper came up, and a few seconds later they were hovering less than ten meters above the hollowed-out eyes of the cockpit. "See anything?"

"No," Mawl answered, scanning the length of the fuselage with his binoculars. "Door's still closed."

"That's why it hasn't gone down. There must be a pocket of air trapped in the cabin."

"Meaning someone could still be alive in there?"

"Anything's possible."

Mawl slammed one of the twenty-round clips into the Uzi, and jacked a round into the chamber. "I can take care of that."

"Hey, be careful with that thing," Chricher warned as he backed the chopper away from the target. "We don't want a ricochet hitting the rotor."

"You just keep this damn thing steady."

Chricher frowned, clearly unhappy with the idea. "I thought this was supposed to look like an accident."

"You pulled the transponder." But even as he said it, Mawl knew Chricher was right, that it was possible they might still find the plane, but a part of him—that almost forgotten young warrior who liked to see blood in the water—wanted to do it. "They're never gonna find the thing." He lowered the top half of the plexi windscreen, steadied himself against the back of the seat, flipped the fire-selector to semi, stuck the

Uzi through the narrow opening, and stitched a neat row of holes along the top of the fuselage. The chatter was deafening, but the gun felt good in his hands. *Really good.* Damn near orgasmic.

Not more than four hundred yards away, Simon was on his knees, frantically waving his good arm and trying to get the helicopter's attention. Behind him, Kyra and Atherton struggled to get the cumbersome six-person raft turned and moving against the incoming waves. Despite the echoing thump of the rotors, the sudden staccato of the machine gun was both distinctive and incomprehensible, momentarily freezing their oars in mid-stroke.

Simon was already on the bottom of the raft, reaching for Kyra with his good arm when she found her voice. "Was that—"

"Get down! If they spot us, we're dead."

She dropped to her knees, but Atherton just sat there—high and dry on the side of the buoyancy chamber, his oar frozen in suspended animation—as if he couldn't decide what to do. Not about to draw the man a picture, Simon reached up and pushed him over the side. "Come on, Rynerson, into the water! We're sitting ducks in this thing!"

"What about your arm? Can you swim?"

"My security case is waterproof. I'll hang on to it."

"Waterproof doesn't mean it will float! Not with you hanging on to it!"

"It's less than a hundred yards to shore. I'll make it." He shoved the survival pack into her arms. "Go!"

For once, she didn't argue, slithering over the side as he grabbed the case and followed her in. The unexpected dip had apparently shocked Atherton back to reality, his expression appropriately fearful. "They're going to see us," he whispered, as if his voice might penetrate the thumping echo of the rotors.

"Maybe not," Simon shouted, struggling to keep his head above water and hang on to the case, which didn't provide much buoyancy. "Not if we sink the raft. There should be a knife in that survival bag."

As the top of the fuselage slipped beneath the surface, Mawl emptied another twenty-round clip into the fading shadow. "Bye-bye, courier man."

Chricher grinned, baring his stained teeth. "I think you killed it, Brick."

Mawl smiled to himself, feeling better than he had in weeks, and closed the windscreen. "Let's get out of here."

Chricher eased back on the pitch lever and the helicopter leaped upward as he swung around toward the coast. "Uh-oh."

"What?"

He pointed at something floating just beneath the surface of the water. "Look at that."

"What the bleedin' hell . . . ?" But he knew—could feel it in his gut.

Chricher nudged the chopper forward and down, until they were hovering only a few meters above the yellow splotch twisting in the bluish-green water.

"Could be debris," Mawl said, but even as he said it, he realized nothing could float that far in such a short time.

Chricher shook his head, his hawk-like eyes already scanning the shoreline, a narrow strip of rocks and sand between the water and a dense jungle of trees. "There!" He pointed to three figures struggling in the choppy surf, the woman and one of the men not more than a few meters from a high outcropping of rocks and boulders, the other man a few meters behind.

"Get on them!" Mawl shouted. "Don't let them get into those rocks." As the chopper leaped forward, Mawl yanked open the windscreen, levered himself up against the back of the seat, snapped the fire-selector to full-auto, and pushed the Uzi out through the narrow opening. "Hold it steady!" He leveled the short barrel on the backs of the two people nearest the rocks and pulled the trigger. He could feel the vibration as the firing pin dropped—a dull snap. "What the . . . ?" He squeezed the trigger a second time, then realized he had emptied the clip on the plane's fuselage. "Sonofafuck!" He yanked the gun inside, pulled the empty clip and jammed his hand into his flight bag, searching for a fresh magazine. "Cut them off!"

Chricher nosed the helicopter toward the water, the rotor only inches from the outcropping of rock . . . the blades whipping the surf into a mini tornado . . . the air swirling with spray . . . the sound ricocheting off the surface: *WHUMP-WHUMP-WHUMP.* From the corner of his eye, Mawl could see the struggle taking place beneath him: the first two figures rising out of the water . . . trying to plow their way through the waist-deep surf . . . falling . . . then rising again, only a few steps from the protection of the rocks. The woman suddenly stopped . . . turned . . . hesitated . . . then started back to help the other man—*Leonidovich!*—who was struggling with a large briefcase and trying to stand. He motioned the woman away, finally managed to get his feet under him, and stood up, the water streaming off the black case as he pulled it into his arms.

"Either that bugger's a bleedin' idiot," Chricher shouted, "or he's got the crown jewels in that thing."

Mawl nodded, more to himself and what he had just decided. Whatever it was, he intended to have it. He slammed a fresh clip into the Uzi, jacked a round into the chamber, flipped the fire-selector to single-shot, steadied the gun on the edge of the windscreen, zeroed in on the back of the courier's head, and took a deep breath. *Slow squeeze.* Everything seemed to happen in slow motion, a slide show of images, the frames clicking off one by one: the woman now hunched in the rocks . . . her soundless scream . . . her finger pointing toward the helicopter . . . Leonidovich turning . . . looking up . . . his expression frozen in a painful grimace . . . his arms coming up, as if to throw the case. Mawl smiled to himself, the bastard had almost made it. Two more steps. Two steps too far.

"Now!" Chricher shouted. "Light him up!"

Slow squeeze . . .

Beyond the thumping sound and swirling spray,

Simon could see the man's shaved head and pale blue eyes . . . could see the short hollow tube aimed at his head . . . and realized they would be the last things he would ever see unless this crazy idea worked. Ignoring the burning pain in his arm, he ducked beneath the case just as the bullet hit, the force of the blow driving him to his knees.

"He's down," Chricher shouted, and immediately began to pull back from the overhang.

"No, wait!" Mawl tried to squeeze off another round before he lost the target, but the helicopter was already moving and the bullet ricocheted harmlessly off the rocks. "The sonofabitch is getting up!" He snapped the fire-selector to full-auto. "Hold it steady!"

Chapter Twenty-eight

An Island in the South China Sea

Tuesday, 10 July 09:58:41 GMT +0800

Still holding the security case over his head, the sand sucking at his waterlogged shoes and the surf pounding at his legs, Simon struggled to regain his footing. Mentally bracing himself for the next impact, he finally managed to stand, to turn, to orient himself. Only a couple more steps, but his legs felt heavy as lead, and the harder he pushed, the deeper his feet sank into the sand, and the more the surf seemed to hold him back.

Thwack-thwack-thwack: three more bullets slammed into the case as a burst of shots pelted the water around him, but he somehow managed to keep his feet, to take one more step before diving beneath the protection of the rocks.

"Simon, are you hit! You okay?!"

Her voice was loud and desperate, but he had no idea if he was hit, and didn't have the strength to answer. Given a choice, he would have closed his eyes and slept, just a two-minute nap, but he knew it wasn't over despite the fading sound of the helicopter.

"Talk to me, dammit!" She grabbed his shirt and pulled him onto his back. "Are you hit?"

"Stop screaming, Rynerson. I'm not deaf."

She sighed, clearly relieved. "You're okay?"

"I think so. Where's Jim?"

She cocked her head to one side. "He's keeping an eye on the chopper."

"Good." He pushed himself into a sitting position. "What about you? You all right?"

"I'm fine," she answered. "What the hell were you thinking? That damn artifact isn't worth your life!"

"It seemed like a good idea at the time."

She opened her mouth, clearly intending to attack that foolishness, but Atherton suddenly popped into view. "They disappeared around the point," he said, his words coming in a rush. "It's obvious they're looking for a place to land." He squatted down, staring at Simon with an expression of disbelief. "You've gotta be the dumbest, luckiest bastard that's ever walked the earth. How the hell did you—"

"Dumb maybe," Simon interrupted, "but it wasn't luck. That case is lined with aramid fiber. The same material used in body armor."

Kyra hooted. "Leonidovich, you are too much! I should have known you wouldn't have done something that crazy without an edge."

Atherton reached over, grabbed the case, and flipped it over, revealing four distinct indentations along the side. "I'll be damned to hell."

"Sooner than you think," Simon said, "if we don't get off this beach. They're going to be coming."

The man leaped to his feet. "You're right. We need to—"

"We're not going anywhere," Kyra broke in, "until I do something with Simon's arm."

"No need," Simon said, struggling to get his feet under him. "I can manage."

"Obviously," she said, her voice flat with sarcasm. "Jim, you keep an eye on the shoreline. That's the only way they can get back here. I'll see what I can do with this idiot's arm."

Atherton frowned, clearly unhappy with the idea of delay. "Okay, but Simon's right. You need to hurry."

Kyra nodded and turned back to Simon. "Let's get that shirt off." She helped him up, unbuttoned his shirt, then gently peeled the wet material away from his skin. She lifted and turned and probed the puffy area between his elbow and wrist. "Does that hurt?"

Like a kick in the testes! "Not much."

"It doesn't look too bad."

"That's what I said." He really didn't like the thought of her playing twisty-pretzel with his arm. "No reason to worry about it now. Let's get moving."

She continued to probe. "At least it didn't break the skin."

"You realize, Rynerson, those funny initials after your name . . . they're for zoology? You do understand the difference? I'm one of those Homo sapiens you might have heard about, the kind of animal that walks upright and has opposable thumbs."

She cocked her head to one side, giving him the fisheye. "Are you afraid, Leonidovich?"

"Absolutely not! Concerned . . . maybe . . . a little."

"What is it with men? You stand out there playing

Roger Dodger with a machine gun, then you wimp out when it comes to a little pain."

"Define 'little.' "

"You won't even feel it . . . once you pass out."

"That's what I thought. And then you expect me to outrun the bad guys?"

She hesitated, staring intently into his eyes. "Okay, you have a point, I won't set it, but we can't leave it like that, you could end up with nerve damage. We'll have to immobilize it."

Immobilize, that didn't sound too excruciating. "Okay. There might be something in the survival bag we could use."

She glanced toward the water. "Afraid we lost it. But—" She squeezed a hand into the wet pocket of her slacks and pulled out the Swiss Army knife. "I've still got this." She lowered herself onto a rock, and quickly began cutting his shirt into strips. "This should do the trick."

"In the movies, the heroine always cuts up her own shirt."

She didn't look up, but smiled and shook her head in mock disgust. "You're a real piece of work, Leonidovich."

"At least I won't freeze. It's like a steam bath out here."

She glanced toward the east, and the towering range of sullen and bruised clouds. "It's about to get a whole lot worse."

"Let's hope. They won't be able to use that chopper in a typhoon."

She nodded. "If we can avoid them for a couple more hours, we should be okay."

He knew better. The storm might buy them time, but people with helicopters and machine guns would not give up quite so easily. "Maybe."

She stood up, his shirt laying in two-inch strips across her arm. "Okay, just relax and let me do this."

Like he had a choice? "I hear that from a lot of women."

"Ha! You should be so lucky."

"What's with all the chitchat," Atherton yelled. "We need to get out of here."

"Two minutes," Kyra answered, as she began wrapping and tying the strips to Simon's arm. "You really think Robbie had a part in this?" It was obvious from her tone, she didn't want to believe it.

"I wasn't sure," Simon answered. "Not until those propellers stopped spinning. Now I'm sure."

She nodded slowly, reluctantly accepting the idea. "He's just a kid. He probably didn't know what he was getting into."

"I'm sure you're right." He wasn't, but she obviously felt hurt and betrayed, and he saw no reason to pour salt into that wound.

She tied two of the strips behind his neck, then wound the others around his back, tightly securing his arm across the center of his chest. "He did try to talk me out of going."

"Yes he did." Which only proved how much he knew, but she would realize that soon enough. On some level, she probably did, but had set up some kind of mental block to avoid the reality. He couldn't really blame her; she had tried so hard to separate herself from the Rynerson juggernaut, only to find herself once again the target of people she didn't know, with an agenda she didn't understand.

"How does it feel?" She looked up at him, her eyes moist, a doe in the juggernaut's headlights.

"Great." He wouldn't have told her otherwise.

Chricher, who was in the lead, suddenly stopped. "We need to go back."

Mawl, who had his head down, trying to avoid the whiplash of branches, nearly ran his Uzi up the man's ass. "Five more minutes, Chrich. We're catching them."

"Yeah," Chricher agreed, "we're catching them all right, but they've still got a thirty-minute lead, and if we don't start back now, we're going to be stuck out here."

Mawl hesitated, reluctant to give up the chase before he had that case in his hands. He couldn't imagine what could be so valuable . . . so valuable Leonidovich would risk his life to save it . . . it had to be worth millions . . . a lifetime pass on the good-time train. He looked up, the thick vegetation reminding him of Cambodia, and tried to catch a glimpse of sky.

"It's coming," Chricher said, as if reading his mind.

"We might be closer than you think. I must have hit the bastard. You saw him go down."

"Yeah, I saw it," Chricher admitted, "but we

should have seen some blood by now. He must have stumbled."

Mawl nodded, though he didn't understand how he could have missed the shot. "It doesn't make sense."

"It's coming," Chricher repeated.

Mawl gave him "the look," letting him know he didn't need to be reminded. "We stop now, we'll lose the trail."

"Will anyway," Chricher answered. "Once that bleedin' rain starts, we've lost 'em."

"There's no way to secure the chopper?"

"Sure, I can tie it down, but that's not the problem. There's no open space on this goddamned rock. Once this shit gets blowin' around, it'll—"

"I get the picture," Mawl interrupted. "Leave, lose the trail. Stay, lose the helicopter."

"You got it."

Mawl hesitated, considering a third option. "Or you go and I stay."

"You think that's a good idea?" Chricher asked, obviously thinking it wasn't. "All you got is a rain poncho, and it's gonna get awful nasty out here."

Mawl smiled to himself, suddenly convinced it was an excellent idea. If he kept moving, he might get lucky, catch them before the rain hit, and that would give him time to hide whatever was in that case before Chricher got back with the others. *No witnesses.* No arguments over a split. "That's what we do, Chrich. We do nasty."

Chapter Twenty-nine

An Island in the South China Sea

Tuesday, 10 July 14:06:21 GMT +0800

They moved along the coast, toward the southwest, away from where the helicopter had disappeared, then turned north, moving inland through a narrow and rising valley of towering trees and thick vegetation, searching for cover and a good place to hide before the storm hit. In the last few minutes, the earth and plants seemed to have lost their color, everything a gunmetal gray beneath the blanket of trees and dark clouds. Atherton, who was in the lead, using the security case to snowplow his way through the dense foliage, glanced over his shoulder. "We need to find something soon. It's going to be a real soaker."

Too late now, Simon thought, as the first drops of rain filtered down through the canopy of trees, a mixture of broadleaf evergreens and palms. A few minutes later he couldn't see four feet, the rain coming in a torrential rush. Another few seconds and the uneven ground had turned as slippery as warm oil, and with only one arm available for grabbing, he could barely stay on his feet. Kyra stumbled into him from behind.

"You okay?" Her voice barely penetrated the ferocious downpour.

"I'm good. Just lost my footing for a second."

She stepped around him, shielding her face with both hands, measuring him with those bar-scanner eyes. "How's your arm?"

"Fine." It was actually numb, better than his legs, which felt like they belonged to someone else. His upper body—every inch of his stomach, chest, and shoulders—was covered with scratches and welts, but it looked worse than it felt. "What about you?"

She smiled, the effort strained. "I'm okay. Where's Jim?"

He looked past her, but Atherton had already disappeared beyond the silver-gray curtain of rain. "He was in front of me only a second ago."

She nodded wearily. "We better wait. He'll come back when he realizes we're not behind him."

"Sounds right," though he knew if Atherton didn't look back within the next couple of minutes, there would be little chance of retracing his steps in such a downpour. "You want to sit down?"

Instead of answering, she collapsed right where she was, sitting cross-legged on a patch of wild grass, her head drooping forward against the rain. Simon leaned in, trying to shelter her body from the onslaught.

"Simon, *please!* Sit down! You're in worse shape than I am."

Before he could answer, Atherton reappeared through the downpour, his blond hair painted to his skull, his tailored clothes hanging like shammy cloth around his body. "What happened?" he shouted. "Twist an ankle?"

Simon shook his head. "We just lost sight of you. Thought we should wait."

He nodded and dropped the case. "Can you believe this crap?"

Considering their elephant-sized trail, Simon thought, *this crap* might be the only thing keeping them alive. "At least it's warm."

"True enough." He squatted down next to Kyra. "How you feeling?"

"Waterlogged," she answered, not looking up.

"You want to rest for a bit?"

"Up to Simon," she answered. "He's the one with the broken arm."

Atherton glanced up. "Simon . . . ?"

As much as he wanted to crawl under a tree and sleep, he realized this was not the place. He dropped to one knee, so they could talk without shouting. "We need to keep moving, but we need to slow down and start being careful where we step and what we grab."

Kyra squinted at him through the rain. "You really think they could find us in this downpour?"

"The way we've been going, a blind man with a wooden leg could track us. We need to get out of this ravine. If we continue like this, they could literally stumble into us. We need to backtrack a ways and then—"

"Backtrack!" Atherton interrupted. "Why would we do that?"

"Simon's right," Kyra answered. "We need to double back and try to find a place where we can climb out of here without leaving an exit sign." She ran a hand through her hair, plowing the water off the back of her head. "I'll take the lead. Jim, you'll need to help Simon up the incline."

"Sure thing," he answered, apparently willing to do whatever she asked. "We can hide the case and come back for it later."

She unfolded her legs and pushed herself to her feet. "Sounds like a plan."

A bad one, Simon thought, for reasons he didn't care to explain. "That may not be a good idea. Another couple of hours, and this area could be under water."

A look of doubt flashed across Atherton's face. "You think?"

"Absolutely," Simon answered, though he didn't really believe it. "Just get me up that incline. I'll take it from there."

The man hesitated, unconvinced. "There's no way—"

"Forget it," Kyra interrupted. "You're asking Dudley Do Right to abandon his mission." She gave Simon a wink, an acknowledgment that she understood. "Trust me, that's not going to happen." She reached down and picked up the case. "I can handle it."

Despite the rain, Mawl knew he was getting close. They were moving like a herd of frightened animals, following the path of least resistance. *Civilians,* he could have closed his eyes and found them, but he forced himself to slow down. Outnumbered three to one, and blinded by the rain, he didn't want to run into them unexpectedly. *No more mistakes.*

Though he didn't understand how it happened, now that he had a chance to consider the ramifications, he was actually relieved to have missed the shot on Leonidovich. Bodies and bullets didn't exactly fit the accident scenario. No more than a fuselage riddled with holes. A mistake he could remedy by planting the bodies fifty or sixty kilometers north, where they would be discovered by one of the local fishing boats. That would put a quick end to any wild speculation, any search near the island, and give Trader his "accident." But, it also made things more complicated. They would have to die from drowning, with salt water in their lungs.

CHAPTER THIRTY

An Island in the South China Sea

Wednesday, 11 July 14:28:16 GMT +0800

"Simon." The man's hushed voice slipped off-balance into his subconscious. He tried to ignore it, to deny its presence, but the harder he tried, the more persistent it became. "Simon, wake up. You're dreaming."

He suddenly recognized the voice, and it all came back, a nightmare of images coming to life in segments: the plane going down, the helicopter, his broken arm . . . *No dream,* he could feel that, a throbbing ache from his fingertips to his armpit. He took a deep breath, the air muggy and thick, and opened his eyes. The rain had stopped, but a blanket of dark clouds still covered the sky, the light thin and gray beyond the overhang of rocks.

Atherton leaned into view, his voice flat with anxiety. "You were thrashing around pretty hard. I thought you might hurt your arm."

Simon tried to suck some saliva into his dry mouth. "Water . . ." The word barely made it past his throat, the choked-off sound of a wild beast being strangled.

Atherton ducked out of sight, then reappeared with a short stalk of hollowed-out bamboo. He looked like a homeless person with a good haircut, his face stubbled with blond whiskers, his well-tailored clothes damp and torn and mud-spattered. He crouched down and carefully trickled a stream of water into Simon's mouth. "Take it slow."

Simon swallowed and coughed, then swallowed again, the flavor earthy and sweet. "Thanks." He still sounded like a frog, but one that could talk.

Atherton sat back on his heels. "You've been running a pretty high temperature. Sweating one minute, shaking the next. How do you feel?"

Numb and foggy, like someone had stuffed his body through a meat grinder. "I'm okay."

"Can you sit up?"

Good question, and though he couldn't remember how he got there, he realized he was lying on a bed of palm branches. "I think so." Using his good arm, he pushed himself into a sitting position. His torso looked as bad as it felt, his upper body ribboned with cuts and scratches, his left arm bound to his chest. "What time is it?"

Atherton glanced at his watch. "Two-thirty. You've been out for sixteen hours."

"Sixteen hours? What happened? I mean . . ."

"You don't remember?"

He remembered walking until dark . . . he remembered finding this semi-dry, semi-sheltered spot . . . he remembered . . . that was it, nothing beyond that point. "Remember what?"

"Kyra setting your arm."

No, he didn't remember that. Thankfully. He glanced around, unable to see much beyond the wall of vegetation. "Where is Kyra?"

"She's been gone over six hours. Said she was going to look for help. I tried to talk her out of it." He shook his head, a gesture of self-recrimination. "I never should have let her go."

Right, as if Kyra Rynerson would let any man dictate her actions. "Don't worry about her." He tried to sound more confident than he felt. "That girl's tough as nails and twice as sharp. She'll be fine."

Atherton nodded, though it was obvious he didn't believe it.

"When did the rain stop?"

He glanced over his shoulder, apparently unaware that it had. "Oh." He extended his hand out beyond the rocks, palm up, as if he didn't believe his eyes. "It comes and goes. Mostly comes. So hard most of the time you can't see a thing."

"I'm sure that's why it's taking her so long." A weak attempt, Simon realized, to convince himself. "She spent three months in the Amazon rain forest. She knows how to take care of herself."

"I guess."

"You find anything to eat?" Simon asked, trying to change the subject. "There should be a lot of berries and nuts in this climate."

Atherton shook his head. "I didn't think I should leave you alone."

"Thanks, I appreciate it." He suspected the man was simply too depressed or too afraid to venture beyond their enclosure. "If Kyra's not back soon, we'll take a look around, see what we can find."

Atherton shrugged indifferently. "I'm not really

hungry." He squatted down, until they were eye to eye. "Mind if I ask you something?"

"Of course not."

"Just between us."

Uh-oh—that meant it had something to do with Kyra. He nodded, though he didn't really want to play keeper-of-secrets in their relationship.

"You and Kyra are close."

Was that a question? "What do you mean?"

"I know she respects your opinion."

Simon smiled, hoping to keep it light. "I told you she was smart."

"I've decided to ask her to marry me."

"Oh . . . wow . . . I mean—" What did he mean? He wasn't *that* surprised; suspected their relationship was heading in that direction, but why now? In this place? "You obviously don't believe in wasting time."

"There's something about going down in a plane that makes a person realize what's important in life."

"Can't argue with that."

"Well . . . ?"

Well what? What did he expect? "I think any man would be damn lucky to have her."

"So you approve?"

Simon chuckled, as if he found the question amusing, though he found nothing about the conversation remotely humorous. "You're asking the wrong person. It's not my approval you need."

"But what you think matters to her. I'd like to know that we have your blessing."

Blessing! "Jim, really, you're placing way too much

importance on my opinion. Kyra doesn't care what I think—not when it comes to love and marriage."

The man's lips disappeared into a tight seam. "So you're against it?"

"No," Simon answered, being careful to keep his tone matter-of-fact. "That's not what I said, and that's not what I mean. I've known you less than two weeks." The same as the proposed bride, he might have added, but restrained himself. "I don't know you well enough to make a judgement. I don't know if you like kids, or if you—"

"Don't," Atherton broke in, "make this complicated. If you're against the idea, just say so. Kids have nothing to do with this. If she wants kids, we'll have kids. It's not an issue."

"I wasn't referring to future children, Jim. Kyra has a child. That's an important *fact,* not an *issue.*"

Atherton rocked back on his heels, almost as if he'd been slapped. "Oh, right. I misunderstood."

Simon nodded, though the man's response seemed disingenuous, his reaction beyond misunderstanding. Did he even remember that Kyra had a child? Was he blindly in love, or an opportunist looking to climb aboard the Rynerson Express?

The object of their discussion suddenly appeared through the foliage, her blouse and slacks caked with mud. "Misunderstood what?"

Atherton leaped to his feet. "Misunderstood how long you would be gone." He gave Simon an awkward, please-don't-say-anything smile. "We were starting to worry."

"Sorry, I wanted to finish scouting the island before dark." She squatted down next to the makeshift bed. "How you doing, Leonidovich?"

"Good." If feeling like a regurgitated hair ball qualified as *good*. "Thanks for setting my arm."

"Ha! That's not what you said last night."

"That was my female side talking. You have to ignore her."

She smiled, just a little, the ordeal clearly having sapped her spirit. "You have sides?"

"Absolutely. Simon and Simone."

"Sounds a little schizophrenic to me."

"We resent the implication of that remark."

She laughed and placed a hand on his forehead. "You're still a bit warm. Have you eaten anything?"

"He just woke up," Atherton answered quickly, his tone a touch defensive. "I was about to look around. See what I could find."

"I might have something." She reached behind her and pulled an olive-green military cargo bag through the foliage. "Compliments of our friends from the helicopter."

Atherton stared at the thing, his eyes devoid of understanding. "They left it?"

Simon knew better. "They're still here?"

She nodded. "Five of them. I didn't see the helicopter, they couldn't use it this weather, but it's the same guys. They were unloading gear from a fishing trawler. Not far from where we came ashore. They've got four Zodiacs and enough supplies to last at least a couple of weeks."

The confusion on Atherton's face deepened. "Zodiacs?"

"Inflatable rubber boats," Kyra explained. "One's pretty good size . . . big outboard . . . would probably hold six, maybe eight people. The others are smaller . . . wouldn't hold more than two. They're setting up camp just inside—"

"They sound like fishermen," Atherton interrupted, his tone hopeful.

"No, they've got guns and—"

"Or hunters."

"Yes, Jim, that's exactly what they are. And, they're hunting us."

"I just don't understand how you can be sure?" he persisted, clearly not wanting to accept what he was hearing. "We didn't really get a good look at them."

"Because—" She took a deep breath, obviously irritated by the interruptions. "Robbie is with them."

"Oh." He slumped back against the rock wall. "Oh, Jesus."

Someone, Simon thought, needed to work on his communication skills before popping the big question. He cocked his head toward the cargo bag, trying to refocus the happy couple's attention. "So, what you got there, Rynerson?"

"I didn't stop to look." She pulled back the zipper and within seconds they were digging through the bag like three kids at Christmas. The contents clearly belonged to one person. The bag contained an assortment of clothes—mostly T-shirts and cargo-style shorts—including an expensive pair of lightweight hiking boots, a cheap pair of flip-flop shower shoes, and a camouflage Boonie hat. There were two smaller bags within the larger: a small toiletry kit, and a nylon accessory bag. The first contained two pivot-head disposable razors, a tube of Marks & Spencer shave gel, a tube of Hedley & Wyche toothpaste, a well-used toothbrush, a first-aid kit, an aerosol can of GreenHead insect repellent, four Safex Delay condoms, a small sewing kit, a washcloth, a laundry line, two sticks of camouflage paint—one loam, the other leaf-green—and a small plastic jar containing an assortment of pills. The accessory bag contained a pair of Steiner 7x50 binoculars, a pair of PVS-7 Ultra night-vision goggles, a SureFire E1e mini-light, a fifty-foot coil of black nylon rope, a clear plastic bottle of dark rum, and an assortment of high-energy snack foods.

Kyra grinned, clearly pleased with herself. "Not bad, uh?"

"Absolutely incredible!" Atherton agreed, obviously trying hard to redeem himself. "How did you get it?"

"It wasn't that hard. They had most of their gear stacked inside the tree line, out of sight from the water. After the trawler left and they started to set up the Zodiacs, I just slipped in, grabbed the nearest bag, and hightailed it out of there."

Simon suspected what she described as "just slipped in" to have been one heart-stopping moment, but he feigned a look of disappointment. "You couldn't have grabbed a gun or two while you were at it?"

"Be careful, Leonidovich, I might have to reset that arm."

"Did I mention what a really fine job you did landing that plane?"

"Smartass."

Atherton glanced back and forth between them, clearly irritated by their mindless sniping. "Hey, guys, we're in trouble here. What's going to happen when they realize the bag is missing?"

"Nothing," Kyra answered. "They'll think they forgot to unload it."

He opened his mouth, ready to argue the point, then apparently realized their situation couldn't get worse, stolen bag or not, and changed direction. "Could you tell what they had planned? Were you close enough to hear anything?"

"Not really," she answered. "Not with all the rain."

"I assume," Simon said, "they were either British or Irish?"

Atherton frowned, a slightly wary look. "And why would you assume that?"

Simon hesitated, not wanting to overshadow the man in front of the woman he intended to marry. "Well, I . . . I just assumed if Robbie was with them, they were from the same country." Probably from the same military unit—ex-SAS, working as mercenaries—but he kept those thoughts to himself. "And most of this stuff—" He motioned toward the toiletries. "—is British."

"Oh, right. Of course. Mercenaries, I'll bet." He turned to Kyra, who was sorting through the pills. "A clear chain of command? One man in charge?"

"No question," she answered. "A real hardass type. Shaved head, late forties, early fifties. Handsome in a rugged kind of way, but not someone I'd want to meet in a dark alley." She selected three identical pills and handed them to Simon. "Acetaminophen. That should help kill your fever."

"Thanks." He popped the pills, swallowing them dry. "You see anything else?"

"Such as?"

"Fishing village? Inhabitants? Boats?"

She shook her head. "Nothing. The weather's too bad to see anything offshore, and the island's deserted. I made it from one end to the other, somewhere around three miles. It couldn't have been more than a mile across at the widest."

"Food?" The question, Simon realized, didn't matter that much; if they didn't find a way to escape this island trap, and fast, they would end up dead long before they starved. "Water?"

"Plenty of wild fruit," she answered. "We should probably save the trail mix for emergencies. And with all this rain . . ." She shrugged, not bothering to state the obvious, and pulled a tube of Polysporin ointment from the first-aid kit. "Here. You need to take care of those scratches. The last thing you need is to get an infection in this climate. You could be dead in a matter of days."

Atherton let out a kind of croak, somewhere between a laugh and the grunt. "Days! How could it take days. There have to be people looking for us."

"I'm sure they're looking," Kyra answered. "The

question is where? Whoever sabotaged the plane knew what they were doing. I'd be very surprised if they didn't disable the emergency transponder as well."

Simon would have bet his left testicle on that. "And this weather won't help matters."

"But what about radar?" Atherton asked. "They must have seen us go down."

"Probably not," Kyra answered. "We never declared an emergency. And since we were flying VFR, it's doubtful they were tracking us."

"VFR?"

"Visual flight rules. We didn't file a flight plan."

A look of dismay flashed across Atherton's face. "No flight plan? Why?"

Not that it made a difference now, Simon thought, but he couldn't blame the man for asking. "A flight from mainland China to Taiwan would have prompted too many serious questions. And with that—" He nodded toward his pockmarked security case. "I couldn't very well explain the Crest of Ch'in to just any old customs agent."

"You're saying no one has any idea where we are?"

"That's very possible," Simon admitted, feeling more than a little responsible. "I should have done this alone."

Atherton waved the apology away. "It's no one's fault. I insisted on coming."

"Hey, it could be worse," Kyra said, clearly trying to put a good face on a bad situation. "We're near the

Lema Channel, so there'll be plenty of marine traffic. Fishing boats as well as freighters." She turned to Simon. "Right?"

He nodded, visualizing the map in his mind. "I'm guessing we're on or near Er Zhou. It's one of the larger islands in the Dangan Liedao chain. And the highest, if I remember right. Once the weather clears it shouldn't be that difficult to flag down a boat."

Atherton rolled his eyes. "This is typhoon season. We might not see the sun for days."

As if on cue, the clouds reopened and the rain began to fall; silver-black sheets instantly transformed the gray afternoon into a charcoal twilight. No one said anything, staring at the downpour in morose silence until Atherton broke the spell. "Okay, let's review our options." He said it as if they had a good selection to choose from.

"Our only option," Simon answered, "is to flag down a boat, and that's not going to happen until the weather clears. And it's not going to happen from here. We need to find a place within sight of the water."

Kyra nodded. "We might be able to find a spot somewhere along the western end of the island. The coastline is pretty rugged over there."

"I agree," Atherton said, sounding very much like he didn't. "Our options are limited, but we're not going to survive out here playing hide-and-seek."

As much as Simon hated to admit it, the man was right. "You have something in mind?"

"Maybe. To start, we need to determine what they want. That's the first step in any negotiation."

"Negotiation!" Kyra stared the wide stare of disbelief. "I can tell you what they want! They want us dead!"

"Yes," he agreed, "but that's only a starting point, and we're interested in the end result." He smiled and gave her a wink. "And I'm a very good negotiator." He turned to Simon, the smile growing wider. "That's what *I* do for a living."

Simon finally realized where the man was heading. "You're suggesting we buy our way out?"

"Why not?" He didn't wait for a response. "They're mercenaries. We'll just offer them a better deal. A better end result."

He made it sound easy, but Simon knew better. The men on the beach might be mercenaries, but the reason behind everything—the accidents at the Pearl, the attack on Big Jake, the massacre at the home of Mei-li Chiang, and the downing of the plane—wasn't *just* about money. "I'm not sure there's enough money to buy our way out of this."

"Are you kidding?" He looked at Kyra and smiled. "I can think of two people who would pay about anything to get their little girl back."

Though Simon knew it was true, it was obvious from Kyra's tight-mouthed expression she didn't like being referred to as a chip on the bargaining table. "Yes, they would," Simon conceded, trying to sound agreeable as he disagreed. "And I'm not saying the idea isn't without merit, but sometimes it's not about money."

"Of course it's about money. It's always about

money. That's what mercenaries do . . . they sell their services to the highest bidder."

"Except that their *services,* as you put it, have already been contracted for. If they let us go, they'll end up being hunted themselves."

Atherton lifted his hands and hunched his shoulders, as if to say this was only a minor detail. "It's a matter of risk and reward. We appeal to their greed. I'll make them an offer they can't refuse."

Simon couldn't decide if the man was being foolishly brave, or showing off for his intended. "You're willing to meet with them?"

"Absolutely."

"And what if it's the crest they're after?"

"Then we give it to them. What's the problem?"

"They'd destroy it. That's why the plane was sabotaged."

"How could you know that?"

"Because no one knew you or Kyra would be onboard." He could see in Kyra's expression that she had come to the same conclusion. "And I'm not important enough to have been the target."

Atherton hesitated, staring into rain, as if listening to something just out of hearing, then shrugged. "So they destroy it. It's certainly not worth our lives."

"Isn't it?" Simon asked, wondering what happened to bravery and honor and showing off for your one true love. "It's the linchpin to the Alliance. A new peace between Taiwan and China. Wars are fought over less. Most people would consider that worth the cost."

"Well, I don't happen to be one of them."

Kyra wrinkled her nose, as though she had suddenly noticed a flaw in what she thought was a perfectly cut diamond. "Speak for yourself."

"You're serious?" Atherton asked. "You'd rather die than give up that broken piece of rock?"

"It's a decision I'd rather not make."

He shook his head, a look of disappointment. "Well, we have to do something. We can't just wait for some boat to happen along. Not in this weather."

"No," she agreed, "we can't." She reached over and picked up the night-vision goggles. "I'm going down there. See if I can figure out what they've got planned."

Chapter Thirty-one

An Island in the South China Sea

Wednesday, 11 July 21:26:28 GMT +0800

Hidden beneath a blanket of darkness and driving rain, her nose not more than an inch off the ground, Kyra edged forward over the slippery leaves, toward the only source of light: a faint glow just inside the line of trees that bordered the shoreline. Above her, the sky was blank and unblemished, not a single star or speck of light, and she couldn't see more than a few feet, the shadowed outline of the trees purple-black against the sand and smoky-gray water. She had tried to use the night-vision goggles, but they were too cumbersome in the muck and she abandoned the effort. Despite the downpour, the air remained hot and thick with the smell of seawater and the fecund scent of earth and rotting vegetation. Too wet, she hoped, for the bugs and nightcrawlers.

She took another shallow breath and pulled herself forward, the mossy green carpet absorbing the sound of her movement. The effort, she realized, would probably be for naught, the sound of the rain too loud to overhear any conversation; but she felt compelled to try, to go back with *something*, to prove she had the nerve. *Prove?* To whom?

Atherton? Maybe, but she didn't like the feeling that she *had* to.

Leonidovich? No, he accepted her as she was—the good and the bad.

Herself? Probably, that same old pressure to "beat the boys." She glanced up, readjusted her angle to the light—*fifty more yards*—then put her head down and slithered forward.

She had barely moved a yard, when suddenly, without so much as a slackening whimper, the rain stopped, as if someone had changed the weather channel. The cathedral-like hush seemed even louder than the downpour, the silence broken only by the irregular patter and drip of water off the trees and drooping ferns. She grabbed a quick peek at the sky, surprised to see an outline of clouds and a floodlight of stars. *Shit,* of all the damn luck!

As her eyes adjusted to the light, a number of large dark shapes began to materialize around her. What the . . . ? Then she realized . . . one-man pup tents, three on one side, two on the other. *God almighty!* She had somehow managed to drag herself into the middle of their camp. *Don't panic!* But even as she thought it, her heart began to flutter and pound, threatening to explode through her chest. She swallowed back the metallic taste of fear and forced herself to breathe, filling her lungs, then letting it go . . . long and slow . . . silent. *Don't panic!* She glanced behind her, measuring the distance, trying to decide whether to move forward or retreat.

You got the guts, little girl? The voice echoed through

her head, her father's words the first day she took flying lessons. Oh, how she hated those words. So easy for him—the invincible Big Jake Rynerson—but that was then, and now he was lying in a coma, maybe dead, and it was up to her. *You got the guts, little girl?*

Yes, Daddy, I do. She put her head down, dug her fingers into the soft earth and started to pull herself forward when a sound not more than ten yards away froze her to the spot. From the corner of her eye she could see a man crawling from one of the tents, naked except for dark-green boxer shorts, and one of those copper arthritis bracelets on his left wrist. He stood up, a big man—his legs the size of small palm trees, his biceps nearly as large—turned his head, then hawked and spit and farted, a loud and rolling eruption that would have registered a good 9.4 on the Richter scale of flatulence.

There was an instant bellow from another tent. "Joisus H. Christ, Paddy, put a cork in that bleedin' hole!"

The big man grinned, took a deep breath, bent forward in a semi-squat, and pushed out another sputtering blast. Despite her fear, Kyra had to bite her lip to keep from laughing. *Men!* Were they all so gross and immature? *Probably*, so why would she want to share her life with one of the beasts? Before she could consider the question, the man pulled out his penis—a female killer if one ever existed—and began hosing down the wildlife around his tent: the male ape marking his territory. He expelled another eruption of gas—not more than a 6.2—wagged his meaty monster back and forth like a windshield wiper, then stuffed it back into his boxers and disappeared into the tent.

She waited at least five minutes, until her heart had regained its natural rhythm, then took a shallow breath and began to slide forward over the wet ground. *Be the snake.* She pulled herself over a hump of a tree root, but as careful as she was, without the rain to cover up the sounds every tiny movement seemed to produce a thundering avalanche of water from the jungle-like foliage, and it took nearly an hour before she was close enough to the light to see or hear anything.

Edging herself between the fronds of two broadleaf ferns, she found herself no more than ten yards from what appeared to be a combination of field kitchen and command center: a rectangular table with aluminum legs, four fold-up canvas chairs, boxes of food and supplies. Everything was neatly arranged within a large canopied enclosure with rolled-up sides. A small lantern, tampered down to a yellow glow, hung suspended within a tightly stacked cove of boxes, which hid the light from the water and the possibility of being seen from any passing ships. Directly below the lantern, sitting sideways to her position, the man with the shaved head sat hunched over the table, absorbed in what appeared to be a small stack of satellite photos. Wearing only a pair of cargo shorts and lightweight hiking boots, his deeply tanned and well-toned body glistened with sweat, reminding her of Yul Brynner in *The King and I.*

He carefully scanned each photo with a six-inch magnifier, marking locations with either a blue or red marker. When he finished, a job that seemed to take the better part of an hour, he set them aside and rolled out a topographical map of the island. He placed a lead sinker at each corner to keep the paper from curling, then pulled a laptop computer from a waterproof duffle lying next to his chair and placed it alongside the map. As the computer booted, he began to transpose the marked photo locations to the map, highlighting and numbering each spot with the same identifying colors. He worked methodically, not stopping until every location had been marked, numbered, and input on a gridlined overview displayed on the screen of his laptop.

Mawl nodded to himself; no way that Houdini Leonidovich would escape this time. He took a deep breath and counted slowly to five, mentally preparing himself for what he would say to Trader, a man who was never satisfied with anything.

No, sir, that wasn't the plan. A little dramatic hesitation. *But you said "get it done."*

No, sir, I didn't know she would be on the plane— Another hesitation.— *but you said you "didn't give a fuck who got in the way."*

Yessir, quite sure, your exact words. Would you like me to play it back?

Oh, didn't I mention that? Everything. Every last word.

Yessir. Thank you, sir. And fuck you too.

Just the thought of it made him smile. He reached

down, pulled his phone from the waterproof duffle, attached the micro-recorder, and punched in the numbers. He waited through the familiar rings and clicks of the router, but then after a few moments the line went to dial tone. What the . . . ? But he knew the answer even before the question formed in his mind. The bastard had heard the news reports, realized what happened, and was now trying to avoid final payment on the contract. Mawl wasn't that surprised, and he certainly wasn't worried. He could find the man—he had a voice print and a money trail—but that would have to wait. First, he wanted whatever was in that black case. That was the golden apple. His one-way ticket to . . . some out-of-synch vibration suddenly broke into his consciousness . . . the faint sound of breathing.

He leaned down, as if to return the phone to his duffle, his fingers closing around the butt of his Beretta. Hunched over, he could now make out the dark shape, realized who it was, and laid the gun on the table. "Enter."

Robbie hesitated, then stepped forward into the yellow light, his body covered head to knee in a rain poncho.

Mawl leaned back and crossed his arms. "Well?"

The kid shook his head, his eyes downcast, like a dog caught soiling the carpet. "I'm sure it was on the boat." He extended his hands out from under his poncho, the stiff material flaring off his arms like bat wings. "I remember pulling out my rain gear on the way over."

Mawl motioned toward one of the fold-up canvas chairs. "Sit down. I believe you."

Though his hangdog expression never changed, the kid's relief was obvious, the tension melting from his face like snow before the sun. He pushed back his hood and dropped into the chair. "Thank you, sir."

"I'm sure the *good captain* didn't think anyone would notice if he helped himself to a little bonus."

Robbie bobbed his head, clearly pleased to be off the hook. "Yessir. That's what I was thinkin'."

"That doesn't excuse it," Mawl snapped, letting the kid know he couldn't dismiss his carelessness so easily. "You should have checked your gear."

"Yessir, you're right. It won't happen again."

There would never be another *again*, Mawl thought, if he could get his hands on that case. "You sure he didn't get anything else?"

"Aye, that was all," Robbie answered. "Just some clothes and things."

"Things . . . ?" Mawl knew exactly what the kid was trying hard not to say. "Such as your NV goggles?"

"Yessir."

"Which you'll pay for."

"Aye."

"What about papers? Prescription bottles? Anything of that nature? Anything with your name on it?"

"Nae."

"Backup weapon?"

Robbie pulled back the edge of his poncho, exposing his shoulder holster and the butt end of his forty-five. "I'm good to go, sir. Really. No problem." He glanced at the map, clearly wanting to change the subject. "Everything worked out?"

"Pretty much," Mawl answered. "I won't be able to finalize exact placement until we're in the field."

"How many infrared?"

Mawl glanced at the count totals on his laptop. "Fifty-three pair. Plus twelve dozen vibration sensors."

Kyra could hardly breathe, her whole body going cold with fear, the way a field mouse must feel when it comes under the shadow of the hawk. What she assumed would be a struggling search through the rain and mud, had suddenly turned sophisticated and high-tech.

Robbie nodded approvingly. "Aye. That sounds right."

"I'm glad you approve," Mawl snapped, irritated by the kid's appraising tone. "They so much as break wind, we'll know it."

"Yessir," Robbie answered quickly, anxious to please. "They're as good as trapped."

"They won't be trapped until the sensors are down and those Zodiacs are in the water. It's gonna be a lot of work, kid, you better turn in."

Robbie hesitated, the shadowed look of a person with something on his mind. "Chrich said you mighta hit one. That courier bloke."

"Chrich talks too much."

"But now you want everyone taken alive?"

Mawl nodded, realizing the kid was circling, building up the courage to ask something.

"Well . . . I was just wondering—" The kid glanced away, avoiding eye contact. "You know . . . what then?"

Normally, Mawl would have verbally swatted the kid for insubordination, but he realized the question would need to be answered soon enough, and this was a perfect time to test the story. "Listen, kid, I take orders, just like you. I just now got off the phone with the client, and believe me, he laid it out real clear. You know that case Leonidovich is carrying?"

Robbie frowned, a puzzled look of confusion. "Aye."

"Well, he finally told me what this is all about. It's full of incriminating papers. Papers that could ruin the client's reputation. He expects me to deliver it intact. Unopened. That's priority one."

"Yes, but—"

"So we need them alive," Mawl went on, getting into the story, feeling the rhythm. "To make sure they didn't hide the case or what's inside."

"Then what?"

Then what? Then it hit him; the kid didn't give a bloody damn about reasons—he was still thinking about the Rynerson bird. "Then we do what the client wants. That's the way we earn our money."

"Well, yeah, sure," Robbie mumbled, though he obviously didn't want to accept it. "But I was just thinkin' . . . you know . . . we could get ourselves a nice ransom for Ms. Rynerson."

"I told you, kid, forget about her. There's not going to be any ransom."

"But—"

"No buts," Mawl interrupted. "We do what the client wants. And he wants their bodies found floating faceup with salt water in their lungs."

For a brief moment the kid said nothing, then the color in his face drained away, as if someone were adjusting the tint on a television. "You mean . . . ? Oh, Jaysus!"

Chapter Thirty-two

An Island in the South China Sea

Thursday, 12 July 00:03:46 GMT +0800

Kyra remained frozen to her spot among the ferns for another two hours, not daring to move until the hole in the sky finally closed and the rain began to fall, an angry spitting that turned into another deluge within seconds. She skirted around the outside of the camp, able to move faster now that she knew the location of the tents, then stood up and ran. It was stupid, the rain coming down so hard she could barely see the trees, but she couldn't stop the blind need to put distance between herself and that maniac who wanted to drown her. Dead was dead, it didn't matter how they intended to do it, but she couldn't convince her feet—not until she had slipped and fallen a dozen times, and gotten so lost it took nearly an hour to find her navigational landmarks.

By the time she found their hideaway shelter, the gray light of dawn was trying unsuccessfully to push its way through the dark clouds. "It's me," she whispered before daring to poke her head through the protective curtain of foliage. Sitting on the bed of palm branches, their backs to the rock wall, the two men jumped to their feet. Even in the dim light, it was obvious that neither man had slept: their eyes bloodshot and weary, their faces stubbled with whiskers.

"Ahh, there she is," Simon said, a relieved lift in his voice.

"We thought they caught you," Atherton said, his tone a touch scolding, parent to child. "Are you okay?"

"I'm fine," she answered, knowing she looked like a train wreck; her legs and arms covered in scratches, her wet and muddy clothes hanging off her body like a filthy layer of old skin. She dropped onto the makeshift bed. "I just need to rest for a minute." The lumpy green surface, with branches poking out in every direction, felt better than any feather bed she had ever slept in. "Then we need to go." She recognized her mistake the moment the words crossed her lips; their single-word response—"Go?"—echoing from both sides. Knowing they would never let her rest until she told them everything, she leaned back against the rock wall, closed her eyes, and began.

No one interrupted or spoke until she finished, and then not for a good minute, until Atherton reached out and patted her knee. "It's settled then."

Settled? She opened her eyes. "What do you mean?"

"They want the case. Isn't that what he said? 'That's priority one.' "

"So . . . ?"

He shrugged, his hands lifting from his sides. "We give it to them. We have no choice. They're going to find us. They're going to get it. We would be stupid not to use it to negotiate our way out of this mess."

"And the trade agreement collapses."

"No," Atherton responded instantly, as if anticipating the argument. "I've been thinking about that. The crest is symbolic. Once the Chinese realize they have no chance of bringing the pieces together, they'll move forward with the Alliance. There's too much at stake. What they want is Taiwan. The Alliance is their foothold. It's all a matter of diplomacy."

"Even if you're right, those men will never let us off this island alive."

"Of course they will. They're mercenaries. They don't care about us. All they care about is collecting their money."

Simon knew it was coming—had known it from the moment the three of them had crawled out of the water—sooner or later they would turn to him, as they now did, expecting him to play arbitrator. A no-win situation, if one ever existed. "Well . . . I guess—" He worked it through his brain, choosing his words carefully, trying to sound fair-minded. "I would have to agree with Jim, it's the crest they're after. And he may be right about the Alliance, it may hold. This whole thing with the crest does seem a bit silly." He said this in an attempt to appease Atherton, knowing it was stupid for any Westerner to underestimate the seriousness of the Chinese when it came to things like superstition and the philosophy of feng shui.

Kyra opened her mouth, then apparently thought better of it and slumped forward over her knees, too weary to argue. In contrast, Atherton tried to hide his feelings of triumph, but it oozed from his pores like fresh sap from an old maple.

"But," Simon continued, "I don't think giving them the crest will get us off the hook. It may, in fact, be the only thing between us and a very large gulp of seawater."

Atherton's pleased expression dissolved into a scowl. "And just how do you figure that?"

"I'm only repeating what Kyra told us. Skinhead wants us alive. He wants to be sure he has the case and the contents before they kill us." He turned to Kyra. "Is that right?"

Her head came up off her knees. "Exactly."

Simon turned back to Atherton. "So we're safe as long as *we* have the damn thing."

Atherton nodded slowly, apparently giving the argument full consideration. "Yes, that's a legitimate point," he agreed. "And I understand your reluctance to try it my way. But I'm willing to take the risk. The two of you can find a new place to dig in. That way they couldn't force me to tell them where you are. Not if I don't know." He turned over his hands, palms up, as if presenting them with a gift. "If I'm right, we all go home. If I'm wrong . . ." He shrugged. "You're no worse off."

The man was either incredibly brave or incredibly stupid, Simon thought, and he certainly wasn't stupid. "Right, except that they would have the crest, and you'd be dead."

"A risk I'm willing to take."

Kyra stared intently at the man, straight into his eyes, as if trying to read his thoughts. "And if I'm not?"

Atherton stared back at her, one of those awkward

expressions people get when they don't have a clue what's being asked of them.

Kyra exhaled, the sound of disappointment, and shook her head. "Never mind."

Two words, Simon thought, that should send any man with half a brain straight to the flower shop. She clearly wanted to know what consideration Atherton gave her feelings and opinions; another way of saying "where do we stand," something he clearly hadn't considered. *Bad mistake.*

"Oh," Atherton said, the internal lightbulb finally blinking to life. "I uh . . . of course I care what you think. That goes without saying."

But it was too late; if her stony expression meant anything, *saying it* meant everything. "I've got an idea," Simon said, trying to save the man from further embarrassment. "Why don't—"

"And why," Atherton interrupted, "don't you stay out of this?"

Kyra turned on the man, her green eyes flashing, but Simon already felt like an interloper and cut her off before she said something she might regret. "Good point. I could use a shower." Before anyone could respond, he stepped through the foliage and into the rain, their words lost in the downward flood. Despite the downpour, it felt good to move, to break free of the thick, moldering air of the enclosure; and though he hadn't really meant it, a shower suddenly sounded like a very good idea.

He found a semiprotected spot beneath a broadleaf evergreen, and carefully peeled off his clothes, no easy task with only one good arm. After hand-washing the mud from each item, he stood in the rain for a good five minutes, letting it pound away at his naked body until he felt completely mold-free. By the time he dressed and returned to the enclosure, he felt invigorated and ready for action, though he had no idea what they could do against such overwhelming odds. Maybe Atherton was right, negotiation was their only option, but something about the proposal felt wrong—something disingenuous about the man's sudden bravery and willingness to walk into the hands of men who wanted to flood his lungs with seawater.

Even in the dim light, Simon could read the somber expressions, and knew what had happened. Atherton, in a lame attempt to redeem himself, had chosen that inopportune moment to propose; a proposal that had obviously been rejected. *Stupid, stupid man.* He almost said, "So, what's the decision," but realized that would not be the most auspicious question at such a moment. "What do you think?"

Kyra took a deep breath, calling on some inner reserve of strength, and pushed herself to her feet. "We need to get moving. They were going to start setting up their network at dawn. We need to stay ahead of them."

Simon nodded. "Jim . . . ?"

Atherton hunched his shoulders, a look of indifference. "Whatever you decide."

"Then we go," Simon said. "If we can't find a decent place to hole up, we'll try it your way." He turned back to Kyra. "You still think the western end?"

"Absolutely. How's your arm?"

"Good." He flexed his elbow to demonstrate. "Better by the hour."

"You should put it back in the sling. It's at least a two-hour walk over slippery ground."

"Yes—" He considered a "ma'am," just to stoke her fire, but decided to save that for a better time. "Good idea."

She picked up the cargo bag. "We should keep our eyes open for things to eat. We won't be able to move around once those sensors are down."

The two-hour walk turned into a six-hour trek through an unrelenting downpour. Exhausted, but unsuccessful in finding a good spot, they stopped to rest beneath a well-protected, but exposed, overhang along the coast. Simon lowered himself to the sand, being careful not to bump his arm, which was throbbing like a bad tooth, and leaned back against a large boulder. Kyra, who hadn't slept in thirty-six hours, curled into a fetal position a few feet away and closed her eyes. "I just need a few minutes."

"Works for me." Now that he had stopped moving, he wasn't at all sure he could get his legs going again.

Atherton found himself a smooth rock and sat down. "Any idea where we are?"

Simon glanced at Kyra, saw that she was already asleep, and nodded. "I think so." He bent forward, picked up a stick, and drew a crude sketch in the sand. "About here, I think." He poked a spot along the northwestern edge of the cigar-shaped outline.

"And where are they?"

Simon brushed the stick along the island's underbelly, almost directly opposite their position. "Somewhere along here." He planted the stick a few inches south. "This is where we came down."

Atherton nodded, apparently satisfied that they were safe for the time being. "Good." He leaned back and closed his eyes.

Within minutes he too was asleep, and Simon realized they wouldn't be moving again until morning. He stared out at the rain, the sound like glass beads hitting the water, and tried to make some sense out of the puzzle and who was behind it. He worked for hours, moving the pieces around in his mind, analyzing their shape, turning them over, inspecting the edges, coming at them from every direction, until finally the answers started to come—at least some of them—before weariness finally overcame his brain, and he drifted off into a hard slumber.

Hours later, when the silence woke him, the rain had stopped and Atherton was gone.

Chapter Thirty-three

An Island in the South China Sea

Friday, 13 July 06:41:21 GMT +0800

Though the rain had stopped, the sky was still leaden and dark, and Mawl knew the lull wouldn't last for long, the air so thick he could almost taste it. As he finished off his granola bar and washed it down with a gulp of warm UHT milk, he amused himself by reading the manufacturer's valiant attempt to convince the consumer its packaged breakfast was something to be enjoyed, not just endured.

> This Ready-to-eat meal (MRE) has been reviewed, evaluated, and assessed for its nutritional adequacy by the Committee on Military Nutrition Research (CMNR). The 3,600 kcal provided by the total ration was designed to meet the Military Recommended Dietary Allowances (MRDAs) for all nutrients.

Yeah, right, nutritious as dog dump, and probably tasted worse. Of course they failed to add that important piece of information.

Shelf stable.

No kidding, it contained enough preservatives to embalm an elephant.

May be eaten hot or cold.

True enough, nothing could make it better. Thoroughly disgusted, he wiped his hands using the towelette, and dropped it into the cup of untouched fruit. There was a day, he recalled, when he actually liked field rations. How was that possible? Or was it the lifestyle? The adventure? Whatever it was, he'd had enough. Once he had his hands on whatever treasure the courier had in that case, he intended to live out his days in luxury. Tahiti or New Zealand. Maybe buy himself a little vineyard.

He pushed the carton away and pulled his laptop closer. Fourteen more sensors had gone active, but everything was taking twice as long as expected. At the pace the men were moving, it would take another day, maybe more, to finish the network. *Bloody fucking rain!* He leaned closer, checking everyone's location, when he realized Blue-6, the designator for Robbie Kelts, was moving toward the camp, not away. Now what? *Damn kid,* you never knew what he would do next.

Ten minutes later Robbie came marching into camp, trying his best to maintain a look of professional nonchalance, but preening like a peacock in heat. "Look who I found—" He jabbed his forty-five between the man's shoulder blades. "—stumbling around in the dark."

Despite his filthy, wild-man appearance, Mawl recognized the man immediately: James Atherton, the chap who had been escorting Kyra Rynerson around Macau. Mawl kept his eyes fixed on the man's face, trying hard not to show any special interest in the black case the man was clutching to his chest. "Good job, kid."

Robbie's proud glow deepened. "Yessir. He knew better'n to give me any trouble."

Atherton turned, glaring at the kid. "I told you, I wasn't lost. I was looking for you."

Robbie gave a sarcastic yip. "Aye. Sure you were."

But Mawl didn't laugh. For some reason, the man showed no signs of intimidation or fear—and that wasn't normal. "Looking for us, uh?"

Atherton turned back, speaking to Mawl as if he were a servant. "That is correct. And you would be . . . ?"

"I'll ask the questions."

"Of course. Why don't I just call you—" He paused, as if to pluck a name out of the atmosphere. "I know . . . you have an accent . . . I'll call you English. Mr. English."

Mawl tried to hide his surprise, the possibility that this might be the client reverberating through his nervous system like an electrical shock. Was it possible? The voice was different, but that could have been altered. It would explain so much: the abnormally long telephone transfers—around the world *and back!*—and the reason no one had answered that phone in three days. Oh, yes, it was possible. It would also explain the man's inexplicable interest in Kyra Rynerson, and how he knew so much. And so fast. There would be no need for a second team in the wings, feeding him inside information. The man *was* inside. "And your name . . . ?"

Atherton tilted his head back, a looking-down-the-nose smirk. "You may call me Joe. That has a nice Yankee ring, don't you think?" He smiled, clearly amused with himself. "Trader Joe."

Robbie yipped again. "Yeah, right! The guy's name is Atherton. James Atherton. He's the bloke been trying to shag Ms. Rynerson."

Mawl nodded slowly, trying to fuse together what he knew about Atherton with what he thought he knew about Trader. "Leave us alone, kid. I'll take it from here."

"But, sir—"

"This man," Mawl interrupted, but once he started the sentence, couldn't decide where to go with it. "This man . . ."

"Works for you," Atherton said, supplying the answer without hesitation.

Perfect! Bloodyfucking perfect! "That's right, kid. This man works for me. He's our inside man."

Robbie stared back, his expression a knot of confusion. "No, he was on the plane. This guy—"

"Stop your blabbering," Atherton snapped, as he set the case on the ground. "That was a mistake. I couldn't say anything to you—you wouldn't have believed me."

"But—"

"Now, listen up," Atherton continued, not giving the kid a chance to think. "I'm going to tell you where to find Leonidovich and that Rynerson bitch. You'll have to hurry or they'll be gone."

Robbie turned to Mawl. "Sir . . . ?"

Mawl didn't really care about the other two—all he cared about was getting his hands on whatever was in that case—and getting rid of Robbie seemed like a good first step in that direction. "That's right, Jocko, you need to move fast." He turned to Atherton. "Can you draw a map?"

Atherton shook his head. "But I know we were somewhere along the northwestern edge of the island. Less than twenty yards from the water."

"That's close enough." Mawl turned back to Robbie. "I'll send Chricher and Big Paddy around in a Zodiac. You link up with Catman, and double-time it over there. You should be able to pick up their trail if the weather holds."

Robbie opened his mouth, but was apparently too stunned by events to put his thoughts into words.

"Go," Mawl snapped. "I'll monitor your progress from here."

Robbie turned slowly, his feet apparently stuck in the quicksand of his thoughts, then he seemed to find his footing and accelerated into a dogtrot. The minute he disappeared into the trees, Atherton lowered himself into one of the canvas chairs. "So, English, we meet at last."

He said it as if that had always been intended, but Mawl knew better. And he also knew that Atherton was too small a fish to be calling the shots on an operation of this scale. "Unfortunately for you."

The man's casual, I'm-in-control expression faded,

his eyes suddenly wary. "What's that supposed to mean?"

"It means the principal is not going to appreciate the fact that their shield has been compromised."

"I don't know what you're talking about."

"Oh, I think you do. Everything was fine as long as a layer existed between the principal and the . . . let me think, how best to describe myself?" He paused, mimicking Atherton's efforts to come up with a name. "I know . . . let's refer to me as *the expeditor.* That has a rather nice ring, don't you think?" A ring—if James Atherton had half a brain—that would leave no doubt about who was in control.

The man hesitated, then tried to bluff his way. "You let me worry about that."

"Yes," Mawl agreed, "you should worry about that. If the principal ever learns your identity has been compromised—" He ran a finger across his throat.

"Listen, you fucking asshole, if that's an attempt at intimidation, you can stuff it. You're the one who should be worried, you created this mess. You're lucky I didn't die on that plane. What the hell was that about? You were supposed to get Leonidovich at the hotel."

Nice play, Mawl thought, stay on the offensive, but he wasn't about to let the man off quite so easily. He leaned down, close enough to count the veins in Atherton's bloodshot eyes. "You call me a fucking asshole again, and a man by the name of Big Paddy is gonna turn *yours* into the Grand Canal." He smiled. "Get it?"

Atherton edged back in the chair, his Adam's apple moving up and down in an involuntary swallow. "What is it you want?"

"I want to know what this is about. I'm tired of being played for a chump."

The man hesitated, his eyes moving left and right, as if rummaging through his mind for an answer that wouldn't get him killed. "You're asking too much."

Too much, Mawl realized, would be the identity of the client. "I'm not asking for a name." *Not yet.* "Just tell me what this is about."

The man hesitated again, still measuring risks, weighing options, searching for a way out, then apparently realized if he wanted to get off the island alive, he would have to give up something. "Okay, but no names."

Mawl shrugged, promising nothing.

"It's about a trade agreement between Taiwan, China, and the United States. I was hired to—"

"Now hold on," Mawl interrupted. "I read the papers. I haven't seen anything about any trade agreement."

Atherton nodded forcefully, as if this fact validated his words. "It's all very hush-hush. They're still crossing the *t*'s and dotting the *i*'s."

"And what's this got to do with Rynerson? Why the hit? Why all the accidents at his hotel?"

"Jake Rynerson is the linchpin. He's agreed to sell China oil from his fields in South America. In exchange, the Chinese have . . ."

Mawl barely listened as the man blabbered on about the Pacific Rim Alliance, and the possible reunification of Taiwan and China. It was true, he could see it in the man's eyes, and there was nothing in it for him. "And you say this ceremony is to take place next week?"

"Saturday the twenty-first," Atherton repeated. "At the Pacific Pearl."

Mawl nodded to himself, everything starting to make sense. "So why stop the accidents? I could have turned that place into rubble if that's all it took."

Atherton smiled in a self-congratulatory way. "When I met Rynerson's daughter . . . well, I realized there might be a better way."

"A better way for you."

The smile widened. "If the Alliance failed and I ended up with the golden fleece, so what? Everyone gets what they want. No reason to wreck the inheritance."

"Right." Only one little problem. "I'm assuming things didn't work out so well between you and the lady doctor."

Atherton snorted, trying to sound amused, but it came out bitter. "She's an idiot. One of those bleedin' heart idealists. Doesn't care a whit about the old man's money."

Mawl had heard enough of bad plots and big schemes. He looked down, noticing for the first time the four distinct bullet impressions along one side of the case. "And what's this?"

"It's just a goodwill offering. Part of an old crest taken from China during the war. It doesn't have any commercial value. Nothing you'd be interested in."

Mawl smiled to himself, like he was going to believe that: something of no commercial value being transported in a special bulletproof case. *Yeah, right.* "Show me."

"The case has some kind of special lock. I don't know how to open it."

The bullshit was getting deeper by the second. "You sure you don't want to think about that?"

"It's true. I saw Leonidovich open it once. It's got some kind of hidden lock on the bottom and—"

Mawl punched the lock button next to the handle and the double latches snapped open with a distinct *click-click.*

Atherton jerked upright in his chair, as if he'd just taken two in the chest. "That's not right! I didn't know. Really! I just assumed—"

Weary of the bullshit, Mawl put a finger to his lips, then reached down and flipped back the fold-over top. "What the bleedin' hell is this?"

Atherton leaned forward, staring into the case with a bewildered look that quickly mutated into outrage. "That fucking Leonidovich!" He reached inside and yanked out the football-sized rock. "That dirty fucking bastard! I'll kill him! I'll kill him with my own hands!"

Chapter Thirty-four

An Island in the South China Sea

Friday, 13 July 06:58:41 GMT +0800

Except for Kyra's breathing and the soft lapping of waves against the rocks, it was quiet and steamy hot, the air sticky as taffy. While she slept, Simon mentally rehearsed the conversation to come, trying to decide how much to say. What did he really know? For sure? Whatever he said, she wouldn't be happy.

The sun—hidden behind a curtain of gray clouds—had been up at least ten minutes when she finally rolled over in the sand and sat up, blinking her eyes. "The rain stopped."

He smiled down at her from his rocky perch; a place where he could see anyone approaching by land or water. "I've always said you were a clever girl, Rynerson."

"Don't pick on me in the morning, Leonidovich. I have an attitude and I know how to use it." She glanced around. "Where's Jim?"

"Gone."

"Gone?" She repeated the word as if it were an unknown expression from another language. "Gone where?"

"He took my case, if that tells you anything."

"Oh, no!"

He nodded.

"Why didn't you wake me?"

He shrugged, ignoring her accusatory tone. "He was already gone, and you needed the sleep. What difference would it have made?"

"None, but—" She lifted her hands and gave them a little toss in the air. "You're right. I should have seen it coming." She stood up, brushing the sand off her clothes and arms, then began rolling her head and kneading the muscles along her shoulders, trying to work out the kinks. "It's my fault."

Uh-oh, he could guess where this was going—a trip he preferred not to take. "It's nobody's fault, Kyra. He—"

"But it is," she cut in, her words coming in a rush. "He did this to impress me. He asked me to marry him and I turned him down."

Good decision, but he wasn't about to say it. Not yet. Not until he was sure. "I figured as much."

She gazed up at him, incomprehension in her eyes. "Figured what?"

"That you turned him down."

She scrambled up the rocky face, agile as a mountain goat, and planted herself on a nearby boulder. "You knew he was going to ask me?"

"He asked what I thought of the idea."

"I'm, uh—" She shook her head, trying to make sense of it. "I'm surprised. I didn't realize you two were that close."

"It was one of those male bonding things."

"So what did you say?"

"I thought he deserved the truth . . . that you were a first-class fruitcake. That he would be better off with one of those blow-up dolls they sell in porn shops. Now that I think about it, he may have gone shopping."

She frowned, clearly in no mood for his ill-timed humor. "He didn't take it very well. Probably thinks if he can save the day, I'll change my mind."

"Probably," though convinced nothing could have been further from Atherton's mind. "Men are stupid that way."

"I'm sorry, Simon. I really am."

Sorry? That was about the last thing he expected. "*You're* sorry?"

"Of course. I know you've never lost a consignment. And something like this . . . all the international implications . . . it'll ruin your reputation."

He almost laughed; in all likelihood they would be floating facedown in the South China Sea before the day was over, and she was worried about his reputation. "You don't need to worry about that. He doesn't have the crest."

"What?"

He leaned back and pulled the small container out from behind a rock. "I removed it from the case."

"Why?"

He shrugged, knowing she wouldn't like the answer. "Truthfully . . . I was afraid he might try something like this."

She leaned forward, her green eyes flashing with

anger, her blond hair in disarray, looking both barbaric and beautiful. "You should have said something! I could have stopped him! They'll kill him for sure."

"No they won't." Of that, he was positive. *Almost positive.*

"How can you say that?"

Careful, Leonidovich, never tell everything you know. "They're not stupid. It wouldn't make sense. He can lead them to us. He—"

"He wouldn't!"

Yeah, right. The only question was whether he would do it voluntarily or at the point of a gun. "Or they'll use him as bait to draw us out."

"You don't really believe that?"

But he did. "As long as we have the crest, he's safe. Which means we need to find ourselves a new place to hide."

She sat there, tapping a finger against her lip, thinking about it. "What if he changes his mind and comes back?"

"That's not going to happen, Kyra. I've been awake for three hours. He's gone."

She nodded blindly, absently brushing sand out of her hair. "Probably couldn't if he wanted to," she said, her voice soft and distant, as if trying to convince herself. "He's no Boy Scout, that's for sure."

In more ways than one, Simon thought, but that was something she would have to discover on her own. "I'm afraid you're right."

"We should stay on the coast," she said. "If we

move inland we're sure to set off one of those sensors."

"I've been thinking about that. These guys are pros. They're going to track us, and it won't be that hard if the rain holds off." He paused, letting the reality of their situation sink in before throwing out his plan. "I think we'd be better off in the water." He pointed to a tangle of storm debris floating among the rocks. "There's some good pieces of driftwood down there."

She looked from him to the floating debris, then back to him. "What exactly are you suggesting?"

"I'm suggesting we head south, scouting the shoreline from the water. It will give us a different perspective." More important, it was an option they hadn't discussed with Atherton.

She nodded slowly, the wheels turning, calculating the risks. "Could you do it with one arm?"

"As long as we stay in close," he answered, trying to sound more confident than he felt. "And the waves don't get too high."

She nodded again, carefully eyeing the shallow waves, but clearly warming to the idea. "They couldn't track us through the water, that's for sure."

"Exactly. But it's still risky. If they catch us offshore with one of those Zodiacs . . ." He didn't bother to say what they both understood.

"Right, but I think it's a good idea . . . worth the gamble."

"Let's do it."

She helped him down off the rocks—which for

some reason proved more difficult than climbing up—then waded out to the debris, while he secured the crest in the cargo bag, and buried the items they wouldn't need. She came back dragging a small tree through the surf, its smooth surface covered with stubby knobs and short projections where branches had broken off. "This should hold us both. You hang on and I'll steer."

"Sounds easy." But he suspected it wouldn't be.

Using the black nylon rope, they tied the cargo bag between a couple of broken-off branches, then waded out beyond the surf and into the gently rolling waves. When the water reached Simon's chest, they began to work their way toward the southern end of the island, tiptoeing and kicking their way over the rocks. Though the waves were gentle, it took their combined strength to keep the tree from rotating toward the shore. Kyra, who was doing the bulk of the work, looked exhausted after only a few minutes. "I didn't think it would be this hard."

"Blame it on Newton."

"You're talking about—" She took a breath. "—Isaac Newton?"

"You got it. The second of his three axioms."

"Which you." Quick breath. "No doubt." Another breath. "Could quote verbatim?"

" 'The alteration of motion is ever proportional to the motive force impressed.' " He paused to grab some oxygen. " '—and is made in the direction of the right line in which that force is impressed.' Something like that."

She snorted and spit a stream of water in his direction. "You need to get a life, Leonidovich."

Surviving one more day seemed like enough of a goal. "Did you say life or wife."

"Same thing." She gulped a breath of air. "How's your arm?"

"Great." So numb he couldn't feel the damn thing. "You okay?"

"Swell." Another breath. "Haven't had so much fun since—" She grabbed a quick mouthful of air. "Hey, look at that!" She pointed toward the island with her chin.

He twisted around, realizing that in his efforts to keep the tree moving in the right direction, he had neglected to keep an eye on the shoreline. "What?"

"That shadow." Quick gulp of air. "Under that ridge of rocks."

"I don't see anything."

"Look down!"

He scanned downward over the sheer rock face, to a small shadow near the waterline. "Okay, I see it. So what?"

"Might be a cave." She grabbed another quick breath. "Should check it out."

He glanced back and saw that they had moved only a couple hundred yards from where they entered the water. "We haven't gone very far."

"So?"

"So that's where they'll start their search. It's too close."

She gave him a look sharp enough to open a vein. "I'm exhausted."

"Well, I don't give a damn what you say, Rynerson. I say we check it out."

She flashed a relieved smile, drew a deep breath, and expelled it through puffed cheeks. "You're a smart man, Leonidovich."

The minute they gave up the fight, the tree rotated around and took off like an arrow toward the shore. "Let it go," Kyra shouted, "I'll steer it in!"

He released his grip, and within seconds she had it heading straight for the dark shadow beneath the rocks. He followed the wake, letting the waves carry him in, his legs so tired they felt like bags of water. By the time he caught up, the tree had wedged itself into a narrow opening between the rocks. Standing in knee-deep water, her breasts exposed beneath her wet T-shirt, Kyra stared into the mouth of a cave-like crevice. "Whataya think?"

He peered into the dark hole, then up at the line of silt running across the rock face. "I *think* the water has carved out a little cavern back in there."

"Exactly. I'll check it out."

"And I *know* it's under water at high tide."

She nodded, already digging through the cargo bag. "I saw that."

"So . . . ?"

"So it doesn't hurt to look." She pulled the Sure-Fire mini-flashlight. "You coming?"

She was right, it didn't hurt to look, and he couldn't have talked her out of it anyway. "Wouldn't miss it."

"You're a sport, Leonidovich."

"And you're half-naked, Rynerson. What man wouldn't follow you into a dark cave?"

She gave him a heavy-lidded, but good-natured look of admonishment. "Well, there's nothing I can do about that, so get used to it."

Such a burden. "I'll do my best."

She started forward, following the flashlight's slender beam into the darkness. The rocks narrowed around them, the light reflecting off the water and throwing shadow ghosts over damp, stone walls covered with barnacles, mussels, crabs, and other crustaceans. Kyra looked back over her shoulder. "Neat, uh?"

Simon nodded, thinking *creepy* would be a more accurate description.

They sloshed forward another ten feet when she glanced back a second time. "Wait here."

Before he could say anything, she ducked beneath an overhang of rock and disappeared, leaving him in near darkness. He took a deep breath, trying to ignore his feelings of claustrophobia, but the air suddenly felt thick and stifling, too heavy to breathe. Then, to make matters worse, he heard them, tiny sea creatures crawling over the walls. "Rynerson?" His voice echoed back and forth, sounding tinny and thin. "You okay?"

The light ricocheted toward him from beneath the ridge of rock, reflecting upward off the dark water. "Come in here."

She held the light steady and he ducked beneath the overhang. *Here* turned out to be a small chamber, about fifteen feet across and equally high, with smooth, dark walls—crustacean free, except for a few stragglers near the waterline. He didn't like anything about the place—it felt like a trap—but had the feeling the lovely Ms. Rynerson did not invite him into the place to discuss the sculpting power of water. He waited, knowing her question even before she asked it.

"So what do you think?"

"I think it's under water at high tide," he answered. "Now let's quit screwing around and get out of here. We need to find a place to hunker down before the next downpour."

"This is it. Look." She focused the flashlight on a shelf about four feet above the opening. "The waterline is below that ledge. Check it out." She ran the beam of light back and forth over the wall. "Dry. It's perfect. They'll never find us here."

Probably, but he didn't like the idea of being trapped in a cage like a rat. "But the opening is *below* the waterline. We'd be stuck in here when the tide comes in. That could be up to twelve hours."

"That only makes it safer," she argued. "We can sleep when the tide's in. Our own private grotto."

"Have I ever mentioned that I have slight problem with claustrophobia?"

"No." She turned the light toward his face. "Really?"

"Really. This *private grotto* gives me the heebie-jeebies."

She directed the light to her own face, giving him

an affectionate and somewhat teasing smile. "I'll hold your hand, Leonidovich."

"Promise?" He was only half kidding.

"Absolutely. If things get too bad, we could swim out. It's only twenty feet or so."

That sounded good, but depending on the wave action, he doubted if they could do it. He reached out, took the flashlight, and scanned the walls. "I don't see any way to get up there."

"Simon . . ." She hit his name hard enough to make it echo, a kind of scoffing ping.

"What?" As if he didn't know. The waterline was less than a foot below the ledge, and she was too smart not to realize they could simply float up when the tide came in.

"We can bring the tree in here. It'll make a perfect ladder."

Even better. "Okay, okay, we can get up there. But—" But what? "But when the tide's out, they could see the opening from one of those inflatable boats. We'd be trapped."

"That's true," she admitted. "But do you really think anyone's going to venture this far back? Would you?"

"I did."

"Only because I'm not wearing a bra."

He gave her chest a flash of light, just enough to acknowledge the point. "I hate it when you're right, Rynerson."

"You really think we'd be safer out there, looking for something better?"

He couldn't see her face, but he heard the sarcastic tone clear enough. *Smartass!*

"I know you love sushi," she said. "You can eat crab three times a day."

Somehow it didn't sound so good when you had to murder the little suckers. "I like to eat 'em, not kill 'em."

"I'll do it for you."

"So, if I agree to this, you're going to hold my hand and feed me?"

"Absolutely. And you're going to stay here and be a good boy while I'm gone?"

He knew it was coming, and didn't need to ask what she meant by *gone.* "You can't save him, Kyra."

"I have to try."

Chapter Thirty-five

An Island in the South China Sea

Friday, 13 July 22:36:51 GMT +0800

Chricher stepped out of the darkness, pulled off his Boonie hat, slapped it against his leg to remove the rain, and dropped it onto a box of field rations. Then, with unaccustomed neatness, he peeled off his rain poncho and very carefully spread it out over a line stretching between two of the enclosure's corner poles. Mawl suppressed a smile, amused at the man's obvious attempt to delay his mission. The men, Mawl knew, had been whispering among themselves, wanting to know about James Atherton—aka Trader Joe—and trying to decide who should ask the questions. With the exception of Big Paddy, Chricher had been on the team longer than anyone, and the obvious choice. Big was muscle, Chrich was brains.

Finally satisfied with his fastidious arrangement of rain gear, Chricher poured himself a cup of tea, then lowered himself into one of the fold-up canvas chairs, never once making eye contact. "I'm getting too old for this shit."

"Yup." Mawl didn't like being questioned, and he wasn't about to make things easy. It was a matter of respect—command and control.

Chricher leaned back in his chair, way back, eyes on the overhead canopy, and folded his hands over his chest, his fingers twitching in a nervous out-of-sync rhythm. Mawl let the man fidget, the quiet broken only by the relentless beat of the rain. After a few minutes of awkward silence, Chricher found his voice. "You get a weather report?"

Mawl reached over, clicked the weather link on his laptop, then rotated the machine around so the man could see for himself.

Chricher rocked forward, eyes on the screen. "Ahh . . . looks like this front is finally ready to move on."

"Yup."

Chricher glanced toward the night sky, as if he could see a parting of clouds through the darkness. "Might even get a few hours of sun tomorrow. The guys could use it."

"Yup."

He leaned forward over his mug, suddenly a reader of tea leaves. "Should be clear by Sunday."

"Yup."

"If we don't find them by then, I could bring in the chopper."

As if he hadn't figured that out, Mawl thought, becoming extremely weary of the man's shifty-eyed avoidance. "What is it you want, Chrich?"

The man looked up, making eye contact for the first time. "Want?"

"You think I'm a bleedin' idiot? Spit it out."

"Well, I . . . the men . . . we were wonderin' about this . . . this Atherton chap. The kid says he was—"

"The kid!" Mawl hooted, wanting to immediately knock Chricher off stride. "You think I'd have bothered to put Catman on his tail if I thought Jocko could figure something out on his own?"

"No, but he was—"

"You think I'm stupid enough to share intelligence with him?"

"Well, no, of course you're not stupid, Brick, but he *was* on the bird's detail. He saw things."

"That's right, Chrich, he saw things. He saw someone trying to get close to Rynerson's daughter. Beyond that, he *assumed*. You're smarter than that. You know I have contacts inside the hotel. Just who do you think arranged all those accidents? How else—"

"Yeah," Chricher interrupted, "but this is different. If he worked for you, why the bleedin' hell did he get on that plane?"

Good question, but obvious, and Mawl was ready for it. "Because the information went one way. I bought, he delivered. Everything by e-mail. I never met the guy till he walked in here and identified himself by his code name."

"But . . ." Chricher paused, thinking about it. "How'd you find the guy?"

Mawl nodded to himself; another question he had anticipated. "Our old friend Madame Chiang." A small fabrication, but one no one could dispute. "That's one of the reasons we needed to take her out. She could connect us to someone inside the hotel."

Chricher nodded, clearly buying the story. "That makes sense."

Mawl waited, knowing there was at least one more question.

"What about that big briefcase? The one that courier chap hauled onto the beach. The kid said Atherton had it with him."

Mawl cocked his head toward the case, which he had purposely left in plain sight; something hawkeye Chricher would have noticed the minute he stepped out of the rain. "It's right there, Chrich. Check it out."

Making an exaggerated effort not to appear overeager, Chricher took a sip of tea, then stretched out and pulled the case onto his lap. "Heavy bugger." He ran his hand over the indentations along the side. "Bloody hell. No wonder he didn't go down. What the bloody hell is this thing made of?"

"Kevlar," Mawl answered. "Or something close to it."

Chricher opened the fold-over double flap. "What the bleedin' hell. Is this a joke?"

"If it's a joke," Mawl answered. "It's on us."

"Any idea what—"

"A worthless artifact, according to Atherton."

Chricher scowled, a look of disbelief. "You believe him?"

"Nope."

"How do you know he didn't just stash whatever was in the thing?"

"We don't," Mawl admitted. "That's why I'm not letting the bastard out of my sight until we've got Leonidovich. It'll take Big about two minutes to make him talk."

Chricher nodded approvingly. "Atherton's sleepin' in your tent, right?"

"Going on eleven hours," Mawl answered. "Hauling that rock around must have tuckered the man out."

Chricher chuckled and stood up, apparently satisfied that everyone was playing on the same team. "Bed sounds like a good idea."

An hour later, during a lull in the downpour, Atherton came sloshing into the enclosure, his eyelids heavy from sleep. Though dressed in clean shorts and a T-shirt confiscated from Mawl's locker, he looked like a street bum in clothes twice his size, his face drawn and stubbled, his blond hair disheveled. "What time is it?"

Mawl glanced at his watch. "Twenty-three, forty-two." He could see the gears grinding, so offered up the answer before the man blew a sprocket. "Eleven forty-two."

"Christ, twelve hours! You got coffee?"

Mawl cocked his head toward the two-burner propane stove. "Tea."

"No coffee?"

"We drink tea."

Atherton scowled, but poured himself a cup. "What about food?"

Mawl kicked the box of field rations.

"That's it?"

"Fruit," Mawl answered, half tempted to shove a banana up the man's ass. "Our chef couldn't make the trip."

Atherton nodded, finally getting the picture, and dropped into a chair. "So what happened?"

"We found where they spent the night," Mawl answered, "but they were gone by the time we got there."

"Shit! That fucking Leonidovich." He mumbled the last, as if talking to himself. "So why aren't your men out there?" he demanded. "You've got night-vision equipment."

The banana, Mawl thought, was sounding better by the second, but he hadn't yet decided what to do with Mr. James Atherton. "They've been out there crawling through the mud for three days. They're not machines."

"But you've got to find them before the storm passes. If they're able to signal a ship, it's all over."

"We'll get 'em," Mawl answered. "After we found the spot, we blanketed that end of the island with sensors. That reduces our search area by two-thirds." He turned the laptop so Atherton could see the grid. "I haven't taken my eyes off that screen in eight hours. They fart just once and we'll have them."

Atherton leaned forward, scrutinizing the screen. "They were planning to stay near the coast."

"And that's the focus of our search."

Atherton nodded, eyes thoughtful. "What if they go in the water? Try to move around that way?"

"Was that discussed?"

"No, but I don't think we should rule out the possibility. That Leonidovich is a clever bastard."

Mawl nodded to himself—he had learned that one

the hard way. "I'll put two Zodiacs in the water. If they—" Something Atherton had said, suddenly burrowed its way into Mawl's consciousness. "How did you know we had night-vision equipment?"

Atherton snorted, the sound derisive and bitter. "Rynerson grabbed one of your cargo bags. She was here when you unloaded your equipment."

Mawl almost laughed; the woman had balls, he had to give her that. "So that's where it went. Why didn't you mention this earlier?"

"Didn't think about it," Atherton answered. "It's nothing to worry about, she won't be back. When she heard what you were planning to do, she ran like a scared rabbit."

"Do?"

"Your plan to dump the bodies where a ship would find them. She didn't much like the idea of death by drowning."

Mawl thought back, retrieving the time and place of the conversation. "She heard that?"

Atherton nodded, took a sip of tea, and grimaced. "Christ, this stuff tastes like boiled piss."

Mawl ignored the gastronomical commentary. "That means she was here more than once."

Another nod.

"Bloodyfucking hell! In our camp! You should have told me!" He grabbed his night-vision goggles and pointed to the lantern. "Put out that light."

Atherton made no move to comply. "You're overreacting. She's not coming back here. You've got them trapped on that side of the island."

Mawl knew the man was right, but it pissed him off and made him feel oddly violated that the woman had penetrated his camp. "Unless you want the pleasure, I intend to drown that bitch personally."

"Me?" Atherton leaned back in his chair, apparently giving the idea serious consideration. Then he shook his head and smiled. "Nope. But I'd like to watch."

Chapter Thirty-six

An Island in the South China Sea

Saturday, 14 July 05:15:18 GMT +0800

Simon adjusted his position on the rock, his backside numb from sitting in one place for so long. He could only guess at the time, but knew it had been at least six hours since she had disappeared into the night. *Damn woman,* just like her mother: smart, beautiful, and stubborn as stone.

He took a deep breath—the moist air heavy with the odor of a large dead fish rotting in the seaweed—and tried to convince himself she was being careful, not careless. A few scattered stars were now visible between the clouds, and he tried to decide if the sky was getting lighter, or if it was just his imagination.

He closed his eyes and started to count seconds—a full two minutes' worth—giving his pupils time to adjust, then looked again. No question, the stars were beginning to fade. He needed to make a decision. If they had her, it wouldn't take them long to find him. Everyone talked, it was only a matter of . . .

She emerged out of the bluish-gray light, the morning fog curling about her bare legs. He saw it all, everything, all at once—in the slump of her shoulders and the way her feet pushed through the water—and knew exactly what she had seen. He crawled down from his rocky perch and hurried out to meet her. "You okay?"

She shrugged, looking sulky and shut down. "Just thinking about my father."

But he could see it was more than that. "And . . . ?"

"And I'm tired, let down, and pissed off."

Uh-oh, he could already feel the heat of that famous Rynerson temper. "So . . . ? Atherton wasn't there?"

She stopped, eyes flashing, her fuse officially lit. "Oh yeah, he was there all right. The scumbag is working with them."

He tried to look appropriately surprised, without overdoing it. "You're sure?"

"Don't give me that crap, Simon. I've had all night to think about it. You knew something."

He shook his head empathically—"No, absolutely not!"—but knew she wouldn't let him wiggle around the truth on this one. "I had a few suspicions. Nothing more."

"A few suspicions?"

"That's right, *suspicions*."

"Then why did you let me go?"

Though he couldn't have stopped her, not with one arm, he had been asking himself that same question all night. "Because you're a pain in the ass, Rynerson, and I thought it would be a good way to finally get rid of you."

"I'm serious."

"And I'm not going to be your whipping boy for what he did. I tried to talk you out of it."

"You could have told me about your *suspicions.*"

"Come on, Kyra, the guy just asked you to marry him. You would never have believed me." Her eyes seemed to confirm it, so he hammered another nail, staying on the offensive. "You would have accused me of being vindictive and insensitive."

She opened her mouth, clearly intending to deny it, then turned and continued toward the rocks and the opening to the cave. "It was never that serious."

"It seemed pretty damn serious to me."

"He was a good dinner companion, nothing more." She reached the rocks, stopped and turned. "Okay, I admit it, I was *hoping* for more. I wanted Tony Jr. to have a man in his life. And with my father . . ." She leaned against a large boulder, out of words—defeated.

"Kyra, for god's sake, you know better than that. TJ's never going to be happy unless you're—"

She cut him off. "Don't say it. I know it was stupid. I was trying too hard, for all the wrong reasons. But, hey, I realized it wasn't right . . . that he wasn't the man for me. I turned him down, remember?" She rolled her eyes, a look of relief. "At least I wasn't sleeping with the guy."

Simon smiled—couldn't help himself.

She gave him the fisheye, though it was obvious her anger had dissipated. "You're enjoying this aren't you?"

Only a little. "Of course not."

"You never liked him."

"What's not to like? Rich, successful, good-looking, well educated . . . okay, you got me there, nothing to like."

Just as quickly as her anger had died, it flared back. "The fucking bastard! He made a fool out of me!" Tears welled in the corners of her eyes and she brushed them away with the back of her hand.

Using his good arm, Simon pulled her against his chest. "He fooled everyone. The State Department. Your parents. All of us."

"Not you."

"Of course he did. Until a couple of days ago, it never even occurred to me that he might have a different agenda. I'm just now putting the pieces together."

She stepped back. "I've been thinking about it all night. It doesn't make sense. What pieces? What did you see that I didn't?"

"Just little things. Some inconsistencies. Nothing remarkable."

"What things?" she demanded. "I want to know."

He hesitated, working it into an order that made sense. "Some of it's in retrospect. I didn't put it together until after he left."

"Such as?"

"The attack at Madame Chiang's. When I found the gun, I realized the attack had something to do with me. That someone wanted me out of the way. Buy why? If something happened to me, another courier could have been brought in. I'm not indispensable . . . it didn't make sense."

"But now it does?"

"It may sound stupid, but I now think Atherton thought we were more than friends."

"Oh." She hesitated, thinking about it. "And why is that stupid?"

It was not a question he expected. "Well . . . because we're buddies. We don't think of each other like that." Embarrassed, he hurried on. "Anyway, I now think he wanted me out of the way. At the time, of course, I only knew there was an information leak."

"And that's why you decided to move the crest early?"

"Exactly."

"That's what I don't understand. If he's been involved from the start, why did he get on the plane? He must have known about—"

"No," Simon interrupted. "I don't think he did. These guys are mercenaries. Atherton said it himself. Something he was very quick to point out, in fact. It's my guess, he's the one who hired them."

"But . . . ?" She faltered trying to put the pieces together.

"He was probably trying to protect his identity. Everything could have been handled by e-mail or phone. No personal contact. There's only one reason he would have gotten on that plane—he didn't know it was going down, and they didn't know he was the man who hired them. It's the only thing that makes sense."

She lowered herself onto a rock, her expression skeptical. "Even so, he would have been putting himself in harm's way. Just being near you and the crest."

"That's right, and I think it bothered him. Plenty.

It was the only time I ever saw the man nervous. I didn't think much about it at the time . . . just thought he hated small planes."

She nodded. "I remember that. I thought the same thing." She cocked her head to the side, dragging a memory out of the closet. "Remember that conversation I told you about . . . the one between Robbie and the skinhead guy?"

"Yeah."

"He told Robbie he had just gotten off the phone with the client. But he didn't. He tried to call someone, but no one answered."

"Now we know why."

"Apparently so." She glanced at the sky. "Maybe we should move inside."

He followed her gaze upward—the stars had faded to a few random light specks—but he was in no hurry to crawl back into that damp, closed-in space. "We've got plenty of time."

"Fine with me. I'm so pissed, I'm not even tired. So, what else? What other *inconsistencies* did I miss?"

He realized she was now internalizing the anger—outraged that Atherton had fooled her so completely. "It always bothered me that he was so anxious to give up the crest and attempt to negotiate our way out of here. It felt wrong, this instant bravery and willingness to walk into the hands of men who wanted to fill his lungs with seawater. If they were so interested in the crest, why sabotage the plane?"

She nodded. "Good point. I still don't understand what it's all about."

"I'm guessing, but when it comes to Atherton, I think it's all about money. There are lots of people, governments even, who would pay a fortune to see the Alliance fail. He's obviously well connected in this part of the world . . . he would have known where to peddle the information."

"What's that have to do with me? Why the mad rush? The proposal . . . ?"

He hesitated, knew he needed to be careful, but she offered up the answer before he could think of a delicate way to express it.

"I guess that was about money too."

"Probably. He saw an opportunity and tried to take it. Probably thought he could destroy the Alliance, and end up married to the golden child."

She made a contemptuous sound, like spitting a bug off the tip of her tongue. "I'm no child."

No, but certainly golden—in more ways than one, and she didn't even know it. "He must have realized time was running out . . . that he needed to make a move."

"So he popped the question."

"Right." And they both knew the result of that. "Enough about Atherton. What did you find out? Did you get close enough to hear anything?"

She took a deep breath and let it go, as if trying to mentally erase the man from memory. "They're concentrating on this side of the island. They've got sensors all over the place. It doesn't sound good."

Exactly as he expected. "I've got an idea . . ." He let the words hang.

She pulled up her legs, planting her feet on the edge of the rock, and wrapped her arms around her knees. “I’m listening.”

“It’s risky.”

“Risky is my middle name.”

True enough, and just what he wanted to hear. “Do they have any special security around their camp?”

“Not really,” she answered. “They think they’ve got us trapped on this side of the island. What do you have in mind?”

“Stealing one of those Zodiacs. Is that possible?”

She sat quietly, staring out at the dark sea, but her mind elsewhere, obviously picturing the camp in her mind. “Maybe,” she answered, her voice as distant as her thoughts. “They pull them out of the water at night. How far depends on the tide.”

“I was thinking we might be able to steal one and disable the others.”

“Disable how?”

“Cut the gas lines . . . ?” He purposely let the question hang, wanting to get her involved in the plan—as committed to the idea as he was.

She shook her head without hesitation. “They’d smell it. They’re camped pretty close to the water, and the wind is usually blowing in. Be safer to puncture them.”

“Whatever works.”

She nodded slowly. “You’re right, it’s risky, but I like it—simple and straightforward.”

“That’s me, Simple Simon.”

She cocked her head, a yeah-right expression. "We wouldn't be able to start the engine until we were quite a ways from the camp. Otherwise they'd hear us and . . ." She ran a finger across her throat.

"Good point." One he had already considered. He held up his bandaged arm. "I'm afraid you'll have to do the heavy lifting."

She feigned a look of disgust, her tone sarcastic and teasing. "I have to do everything."

"The curse of being a Rynerson."

She glanced again at the sky, which was growing lighter by the minute, and jumped off the rock. "Maybe I can do something to improve our odds."

"How's that?"

"Where's that cargo bag?" She started toward the cave, not waiting for an answer. "I saw some things that might help us."

Things? "What kind of things?"

"It's going to be light soon. I'll explain when I get back."

"Back from where? Where are you going?"

"Hunting."

Chapter Thirty-seven

An Island in the South China Sea

Saturday, 14 July 14:31:14 GMT +0800

Though still hidden behind a layer of gray-white clouds, the sun seemed to be gaining strength, the storm slowly giving way. Simon retreated deeper into the rocks, ahead of the tide, which had begun its relentless march up the sand. Where in the hell was she? *Hunting*—what did that mean? What if she didn't make it back before the tide came in?

He was still chewing over the same questions, the water over his ankles, when she appeared between the rocks, the cargo bag slung over her shoulder, a dark silhouette against the leaden background of the sky. "Sorry it took so long."

He took a shallow breath, hiding his relief. "I didn't notice."

"You're a lousy liar, Leonidovich." She plowed her way toward the entrance to the chamber. "We need to get inside, there are two guys in a Zodiac working their way up this end of the island." She ducked beneath the overhang of rocks.

Simon snapped on the flashlight and followed. "What do you mean by 'working their way'?" He focused the light on their tree ladder.

"You know what I mean." She started to climb.

Unfortunately, he did. "Are they staying in the boat, or actually walking the shoreline?"

She glanced over her shoulder. "They were both in the boat, but I didn't stick around to watch." She tossed the cargo bag onto the ledge, then backed down. "Once the tide's up, we'll be okay."

"Right."

She stepped back into the water. "Just take it slow. No hurry."

He handed her the light, waited for her to refocus the beam, then started to climb, an awkward maneuver with only one hand. "Did you find what you were looking for?"

"I did."

"Which was?"

"A nice patch of Psilocybe Aucklandii."

"Ah, my favorite." He edged his way upward. "What is it?"

"Mushrooms."

"Great. I love mushrooms."

"They're hallucinogenic."

"Even better." He paused to catch his breath, the air so dense and muggy it was hard to swallow. "I prefer to be stoned out of my mind when they drown me."

"You always start joking around when you're scared."

"I'm not scared. I'm appropriately concerned."

"Whatever."

He inched forward, hugging the wet tree with his legs. "So, what's with the mushrooms?" As if he couldn't guess. "And don't tell me you're going to try and sneak it into their food."

"It would give us a nice edge."

He looked down, but could barely make out her features in the reflected light. "Forget it! It's too risky."

"Don't get your testes in a twist, Leonidovich. I wouldn't try anything unless the opportunity was right."

Opportunity was right! She made it sound like a business investment. "There's isn't going to be an opportunity . . . not unless they eat at two in the morning." He reached up, found the broken-off stub of another branch, and pulled himself onto the ledge. "We're going to be stuck in this damn place until midnight."

"I realize that, but you never know what's going to happen. So I grabbed them. End of story." She put the mini-flash in her mouth and began to climb.

Within a minute they were both sitting directly over the entrance, the cargo bag between them. She reached over and gave his hand a little squeeze. "Ready?"

"For what?"

She snapped off the light and Simon instantly felt the chamber close around him. *Shit.* He leaned forward, staring down at the shadowy light reflecting off the water beneath the overhang, and tried to ignore his growing sense of claustrophobia. "Spooky." His voice echoed through the darkness, sounding unnaturally tight and ghostly.

"Cozy."

He closed his eyes, determined to overcome his phobia, when he felt the cargo bag shift against his leg. "Uh . . . Rynerson?"

"Yes."

"Did you just move the bag?"

"No."

"Well, unless those mushrooms are still growing . . . growing really fast . . . there's something alive in that bag."

"Is there?"

"Rynerson . . . !"

"Trust me, you don't want to know."

Great, that's just what he wanted to hear. "Is that what I think it is?"

"You don't bother it, it won't bother you."

"A snake, right?"

"A beaked sea snake, to be exact. Just a baby."

"Define baby."

"Less than eighteen inches."

Right, eighteen inches and a baby. He didn't want to think about mom and dad. "And poisonous, I suppose?"

"Very."

"Why in the world would you—"

"It's my secret weapon," she cut in. "If I get a chance, I'm gonna slip this little guy into Atherton's tent."

"A charming thought, but he's damn near in my lap!"

"Relax, I've got him in that nylon accessory bag. He can't get out."

"You know I don't like snakes."

"Snakes are cool. You just don't understand them."

"What's to understand? They're cold-blooded and they bite. That's enough for me."

"Don't be a wuss, Leonidovich, snakes are fascinating creatures. This species especially."

"Uh-oh, I feel a lecture coming on."

"I'm serious, snakes are the most recently evolved of all reptiles. They descended from mosasaurs, marine predators that disappeared about the same time as the dinosaurs. This species actually evolved from terrestrial snakes, so they only recently returned to the watery realm of their ancestors."

"Really." Normally, he would have said something sarcastic, but the sound of her voice kept his mind off the fact that they were about to be sealed in a watery, dark room with a sea snake. "That is interesting."

"Sea snakes are air breathers, but they have an extra lung that leads directly into their true lung, which in turn connects to an elongated air sac used for oxygen storage. Much like a diver's aqualung. Are you going to tell me that isn't interesting?"

"Absolutely not."

"They can even absorb oxygen through their skin," she continued, her voice rising with enthusiasm. "Directly from the water."

"Fascinating."

"Don't be a smartass, Leonidovich."

"No, really, I'm serious. It's all very interesting, but that doesn't mean I want one for a pet."

"You'd be surprised."

He knew better. "You know the problem with reptiles?"

"I have a feeling you're going to tell me."

"They have no expression. You don't know if they're looking at you as their next meal, or as a friendly provider. I like my pets furry and cuddly."

"I thought that was your choice in women."

"Absolutely not. I like women *smooooooth* and cuddly."

"See, you like smooth skin. If you would—"

"What . . . ?"

"*Shhhhh.* You hear that?"

For a moment, he heard nothing but the soft lap of waves, and then the low and unmistakable hum of a small outboard. He looked down, staring at the shadowy light, trying to measure the gap between the water and the overhang: two feet, maybe three. *Not good.*

Kyra leaned across the cargo bag, her voice low and tight. "They're slowing down."

"They won't see the opening," he whispered back, trying to sound confident, though his heart had already kicked into overdrive.

She reached out, found his hand, and squeezed. "We'll be okay." Her words sounded hollow and full of wishful thinking.

"Of course we will." He cocked his head to the side, straining to hear, to calculate the distance. Twenty, maybe thirty yards, but with the wave action it was difficult to judge.

The engine suddenly went silent, the hush so quick and unexpected Simon found it difficult to breathe. The seconds ticked slowly by, the silence intense and electric, then the scrape of rubber against rock, followed by the double splash of two men stepping into the water, the sound shockingly clear.

"There's nothing back in there, Big. Let's move on."

"You stay with the boat," the other man answered, his voice a raspy growl. "I'll check it out."

"That's the one they call Big Paddy," Kyra whispered.

Simon leaned close, until his lips touched her ear. "To hell with Atherton. If you can handle that snake in this light . . ."

She nodded and placed a finger to her lips, as the sounds of a man sloshing through the water drew closer. He seemed to move past the opening, then stopped and came back.

"Hey, Chrich, come here!" The man's deep voice echoed through the chamber as a beam of light skipped off the water beneath Simon's feet.

As the second man splashed toward them, Kyra slowly unzipped the cargo bag, the metallic *click-click-click-click* loud as a rivet gun in Simon's ear. He leaned back against the stone wall, forcing himself to breathe, to gain control of his heart, which felt like it was about to explode.

The light flashed again, bouncing off the back wall. "Take a look."

Holding the snake just behind its head, Kyra

pulled the angry reptile free of its enclosure. Despite the woman's penchant for risk, she looked almost catatonic with fear, her hand shaking nearly as hard as the wiggling monster she was trying to control.

Another flash of light. "I think you better check it out."

"Me! Why me?"

"Because you're smaller'n me, asshole."

"Bloody hell. I'm not going in there."

"Brick said to check everything."

"So you do it," the other man snapped. "You're the one's always actin' like a badass."

Big Paddy answered with a scornful grunt. "And you're nothin' but a chicken-ass flyboy. Gimme that Uzi."

"That's Brick's gun. You get it wet, you clean it."

Another grunt, another flash of light, and then Big Paddy was in the chamber, standing directly below Kyra. He swept the flashlight from side to side, then up and down the walls, past the tree . . . then back . . . the light hovering over their makeshift ladder. Simon could almost see the gray matter bubbling in the big man's head, and realized it would take him only a second or two to put it all together. *Do it now! Do it now!* Then he realized she couldn't, her entire body rigid with fear. The snake looked equally incapacitated—either oxygen-starved from Kyra's death grip, or simply waiting for its opportunity to strike—its long body hanging limpid and straight. *Ohhhhh, shit!* He reached out, grabbed the beast from her hand, leaned forward, quickly adjusted his aim, and let it go. It seemed to hover for a moment, its body twisting frantically, searching for solid ground, then dropped straight down, landing across the man's shoulder.

Big Paddy let out a yelp and the snake reacted, striking the big man's neck before he could grab it and fling it against the far wall. He stumbled back, blindly firing the Uzi—briefly turning the chamber into a storm of flashing thunderbolts—before disappearing beneath the overhang.

Deafened by the jarring reverberations, it took a few moments before Simon could hear anything, and then inexplicably, it was the sound of receding laughter.

"It ain't funny, Chrich! The damn thing bit me."

"Don't go all barmy. I'm sure it was harmless. You just scared the little thing."

"It wasn't so fuckin' little, asshole!"

Simon reached out, found Kyra's hand, and gave it a squeeze. She squeezed back, holding on until the sound of the Zodiac faded, then she laughed, a great relieved chuckle. "Sorry, I don't know what happened. That man . . . the thought of being trapped . . ."

But Simon knew exactly what happened—a flashback to El Pato prison—a memory that would make anyone freeze up. "Happens to everyone."

"Not you."

"Trust me, Rynerson, I reacted out of fear, not courage."

She chuckled again. "Told you snakes were cool."

"You think it's still alive?"

"Probably."

"And more than a little pissed off, wouldn't you say?"

"Royally."

He glanced down at the narrow band of light still visible beneath his feet. "Wonderful." He didn't try to hide the sarcasm.

"What's the problem?"

"Another couple of minutes and we're going to be trapped in here for the next nine hours with a pissed-off snake. *That's* the problem."

"They're really quite shy." She gave his hand a reassuring squeeze. "Nothing to worry about."

Right, except that wasn't the only snake he was worried about.

CHAPTER THIRTY-EIGHT

An Island in the South China Sea

Saturday, 14 July 20:01:14 GMT +0800

Absorbed in thought, Mawl didn't notice Atherton had gotten up from the table until he spoke. "What the hell is that?" It was obvious from his tone that whatever it was, it wasn't good enough for him.

Mawl let it go—for the moment, the man remained the client—but that would change soon enough. "Irish stew. As close as I make it with all this canned shit. I thought the boys might appreciate a decent meal."

Atherton glanced toward the three men huddled in the trees. "I don't think it's food they're talking about."

Mawl nodded, it was true, they were doing more talking than digging. "They just need some time."

"Time," Atherton repeated, his tone mocking. "We're out of time." He cocked his head toward the west and the hazy yellow globe that hung above the horizon. "That's the first time we've seen the sun in four days. This storm is over. By midday tomorrow, there's going to be search planes all over this area."

Mawl nodded, as if he needed that fact shoved in his face. "And I intend to have all four boats sitting off that end of the island by daybreak. If they show their heads, we'll see them first. We'll get them."

"So you say."

Mawl ignored the sarcasm. "The accident set us back." A weak excuse, he realized, but it had, in fact, cost them half a day. Big Paddy had not gone easily—putting up an agonizing and ugly fight that lasted six hours—and that left the men somewhat reluctant to go sticking their heads into dark spots. "They'll be ready to go by morning."

"I'm sure," Atherton said, tilting his head back in that superior way he had of speaking while looking down his nose. "But I've been thinking about it, and I'm not so sure it was an accident."

"What are you talking about?"

"Snakes don't jump on people."

"It's not common," Mawl agreed cautiously, not sure where Atherton was heading. "But it happens."

"Out of trees, maybe. Not out of the water. Are you telling me a snake jumped out of the water and bit your big guy on the neck?"

The way he said it, in that patronizing tone, it did sound a bit implausible. "What are you saying?"

"Don't you know what Kyra Rynerson does for a living?" He didn't wait for an answer. "She's a zoologist. Think about it."

That's exactly what Mawl was doing, and he couldn't decide which sounded more implausible, that a poisonous water snake had somehow bitten Paddy on the neck, or Kyra Rynerson had somehow used the snake as a weapon. He reached over and snatched his two-way off the table. "Chrich—" As if connected to the same electronic string, the heads of all four men turned toward the enclosure. "—come over here." Mawl turned back to Atherton. "You better let me do the talking. The men don't exactly trust you."

Atherton smiled, a smug upturn along one side of his mouth. "It's mutual."

Chricher, who apparently thought he knew why he was being summoned, began talking even before he stepped beneath the canopy. "It's not my fault, Brick. We got ourselves a problem."

Great, as if he didn't have enough. "What kind of problem?"

"The guys are pretty upset. They don't think we should be leaving Big out here on this godforsaken island."

Mawl nodded to himself. He wasn't that surprised, it was part of their training—the old warrior's code—to take their fallen with them. "And what is it they think we should do with him?"

"It's pretty much a majority," Chricher answered, clearly wanting it understood that he wasn't alone in this opinion. "They all think we should be shipping him home."

Bloody hell, that's all he needed—a fucking mutiny. "And just how are we supposed to do that, Chrich? If we try to ship his body there's gonna to be a thousand bloody questions."

"I understand that, but—"

Mawl cut him off, not about to let the idea gain momentum. "Paddy hasn't been back to Ireland in fourteen years. He doesn't have a family. There is no *home.* Just where in the bloody hell are we supposed to ship his body?"

"I'm not disagreein', Brick." Suddenly he didn't seem so concerned about the majority opinion. "I'm just the messenger."

"And you're second in command now." Of course there had never been a second to his command, but it sounded nice, and seemed like a good way to gain support for his decision. "Just get it done. They'll listen to you."

Chricher hesitated, noticeably surprised at his sudden promotion. "Uh . . . sure, Brick. I'll handle it." He started to turn away.

"Just a minute, Chrich. Let me ask you something. What exactly was that cave like?"

Chricher shrugged evasively. "Can't really say. Dark as the inside of a whore's box, I can tell you that."

"Did you go in?"

"Well, not all the way," Chricher admitted. "You know Big, he doesn't . . . didn't . . . he didn't like to sit anything out."

"So what *did* you see?"

"There really wasn't much of an opening between the water and the rocks, but you could see the back wall . . . no more than four or five meters, I'd say."

"Uh-huh. And how deep was the water?"

Chricher shrugged again, his eyes a combination of curious and cautious. "'bout to my ass, I guess. Why?"

Mawl ignored the question. "About to Paddy's knees, then?"

"Yeah, that's about right." His eyes shifted from Mawl to Atherton, then back again. What's this about, Brick?"

"Paddy was over six foot. That's a bloody big jump for a snake."

"Oh, that," Chricher said, a relieved lift in his voice. "The snake didn't jump. It landed on his back."

"Landed?"

"That's what he said. Said it dropped right on top of him."

"Okay, that would explain it," Mawl said, though he knew it didn't.

"Yup."

"Dropped from where? That's what I'm wondering."

Chricher's expression went blank, a clock without batteries. "That's a bloody good question." He paused, thinking about it. "He did say something about a tree."

Atherton spoke for the first time, making no attempt to hide his skepticism. "A tree inside the cave?"

Chricher nodded. "That's what he said."

Mawl gave Atherton a look, trying to warn him off. "Yes, that would explain where the snake came from."

But it was too late, Chricher was already putting the pieces together. "Bloody hell, you think that's were they're hiding."

"No," Mawl said, "I don't think that, but it's worth checking. Can you draw me a map?"

"I'll take you there."

But that wasn't what Mawl wanted. If they found

Leonidovich, they would find that "worthless artifact"—something he didn't believe for a second—and he preferred to make that discovery on his own. "No, you need to stay here. Make sure this problem with Big Patty gets handled properly."

Atherton smiled, just a little, that I-know-what-you're-thinking smirk. "I'll go with you."

Mawl nodded—that would only make it easier to get rid of the arrogant bastard—and turned back to Chricher. "About that map . . . ?"

"Sure, Brick, but even if you're right . . . even if that's where they're hiding . . . you won't find them. Not now."

"And why's that?"

"The tide's up. If they're in there, they're trapped until it goes out."

"You're sure?"

Absolutely," Chricher answered. "The waterline was at least a meter above the opening."

"When's ebb tide?"

Chricher pulled a small *Tide and Pilot Guide* from one of the oversized pockets in his shorts. He thumbed through the pages, found the one he was looking for, then traced down the column with his finger until he found the right date. "Looks to me . . . lemme see here . . . yup . . . looks like it'll be another four . . . maybe five hours before that thing opens up."

Mawl glanced at his watch. *Midnight.* And he planned to be there.

CHAPTER THIRTY-NINE

An Island in the South China Sea

Saturday, 14 July 20:22:14 GMT +0800

Kyra stopped her forward stroke, put a finger to her lips, and motioned for Simon to move up.

He propelled himself through the tepid water, trying to maintain that perfect point of buoyancy where he could walk on the bottom, maintain control, and not have to use his broken arm. "What's up?"

"We're getting close," she whispered. "You okay?"

He nodded, feeling better now that the sun had disappeared over the horizon. "Just tired."

"Don't complain to me . . . I'm the one who wanted to stay put and get some sleep."

"I'm not complaining."

"Fess up, Leonidovich, you were just afraid to stay in that cave with my snake."

True enough, but he was getting tired of hearing about it, and he couldn't resist a little retaliation. "Despite what you *now* think of him, Atherton is no fool. He knows you're a zoologist. He just might put you and that damn reptile together."

"Yeah, yeah, good story. You ready to get out of here?"

He glanced at the sky, the few remaining clouds

still amber-lit along the bottom. "How close are we?"

"It should be right ahead." She pointed her chin toward an outcropping that looked vaguely familiar. "Just beyond those rocks."

He suddenly remembered the spot, the place where they had come ashore only four days before, but which felt like another lifetime. "You sure they don't have motion sensors around the camp?"

"Pretty sure. Thanks to that *sonofabitch—*" Her new pet name for Atherton. "—they're concentrating all their efforts on the other end of the island."

"I hope to hell you're right, Rynerson."

"Yeah, me too. Let's get out of here before we turn to seaweed and the fish start nibbling on our toes."

"I'll go first." He gave her a don't-screw-with-me look, letting her know this issue was not open to debate. "Wait until I'm past the rocks and into the trees. Then wait another five minutes . . . just to be sure." He pointed toward a lightning-struck tree among the gray silhouettes that lined the shore. "Then head for that tree."

"Yessir, boss."

"I mean it, Kyra. You hear anything, you swim like hell."

She reached out, pulled him close, and kissed his cheek. "For luck."

He nodded—had a feeling they were going to need it—and pushed off toward the shore, never taking his eyes off the tree line. He waited until his knees brushed the bottom, then stood up, waited for the initial rush of water to stream off his clothes, then as quickly and quietly as possible, made his way through the rocks and into the trees. Five minutes later, clutching the cargo bag to her chest, she dropped onto the ground beside him. "That was easy enough."

He nodded, but *easy* always scared him; it was that old fear that some cosmic force controlled the balance of life—measuring good against evil, easy against hard—just waiting to nudge the scales in the opposite direction. He pointed up, at the burned-out hulk he had used as a target from the water. "Could you find this tree again, if you needed to?"

"Sure. Why?"

"Because this is where I'm going to leave the crest." He pointed to a cavity near the base. "Just in case."

"In case of what?"

"In case we're caught. If they get us, I don't want them to get the crest too." He actually had something else in mind, a little insurance in case the cosmic gods decided to tilt the scales away from easy. "If we're able to grab one of those nice rubber boats, I'll pick it up on the way out."

She shrugged. "It's your responsibility." She fished the black case with the Smithsonian logo out of the bag. "Your call."

"Yes it is." He tucked the case into the hollowed-out cavity.

"But I suggest we *don't* get caught."

"I agree. But just—"

"Yeah-yeah, I know . . . just in case. You ready?"

He checked the sky, which in the last few minutes had gone from a kaleidoscope of color to a hazy charcoal. The world, he thought, might be getting darker, but it wasn't getting any cooler. "Lead the way."

She stood up, hooked the bag over her shoulder, and began moving in a northwesterly direction along the coast, staying well back in the trees. The ground was soft and spongy, everything saturated from four days of rain, the thick vegetation absorbing the sounds of their movements. By the time they reached the encampment, the night had settled in; that brief period after the earth had lost its color, and before the stars appeared. Kyra lowered herself to a prone position, then slithered forward to the edge of the clearing. Being careful not to put pressure on his broken arm, Simon lowered himself to the ground, edged onto his right side, then slid forward until they could whisper mouth-to-ear. "What's going on?"

She pointed to a light about fifty yards ahead: a canopied enclosure with the sides rolled up. Sitting at a small table surrounded by boxes, were two men: James Atherton, and the man with the shaved head. "That's Bricker, the head honcho." She moved her finger to the left, toward a grouping of dark shapes. "Their tents." Another finger adjustment, toward a hazy yellow light back in the trees, and the shadowed silhouettes of three men, one on his knees. "Something's going on back there."

Simon nodded. "That's five. I don't see the big guy."

"Probably in his tent," she whispered. "Dead or wishing he was."

That's when Simon realized the third man wasn't

on his knees, but in a hole. "Then I think he got his wish. It looks like they're digging a grave."

She leaned to the side, trying to get a better view through a gap in the undergrowth, then emitted a low grunt of satisfaction. "Snakes are *sooo* cool."

"That's six, then . . . all accounted for."

She nodded, her lips curling into a I-told-you-so grin, and he knew exactly what she was thinking—*all here, no one sitting outside the cave*—but at least she didn't say it.

"So where are those inflatable boats?"

She pointed toward the water. "Just beyond those trees."

Being careful to keep a thick buffer of plants between themselves and the clearing, it took them only a few minutes to cover the short distance. As they edged up behind the last protective barrier of trees, the night seemed to grow brighter, the rocky shoreline awash beneath a galaxy of stars, the ocean a shimmering pool of oily luminescence. All four of the inflatable boats were clearly visible: the three small craft staked side by side near the water's edge, but the fourth and largest, had been pulled onto the rocks, to within twenty yards of the canopied enclosure. "We're screwed," Kyra whispered. "If we can't disable that big one . . ."

He nodded. "Is someone always around that shelter?"

"Always," she answered. "That's where they monitor their network of sensors."

He couldn't imagine how she got so close. "You were close enough to see all that?"

"It wasn't like this. I swam through the mud in the middle of a typhoon. We couldn't get within twenty yards of that place in this weather."

It was, he realized, that perfect after-storm lull: calm sea, clear sky, quiet as a— He glanced toward the shadowy light back in the trees. *Cemetery.* "Any brilliant ideas?"

"Retreat," she answered without hesitation. "Wait till morning. Try to signal a ship."

But he knew what that meant—*back to the cave*—and that was not something he wanted to do. Sooner or later, Atherton would put things together—*Rynerson plus snake*—and come looking. "Why don't we wait awhile, just—"

"Yeah, I know," she interrupted. "Just in case."

"That's right. You sleep, I'll keep an eye on things."

"Now there's an idea." She curled into a fetal position, her head on one hand, and closed her eyes.

"Just tell me I don't have to worry about snakes."

"You don't have to worry about snakes," she repeated, her voice already drifting toward slumberland. "It's the centipedes you should worry about."

"Damn you, Rynerson, did you have to tell me that?"

She smiled, just a small upturn of the lips, as if lacking the strength for more. "It makes me feel superior."

In less than a minute she had drifted off, her breathing soft and regular. Though he hadn't slept more than a few hours in three days, he didn't feel tired, his brain too energized with plans and schemes and dreams of escape. Ironically, he felt more in control now, where he could see the enemy and take advantage of their movements. And there would be movement. He knew the laws of physics, and nothing remained static for long.

That first movement came twenty minutes later. Simon placed a hand over Kyra's mouth, and nudged her awake. Her body stiffened and her eyes flew open, then she realized who it was and relaxed. "What's happening?"

"Skinhead just got a call on his radio." He pointed toward the silhouetted shapes of Atherton and Bricker as they moved toward the burial site. "I think they're about to plant the guy."

"You want to go now?" she whispered, her voice edgy with excitement.

A question he had already asked himself. "If I had two arms, I'd say yes, but I doubt if we'd have enough time to disable three boats and get away before they spot us."

She nodded, a look of disappointment. "You're probably right. We'll stand a better chance once they're asleep."

They watched as the five men gathered in a circle around the light. Though too distant to make out the words, a cacophony of voices filtered back through the trees. "Can you believe that?" Kyra whispered. "They're having some kind of ceremony . . . as if God would welcome one of those bastards into paradise."

"I think it's a military thing. Band of brothers, that sort of thing."

"Yeah, brothers, and that sonofabitch is right with them." She rolled over and began digging through the cargo bag.

"What are you doing?" But he knew the answer as soon as he asked the question. "Don't even think about it."

"It's perfect," she said, yanking out her bag of magic mushrooms. "With all that digging, they may not have eaten yet."

"It's too risky. You don't even know if there's anything you can put them in."

"One way to find out. We need some kind of edge if we're going to make it out of here. If they see me, I'll take off down the beach in the other direction."

"Come on, Kyra, don't be foolish." He grabbed her wrist. "You know what these guys will do if they catch you."

"And that's why I won't let them. If I have to, I'll take my chances in the water. I can swim like a fish." She glanced toward the burial party. "Now let go of my arm. We don't have much time."

Short of wrestling her to the ground—which he doubted he could do with one arm—he could only agree. "Be careful." The words sounded hollow and foolish, like the warning to a child who thinks they're invincible, but he couldn't think of anything better.

She nodded. "If something happens, I'll meet you back at the cave."

"No. Where I hid the crest. We're safer here, than in that damn cave."

She nodded again, anxious to go.

"You see any guns lying around, you might consider borrowing a couple."

"Ten-four." She gave him another one of those nice little pecks on the cheek, then was gone, crawling straight toward the water until she had dropped below the men's sight line, then turned, moving low and fast toward the canopied enclosure.

Simon watched her go, glancing every few seconds toward the burial party, and feeling helpless. *Should have arranged some kind of signal. Shouldn't have let her go.* But it was too late, too many shoulds and shouldn'ts to count.

She reached the enclosure in less than two minutes, momentarily visible before disappearing behind a stack of boxes. Every moment felt like an hour, until he had no idea how much time had passed, his body numb with the agony of helplessness. *Come on, come on! Get out of there!* Then, at the edge of his consciousness, he realized the murmur of voices had died away—the burial party breaking up. He could see Atherton and Bricker moving through the trees, heading straight for the enclosure. *Oh, Jesus! Get out of there! Run!* For several eternity-in-an-instant heartbeats he knew she'd be caught, and then he saw her, crabbing her way along the tree line. *Thank you, Jesus.*

She crawled in beside him just as the men reached the enclosure, her face dripping with sweat, hands and knees bleeding. She expelled a heavy sigh and rolled onto her back, panting and gulping for air.

"You okay?"

She nodded. "Sorry—" Quick breath. "—no guns."

He kept his eyes on the men, watching for an indication that they might have seen something. "So . . . ?"

"It was perfect." She swallowed, still trying to catch her breath. "Big pot of stew."

Stew—these guys were serious carnivores—only an animal would eat stew in this kind of heat. "How much did you put in?"

She pulled the half empty bag from her pocket. "Just the little ones. I was afraid they might notice if I did more."

"So what now?" He watched as Atherton and the other man settled into their chairs, their heads tilting forward in conversation, oblivious to her visit. "What will the effect be . . . assuming they eat?"

She shook her head. "I'm no expert. Mushrooms are normally eaten raw or dried. I'm not sure what effect cooking will have on them."

"Best guess?"

"Nausea and vomiting, followed by a kaleidoscope of possibilities, ranging from paranoia to a nice Alice-in-Wonderland field trip, a kind of dreamy state of consciousness with lots of colors and patterns. The effects can last from four to six hours."

"You're right, doesn't sound like you know much."

She smiled, making no attempt to deny the implication of his words. "When I was in the Amazon, most of the interns tried them."

"Sounds like fun. Especially that vomiting part."

"It's not pretty from the outside," she agreed. "Once was enough for me."

"Let's just hope—" He watched as another man entered the enclosure. "We've got a new guy. Some kind of pow-wow."

Kyra rolled onto her side, peering through the undergrowth. "That's Chricher. The chopper pilot."

A few minutes later, apparently leaving Chricher in charge, Atherton and Bricker loaded one of the small Zodiacs with gear and headed south along the coast. "What do you think?" Kyra whispered.

"Our odds just got better."

"You think they're going back to the cave, don't you?"

Of course that's what he thought. "It makes sense. The tide's going out."

"If you're right, we need to make our move before they discover we're gone and come back." She pointed toward the enclosure as Robbie and the third man joined Chricher. "That's Fosseler. The one they call Catman."

Obviously. Thin and wiry, the man had a way of walking, an effortless kind of glide, like a cat ghosting through tall grass. "Let's hope they're hungry from digging."

Two hours later they were still hoping, the men apparently too upset with the loss of Big Paddy to think about food. They huddled around the table, drinking beer and telling stories: *Big* the only discernable word that made it into the trees, the man growing "bigger" by the minute. Finally the stories seemed to run out, and after a few long minutes of silence, Robbie and Catman-Fosseler retreated to their tents, leaving Chricher to stand guard.

"How long," Kyra whispered, "you think we have before they get back?"

He studied the waterline, trying to gauge the ebb since Atherton and Bricker had left. "An hour . . . two at the most."

"I'm thinking one. That's our window. We need to do something before then."

He nodded, but saying it and doing "something" were two different things. "I don't see how we can disable that large Zodiac. Not as long as he's—" He was about to say "just sitting there," but suddenly realized the man wasn't *just* sitting, but had his head bent forward. "Is he eating?"

She edged forward, trying to get a better view. "Maybe . . . I think so . . . yes . . . no question about it."

"How long will it take for something to happen?"

"If it works . . . not long."

Ten minutes later the man was on his knees in the sand, experiencing the first euphoric effects of hallucinogenic mushrooms: regurgitated stew. Until that moment, Simon didn't give the plan much of a chance, but now it actually seemed possible. Those positive feelings dissolved almost instantly when Chricher suddenly bounced to his feet, apparently purged of his demons and ready for his next adventure on the magic carpet. He wandered toward the water, his gait dysrhythmic, his arms floating about his body like disengaged appendages. After a few aimless trips to nowhere, first in one direction and then the other, he began to circle the large Zodiac in a kind of slow-motion, tango-around-the-temple dance, babbling incoherently and staring at the stars, seemingly dazzled by the light show, most of which, Simon assumed, was taking place inside his head. "Will he pass out?"

Kyra shook her head. "He's actually in a heightened state of awareness. Unless he suddenly wanders off, this may be our best opportunity."

"What opportunity? There's no way we can get to that boat."

"I'm talking about your backup plan."

"I don't have a *backup* plan."

"Don't give me that, Leonidovich, you're usually on the fourth move before anyone else realizes they're playing chess and not checkers."

"I appreciate the flattery, Rynerson, but it's not true." Which, of course, wasn't true, and she saw it, giving him one of those hooded, give-it-up stares he could never resist. "Well . . . it's just an idea . . ."

"Stop stalling, Leonidovich. I get it. It's risky. Spit it out."

"While he's over there tripping around in psychedelic heaven, we might be able to float one of the smaller boats out of here."

"And what good will that do? They'll hear us the minute we start it up."

"That's the idea."

"I don't get it," she admitted. "They'd run us down in that big monster before we got half a mile."

"It's a diversion. We won't be in it. They'd be chasing an empty boat. By the time they catch it . . ."

"Oh." Her eyes suddenly brightened. "We've gotten away in the other boat."

"Exactly."

She nodded slowly, thinking about it. "How long do you think it would take them to catch the thing?"

"They would have to keep shutting down their engine to listen. That's the only way they could track it—by sound. I would guess somewhere between five and ten minutes, which would give us from ten to twenty minutes before they got back. But—" He paused, letting her know this was a very big *but.* "—that's assuming the boat continued in a straight line. If it got turned in the waves . . ."

She glanced at the water. "It's dead calm."

"Right, and we could lock down the engine, but there's still a prevailing current. We could compensate for that, but it would be a guess at best."

"And what if they leave someone behind?"

"Then we're in no worse shape than we are now."

She let that percolate for a few seconds. "You really think we could pull it off?"

Probably not, but they were running out of options. "Why not?" A cop-out answer if one ever existed.

"Okay, we have nothing to lose. Let's give it a try."

"You stay here. I'll—"

"Forget that," she interrupted. "You can't get that thing in the water with one arm. Not quietly, anyway. If he spots me, I can at least swim. You get the crest, I'll get the boat."

It was another one of those you've-only-got-one-arm battles he could never win. "Okay." He fished the mini-flash out of the cargo bag. "Let's go."

They backtracked through the trees, just far enough so that she could enter the water without being seen. "I'll meet you right here."

"Don't do anything crazy, Rynerson. If you can't get it, we can still try to signal a ship."

She nodded and slipped into the water. He waited until she was out of sight, then hunkered down in the rocks, nothing to do but run through the mental checklist and hope for the best. As he started down the list, the moon suddenly bulged over the horizon, huge and white, as if God had decided to turn on a spotlight so as not to miss the action. *Thanks a heap.*

In answer, something broke the surface of the water, a sudden pop and splash, and for a moment Simon thought his heart had abandoned ship. *Sorry, God.*

The night seemed to absorb everything, a giant sponge sucking everything into its vortex, until he had no sense of time or its passage. Surprisingly, though his five senses were working overtime, he didn't hear or see her until she was less than twenty yards away, her head hidden behind the black rubber surface of the boat. He waded out and helped her pull it into the shallows. "Any trouble?"

"Not a bit," she whispered. "He's still riding that magic dragon. You get the crest?"

"I decided to leave it."

"What!"

"Keep your voice down, Rynerson. If we get away, I can always come back."

"Come ba . . . oh, I get it. In case we get caught, you don't what them to get that too."

An implied question he had no intention of answering. "You need to rest?"

"No. Let's get out of here before that sonofabitch and his buddy get back."

"Sounds good to me. You climb in—" He handed her the mini-flash. "—and drop the engine."

"Yessir, boss." She put the light in her mouth and shimmied over the side.

"There should be some way to lock the steering arm."

She snapped on the light, shielding the beam with one hand as she dropped the engine with the other. "Yeah, I see it."

"Okay. Lock it straight ahead. I'll line you up."

"Ten-four."

"Once you start it, you'll have to let it idle a bit. You don't want to kill the thing when you open it up."

"I'm a pilot," she hissed back, "you don't think I know how to warm up an engine?"

"Oh, yeah, that's right. I try to forget that." He held up his broken arm. "Did I mention that problem you have with landings?"

"Screw you."

"I get so excited when you talk dirty, Rynerson."

"Now I know we're in trouble, you're starting to joke around."

He ignored the commentary; so he had a little avoidance quirk, who didn't? "Don't forget to lock the throttle before you bail out."

"Yessir, boss."

"Come straight over the back, or you'll throw the thing off course."

"I have to do everything."

"Don't let it go to your head, Rynerson. You're muscle, I'm brains."

"Yeah, yeah, let's get this party started, Einstein."

"You're all lined up. Give it a rip."

She yanked the starter cord and the tiny engine began to cough and sputter—a heart-stopping clatter that seemed to last for minutes, but couldn't have been more than five or ten seconds—then settled into a wake-the-dead whine. While Simon tried to keep the boat aligned, Kyra worked the throttle, goosing it higher and higher until it was screaming, then she backed it off, gave him a nod, and dropped it into gear. The boat lurched forward as she opened the throttle, and was nearly thirty yards away before she could jump clear, a graceful dive directly over the stern.

Simon could hear the men shouting even before she reached the shore, their frantic words indistinguishable beneath the fading whine of the engine. "You okay?"

She nodded, grinning like a schoolgirl on prom night. "That was fun."

The woman, he decided, had a serious risk addiction. "We still need to be careful. They might leave someone behind."

She nodded again. "Let's go."

The giant outboard roared to life just as they

reached the encampment. A second later the boat was accelerating across the water, the huge engine throwing a roostertail, Catman Fosseler at the wheel, Robbie stretched out over the bow with a spotlight, its beam cutting a wide swath through the darkness. "I only see two of them," Simon whispered, then realized he could have shouted and the men wouldn't have heard him. "Where's the zombie?"

"He's with them," Kyra answered. "Lying on the deck. I caught a glimpse of his head."

"Let's hope they don't start wondering what's wrong with the guy, and start putting two and two together."

"I think they're more worried about what Bricker will do if we get away."

"Yeah, you're probably right." So why did he have that feeling things were going *too well*—that the cosmic gods were about ready to tilt the scales? "Let's do this."

They ran across the open stretch of beach, but when they reached the boat, he suddenly realized the sound of the engine seemed to be growing louder, not fading. "It sounds like they're coming back!"

Kyra, who was already pulling the inflatable toward the water, stopped and cocked her head. "It's just the night air. The sound reverberates off the water."

He hesitated, not convinced—it was too loud, too close—but before he could argue the point the sound faded, as if the boat had suddenly slipped over the horizon. "Okay, let's get out of here."

"I don't think so."

The soft but threatening words seemed to float across the water, and Simon realized instantly why the sound of the motor had seemed so close.

Chapter Forty

An Island in the South China Sea

Saturday, 14 July 23:14:38 GMT +0800

Simon had two oddly discouraging thoughts as the black inflatable slid silently into view: that his insurance plan would never succeed against two men, and only a fool would put a gun in the hands of James Atherton. To survive, one problem would have to cancel out the other.

As the boat scraped along the bottom, Atherton stepped into the water, a small automatic leveled at Kyra's chest, his eyes on Simon. "I finally figured you out, Leonidovich. Point one way, go the other."

The man with the shaved head, a small Uzi hanging below his right arm, grabbed the tow line and began pulling the boat out of the water. "Cut the bloody chitchat. We need to do this quick, before the others get back."

Atherton smiled, a cat-like smirk. "Before the others get back? Now why would you say that, Mawl? They're your men."

Mawl realized he had made a mistake, it was written in the sudden stillness of his eyes, but he tried to bluff his way past it. "I only meant—" He turned and bent forward, as if to stake the boat, his hand moving toward the Uzi. "—we should—"

But Atherton wasn't fooled and he didn't hesitate—*BANG-BANG-BANG,* firing so fast it sounded like one loud eruption—blowing away half the man's head before his hand reached the Uzi. He pitched forward into the sand, his body folding up like a discarded suit of clothes. Even before the sound echoed away, Atherton had his gun back on Kyra. "I was on the pistol team in college." Then he laughed, a kind of mirthless bark. "I may have forgotten to mention that when he gave me the gun."

She glared at him. "Apparently you forgot to mention a lot of things."

"Well, hello-o-o, sweetheart. Found your tongue, did you?"

"Fuck you."

Atherton grinned, an expression of detached pleasure. "You should have. We could have had everything. The whole enchilada. Now look where you are." He flicked the barrel of his automatic toward Simon. "You and the loser. Oh, well . . ." He shrugged and glanced over his shoulder, a quick scan of the dark water. "But the late Mr. Mawl was right about one thing, we do need to hurry. Where's the crest?"

"We don't have it," Kyra answered, her response a little too quick. "We lost it in the water."

"Really?" Atherton shifted his focus to Simon. "Now why don't I believe that?"

"It's true," Simon answered, knowing the man would never believe him. "We don't have it."

"Now there you go again, saying one thing, meaning another. Of course you don't have it. I can see that. But did you lose it?"

"Yes," Kyra snapped. "That's what I said."

Atherton never took his eyes off Simon. "Okay, I don't have much time, so we'll just have to do this the quick and dirty way. On the count of three, she dies. It's up to you, Boy Scout. One! You know I'll do it. Two!"

Yes, Simon realized, the bastard would do it without a moment's hesitation; he had enjoyed the first experience too much. "Okay, you win. I'll take you to it."

"No, Simon! Don't do it. He's going to kill us anyway."

Atherton smiled at her in an understanding sort of way. "That's just not true, Kyra. All I want is that piece of broken rock."

"Tell that to your friend with no face!"

"Unfortunately, Mr. Mawl wanted the same thing," Atherton responded, his tone indifferent. "But I have no reason to hurt you or Simon. No reason at all."

"I believe him," Simon said, trying hard to sound sincere. "Killing the daughter of Big Jake Rynerson would attract too much attention." He gave Atherton a disgusted look. "Our Jimmy boy is too smart for that."

"That's right, Boy Scout, and I'm smart enough to know when you're stalling for time. Now where is it?"

"Please, Simon, don't do it. He's crazy."

"It'll be okay," Simon answered, trying to send her

a signal without making it obvious. "He's not going to hurt us if we do what he wants." He turned back to Atherton. "It's up the coast a ways. Follow me." Something he knew the man would never do—not in the dark.

Atherton turned his head, listening hard to the distant drone of the Zodiac. "I don't think so." Keeping his automatic leveled on Kyra, he crouched down, unclipped the cell phone from Mawl's belt, and picked up the Uzi. "I'll give you five minutes." He glanced at the watch. "If you're not back by—"

"I'll be back," Simon interrupted, "but it will take at least fifteen minutes." Kyra stared at him, knowing it shouldn't take half that time.

"Five minutes," Atherton snapped. "I suggest you run."

Simon didn't move. The man was clearly growing impatient, and impatience led to bad decisions. "Five minutes isn't long enough. Not on foot. It might be possible if we—" He purposely said *we,* knowing Atherton would resist any suggestion. "—took one of the boats."

Atherton hesitated, his expression going from wary to appraising. Simon silently held his ground, letting the pressure of time wear on the man. "Five minutes," Atherton repeated. "I don't give a fuck *how* you do it."

"I'll take this one," Simon said, moving toward the boat still partially in the water. "It's warmed up." He reached down, yanked the tow line out of Mawl's lifeless hand, and pushed off.

"Don't do anything stupid," Atherton warned, "and we can all walk away from this little adventure."

Though he didn't have a watch, Simon doubted if it took him more than three or four minutes to retrieve the crest and start back, but he knew that was the easy part—that things were about to get hairy. As he came around the last outcropping of rocks, he could see the two of them silhouetted against the sand, Atherton now standing behind Kyra, using her as a shield. Before he got too close, Simon adjusted his course to a spot about thirty feet offshore, then cut the engine and slipped over the side. Using the crest's Frisbee-sized container to maintain direction, he wrapped his broken arm around the prop shaft, and ducked as low as he could behind the engine.

"Don't start playing games," Atherton yelled. "I can see you, Leonidovich, and you know I'm a very good shot."

Simon held up the crest, the golden sunburst clearly visible in the moonlight, letting the man see the prize. "You shoot me, you lose this."

Atherton placed the tip of his automatic below Kyra's ear. "I'm going to start counting, and if—"

"Cut the bullshit," Simon shouted back. "You want this crest, you'll have to do better than count."

"I'm not kidding!"

"You think I am?

"One!"

"You kill her, you think I'm going to give you the crest?"

"Two!"

Kyra closed her eyes, the moonlight pale against her face, and Simon hoped to hell he wasn't making a mistake. "You told me the first step in any negotiation was to determine what the other person wanted."

"I'm not negotiating."

"Then you lose, because when you say 'three,' I'm dropping this thing in the ocean. Is that what you call a 'successful end result'—no one ends up with anything? Sounds like lose-lose to me."

Atherton hesitated, a man sifting through his choices, looking for the best one, then apparently gave up. "What is it you want?"

"You know what I want. Release her."

"I will. Put the crest in the boat and shove it over."

"That's not going to happen, Jim. I'll trust you with my life, not hers. You release her and you can have the damn thing. You have my word."

"I'm going to start counting, Leonidovich!"

"Don't try and play the stupid card, Jim. It doesn't work for you. I'm making you a good offer and you know it. You get me, you get the crest. I heard you say it, 'you've got to give up something to get something.'" Actually, he didn't remember Atherton saying anything of the kind, but it sounded reasonable. "And I suggest you make up your mind . . . I don't think your new friends are going to be too happy about what you did to their boss."

Atherton smiled awkwardly, the expression of someone feeling outmaneuvered but having to act like it was all for the best. "Sure, let's do it that way." He pulled the gun away from Kyra's head, then carefully leveled it on Simon before releasing her.

"Go on!" Simon shouted. "Get out of here."

She hesitated, their eyes making a brief connection, then she turned and sprinted into the trees.

Atherton steadied the gun with his free hand. "Come on, come on! You got what you wanted."

"Don't get trigger happy," Simon warned, holding the crest above the boat where Atherton could see it. "You hit me . . . *or the boat*—" He emphasized the words, making sure Atherton got the picture. "You'll lose the crest."

"Just bring it here."

"Hang on, I said you could have it." He began to rotate the boat around, making a production of it and filling his lungs with air. As the bow came about, shielding his body, he dropped the crest into the boat and slid beneath the surface. Muffled by the water, he barely heard the eruption, but realized it was only a shriek of anger, the man not daring to fire with the boat between them.

Ignoring the pain in his arm, Simon began to kick and stroke his way into deeper water, not surfacing until it felt like every capillary in his lungs would explode. He grabbed a quick breath and dove again, moving to his right with the current. When he surfaced again, he grabbed a quick look around, surprised to find that he wasn't more than fifty feet from shore. Atherton had already retrieved the boat and was pulling it onto the beach. He reached inside, grabbed the container and snapped it open. Though too distant to read his expression, Simon could well imagine the triumphant smile.

As if hearing the thought, Atherton looked up, scanning the surface of the water. "I know you're out there, Leonidovich! Nice move! Unfortunately, you're not going to live long enough to enjoy it." He stepped back and fired three shots into the inflatable. Then he laughed, the sound high and maniacal. "I'm only sorry I won't be here to see what they do to you."

Chapter Forty-one

An Island in the South China Sea

Saturday, 14 July 23:34:16 GMT +0800

By the time Simon reached shore, his arms and legs had gone numb with fatigue. "You realize this is the second time I've had to crawl onto this beach?"

Kyra squatted and ducked her head beneath his arm, trying to pull him up. "Come on, Leonidovich, we need to get out of here."

"Give me a break, Rynerson, I just saved your puny butt."

"For which you shall be thanked and rewarded for the rest of my life."

Thanked and rewarded—that didn't sound too painful.

"Which won't be very long, if we don't get moving!"

Though his legs felt like Silly Putty, he finally managed to get his feet under him and stand. "Just give me a couple minutes. I need to catch my breath."

"I'm not sure we have minutes." She pulled him around, pointing toward a bouncing speck of light, the sound of the Zodiac's huge engine reverberating over the water. "Once we're in the trees we'll be okay."

He felt two rubbery legs short of *okay*. "You go. We stand a better chance if we split up."

"Don't give me that crap, Leonidovich. You mean *me,* not *we!* We're a team, remember? Muscle and brains. Giddyup, cowboy. Let's go!"

A disembodied voice put an end to the debate. "Brick! Come in!"

For one heart-stopping moment neither one of them moved, their feet cemented to the sand, then the tiny radio on Mawl's belt gave a beep, and they realized where the voice had come from. "That was Robbie," Kyra whispered, as if he might hear her.

Simon stared at the light, which now hung steady over the dark water, the sound of engine reduced to a low idling rumble, and realized they had stopped to use the radio. And he realized something else, it was right there, as clear as Mawl's body lying in the sand: the cat-and-mouse game was over, or it should be, there was nothing in it for mercenary soldiers without a leader. "Give me that damn thing."

"What?"

"I've got an idea."

She cocked an eyebrow. "You sure?"

Beep. "Brick! Come in!" *Beep.*

"Rynerson, if we're going to be a team, you need to get past this questioning every one of my little life-and-death decisions."

She hesitated, then dropped his arm, ran to Mawl's body, pulled the radio off his belt, and rushed back. "I just hope you know what you're doing."

Don't we all. He pressed the TALK button, trying to sound almost giddy with confidence. "Hello-o-o, Rob-bie."

There was a long pause before Robbie answered,

his voice tentative and muted, as if filtered through cotton. *Beep.* "Mr. Leonidovich?" *Beep.*

"You got it, Robbie boy."

Another long silence. *Beep.* "Where's . . . where did you get that radio, Mr. Leonidovich?" *Beep.*

Kyra smiled and shook her head, as if she couldn't believe what she was hearing. "You gotta admit, that boy sure is polite."

"Sure is."

"Now what?"

"Now I give him the bad news." He pressed the TALK button. "Sorry to break it to you like this, Robbie boy, but James Atherton just killed your boss and took off in one of those small inflatables."

Beep. "That's a bloody lie!" *Beep.*

"Oh, it's true, Robbie. How else would I have gotten his radio? Not to mention his machine gun and his cell phone." He released the button. "That should make them think twice before storming the beach."

Kyra nodded. "Remind me not to play poker with you."

Beep. "You're full of blarney! You snatched the radio! We ain't stupid!" *Beep.*

"You may not be stupid, Robbie, but you're damn lucky."

Beep. "Lucky?" *Beep.*

"Atherton tried to kill all of you. He put something in your food."

Kyra chuckled. "Nice touch. Chricher is now hanging over the side of the boat trying to barf up the last of his dinner."

There was another long pause before Robbie came back, his voice subdued. *Beep.* "How do we . . . you know . . . how do we know . . . ?" *Beep.*

"He's lying right here," Simon answered, "if that's what you're asking." He began moving toward Mawl's body. "Why don't you think of a good question? Something that will prove I'm not feeding you a line."

While they waited for a response, Kyra searched Mawl's pockets. "Just this." She held up a digital micro-recorder. "No ID."

Simon slipped the recorder into his pocket. "Can you flip him over?"

"I knew you were going to ask that." She grabbed the man's belt and pulled him onto his back. "Ugh!" The front of his skull had been completely blown away, his face nothing but a mass of chunky red globules covered in sand. "I'll never eat cherry pie again."

Beep. "Mr. Leonidovich?" *Beep.*

"Go ahead, Robbie."

Beep. "He has a tattoo on the underside of his right arm. Can you describe it?" *Beep.*

"Sure." At least they didn't ask for eye color. "Hold on." He squatted down next to the man's body as Kyra turned his arm and wiped away the sand. "Yeah, I see it. It's a double-edged commando knife over a pair of wings. There's a banner across the blade that reads 'who dares wins.'"

Beep. "Okay . . . I uh . . . I'll get back to you." *Beep.*

"There's nothing more we need to talk about, Robbie. You've got two men down, and another one who needs a doctor if he wants to live. It's time to cut your losses and go home."

Kyra nodded toward the water. "They just turned off the light."

"Doesn't matter. We'll hear them if they crank up that engine."

She cocked her head, listening to the faint drown. "You're right. Now what?"

"Now we call in the Marines."

"And just how are we—"

"You said they used a laptop to monitor their network of sensors. That means it's wireless. Which means—"

"Ohmygod, the Internet!" She spun around, her feet digging into the sand. "I should have thought of that!"

He tried to keep up, but his legs were still a bit shaky, and by the time he reached the enclosure she was at the laptop, a finger tapping impatiently on the mouse pad. "It's in hibernation."

Naturally, no reason for the cosmic scale-master to start making things easy. "That could be a problem."

"Meaning a password?"

"Most likely." He made a slow three-sixty, scanning the supplies. Everything looked neat and tidy, very military—cases of ready-to-eat meals and boxes of canned fruit; twenty-liter containers of gasoline and cans of marine motor oil—everything but the true essentials of military life: guns, ammunition, and hand grenades.

Beep. "Mr. Leonidovich? *Beep.*

"Yes, Robbie." He paused and took a breath, trying

to sound more confident than he felt. "What can I do for you?"

Beep. "We need to pick up the body." *Beep.*

Need, not a good sign. "Forget it, Robbie. You set foot on this beach, and I'm not going to hesitate to use this machine gun."

Beep. "Nae, I don't believe you would." *Beep.*

"Don't test me, Robbie. I've been out in the rain and mud too long. I'm in a pretty grouchy mood right now."

Beep. "Sorry, my friends insist. We can't leave him." *Beep.*

Kyra waved a hand. "It's waking up." Her green eyes glowed hopefully in the reflection of the screen, then suddenly dimmed as if someone had switched off the power. "Shit! You were right, it wants a password." She looked up. "Unless you know some magic . . . ?"

"What operating system?"

"Vista professional. But the header on the dialog says Drivecrypt."

"Forget it. That's a military encryption program. We couldn't break it if we had two lifetimes."

Beep. "Mr. Leonidovich?" *Beep.*

"They're calling your bluff," Kyra said, holding out her hand. "Let's see if I can do any better."

He dropped into one of the canvas chairs—he couldn't remember a chair ever feeling so good—and slid the radio across the small table. "Good luck." But he had a bad feeling it was going to take more than luck and a bluff to get them out of the game.

She studied the keys a moment, then pressed the TALK button. "Robbie, it's Kyra Rynerson."

Beep. "Aye," he answered, his voice rising with a sudden vibrancy. "You okay, Ms. Rynerson?" *Beep.*

"Yes, Robbie, I'm fine, but I don't feel very good about you wanting to kill me." She gave Simon a wink. "I thought we had a good relationship. Did I do something wrong? Did I mistreat you in some way?"

Beep. "No, ma'am . . . I mean . . . I didn't . . . I'm sorry about all this . . . it was—" There was a faint *whap,* the edge of a hand coming into contact with exposed flesh, and when he continued his voice had gone flat and sullen. "We need to pick up that body, ma'am. It's . . . it's important." *Beep.*

Kyra looked at Simon. "Someone else is calling the shots."

"Absolutely, you can forget about Robbie. You need to speak as if you were talking directly to the decision maker. Let him know this isn't a negotiation."

She nodded and brought the two-way to her mouth. "Sorry, but that's out of the question. You need to do the *smart* thing, Robbie. You need to get out of here while you can. We've already spoken to the authorities in Hong Kong. They're on the way."

There was another short delay—pow-wow time—before Robbie responded. *Beep.* "With all due respect, ma'am . . . on the way where?" *Beep.*

Kyra looked at Simon and grimaced. "You need to stay firm," he warned. "You need to convince them."

"Robbie," she said firmly, as if to question her word was not only ill-advised, but foolish. "I'm a pilot. I may not know the name of this island, but I know where we came down. I gave them our final coordinates."

This time the delay was longer—long enough to suspect the men were arguing about what they should do. "I don't understand it," Kyra said, more in denial than confusion. "They're willing to risk their own necks over a dead man?"

"Apparently," Simon answered, but suspected it was more than that. "Or it's their necks they're worried about."

"What do you mean?"

"They can run, but they can't hide . . . not as long as we're around to identify them."

Beep. "Ms. Rynerson?" *Beep.*

"Go ahead, Robbie."

Beep. "We're leaving." *Beep.*

"Good decision, Robbie. Good luck."

Simon nearly choked—*Good luck!*—the kid might be polite, but that hardly excused his actions.

Beep. "Aye. Thank you, ma'am. I . . . uh . . . I'm sorry." *Beep.*

Kyra opened her mouth, about to respond, but Simon caught her hand. "Don't you dare tell him 'it's okay.' Let it go."

She hesitated, then nodded and laid the radio on the table. "You're right."

"Screw 'right.' I just don't want you giving that kid a moral pass. He's a—"

"*Shhhh.* Listen." The low idling rumble of the engine quickly accelerated, its steady drone echoing through the darkness, then slowly began to fade. "I can hardly believe it," she whispered, as if saying it out loud would make it less true. "They're actually leaving."

Simon nodded, though something about the situation felt wrong. "They gave up too easily."

"You're being paranoid."

Probably. "Why are they heading south? It's the long away around the island. The long way to Hong Kong."

"And what make you think they're going to Hong Kong?"

"It's their home base," he answered. "The Kowloon Security Service."

"All the more reason they wouldn't go there. Besides, they can't sneak up on us in that boat . . . you can still hear the thing, and they've got to half a mile away by now."

"What about the other boat? We'd never hear it over the sound of that big outboard."

She stared at him in bewilderment. "What other boat?"

"The one we sent them after. They must have caught it. They wouldn't leave it out there."

"Come on, Leonidovich, they left." Her voice was almost pleading, not wanting to hear it. "Relax. We've got food . . . we've got beer. We should be celebrating."

But he couldn't. Everything felt wrong. Even Robbie's final words: *I . . . uh . . . I'm sorry.* It sounded like regret, not apology. Regret for everything that happened? Or regret for what was about to happen?

Chapter Forty-two

An Island in the South China Sea

Saturday, 14 July 23:56:16 GMT +0800

"I still think you're being paranoid."

Not ten yards from where he was lying, her voice barely penetrated the waterproof tarp. *Or crazy,* Simon thought, the sweat pouring off his scalp. He turned his head, peering through the tiny eye-slits to where she was sitting—in the open, a few yards beyond the enclosure—easily visible from any direction. "Don't look at me when you talk."

She turned, facing the water, her back to the enclosure. "I can't believe I let you talk me into this." She stooped forward, filling another beer bottle from the container of gasoline.

"Quit bitching, Rynerson, you wouldn't believe how hot it is under this damn thing."

She twisted a rag saturated with oil down the throat of the bottle, leaving a good six inches hanging out the top, then placed it in the small box next to her chair. "That's two."

"Six should be enough."

She popped the top on another bottle, tipped it back and took a gusty swallow. *"Ahhhh."*

The woman had no compassion. "Just keep talking, Rynerson." If somebody showed up, he wanted to draw them in. "I'm signing off."

"You betcha, boss man." She poured the rest of the beer in the sand. "This is all for nothing you know."

He ignored the comment, adjusting his position so that he was facing into the trees, being careful to keep the weight off his broken arm, and slipped on the night-vision goggles. The world instantly turned to green and black, everything suddenly sharper and more defined. If he came—and Simon was certain it would be no more than one—he would come from the rear, out of the trees. Chricher was in no condition to do anything, and Robbie would stay with the boat, so that left Fosseler—the one they called Catman.

Kyra settled into a meaningless patter, pausing at sporadic intervals, as if listening to someone's response, then continuing. When she started into a discussion on the "coolness" of snakes, Simon tuned out the words. *No compassion.*

He had no idea how much time had passed—it felt like an hour, but he suspected much less—before the hot, muggy air had turned his tiny hollow into a steam box and he began to feel lightheaded. He reached up, about to pull off the goggles, when he saw something move in the trees. Or did he? He waited, afraid to even blink away the sweat, staring at the spot for what seemed an unbearably long time, but couldn't have been more than seconds, before he saw it again, a shadowy silhouette, there and gone, like a panther stalking prey. *Catman Fosseler.*

Not more than fifty yards, Simon estimated, too

close to warn Kyra, who was now feigning a telephone conversation with her mother. Simon took a deep breath, forcing himself to breathe, and carefully scanned the area, confirming the man was alone before slipping off the goggles. *Slow and easy.* He slid his good hand along the edge of the tarp, found the trip rope connected to the canopy's corner poles, and twisted it around his fist.

The ghost-like figure now seemed to be moving faster . . . *forty yards* . . . familiar with the ground . . . *thirty yards* . . . pausing, listening . . . then moving forward . . . *twenty yards* . . . obviously feeling confident . . . coming straight on . . . approaching the enclosure directly from behind. He paused again . . . *ten yards* . . . black automatic pistol in his right hand . . . listening to the chatter . . . eyes moving, sweeping the area. Satisfied, he stepped to the edge of the canopy, then stopped again, apparently wondering what happened to the table.

Simon curled the rope one more time, taking up the last bit of slack. Despite the rivers of sweat running down his face, he felt stiff with cold, a numbness that spread across his chest and arms. *Don't lose it, Leonidovich. Wait! Wait!*

Fosseler tilted back his head, nose in the air, as if trying to make sense of the heavy smell of gasoline, then, without warning—moving with the confidence of a cat that had measured the distance between the floor and counter—he silently sprang across the open space before Simon could react. *No-no-no!*

Crouching behind the low wall of supplies, Fosseler paused again . . . listening . . . cautious as a wild animal . . . then stepped around the boxes, the gun pointing directly at Kyra's back. "Don't move, lady." Though spoken in a whisper, his words sliced through the night air. "Don't even twitch."

Startled, a tiny tsunami rippled up Kyra's frame before she managed to gain control, her body going stiff as a statue.

"Where's your friend? The guy with the machine gun."

A question, Simon knew, Kyra was asking herself at that very moment.

"I—" She faltered, her voice catching in her throat. "I'm not sure."

"Yeah, right. Extend your arms straight out, then stand up and turn around. Slow."

She did as instructed, a wooden cross in the moonlight.

Fosseler glanced left and right, then down at the small cardboard box. "Whatcha planning to do with the Molotov cocktails?"

"I uh . . . I'm alone. I thought I might need a weapon."

"Yeah, I can see you're alone. Where did your friend go?"

"I told you . . . I don't—"

Fosseler raised his gun, pointing it directly at her face. "I'm not asking you again, lady."

"He went looking for his case."

"His case?" Fosseler repeated. "Are you talking about the black case that Atherton guy carried in here?"

Kyra stared back at the man, a look of utter astonishment. "He brought it here?"

Fosseler ignored the question. "What's so bloody important about that case?"

"I—" She hesitated, as if reluctant to say, then seemed to realize she didn't have a choice. "It contains a set of rare Chinese medallions. Ming dynasty. Gold. They were hidden in the lining."

"That right?" Fosseler said, his tone a mixture of interest and skepticism. "How rare?"

"One of a kind."

"What the bloody hell are they worth, lady? That's what I'm askin'."

Kyra hunched her shoulders. "Eighteen . . . twenty million . . . maybe more."

Fosseler nodded slowly, thinking about it, then he stepped back, moving into the middle of the enclosure but not taking his eyes off Kyra. "Don't move." He glanced around, eyes searching. "Trust me, lady, I won't hesitate to shoot."

"I believe you," she answered, "but that would be a terrible mistake. For you, I mean." The man narrowed his eyes and she pointed toward the canopy above his head. "Can't you smell it?"

He glanced up just as Simon yanked the rope, the heavy material collapsing over the man before he could move. Kyra dove behind the wall of supplies as Simon threw off the tarp and scrambled to his feet. "You hear me, Catman?" He could see the man's crouched form, the barrel of his gun poking against the stiff fabric. "You move and I'll open up with this machine gun!" Simon started to circle, watching as the man tried to follow his voice with the gun. "You smell it? That canopy is soaked with gas!" He reversed direction, not giving Fosseler a chance to anticipate his movements. "You understand?"

"You can bloody well go to hell!"

"You fire that gun and that's just exactly where you're going—a one-way trip to the big furnace! You get the picture?"

The man growled a response, the words incoherent.

"I didn't hear that!"

"Yeah," the man screamed, "I hear ya!"

Simon kept moving, not letting Fosseler get a fix on his location. "On the ground! Hands stretched out in front of you!"

The man hesitated, the barrel of his gun jerking first in one direction, then the other.

Kyra poked her head around the wall of boxes. "Go ahead, Simon! Light him up!"

"No!" Fosseler screamed, his body dropping to the ground. "I'm down! I'm down!"

"Okay," Simon yelled, circling around behind the man. "You can crawl toward the edge, but if I see anything but the butt end of your gun emerge from that tarp, I'm going to open fire. You understand?"

"These bloody fumes are killing me! I can't breath!"

"Then do as I say," Simon shouted, "and you'll survive!"

The man began to slither forward, coughing and choking.

"Take it slow!" Simon warned, trying to create a verbal distraction as Kyra crept forward to take the gun. "Don't do anything stupid! That's far enough! Push the gun out!"

The butt end of the gun emerged from beneath the material and Kyra snatched it away.

"Okay," Simon yelled, "you can come out!"

He came out spitting and gagging, his eyes so burned from the fumes he couldn't open them until they had him zip-tied to a chair and doused his face with water. He stared up at them through red narrow slits, his hands clenching and unclenching. "You're gonna pay for this. You can start thinkin' about that."

Kyra leaned close, staring at the man as if she had just discovered a new subspecies of primate. "Not very smart."

"Up your bleedin' ass, lady."

"Downright ignorant," Simon agreed.

"I'm gonna watch your balls rot off."

It was time, Simon decided, for a little attitudinal correction. He reached down, plucked one of the Molotov cocktails from the box, pulled out the rag stopper, and poured the contents onto the man's lap. "Let the rotting begin."

"You fuckin' asshole!"

Simon held up the oily, gas-infused rag. "The next time you speak, this is going in your mouth."

The man glared back his response, his face purple with the effort of not saying what he clearly wanted to say.

Simon leaned down next to the man's ear, speaking in a low voice, a little man-to-man secret sharing. "Here's the deal, Catman . . . I don't like you . . . I don't like your friends. But, because of her—" He nodded toward Kyra. "I'd kinda like to show off my benevolent side. So, I'm going to give you a chance. One chance only. And just between you and me, I hope you screw up, because I really do wanna see you burn." Simon chuckled softly, trying hard to sell his craziness. "I want to hear you beg and scream. I want to hear your balls pop and your skin crackle. You get the picture?"

The man nodded, eyes wide, as if seeing Simon for the first time.

"So, I'm going to ask you a number of questions. And you're going to answer them truthfully and without hesitation. If you do that . . . well, shit, then I don't get to see you do that screaming Joan of Arc thing." Simon dropped his voice to an even lower whisper. "But if you screw up, if you hesitate—" He chuckled again, the sound a bit maniacal even to his own ears. "Then I'm gonna toss a match. Clear?"

Fosseler nodded rapidly.

Simon straightened up. "Okay, first question. Where did you leave the boat?"

The man hooked his chin toward the south. "About two hundred yards."

Kyra handed Simon the gun. "I'll check it out." She took off at a run.

Simon tucked the automatic into his waistband and turned back to Fosseler. "And your buddies are sitting out there waiting for an all-clear . . . ?"

Fosseler nodded again. "I'm supposed to call 'em on the radio."

"And say what?"

"We didn't have a code, if that's what you mean."

"Okay, here's what you're *going* to say: 'I got the bloody bastards. Come on in.' I suggest you say it with meaning. You think you can do that, Catman?"

"I ain't bloody stupid."

Simon gave the man a little smile. "You better hope so." He pulled the chair around, so Fosseler's back was to the beach, then placed one of the twenty-liter containers of gasoline next to his chair. "I'm going to be sitting right behind you in the rocks. If something goes wrong . . . you try to warn them . . . my first shot—" He kicked the side of the container. "—right here. And just so you know, I was captain of the pistol team in college." *Thank you, Jimmy boy.*

The man nodded, his head drooping to one side, like a sick animal.

Kyra came trudging up the beach, panting and out of breath. "It's there."

"Fuel?" Simon asked.

"Almost full."

"Then let's do it." He held the radio up to Fosseler's mouth. "Be smart," he warned, and pressed the TALK button.

"I got the bloody bastards," Fosseler growled. "You can come in."

Robbie responded within seconds. *Beep.* "What happened?" *Beep.*

"Tell him he's breaking up," Simon said. "Just keep

saying the same thing: 'It's okay. You can come in.' "

Fosseler did as instructed, repeating the message twice before Robbie gave up. Kyra looped a piece of rope over Fosseler's head, pulled it into his mouth, and tied it behind his head. "Be good, now, my friend's an excellent shot." She gave Simon a wink, then picked up the box of homemade bombs and headed toward the outcropping of rocks where they had first come ashore.

Simon gave Fosseler a little wink, then reached down and tapped the red container with the pistol. "Nice target."

By the time he reached the rocks, he could hear the faint whine of the outboard. "You better take off, Rynerson, we've only got a few minutes."

"I'm still not convinced these things will break when they hit that rubber boat."

"It won't matter. The jolt will be enough to release the gas." *Hopefully.* "They'll be trapped here."

"Maybe you should use the gun."

"I've never fired a pistol in my life. Chances are I'd never hit the damn thing." He picked up one of the bottles, testing the weight. "This is perfect."

"I could try. I don't think Robbie would shoot me."

"Forget that." He had a feeling she would make the suggestion. "We can't be sure where they'll come in, and I can throw farther than you." He pulled the automatic. "Take this."

"Don't be crazy. You might need it."

"I have no intention of sticking around long enough to use it, and I'm not about to get into a gun-battle with professionals." Those professionals, he realized, were getting closer, the engine whine growing louder by the second. "If something goes wrong, you take off. Don't put yourself in jeopardy."

She hesitated, reluctant, then took the gun. "You sure?"

"I'm sure. The minute you hear the explosion, start the engine, I'll be coming fast."

She leaned forward and gave him a sisterly kiss on the cheek. "I'll pull the boat this way as far as I can."

He moved deeper into the rocks—a well-protected spot with a good escape path—placed the bottles and a half-dozen wooden kitchen matches within easy reach, then hunkered down to wait. The engine was now a high-pitched wail, the light bouncing over the surface of the water and coming straight on, the men apparently oblivious to any threat.

Threat, was he really a threat? The plan had sounded reasonable, but now that it was about to happen, it seemed full of holes and wishful thinking. What if they stopped offshore and tried the radio again? What would they do when no one answered?

What if he couldn't make the throw? What if he missed? Would there be time for a second?

Then it was too late to second-guess . . . everything going silent as Robbie cut the engine, the Zodiac scraping onto the sand, half in, half out of the water. Robbie jumped out of the boat, Chricher only a step behind, apparently recovered from his trip to la-la land.

Simon waited until the men were halfway up the beach, then lit the rag on the nearest bottle, stood up, took careful aim, and let it fly. The bottle rotated slowly in the air, end over end, like a Fourth of July pinwheel, then bounced off the side of the buoyancy chamber and splashed harmlessly into the water. *Damn!* As he crouched down, Simon saw Robbie spin and drop, gun extended, searching for a threat.

One more, he had to try. He took a deep breath, pictured the throw in his mind, recalculated the arc, then lit the second bottle and stood up. Robbie leaped to his feet, taking aim, but Simon forced away the image, extended his arm back behind his head, then stepped forward and released just as Robbie fired. *Br-rrang!* The bullet ricocheted off a large boulder behind Simon's head, spraying rock fragments across his back, but he couldn't turn away . . . had to watch the bottle as it arced toward the boat . . . *too long* . . . but only by a couple of feet, the bottle hitting the outside chamber and bouncing back into the air. It seemed to hang for a moment, then dropped into the bottom of the Zodiac with an impotent *thump.* Simon hesitated, considered one more try, then realized Robbie was on the run, closing the distance between them. As Simon spun around, already picturing his route through the rocks, he heard a muffled *WHUMP* as the gas ignited. *Thank you, Jesus!*

He could now hear the small outboard, not more than hundred yards, but Robbie was less than fifty back. *Run, Leonidovich! Run!* It felt like he was plowing through crusted snow, the sand dissolving into tiny sinkholes beneath his feet, the harder he pushed the deeper the holes. Now he could see the small inflatable . . . *fifty yards* . . . idling just offshore. *Brrrang!* A bullet whistled past his ear, and he swerved to the left. *Brrrang!* Then Kyra opened fire, the gun pointing at the sky—*pop-pop-pop*—the sound less deadly, her voice rising above the reverberations. "Don't do it, Robbie! You haven't killed anyone! Please! Don't do it!"

Simon plowed through the water, grabbed a quick peek over his shoulder—shocked to see Robbie less than ten yards behind—and dove into the boat. Kyra opened the throttle, and the small Zodiac leaped forward. Simon pushed himself into a sitting position, helpless to do anything as Robbie stopped and cradled his gun . . . taking careful aim . . . then his shoulders slumped and he dropped his arm, watching until they disappeared into the darkness.

Kyra threw back her head and howled, a mixture of relief and triumph. "We made it!"

Simon nodded, too exhausted to feel anything.

She cranked back on the power, her expression mutating from elation to self-reproach. "Sorry. I wasn't thinking. I should have realized you wouldn't feel much like celebrating."

Sorry? "What are you talking about, Rynerson?"

"You know . . . losing the crest . . . the publicity . . . all that. What it will do to your reputation."

He smiled to himself, barely able to keep from laughing. "Well, you don't need to worry about that, Rynerson. The only thing I lost was one of those fake reproductions from the Pearl."

Her mouth went slack, as if caught between expressions.

"There was obviously an information leak," he went on quickly, realizing he had just taken a giant step onto thin ice. "I couldn't take the chance of losing the thing, so I made other arrangements to have the pieces picked up and delivered."

Her nostrils flared, as though she had just gotten a whiff of deceit. "Other arrangements! Are you kidding me? All this time we've been carrying around a fake? Risking our lives for—"

"No," he interrupted, "it wasn't like that. That piece of rock was the only thing keeping us alive. As long as we had something they wanted, we had a chance."

"So we were—" She faltered, clearly struggling to put it all together. "What? A diversion?"

"Not *we.* You weren't supposed to be on the plane. I tried to talk you out of it."

But it wasn't enough, her green eyes flashing in the moonlight. "We almost died!"

"Come on, Kyra, if I knew that plane was going down, do you think for a minute I would have let you go? I never thought anyone would actually try to bring down the plane. *Especially* if they thought the crest was on board."

"You could have told me! I would have understood!"

But he knew better; not when she realized her mother might be behind everything.

Chapter Forty-three

US Consulate Office, Hong Kong

Sunday, 15 July 11:44:29 GMT +0800

Simon cut a glance toward the small gathering of onlookers—a professional group of well-meaning, but gawking staffers who had been called in to "assist in a special repatriation"—then turned to the Consul General, a distinguished-looking gentleman who had just arrived on the scene dressed in a snowy white tennis outfit. "Before we get started, is there somewhere private where we could make a call?"

The man, who looked somewhat overwhelmed to have the lost daughter of Big Jake Rynerson suddenly thrust into his care, couldn't move fast enough. "Of course, of course. Please." He extended his arm like the maitre d' in a fine supper club. "Right this way."

He ushered them into his personal office, a spacious room decorated with flags, national mementos, and a photographic array of foreign dignitaries, all clearly intended to remind visitors of the power and might of the government he represented. "Please make yourself at home. Use the red phone. It's a secure line, direct to the outside." He flashed a set of teeth slightly more dazzling than his tennis togs. "Take all the time you need. While you're doing that,

I'll check with the Chinese authorities . . . make sure those three men have been picked up." He flashed another smile, this one directly at Kyra, and backed out of the room.

Simon waited until the door clicked shut before speaking. "I think he likes you."

She smiled, the effort somewhat strained with weariness, and held out her arms. "What's not to like?" Dressed in the clean but shabby garb of a deck-hand from the Chinese freighter that had picked them up, she looked a bit like Charlie Chaplin as *The Tramp.*

"My sentiments exactly."

"Simon—"

Simon, that didn't sound good. "Yes."

"I'm sorry I snapped at you last night. I was so shocked . . . so—"

"Forget it. I should have told you."

"No, you were right. I see that now. If Jim had found out—" She shivered, as if old man winter had just blown across the back of her neck. "I don't even want to think about it."

He nodded, more than happy to leave that subject behind. "You better make that call. Our rescue is going to be all over the news within the hour."

"I can't."

"Can't? Why not?"

"Because . . ." She hesitated, as if she couldn't decide how to say it. "Because I have a bad feeling. I know it's been only five days, but it seems like a month. I'm afraid . . . it's hard to explain. I'm both excited and scared. I don't know if it's a good day or a bad day. Should I be happy or sad? I can't very well say, 'yippee, I'm back,' then find out my father's dead." Her eyes glittered with tears.

Tears, Simon realized, she had been fighting to hold in for too long. "It's okay, Kyra. I understand. I'll do it." He circled around behind the desk—an early American museum piece—pressed the SPEAKER button on the red phone, and punched in Billie's cell phone number.

She answered on the second ring, her voice lacking its usual vibrancy. "Billie here."

"Hello, Billie."

"Simon!" Her voice suddenly filled the room. "Ohmygod, is it really you? Are you okay? Where are you? Where's Kyra? Is she okay?"

"Slow down, Billie. We're okay. We're at the American Consulate in Hong Kong."

"Oh, thank God! Thank God! I was so . . . so—" She momentarily ran out of steam, then quickly recovered. "This is wonderful news! Wonderful! Just what Jake needs to get his head out of the weeds."

Simon gave Kyra a cautioning look, thinking it was the kind of news Billie hoped might somehow revive her husband. "What's happening, Billie? How is Jake doing?"

"It happened just like you said. Remember?"

"Uh . . ."

"You said he would sit up when he felt good and ready, and not a minute before, and damned if that ain't just what he did. Sat right up . . . scared me half to—"

Kyra lurched forward over the desk. “Mother—”

“Kyra! It’s so wonderful to hear your voice! What happened? Where—”

“Is it true?” Kyra cut in. “Is Daddy really okay?”

“Well, he’s not exactly back on his feet yet. You being lost at sea didn’t help matters, but believe me, when I tell him you and Simon are safe, he’s going to be up and out of that bed before . . .” She released a huge sigh. “Holy damn, this has gotta be the happiest day of my life.”

“Me too, Momma. Me too.”

“What about Mr. Atherton?” Billie asked. “Is he with you?”

Kyra gave Simon a nod, indicating that he should answer. He hesitated, knowing all calls out of the office might be recorded, whether the Consul General knew it or not. “Well, uh, that’s kind of a long story, Billie. But he’s . . . he’s uninjured. We’ll tell you all about it when we see you.”

“And it better be damn quick, Simon Leonidovich. You hear me, now?”

“Yes, ma’am, we hear you loud and clear. We lost everything in the plane, so we need to fill out some paperwork before we leave here. As soon as they give us temporary passports, we’ll catch a flight to Bangkok.”

“We’re back in Macau. Flew in this morning. We’re at the Pearl.”

Kyra frowned. “Shouldn’t Daddy be in the hospital?”

“Well a course he should be in the hospital,” Billie snapped back, clearly venting an old argument. “But you know your father, he wasn't about to sit around any hospital with you missing in the South China Sea."

"But—"

"Now don't you worry, honey. Dr. Yuan is here with an army of nurses."

"But—"

"Nothing I could do," Billie cut in, her tone suddenly defensive. "That old fool, thinks he's gonna take charge of the search."

Simon smiled to himself; somehow, coming from Billie, "that old fool" sounded warm and endearing. "What's happening there, Billie? Are you going to make the grand opening?"

"We damn well better! The President is due here in two days."

If anyone was listening in, Simon thought, that should make them sit up and take notice. "Is the hotel ready?"

"Well, y'all just better come see for yourself."

Chapter Forty-four

The Pacific Pearl, Taipa Island, Macau

Wednesday, 17 July 11:46:28 GMT +0800

Simon instantly recognized the young man standing post outside Jake's suite, a regular from his Las Vegas detail. "Hey there, Tomás, how you doing?"

"Good, Mr. Leonidovich." He reached out and gave Simon's new plastic cast a playful rap. "Rumor has it you can't stay out of trouble."

"Could have used your help, that's for sure."

"Next time you call me, okay?" Tomás pulled a keycard from the pocket of his sport coat, slipped it into the magnetic reader, and pushed open the door. "You're expected."

The suite's living area had been transformed into a mini MASH unit, with enough medical paraphernalia to equip a small hospital. Dr. Yuan and three female nurses were sitting at a game table playing mah-jongg. The doctor leaped to his feet as Simon came through the door. "Mr. Leonidovich." He dipped his head. "A pleasure to see you again."

Simon returned the bow and extended his hand. "Dr. Yuan. How's the patient?"

Yuan rolled his eyes heavenward. *"Ayeeyah."*

Simon smiled to himself, not the least surprised. "A little difficult, eh?"

"Little? Nothing about Mr. Rynerson is little."

"You got that right." Simon hooked his chin toward the hallway leading to the master bedroom. "He's in there?"

Yuan nodded. "*Hai*, with both Mesdames."

Hearing Kyra referred to as a *Mrs.* always gave Simon a start, and conjured up a memory he preferred to forget. "Thanks, Doc."

The door to the huge bedroom was open, but Jake's booming voice stopped Simon before he could get past the threshold. "I'm not using that damn chair!" He was in bed, propped up against a mountain of pillows, his chin covered in shaving cream, his verbal assault directed at Billie, who was standing arms akimbo alongside a shiny new motorized wheelchair.

"Don't you raise your voice to me, Jake Rynerson! Dr. Yuan says you're to use it or stay in bed, and that's just what you're gonna do."

"Like hell I am!"

Kyra, who was sitting on the edge of the bed with a towel and safety razor, leaned back, inspecting her handiwork. "Yes, Daddy, you will."

It was an argument Simon wanted no part of, but before he could retreat Jake spotted him. "Simon boy! You're just in time to even up the odds a bit."

A bit and a bazooka wouldn't do it, Simon thought, not against those two. "We might be able to handle one, Jake, but you know damn well we can't beat the two of them."

Jake feigned a look of disgust. "Well, shit fire and save matches! Things are getting pretty bad when these two start agreein' on things. So how are you, boy?"

"I'm good. The question is, how are you?"

"Lucky to be alive," Jake bellowed back, "and feeling pretty frisky about it."

"I hear that. You do look better than when I saw you last."

Jake grunted, as if to say, ain't that the truth. "Everyone assures me I have a very attractive drool."

"Far be it from me to contradict popular opinion."

"Spoken like a true politician." As Kyra wiped the last of the shaving cream off his chin, the big man levered himself higher against the pillows. "Guess I missed a bit of excitement."

"It was a little hairy at times." Simon held up his arm, showing off his new cast. "Turns out your daughter can't land a plane."

Kyra stuck out her tongue. "I've had enough abuse for the day. I'm leaving now."

Billie glanced at her watch. "Oh dear, we need to hurry." She cocked her head and flipped back her silver-blond hair in an exaggerated gesture of self-importance. "*The President* has invited us to lunch." Then she laughed, a typical Billie Rynerson life-is-good rib-scraper. "Wanna join us?"

Simon didn't need to think twice about that; he had met one president, and that was enough for a lifetime. "Sounds great, but I have an appointment to look at a piece of art I saw advertised in the paper."

Kyra gave him a puzzled, somewhat disbelieving look. "You, the great anti-shopper . . . the man without a home . . . buying art? What's this about?"

"It's something I thought Lara might like for her new office." He knew better, but that had nothing to do with it.

A moment later they were gone, which was exactly what Simon had wanted; a very private talk with the big man himself. "You feeling up to a little conversation?"

"Hell, yes, I've had enough female chatter these couple days." He pointed to a chair. "Set your butt." He sighed, and leaned back into his mountain of pillows. "It's still hard for me to believe . . . Atherton and all that. Not that I especially liked the boy. All foam and no beer, in my opinion, but I sure didn't think he was the type to . . . you know."

Simon pulled the chair up close to the bed. "Yessir, he fooled us all."

Jake snorted. "That's not the way Kyra tells it. Says you were ahead of him at every step."

"You know women, they embellish."

"Not my daughter," Jake snapped back. "That girl tells it straight . . . like it or no."

"You're right," Simon conceded, "but believe me, he had me fooled most of the way." He paused, gently tossing out the hook. "There's *still* a few things I haven't figured out."

Either Jake missed the hint, or purposely avoided the bait. "So what did the security people say?"

"They're hot on his trail, as you cowboys like to say. They figure he's in Taiwan or China."

"China's a big place."

"I doubt they'll find him, but I don't know that it matters. His employers aren't going to be too happy when they discover that piece of rock is a fake."

Jake smiled, clearly amused at the thought. "Any idea who those employers are?"

"They obviously have money. The investigators believe it's either a group of dissident Chinese politicos, or a Taiwanese business faction. They've already traced the source funds to a numbered account in Switzerland."

Jake expelled a deep breath, the sound of hope taking a nosedive. "Figures. The Swiss don't give up that kind of information."

"Usually, but after all the bad publicity they've had over the past decade . . . all the Holocaust stuff . . . they're not exactly standing on firm moral ground. There's going to be pressure, both from our government and from the Chinese. Trust me—" He tried to put a little warning into his voice. "—they'll get the information."

Jake nodded thoughtfully. "You said, 'the investigators believe.' You're not convinced?"

"Not completely," Simon admitted. "How much do you remember about the night you were shot?"

"Ha! If I was smart, I'd tell you what I told the police. Nothing. Nada."

Simon waited, letting the man get to it under his own terms.

"But just between you and me—" His eyes augured in, letting Simon know the limits. "I pretty much remember everything until I reached the hospital."

"So you know who shot you?"

"Of course."

"And you could identify them?"

"Identify *them*," Jake repeated. "Now that sounds like more than one."

"Yes, it does."

Jake smiled, another sly grin. "Course I didn't know the name of one of *them* until yesterday."

"Bricker Mawl. And the other one?"

Jake considered his answer, then apparently decided to avoid giving one. "What do you think?"

Simon realized he was teetering on the edge of trouble—that Jake wasn't about to make this easy—but he couldn't back away, not before he had the answers. "It was Billie."

For a moment Jake said nothing, his face showing neither shock nor outrage, then he chuckled softly, as if amused, though nothing about his expression supported such a sentiment. "And what makes you think that?"

Not easy at all. There were actually a number of reasons—the fact that Billie failed to mention her husband had been shot with two different weapons, from two different angles, and then, most damning, her denial of a second shooter—but those were all things she could explain away as heat-of-the-moment oversights. What she couldn't explain had come from another source. "Madame Chiang inferred your meeting was a romantic liaison."

"What! That old witch! You can't be serious. You believe that?"

"No," Simon answered. "I don't. It's ridiculous. But I realized she would never have made the accusation if Billie had been there."

"But she was there. She told ya that. I'm telling ya that."

"Yes, but not *with* you, Jake. Madame Chiang never saw Billie, because Billie was in the shadows. She was one of the shooters."

"And you think my wife shot me?"

A question, Simon realized, not a denial. "Yes, Jake, I'm sure of it."

"But that's not the worst of it, is it? You think Billie might be behind this whole thing? That Atherton worked for her?"

"No, that's not what I believe." Certainly nothing he *wanted* to believe. "But it does make sense."

"Right, the wife is always first on the list. The one who stands to benefit the most."

"It's more than that, Jake, and you know it. You can't deny giving her a few good reasons over the years."

"A few extra wives in between, you mean? That was nothin' but a temporary loss of sanity. Billie understands that."

"This isn't funny, Jake. If I kept my mouth shut, I wouldn't be your friend."

"Hell no, it's not funny," Jake bellowed, though he looked throughly amused. "So that's why you told Billie about the flight to Taiwan, but didn't tell her about using another courier to transport the crest?"

"Exactly."

"So you set up my wife, and used yourself as bait?"

"Yessir, I'm afraid I did. Of course I didn't want it to be true, but when the plane went down, and Billie was the only one who knew about the flight . . ."

Jake howled like an old wolf. "Man-oh-man, that *is* rich. Billie's going to get such a kick out of this."

Was the man putting on a show, or was he serious? "Just tell me it isn't true, Jake. Whatever you say, I'll accept."

"Hell no, it's not true. Here's the deal, Simon boy. Billie tried to talk me into taking security, but I refused. Well, you know Billie, she doesn't take no for an answer, and decided to follow me herself. She saw the guy come out of the shadows the same time I did, and here she comes, charging over those cobblestones, wavin' and firin' that little peashooter like an old momma bear protectin' her cub. She must have hit the guy or he would have finished us both off. Unfortunately, she hit me too."

Simon flashed on the moment, pulling his conversation with Madame Chiang from his memory file. *Bang-bang-bang*—three shots.

"So, yes," Jake continued, "she shot me. And she saved my life. She was on her cell phone almost before I hit the ground, calling for an ambulance, applying pressure to my wounds, and cussing me every minute."

Simon slumped back in his chair, feeling like he could breathe for the first time in a month. "I can't tell you how happy I am to hear that."

Jake howled again. "And I can't wait to tell her."

"Come on, Jake, I'll never be able to look her in the eye."

"Oh, don't you worry, she's gonna give you some grief, son, no getting around that, but you know Billie, she'll think it's all just—" He stopped, his eyes suddenly serious as ice picks. "You can't tell Kyra. Ever! That's why Billie wouldn't say anything. She was afraid Kyra would blame her if I died. You know how those two are, oil and water. Kyra would never forgive her."

"I'll make you a deal. You don't tell Billie, I won't tell Kyra."

"Stop worrying about Billie. It's my daughter you should be thinking about."

"What do you mean?"

Jake shook his head, a look of disgust. "I do believe Billie's right. Men are stupid."

Her exact words, Simon recalled. "I don't understand."

"For someone so godawful smart, you sure are a dummy when it comes to women, Leonidovich. Kyra's got a thing for you, son. You too blind to see that?"

He wanted to see it—wanted more than anything to believe it. "Are you sure?"

"Hell yes, I'm sure. Even a dummy like me can see that. Every time your name gets mentioned she turns all flushy-faced."

"Well I . . . I guess I'd like to know what you think about that."

"What do I think! Hell, man, she's my daughter! I might be a tad biased, but I damn well think you could do worse."

Worse! "No, sir, I can't disagree with that, but I'm asking if you think she could do better?"

"Well, first of all, son, if you know anything about the women in this family, you know it doesn't much matter what I think. But between you and me, nothing would make me happier."

Chapter Forty-five

The Pacific Pearl, Taipa Island, Macau

Saturday, 21 July 19:41:06 GMT +0800

The waiter pulled back the last vacant chair at the front table, and Simon took his seat between Li Quan and Kyra, who was holding T.J. on her lap. The boy looked over and grinned, obviously very pleased to be back in his mother's arms. A mother, Simon thought, who couldn't have looked any more spectacular. Dressed in a simple midnight-blue cocktail dress, she had her hair pulled back in a way that accentuated her face and gave her a somewhat regal appearance. Overall, she looked sleek, sophisticated, and sexy. "You don't look too bad in a dress, Rynerson."

She cut him a little sideways look. "Was that supposed to be a compliment, Leonidovich?"

"I was simply comparing this look to that fashionable wet T-shirt thing you wore on the island. This is nice, but . . . well, not quite as spectacular."

She chuckled, the sound low in her throat, her eyes taking in his new Armani tux, which had been custom-tailored to accommodate his cast. "You clean up pretty well yourself, Leonidovich."

Within minutes, all the invited guests—a confluence of world politicians, business leaders, and international celebrities—had taken their seats, and the doors were now closed, tuxedoed security agents from three nations circling the giant ballroom. Architecturally, the room looked like it might have been plucked from the palace of Versailles: the walls covered in pale blue silk, the ceiling awash with gleaming prisms of cut crystal. Even the tables and chairs looked vintage. The flags of China, Taiwan, and the United States hung over the dais, empty except for a long table covered in ivory silk brocade. At the center of the table, encased within bulletproof glass, sat the hallmark of Shih huang-ti, First Sovereign Emperor of a united China: the Crest of Ch'in.

Simon turned to Li Quan, who looked ready to burst with pride. "The place looks spectacular, Mr. Quan. Congratulations."

Quan smiled and dipped his head. "Very good *joss.*"

Plus four billion dollars and a lot of hard work, Simon thought, as the din of conversation suddenly faded. A moment later, everyone rose to their feet as a military guard escorted the three presidents, Jake and Billie Rynerson, and a brigade of political functionaries onto the dias. Simon reached over and gave Kyra's hand a squeeze. "I see your father talked his way out of that wheelchair."

She nodded, her eyes brimming with tears. T.J., who until that moment had been remarkably composed for a two-year-old, suddenly spotted his grandfather. "Poppy!"

Big Jake winked and gave his grandson a thumbs up as a ripple of laughter pulsated across the room.

James Atherton watched the three presidents toast their great accomplishment—the Pacific Rim Alliance—and knew he was in serious trouble. He turned away from the screen, looking down the length of the conference table to the slab face of Tureyuki Yakamaro, chairman of Yakamaro Industries and titular head of the consortium of Taiwanese businessmen who had paid to see the Alliance fail. "You can't blame this on me."

Yakamaro picked up the tiny remote, the sole object on the long glass table, and muted the sound. "Of course not."

Just the way he said it—*of course not*—as if the matter were of little consequence, made the hair rise on the back of Atherton's neck. "That's not the real crest, you know. Not all of it, anyway." He tried to remain calm, but could hear the tightness in his voice. "I can't help it if Beijing decided to go ahead without the real thing."

"Of course not."

Jian-min Weng—the only one Atherton had ever met or talked to before that day, and the only other person present in the room—stood and bowed to the chairman. "Yakamaro, *xiansheng.*"

"Hai."

Weng stepped forward, laid the black case with the Smithsonian imprint on the table, then stepped back, bowed again, and left the room.

Atherton swallowed, trying to draw some saliva into his mouth. "That's the—"

Yakamaro held up his hand and turned to the window, a spectacular overview of Taipei and the Pacific Ocean beyond. The sun was just going down, a disk of orange fire slipping into the water beneath a salmon-pink sky.

Some kind of ritual, Atherton thought, as he tried to appear appropriately impressed with the colorful display. Then, just as the sun winked below the horizon, Jian-min Weng hurtled past the window, his suit coat flapping behind him like a pair of broken wings, his face oddly serene. Atherton leaped to his feet, staring in shocked disbelief as the man plunged toward the sidewalk, fifty-three stories below. "What the . . . why . . . ?"

Yakamaro showed no emotion, his dark eyes as dull and dangerous as a shark. "He failed in his mission. The decision was appropriate."

Appropriate! Atherton sank back into his chair, trying to decide what he needed to do, how he could save himself—*It wasn't my fault, I got the crest*—but his mind felt like a lump of dough, beyond any ability to reason.

Yakamaro reached down, picked up the small black case, and twisted open the lock. He studied the piece for a long moment, then carefully pried the carving free of its molded impression. About the size of his massive hand, he bounced it in his palm, as if estimating the weight, then turned it over. For the first time, his face showed a flicker of emotion, his eyes narrowing as he leaned forward, his face only inches from the back of the carving. Then his lips curled upward and he started to laugh, a kind of rolling, mirthless bark.

Though he knew better, Atherton couldn't stop himself from asking. "What?"

"It's a fake," Yakamaro screamed. "A reproduction."

"That's not possible. It was on the plane. It's the same one. I was—"

"You were tricked," Yakamaro interrupted. "That courier played you for a fool."

"No. That's not possible. How can you be sure? You hardly—"

As if it was nothing more than an oversized hockey puck, Yakamaro slid the crest down the surface of the table. "You're a clever man." He made *clever* sound like an insult. "You figure it out."

Atherton picked it up, barely able to keep his hands from shaking, and read the words stamped in clear English along the bottom edge.

Made in Taiwan

A ticket, he realized, to the next flight off the Yakamaro building.

Epilogue

The Pacific Pearl, Taipa Island, Macau

Saturday, 22 July 23:04:15 GMT +0800

Kyra rolled off his body just as the crescendo of fireworks reached its peak; the night sky an eruption of brilliant explosions and pulsing claps of color. Simon struggled to catch his breath. "Holy Jesus!"

She stared down at him, her skin pink with the afterglow of good, adventurous sex. "That's all you can say, Leonidovich? Holy Jesus?"

Bitch-bitch-bitch—after two hours, she was lucky he could talk. "That's what I call timing."

She glanced toward the windows, a panoramic view of Macau and the contrails of a thousand colored sparklers. "It's been a while. I was ready."

"Any more ready and I'd be dead."

She grinned and crossed her legs—as naked and shameless as a child—her scent sweet and wild. "You know, Leonidovich, the Secret Service is out there in helicopters."

"Swell. I feel very well protected."

"You sure they don't have some kind of special equipment that allows them to see through this reflective glass?"

"I'm sure." Thermal imaging, yes—and there had

been enough heat to make the room glow like a plutonium stockpile—but she didn't need to know that.

"You better hope so. If my bare ass shows up on the Playboy Channel, I'm going to break your other arm."

"Trust me, Rynerson, if your ass shows up on television, it won't be on the Playboy Channel."

"Oh." There was a dangerous chill in that *Oh,* like the first snowflake of an approaching blizzard. "You don't think it's good enough?"

"Not for Playboy." He gave her a little smile. "You most definitely have a Magic Kingdom ass."

She laughed—*haw haw*—and then they were both laughing and rolling around on the giant bed in a kind of postcoital frolic: a celebration of their survival and freedom, and maybe—though it was still unspoken—a future together. Finally, their energy spent, they drifted off to sleep, the lights still on, their arms and legs intertwined. They didn't move for two hours, until his new cell phone began its annoying chirp. "Sorry, I have to take that."

She sighed and cracked an eyelid. "How do you know?"

"Besides you, Lara's the only one with the number. If I don't answer, she'll call your mother."

"At this hour!"

"That's my sister, Ms. Determined. And then your mother will call you, asking if you know—"

"Say no more." She released her death grip and rolled over, stretching her lean body like a cat across the bed. "Let's keep this between us for a while."

"Good idea." At least until they knew if it was going to work. He rolled over, snatched the phone off the bedside table, and growled into the receiver. "Simon says, leave me alone. It's two o'clock in the morning."

"And may I," Lara snapped back, "be the first to wish you a wonderful day."

"Give me a break, Sissie. What is it that couldn't wait till morning?" As if he couldn't guess.

"I've just taken receipt of a very large air-priority shipment."

"Oh?"

"Don't play Simple Simon with me, Boris. What the hell am I supposed to do with this thing?"

"I thought you might like it for your new office."

A slight pause, then a hopeful "You're kidding, right?"

"You don't like it?"

"That's an understatement. What the hell did you pay for this thing?"

"Ninety-six thousand *pataca.*"

"And what's that in real money?" she demanded.

"About twelve thousand dollars."

"Twelve thousand dollars!"

"Give or take. A real bargain."

"Bargain! This thing is absolutely Orwellian."

"It's a bit depressing," he admitted.

"So what am I supposed to do with it? Really?"

"Donate it to the charity of your choice."

"What? You paid twelve grand and shipped it air priority halfway around the world just to give it away?"

"Take it home if you want."

"Yeah, right."

"One thing, Sissie, before you give it away . . ."

"I'm listening."

"You see that third smokestack from the right?"

"Yeah." Her voice changed as she moved closer. "What about it?"

"Get a good grip on the thing, then give it a jerk. Straight up."

There was a momentary pause, then a determined grunt, followed by the metallic scrape of metal against metal. "The missing gun!"

"That's the one. Ask your friend Mr. Rapp to dispose of it, will you? The sooner the better."

"Sure. Okay. He's coming by for lunch, I'll give it to him then."

"Good." It was an admission, he realized, to her blossoming relationship with Bill Rapp. "Very good." And now, he had his own blossoming relationship to worry about. "If you don't mind, I'd like to go back to bed."

"When are you coming home?"

Home, where exactly was that? He glanced over at the alluring form stretched out across the sheets. "Kyra's flying back tomorrow. I'm hoping to catch a ride."

"Sounds good, Boris. Get some sleep. I won't bother you again."

"Great." But it wasn't sleep he was thinking about. "Talk to you tomorrow."

Kyra pushed herself up on one elbow. "Hoping to catch a ride, were you?"

Among other things.

"What was that all about? A smokestack?"

"Madame Chiang had this futuristic cityscape of black tubular steel in her panic room. I managed to buy it before—"

"Ah-ha!" She bounced into a sitting position. "So that's where you hid the gun!"

"At the time, it seemed like a decent idea. But, sooner or later, someone was going to find the thing, so I made arrangements to buy it prior to the estate auction."

"At a price they couldn't refuse."

"Something like that."

"You're a clever man, Leonidovich."

"Lucky too." But he wasn't thinking about the gun, and he couldn't stop himself from smiling.

She cocked an eyebrow, her green eyes suddenly suspicious. "Okay, what's going on in that devious male processor?"

"Actually . . . I was thinking I wouldn't mind trying that twisty thing again."

She grinned and swung a leg across his midsection. "I have to do everything."